MR WHIPPY GOES TO SCHAUMBERG

A novel

By Robin Tudge

To Dawn, Ringo, and Ben.

New York

With a towering view over a towering city, who could fail to get a snog up here? Eighty-six floors up above New York, visibility 80 miles in every direction, across New Jersey, Pennsylvania, Connecticut, Massachusetts – say those names! – and all New York. Surely no-one could resist a pass up here, up a man-made monolith more than a thousand feet closer to the Sun and the Heavens. High above the bad air, bad noise and bad temper of the city, high up on another plane where the Sun dazzled and the winds ripped through to your bones. And of the thousand towers in New York, the Empire State beat them all for its power and majesty, pride, daring, its insolence, the defiance with which it scraped the sky. It had taken decades of every kind of extreme weather thrown at it. Even when struck by lightning bolts powerful enough to fry every New Yorker, innocent and guilty, the Empire would glow and scream in victory as God had tried and failed again to punish its audacity.

But not everyone who came to the top of the Empire had got such a rise out of this great concrete cock. How many people had come here and thought, yeah, this is it, before high-diving off into the hands of their own man-made fate? All around the observation platform where Elly and I stood under the midday Sun was a high wall topped by a gleaming steel trellis to stop the suicides, which was slightly depressing.

But no matter, what a view! We could see the Statue of Liberty, that green Goddess who welcomed the oppressed and poor at the end of their desperate voyages to a land of giddying wealth, violence and power. Here, some built their way to Heaven, others built their way up to drag Heaven down to Earth; but all built skywards, creating a concrete landscape of peaks, mountain ranges and canyons. All were free to come and have a go and succeed. In London, all the tall buildings were structures of power, St. Pauls, the NatWest Tower, the Shell building, Parliament. But in New York, height gave no clue as to purpose or position. They were all flash, brash, and soaring as they fought for supremacy in a land where anyone can be king.

Even at night these towers sought order on the wilds of the universe. The evening before, from our sweat and oil-reeking taxi from JFK into town, Elly and I saw Manhattan's skyscrapers like giant holding pens of stars, all herded and stacked, given a price, the skyline marking a jagged frontier between man-made order and stellar wilderness.

God, New York was beautiful.

God, Elly was beautiful.

And it was all so new, you could imagine how recently this was an island of trees, fishermen and natives scraping along, year in, Millennia out. Before the foreigners came and claimed it all, drew it on a map with a million squares and built the city thus, building east, west, north, south, under, and over, over and over, up and up and up, the city planned by a man with a ruler lining up the road and blocks, going *pht pht pht* with his pen across the page. A city built so fast in a land without history the streets had no names, just numbers, so the Empire stood on the meeting point of fifth and thirty-third east, or *fifth and thoidy-thoid east* as the locals said. They called this abstract grid of numbered lines 'real estate' – such an American term! 'Real estate, Gorrrdamn, nyadder-nyadder-nyadder' – they were just too Goddamn busy to think up some cockamamie street names. 'Shtreet noim? Wad? Nyadder nyadder ged oudda my way, I godda skyscraper to build, asshole!' And they did, building up and up to convert God's heavenly island and its blue vaulted sky into their own man-made mountain scape.

And here we were, en route to Chicago for a summer of selling ice-cream, and like you do when you're jet set and fucking cool, you stop off in New York for a day of sight-seeing – *Noo Yoik!* – done best from up here, looking down over the mean city streets of the sprawling metropolis, like Batman, out on the ledge, one foot up on the head of some stone lion head.

I tried to say something like all that to Elly, reckoning that surely here, of all places, we'd have to snog. But here, of all places, still she would not be wooed.

This was our first morning in *Noo Yoik*, we'd just flown in from Heathrow to JFK the evening before, and everything was brilliant. Everything! Even passport control, where a fat, bearded man not only checked my passport but then interrogated me about what I was doing in the US, how long I'd stay, where was I going, how much money I had, how I got it, where I'd worked, what I'd earned an hour, all questions I answered with lies: I was here on holiday, to stay with a friend, for a month (lucky he didn't ask for my 'friend's' address, nor to see my return ticket, as I had neither, I only had the phone number of the guy I was going to work for, but calling him to vouch for me would have backfired). That I had loads of money, from working in McDonalds, was obviously bollocks because McDonalds' pay was shit, and I really had only a couple of hundred dollars on me – because we were off to make millions from selling ice-cream! The lies and the heat made me sweat, and the fat bearded man's tone became sharper with each question, so I was sure any second he'd declare, 'I know you're lying! You're going to Chicago to work illegally! *You're busted – I got your ass*!', but instead he stamped my passport and said, 'Welcome to New York, have a nice stay.' Moreorless what I'd thought he'd say at the outset.

Anyway, I'd made it in, and so had Elly! And here we were at the brilliantly grim JFK airport, filled with brilliant muggy summer heat. The phones needing quarters – *kwaaders*, as they said on *Sesame St* – were brilliant, the *Noo Yoik* accent of the hostel receptionist I spoke to to book a room was brilliant, the cops standing around with their black uniforms and huge guns were brilliant. While we were snail-like with our heaving rucksacks on our backs, there were people at the airport going around with only small suitcases or briefcases – these people commuted by plane – so extravagant! Brilliant! The line of oily, dented yellow cabs with their dorsal fin adverts waiting to take us *where we wanna go, man* along a yellow river shimmering with red tail lights was brilliant. Even the traffic tailback to the toll-gates was brilliant with the continuous angry beeping of car horns as drivers jostled into queues, the distant insults of '*move it asshole*', '*hold your horses, bitch!*'!

The drive into Manhattan, like a dream.

The hostel, a tall, thin building with cracked walls and rooms barely wider than the bunks, was brilliant, as was the endless cacophony of car horns, sirens and yells from the streets throughout the night as we sweatily tossed and turned in the mean city heat.

Breakfast in the hostel canteen, all blueberry muffins, pancakes and endless cups of coffee, was brilliant. The shop selling a hundred varieties of unknown cigarettes was brilliant, with its massive fridge heaving with Coke, diet Coke, caffeine-free, diet caffeine-free, cherry, diet cherry, caffeine free cherry, and weird stuff like Mountain Dew. Hershey Bars! Which I thought would be delicious, because Americans do shit better than everyone, but were horribly bitter. And the trek to the Empire State building was brilliant, the streets littered with film props, an empty half-bottle of whisky in a little brown paper bag, the yellow cabs, the black and white police cars – smoking manholes! I wanted to scream! *Noo Yoik* was everything *Cagney and Lacey* made it out to be. And as we traipsed the streets, ahead in the distance, in a light grey haze against the blue sky up, loomed the Empire State building – for real!

And at the top the gallant hero (me) would sweep the girl (Elly) off her feet, their lips meeting and parting across the blinding backdrop of the almightiest nuclear explosion, like in *True Lies*, but this time the Sun itself. Who could resist a snog here? Who? Who? On top of the world, on top of the New World, what else was there to do except snog and celebrate being able to see all around and touch the sky? Who wouldn't swoon to such a view? Who would dream of doing anything else, but snog?

Her, for one. Every time I got near, her staggeringly beautiful eyes, as blue as the sky around, as enveloping as the deep end of a swimming pool on a sunny day, those arrogant eyes, filled with the sentiment, 'I'm not impressed. You're barely amusing me, and that's all.' That little nick of a smile at her perfectly pouted lips, said, 'I'm not rewarding what's hard work for you.' Her posture, her gait, the way she sauntered, it all screamed, 'you're going to have to do more, much, much more,' with the unspoken certainty that none of it would work, but I was welcome to keep trying.

Not only was she not blown away by being up here, atop one of the greatest cities in the world, atop these sheer, diamond-crusted canyons and the shimmering canals of cars, and worse, something told me she was underwhelmed because of something I'd done, or not done. Maybe if I'd just grabbed her and held her and kissed her that would have worked, but being a gutless fucker I preferred endless preparation instead of seizing what chances came my way. Maybe she wasn't being hard on me, it was me being hard on me, but gutless fuckers turn on themselves first and worst.

4

Still I hoped that with just the right effort, somehow, with just the right twist, wisecrack, factoid, that oh-so-elusive something, she'd fall for me, fall into my arms.

She nearly had. While she'd been indifferent to my efforts of the previous ten months back at uni, at first we'd really fancied one another, gone out on a date, and she wanted another, but somehow, somehow … I bottled it. She was upset. Then by the time I'd got the guts to try and reprise things, she'd lost interest.

So we become friends. Very good friends. But for her, I was just a friend. For me, she was everything I wanted and so very nearly had. And she sometimes got epically pissed off with me, life and everything for that, but she must have had a reason for rejecting me. What was it I lacked? If I could just find out what it was, I could rectify it. I was like a scientist in his lab, going mad in his search to develop that superpower turning him from a geek into a superhero.

I must have done something wrong at some point, because I'd been that close. And I mean, that close. No-one fucking believed me. But I had been, but somehow I'd blown it. How?

How elusive was that 'thing' that would open her heart *ZZ and open her satin-smooth legs to reveal her vagina dripping with clear, viscous fluid of desire* …. What was that 'thing' I'd lacked that led her to reject me? I spent countless nights blacked out on pints drunk at Formica tables in shitty student bars, all so vibrant the first weeks, then emptied over the year, then dark days wondering where I'd gone wrong and how I'd got so close to winning over this Goddess, then missed.

I had asked her out, she'd said yes, we had a lovely evening, she really enjoyed it. But then I got afraid, and backed away, and she was shy, and so was I … and I couldn't even speak to her in the studio … and I saw her look at me once, her eyes so sad.

Weeks later we found ourselves getting drunk together and she asked why I'd lost interest and I said I hadn't at all, I'd just become overwhelmed by shyness, and then we nearly snogged, but didn't, I held back. We hung out a bit over the coming days and I got this strong sense we would get together, but then she said she liked me as a friend, and it was too late: on our first date she'd met my best mate Mark, and now she really liked him.

Ah, fuck.

And as I spent the rest of the year wondering what he had, I cooked up any number of new identities to try and win her over, and none worked, all those new characters became ever growing casualties in the appalling civil war in my mind, that concluded I was a useless bastard, proven by fighting myself in this kind of stupid war, a war with myself that I was losing. Holy shit. And yet just one kiss from her could have brought peace and order to my world, would have healed all the pain. If she'd just once taken me in her arms and brushed her lips against mine, all would have been resolved.

But it wasn't happening. My role was to entertain, whichever side of the Atlantic we were on, and again, I was failing, for which she wasn't going to reward me with a smile, let alone a fucking snog.

'I wonder what the other architects are up to?' I wondered aloud over the hum from the streets so far below. 'Fred's working on a farm this summer, isn't he? Somewhere in Hereford?' I knew Elly had fancied Fred, and strongly suspected she'd done something with him, either way it was good to highlight that he could be up to his knees in pig-shit.

ZZ! But she'd be with him, on her knees, rosy cheeks filled with his pork saus – stop! Stop! Another terrible sex pun electrocuted my mind. Damn, I thought they'd stopped. I had to press on.

'Peter's going grape-picking,' I said.

'Really? I thought he was Billy-No-mates?'

'Oh, he is. He's going alone,' I chortled.

'That's nice. You're supposed to be his friend, aren't you?'

Not only did she know I hated Peter, but she hated him too. He wasn't a bad bloke, except he wasn't a bloke, he was a child in the body of a 19-year-old who'd latched onto me from day one and wouldn't leave me alone, but proved so pitiful I hadn't the heart to tell him where to go. A youth you'd have a beer with out of pity or boredom and just wanted somebody present while you got pissed, and probably subject to a load of verbal abuse as the drinking wore on, which he'd just take, sitting there, until your real friends turned up and you could happily side line him, but he'd get his revenge by introducing himself as your best mate and going into prat overdrive and you'd see it in everyone's faces, they were thinking, 'Christ, is this guy a friend of yours?'

Pretty much what Elly was thinking now.

'Errm, yes, up to the point that I think he's a complete twat.'

'Does he know that's what you think?'

'Well we're not spending summer together and I've always refused to give him my home address, so he might work it out.'

She smiled lightly. Having deigned to engage in this barely interesting natter, she'd effortlessly shown me up to be a bit nasty.

I changed tack.

'And here we are. New York, *Noo Yoik*!' I beamed, outstretching my arms as if to embrace the city's panorama, then I turned to embrace her, but she was out of range.

'I'm getting hungry,' she said.

'Brilliant! Lunch it is!'

'All right,' she looked at me, 'like?'

'Like, whatever. What are you up for. You can get anything, that's *Noo Yoik*!' I outstretched again. She just shrugged. This was getting demoralizing.

6

We took the rocket-lift down, and looked up and down the street for possible food outlets.

'I thought there'd be McDonalds and stuff on every corner,' I said.

'Don't want a McDonalds.'

'Well nor do I. I know, why don't we just head for Central Park and see what we can pick up on the way?'

'Can we just find somewhere to eat? I'm hungry.'

'Yes, that's what I'm suggesting. There must be something on the way to the park. We could try and knock up a picnic.'

ZZ go on a picnic and knock her up.

Another evil pun electrocuted my mind. A storm of sex puns, and an accompanying headache, were heading my way.

I got the *Rough Guide to the USA* out of my khaki canvas rucksack, then Elly hissed, 'put it away, we'll get mugged as tourists, fucking idiot.' So with only a best guess as to the direction of the park, we started to walk.

And walk.

And walk.

From the Empire to Central Park was far further on the ground than it seemed from up on the Empire's observation platform, and the speedy crowds with their *ged-oudda-my-way* look in their eyes, the *Walk–Don't Walk* signs, the hot-dog stands and all the other familiar stuff from TV were of no interest as hunger took over. Then over the road I spotted this place called Joni's Deli. A deli! A brilliantly American food joint!

'Look there you go, perfect. Come on, let's jaywalk,' I said. Another sarcastic great-time-party look from her, but she was wrong. The idea of getting busted for crossing the road was brilliantly exciting and ridiculous.

People were pushing past each other in and out the deli, with a long high-stool bar along its plate window lined with all people churning into heaving plates of stuff.

'Get me something. I'm staying outside,' said Elly.

'Right, what do you want?' I clapped and rubbed my hands with anticipation.

'Anything.'

'Well give me some idea?'

'Anything.'

'OK. Pastrami on rye, hold the mayo?'

'What the fuck is that?'

'Something Noo Yoikers eat!' my mouth agape in excitement.

She looked disdainful.

'Cheese and pickle?' I said.

She tossed her hand up. 'Yes, whatever.'

Inside, the deli went back forever, with two long rows of tables and wide, brown leather double seats going down the left side, a chessboard-tiled aisle, then a long, long glass counter containing buckets and plates and trays of meats, salady stuff, God knew what. It was packed, the noise was incredible, every table was full with people from business types to old ladies, scoffing, chattering, clattering their cutlery, while the folk in the long queue along the counter shouted orders to the half-dozen women in white bustling behind the counter, scribbled on bits of paper, shouting at one another over a row of cracking crockery and hissing coffee machines, and scooping heinous mounds of fluorescent stuff onto a dazzling variety of breads, rolls, bagels. And all at such speed. Most of it looked delicious, but totally unidentifiable, and as I moved slowly along the queue, I was increasingly baffled by the choice of foods. And this was just for sandwiches and salads!

A suited man in front of me fired orders of rocket science complexity, 'Two Danish and an open with lettuce and hold the mustard side pickle and honey ham on high and toasted and pastrami on one Danish butter on the other *on-de-udder nyadder -nyadder-nyadder waah waah nyadder-nyadder ... .*' The words were lost in the noise of jets of steam, clanging, clattering, shouts of *hey dis, hey dat ... nyadder-nyadder to go! C'm orrrrn let's moiv! Gatcha oider heyerr* from the sandwich women. That's what I thought I heard, but not only was all that movie-speak I'd heard real, but I'd never really understood it, as his order was sliced and splatted together with such speed, then this well-fed olive-skinned woman said loudly to me, 'Hey mister, take your order?' or '*oidah*'.

'Erm ... errr ... do you have ... err', I said, gazing blankly at all the food buckets, trying to see something I recognised and wanted to eat. I should have chosen by now but it was all so confusing!

'What do you want, mister?' – *waddya want, mistah?* said the sandwich woman. Others queuing behind tutted and hummed loudly, and I got nervous and stared hard at the long menu on the wall above the counter for help, but random words like 'kraut', 'knishes', 'rye' (brilliant!) 'Burrito', 'pita', 'pastrami' (brilliant!) stuck out and I couldn't see good old cheese and pickle or egg and cress anywhere.

She tapped the glass top, hard and loud, looking unimpressed. 'Don't keep me waiting now!' – *waidin' now.*

'Have you got ... err.. .. could I have egg and cress rolls?' I said. They sold egg and cress sandwiches at the café at the top of Peter Jones' shop on Sloane Square, ma used to take us, and I'd look out at all the ornate Victorian flats with the natural child's assumption that because I wanted one of those flats, one day I'd live in one.

'What?' the sandwich woman bawled, or rather, *wad?*

'Egg and cress rolls.' O come on, everybody knows egg and cress, surely.

What's dis guy's problem, someone in the queue said, so I thought I heard.

'Egg and cress what, open, Danish, wrap? Wad, mister?'

Eh? I said rolls! 'Well what's the difference?' I said, eyes wide. Rolls, woman! Egg and cress rolls!

'What kind of rolls?'

Aww, c'm awwwn, someone said.

'Normal rolls!' I said in exasperation.

'Man I want to know do you want normal, open, Danish, wrap, on what kinda bread?' she barracked, as a minor chorus of *Jeez, Goddamn, wad's wid dis goi*, grew louder behind me, or so I thought, someone was saying something aggressive at me, I bottled it and left.

Outside, Elly was conspicuously bored. 'Where's the food?' she snapped.

'It looked terrible, covered in rats and cockroaches. Let's find somewhere else.'

'Where's the food? Come on.'

'It was really busy. Everyone was really sort of ner-r-r-r-ruur-ururur and jostling and stuff and ordering weird shit and being ill-mannered.'

So? only her eyes said.

'It was complicated.'

'Sandwiches are complicated?'

'Yes, not your Marmite rolls in there, matey,' I started laughing, but she didn't.

'You didn't ask for Marmite, did you?' she said, with a good slice of disbelieving contempt. 'Useless. You're useless!' then she laughed. A laugh! Well that was progress.

We trekked on, stopping off at a store to get some Diet Coke, not caffeine-free Coke or Cherry Coke, nor Tab – Tab! Eventually on the edge of Central Park we found a food shop, with endless arrays of jars of olives, alien pickles strange-looking breads, not a loaf of Mothers' Pride in sight. What was it with these people and their bread? Our picnic of cheese, the most normal looking bread we could find, tomatoes and this big jar drink thing called Schnapples or something, in like grape and blueberry – why?– was loaded into a large brown cuboid paper bags – brilliant – solely for the groceries from *de shtoor* (brilliant!) and finally we got to Central Park – brilliant! – a row of coaches and horses, or *hosses*, in sight. Beginning to wilt under the sharp sunshine that burned the colours out of everything, we found a bench next to some baseball pens and ate to the sound of players shouting *STRI-I-KE*, *awesome*, and *dumbass*, while lithe women and men on roller blades scythed past - brilliant!

Elly's mood improved and we got on almost like we used to, when were we out getting hammered, but I was still having to think hard of things to say. Then I saw in the distance an open-top tour bus offering a tour for $10.

'Why don't we get one of those tourist buses? Over there? $10 for three hours, see everything, it'll take out the afternoon, and then we can get pissed somewhere.'

'Don't spend all your money here,' she replied.

'It's only $10. It'll be fun.' She didn't reply. 'Don't you think?' She didn't look enthused. 'What do you want to do?'

'I'm not really interested,' she said.

'Not interested in what?'

'I'm not really interested in seeing New York,' she said.

'Eh?'

'I've seen it before. New York. It's not new,' she said.

'You said you'd never been here before. What do you mean it's not new? Of course it's new, it's New York!'

'So, I haven't been here before,' she replied, her tone all yes-you're-right-but-so-fucking-what.

'So how have you seen it before?'

'In Canada, in my year-off. I told you,' hinting as she often did that I'd forgotten this and so wasn't listening in the first place. She often said, 'you don't listen'.

Like I was her boyfriend.

Which I wasn't.

But wanted to be.

'Oh yeah, Canada,' I said. Canada, land of trees, being chopped down. maple syrup and bears. Canada, as in Canada, not New York. 'Did you come down from there to here?'

'No.'

'So when did you come here?' I was confused.

'I've been to Toronto, silly. I was there for three months, like I told you.'

I looked at her, baffled.

'It's the same as here,' she continued, 'There's nothing here for me to see.' She actually said this with a straight face. She said it so matter-of-factly, as if this was reasonable behaviour from a tourist with only a two evenings and a day to see this incredible place. She'd been to Toronto, and so she didn't need to go round New York. She was comparing Toronto to New York. New York? *Noo Yoik*? What the fuck. I picked up the guidebook and showed it to her, pointing out the emboldened highlights on the maps.

'There's stacks to see. What about Soho, or Greenwich Village, or that lot. Look, from here, they're on the way to the World Trade Centre by Tube, or the subway, the *shubway*. It'd be a piece of piss to get there.'

'So go and see them,' she said.

'But you're not coming?' I said, feeling my voice die.

'I'm not really bothered. You go if you want.'

Not bothered? New York? People had died to get here. People had killed to get here. I'd had to get my mum to lie to her dad so he'd allow her to stop over here. Her folks thought she was flying direct to Chicago, whereas the cheapest tickets involved a two-night stopover for which Elly was thrilled, but she said her dad wouldn't let her stay in New York, and he also wanted to talk with my mum about the whole trip, so I got her to tell him I was a nice boy – true – but also to lie that we were going straight to Chicago, which poor old ma had been very, very reluctant to do. But she did it, for me, knowing how I felt about Elly. And for nothing.

10

Then we'd had to lie to get through passport control, pretending we were tourists and not spending a summer selling ice-cream on non-existent work permits. That all came about through my mate Christian, a medical student who lived next to us in halls. He'd been on holiday in the US the year before and stopped off to see a mate in Chicago who was selling ice-cream on a student visa. Business was great, drivers too few, and Christian was asked if he wanted a go, and he had such fun and made so much money he wanted to come back this year on a veteran rate, and asked if I'd like to come. Hell yes, and as the year collapsed into a self-hating black Hell of drink and dope, it was the one thing worth looking forward to – especially when one boozy evening with Elly she asked if she could come, and of course I said yes, (or 'abso-fucking-lutely yes fucking A!'), making the whole trip wondrous and cool and legit. Things were worth doing if she was there. And I'd phoned the owner of the ice-cream company, this guy Hank, and he sounded really cool and nice, speaking with this long relaxed drawl (Christian said he was very laid back), and he was prepared to take a punt on having us without permits … and now we were on our way there, stopping off in one of the most incredible cities on Earth.

But now she couldn't be bothered.

'This is the only day we're here. We've only got one day here,' I said, no longer bothering to hide my bafflement and disappointment. And for the first time ever, some anger. I never got angry with Elly. She couldn't do any wrong in my eyes. She got angry with me, but I was useless so it was fair enough.

But she just shrugged. New York wasn't a city she was bothered with.

'So what are you going to do then?' I asked.

Another shrug. 'Go back to the hostel. Write letters to people.'

'Write letters? You're going back to that cupboard of a hostel room, to write letters?' I sounded like Robert Redford in *A Bridge Too Far*, barracking the British tank brigade who refuse to advance, "'I lost half my men to take that bridge, those are Briddish troops dying in Arnhem … and you're just going to sit there? And … drink tea??'"

Oo, don't take that tone of voice with me, her look said. 'Yeah, in the coffee bar, or in our room.'

'What are you going to write about? "Having a lovely time in New York lying in this bunk bed writing to you, but having refused to see anything here, I've actually got nothing to say, so … um".'

Me being sarcastic with her was daring … I was frightening myself. She looked miffed. But I didn't care, I was going to interrogate her on this because her lack of interest was staggering.

'And who are you going to write to?'

Oh no, let me guess.

'Richard,' she said, and she said it with barely disguised glee that it'd hit me like a fish in the face.

Richard.

Always Richard.

11

Amazing Richard.

God-like Richard.

Super Richard.

Her ex from her Colombian adventure the year before. The one she'd had a whirlwind, three-month romance with in the heady South American jungle. *ZZ he'd been in her jungle.*

Well this wasn't Colombia, it was New York. And here we were, now having a perfectly shit time.

'Presumably you'll tell them about the great time you're having in New York.' I couldn't disguise the sarcasm.

'And that I'm having this wonderful time with you,' she could have said, but chose not to sink to my level.

'What you going to do, then, tourist?' she asked, saying 'tourist' like I had the problem.

'Look around,' like, apparently, stupid people do when they're in a city on holiday. This was crazy.

But if she wasn't interested, she wasn't interested. My head was beginning to hurt. If we split up I might be able to find some inspiration round town for a later chat that would woo her, make her realise what a truly great guy I am.

I stood up from the bench and made up some vague plan about going to the World Trade Center. Have a good time, she said. We parted.

I would have checked the guidebook again about getting to the World Trade Center, had Elly not made me so self-conscious about getting the book out, but I knew it was pretty much due south, and there was just enough angle off the Sun to gauge the direction, so just started walking.

I saw a big black cop, or *cahp*, on the *sidewalk* across the road, I crossed at the crossing – *walk, don't walk* – and went up to him. 'Excuse me, Mr Policeman sir, could you tell me which way is the World Trade Center?', half hoping this *cahp*, who investigated *moidahs* and shot felons before his morning coffee and doughnuts, would tell me 'go buy a goddamn map!' Instead he looked at me kindly, and said, 'the World Trade Center is, gee from here, it's at least fifty blocks, that way,' and pointed down the canyon of tall buildings to the point on the horizon where they disappeared and where I couldn't see WTC sticking out, but surely a block wasn't a great unit of distance.

'OK. How long's that on foot?'

'You gonna WALK?' he said incredulously.

Hooray, a reaction! From a *Noo Yoik cahp*.

'Yes!'

'That'll be, er, about an hour anna' half, maybe, two hours?'

'OK thank you very much,' I said.

'You're welcome, take care now,' he replied, smiling.

It was a long way south. I didn't see much if anything by way of crime or shootings or whatnot. Turning down a shaded street, a down-and-out looking chap accosted me. Was he a hobo?

'Hey man, I need some money, man, give us some money.'

Shit, was I being mugged? First full day in *Noo Yoik* and we've got a mugging! Brilliant! Emboldened by the excitement, I said: 'I haven't got any money. Do you want a cigarette?'

'No man, I need money, to eat, for food,' although he had a long salady baguette thing in cling film under his arm.

'You've got a sandwich already.'

'Dat's for now. Come on.'

With my most vice-like grip I opened my wallet, keeping the notes' slit out of his view and gave him a couple of dollars.

'Nyrrr, two bucks? Is that all?' he grizzled.

'Do what? That's loads.'

'Nyrrr, anna' cigarette.'

'Tsk! I asked if you wanted one and you said no.'

'Nyrrrr!'

He took one and I lit it. And off he went without thanks! 'Anytime!' I called.

'Nyrrr!' he replied, punting a fist skyward.

Was that a mugging, or were *Noo Yoik* beggars – or rather, hobos – just much more aggressive than Londoners' 'spare us some change'? Was he going back to his burning brazier to stand with his friends, all wearing flat hats and fingerless gloves? I didn't have time to follow him and find out, but how exciting! A real life *Noo Yoik* hobo, and I had a showdown with him!

Exciting though that was, the trek along the long, long sidewalks south were getting my feet all hot and bothered, and I decided to try and take the *subway*, going down the steps to a really grotty underground station, all dirty tiles, like something off *Death Wish*. There it got weird because instead of ticket machines and then feeding the ticket into the big padded chomp-chomp gates they have on the Tube, they had these crappy turnstiles operated by tokens. Then the Tube map was unintelligible, so were the line maps on the dingy, ugly platform, all broken up by vertical steel girders. It was as dour and oppressive, but worse was when the train came in, and it was all clean steel! Not a single squiggle of graffiti on it, let alone an incredible 100-yard long work of spray can art about 'DIE HONKY SH-I-IT' that I'd expected to see squealing past at horrible speed which you'd expect from Noo Yoik! .

I'd no idea what train to take, or what the map destinations really meant, I couldn't see anything that simply said World Trade Center. The trouble was I was so self-conscious about staring at the maps or getting the guidebook out, standing there looking all lost and confused like a tourist until someone somebody would come over and I'd be shot.

13

As fun as being mugged was I was now worried about being robbed, or *rorbbed* and shot, and obviously asking anyone for help might lead to all that anyway if they hadn't taken offence cos I'd looked at them funny, as *Noo Yoikers* seemed more excitable than Londoners, and then I'd get shot for that as well.

Plus I wasn't entirely sure if I was in fact heading for the World Trade Center and instead might be heading for Pelham or the Bronx, where I'd get shot.

But then if I got on a random train and got out at some distant destination looking all bewildered I'd probably be spotted and shot anyway, if somebody hadn't already shot me on the train, and there were none of these famed Guardian Angel chaps in sight! Oh my Gahhd!

I got the next train. The carriage was pretty busy, and unlike the Tube it was all high enough to stand in, no need to crook your neck if next to the door. There was one free seat down one side of the carriage, but I didn't take it in case doing so transgressed some unstated subway rule and someone had already laid claim to it and I'd get shot. I wondered if we'd be hijacked like in *The Taking of Pelham 1-2-3*, which would normally be brilliant, but I'd miss my flight out the next morning. So I stood and tried to look uninterested.

A few seats down the carriage towards the next set of doors, I could see a hobo, slumped in a seat at the end of the bench, with one arm draped along the back of seat and his head hanging down, his chin almost touching his chest, with a tiny cable of drool bungee-jumping from his mouth. His clothes were 1980s, but worn and stained several shades darker by the dirt holding them together. The few clearings of his face visible through a jungle of beard and knotted hair showed an AZ map of broken veins, like a city gone to ruin. Next to his feet on the floor was a brown paper bag – brilliant! – that clinked every time the train jostled, and threatened to trip up more than one passenger teetering past. He was taking up two seats as no-one wanted to risk sitting next to him, and his smell and the drool created a standing cordon zone around him in case he was sick, or barfed his cookies. I heard someone say, 'Goddamn bum', and something about get the police. Then the train pulled into a station and stopped sharply, jolting everyone into one another, and causing the hobo's head to flip up and then bang sharply towards his shoulder, whereupon he suddenly awoke, reared up, eyes half-closed, and, with an arm outstretched, filthy hand gnarled into a claw, shouted in a voice more gravelly than James Coburn, but *so* loud, 'Mere-diiiith … *WHY?*'

Everyone turned and stared at him in shocked silence. The hobo, having woken himself up, now glanced embarrassedly around, hoicked his bag onto his lap and muttered 'sorry, sorry'. No one commented after that.

I'd only travelled a few stations when I decided to get out and press on on foot. The traffic never stopped, the blocks never ended, the sunshine blazed away, and though I hadn't really stopped since Central Park, I still didn't seem anywhere near the World Trade towers. To cope with the pedestrians I had to almost get in-lane then stick to it, no weaving or ambling along. There was all the street furniture, the little red fire hydrants, the guys in long coats and peaked hats outside posh shops and hotels, shop signs that just said LIQUOR, but none of it was as much fun by myself, and I was tiring and getting pongy.

Maybe Elly was right, this was boring. No doubt Richard would have come up with something better and fun that she would have jumped at. Probably the same as this, but because he thought of it, she'd think it incredible and great. A headache clouded in and I started thinking about their lust in the dusts of Colombia. He who'd come out of the sunset and saved her, she'd been lost and alone in the expanses of South America until he'd come along and they joined up *ZZ O yes didn't they fucking just, just fucking*, and spent months battling to save the poor little orphans of South America. He who'd rescued her from all the sexual predators and weirdoes lurking in the hillsides waiting to abduct her, ravish her, then spear her open and eat the remains. He who'd betrayed his fiancée – oh yes he did! – to have a doomed Mills & Boon affair with Elly. An affair! Elly had been a Mistress, of all the exciting things, a Scarlet Woman, a woman whose love (*ZZ and lust*) had led her to dare to endure the cruel slurs of a Puritanical world. And this added to her sense of being a woman, for those mocked and denounced as whores, she now knew too were women of feelings and love, who could be hurt, and weren't they, and the sex, all the more incredible for it.

Fucking Richard – *ZZ yes fucking Richard!* – at Cambridge now, doing his wonderful, intelligent degree in anthropology, the subject Elly was now switching to having decided architecture wasn't interesting, and by extension, I lost interest in it too, graduating from top student to total fuck up in less than a year, and thought of doing anthropology but realised it'd look so lame if I did.

Ah, Richard, nobly and honourably still burdened with this fiancée he was duty-bound to marry for some piss arse scam, a marriage of convenience that was nonetheless keeping him from Elly, or so Elly said. What a heroic sacrifice Richard was making! How eye-wateringly tragic that had made their shag-fest, it was beyond any level of romance and tragedy seen in *Out Of Africa*, although when I said *Romancing The Stone* was more appropriate, she said 'you're just jealous', and I was.

Brilliant Richard. Profound Richard. Brave Richard, who'd fought back from months in bed suffering from ME. 'Oh God it's Hell being ME, I'm positively bed-ridden with angst', Richard lamented every day, while Elly wept at his heroic lethargy *ZZ and so always went on top to save his energy*.

You want to try being ME, Richard, you big-nosed git *ZZ a nose big enough to lance deep into her when he's licking her from behind*. You see, Richard, try being me. You'd never fucking get up again. *ZZ – big nose, big willy, don't forget*.

How many times had she told me this story, crying her eyes dry while I heaved my guts drier, bloody Colombia, bloody orphans, bloody rescuing her (from nobody) and shagging and getting hammered and shagging. Richard, who

15

I was often and always unfavourably compared with, although he was her boyfriend, and I never was.

Richard, who from the photos I'd been (often) shown actually looked a bit too much like Richard 'Gerbil' Gere for my liking. But apparently that beat my vague resemblance to Colin Firth, as did every other thing about the sensuous, super-insightful, seductive but sensitive philanderer Richard. The benchmark to - *ZZ-bedpost mark* – for her perfect man, a benchmark I'd never reach, no matter how hard I tried, and yet I still tried, and she still let me, me hoping, her knowing there was none.

All this flitted through my mind as I walked on and on. The cool breeze that had made the morning so fresh had long gone, the sun had already arced over and scorched both of the never-ending walls of the canyon, and remained a heat trap even as the buildings began to sink under the rising tide of shadows. My feet were hot and fat as burgers. The roads still ran straight as arrows in the four directions, with humans and vehicles kept in sharp geometric flows by the soaring walls of buildings. I realised I was nowhere near anywhere, really, and all alone I didn't really feel much reason to go any further. I had a camera but was too self-conscious as a tourist to take any pictures in case I got shot, and I didn't have a huge amount of film.

I found a café and from another dizzying array of coffee stuff, mocho or macho, coffee without caffeine, iced coffee, coffee with canned cream stuff shat all over it, and chocolate dust, from all of which I managed to get just a simple black coffee, and reviewed my location. I was really just a few blocks from the hostel, so I thought 'ah fuck it', went back and found Elly on her bunk, postcards new and written on her pillow. She looked up and smiled.

'Did you have a good time?'

'It was all right. Didn't get to the World Trade Center, though.'

'Shame. Do you want to go out and find a bar?'

'Yes!'

Maybe it wasn't so shit. The Sun was still up but on its way out, and we wandered along and found a bar with a sign pointing down a flight of stairs, leading to a dark-wooded bar like that of *Cheers!*, but dingier.

I asked for two beers. 'Are you a minor?' the barman asked.

'No, I work above ground,' I said, grinning.

He replied curtly, 'ID'.

I burrowed in my bag for my ISIC card, carefully doctored with a pencil to make me over 21, and which I'd worried would be found at JFK customs and I'd be busted.

'What is this ID?' he said.

'It's a student card.'

'Is this valid?' he asked.

'Yes!' I said, wondering if he'd expected me to say 'actually, no! You got me!'

'OK,' he said.

I told this to Elly and she laughed, and we ended up whiling away a couple of pleasant hours getting sozzled, just me and her, which was all I wanted really. But the day was still squandered and the beer quickly went to my overcooked head.

Heading back to the hostel we decided to get a six-pack of bright yellow lager. Our room was as filled with the noise and heat of *Noo Yoik* as the night before, but Elly now didn't want any of the beers, so I drank them in bed, for some reason telling her about the attack of the ants in the film *Phase IV*, until she told me to shuttup, and then all the beer I'd drunk to fuel my courage to make a move on her now worked to knock me out without trying. This wasn't brilliant, it was crappy.

On to Chicago

I felt groggy as shit in the cab back to JFK early next morning, to fly on
to Chicago. We left early in case we ended up marooned in some steaming
yellow stream of taxis backed up to Manhattan to a soundtrack of car horns and
abuse, while somehow seeing our plane beetle away into the distant sky. In fact,
we barely stopped and hit the airport not only well early, but then we saw on the
almighty departures' boards our flight was delayed, leaving loads of time to get
bored and spend our few dollars on over-priced coffee and water. Elly didn't
blame me for this, but did say, 'We could have spent the morning looking at
New York,' to which I thought, you cheeky cow. You bloody cheeky cow.

The delayed flight meant getting a later train from Chicago to
Schaumberg, where Hank was going to pick us up, so I phoned him to say we'd
be late, and he luckily pointed out we had to go to Shorewood, not Schaumberg.
We still had hours to kill and mill around until check in, so I went and stared at
the departure boards, in case glaring at it made our flight move up the queue.

There were flights to every American city I knew, many I didn't, and then
the whole world, by so many airlines I'd never heard of. It certainly wasn't all
TWA and American Airlines. No Pan Am, they'd already gone bust over
Lockerbie.

The departure board showed all the destinations, flight numbers and gate
numbers printed in neat little white letters on a morass of little black slats, and as
each flight left, its departure was marked by its slats at the top of the queue
flipping to black, *phtphtpht*, shortly followed by a mass cascade across the board
as the other flights shuffled one along,
phtphtphtphtphtphtphtphtphthtphtphtphtphtphtphtpht, like when one bird takes
off and the whole flock suddenly follows, or maybe they were just giving the
departing plane a massive round of applause.

I fished out of a bin, or the *garbage*, a slightly soiled New York Times,
while Elly started to read the book I'd given her back at Heathrow about some
girl who, like her, had done a gap year in South America. We'd broken up from
uni only a couple of weeks before, I'd gone home to London and her to Bristol,
and I'd found this book I thought she'd like. She was very happy about it, but not
read it on the London-JFK leg cos she'd been busy being chatted up by this
bloke next to her who kept on showing her pages of *Viz*. He didn't even speak to
me, just looked at me like I was a nob. Fucking mutual, mate.

Anyway. We checked in, walked down this walkway to infinity to our
departure gate, where she got out the book, and I looked at the planes.

There were 747s, some long, some fat and stubby, and countless 737s,
like the one that had burned out at Manchester. A few pencil-like 757s, and a
727, so small and dinky compared with the others. There was a chunky
Lockheed TriStar, and at least one Airbus. A DC-3 Dakota which was lovely to
see, although Elly didn't share my enthusiasm, and an old four-engined jet that
was either a DC-8 or a 707, it was certainly other-era-ish, then two DC-10s –
which I thought had all crashed. I'd been mad keen on being a pilot since being a

18

kid, and had joined the school RAF cadets, but then the Gulf War broke out and when I saw one of the boys in the army section, only 13 or 14, sauntering along in his camo gear, wielding a rifle, I thought, 'this is how it starts, how they get us to go die for them.' I wasn't going to go kill or get killed for the likes of John Major, and left, never joining the service for real.

Boy, did I regret that. My first and bestest friend at uni was Mark, interested like me in economics and politics, but he was also an ATC pilot, as by then I would have been, and who'd also met Elly on our first and only date.

After I fumbled it, and she'd lost interest, she was after him, partly dazzled by his heroic uniform. Time and again she she'd begged me to bring him out clubbing or whatever, and bit by bit he got the message.

I saw the looks pass between them.

Saw them holding hands.

Saw them clench and kiss.

I'd even thought of rejoining the RAF to impress her, but this plan ended up on the towering scrapheap of futile efforts, with every week starting with a new plan, and every week ending with disappointment and drink, then spliff, then drink and spliff every night.

There was no escape. She was on the course, with my mates, then round the flat. Mark's room overlooked the courtyard above the main door and even walking back I could see them in his room. Then inside I heard them fucking, as so lost in lust they'd left his door ajar. I'd gone into my room and banged my head against the brick wall.

The self-hatred.

Wow, the self-hatred.

The black, black Hell of the hate. Weeks, months of screaming torture in my mind: *Zz yep she'd been on his joystick on that cockpit zzz he'd elevated her flaps – zzz undercarriage up zzz – mile high club zzz.* Luckily he dumped her after only a few weeks, and she consoled herself by telling us he had a tiny cock and was shit in bed. But even that was Hell to hear.

I'd written the notes, how many times had I hung out of one of 20th floor windows of the student tower. Something pulled me back in, but more I screamed within of cowardice, the self-hatred and wanting to die battling the self-hatred of its selfishness, how bad everyone would feel, and the thought I'd just fuck that up as well and just end up crippled for ever.

I wasn't sure I hadn't binned my first-year exams just to get her attention. And here, in the Land of the Free, on this beautifully sunny day, en route for a summer of adventure thousands of miles from home, still yet I couldn't escape the storm of disappointment brewing in my mind.

Those fabulous machines I could have been flying by now.

Finally, we boarded the plane, and over the intercom the pilot said in an American drawl, 'Ladies and gentlemen, welcome aboard this flight from JFK to Chicago O'Hare, I'm Captain Jack Andrews and –'

19

'Oh no, not crasher Andrews!' exclaimed Elly, and we laughed. Our plane taxied this way and that, until nosing up to the back of a long queue of planes, all impatiently waiting to get the clear from Tower before each plane might remark to the other waiting planes, 'right, guys, watch this!', then barrel down the runway, reach the roll point and then vault up off the ground. Through the heat shimmer and engine wash we could see the planes as they lifted off the far end of the runway, then rise like vertically into the sky, aboard some invisible lift. The queue of planes jostled forward, everyone itching to show their stuff, to get on their way.

Finally our turn came, we slowly rolled into position at the end of the runway, then the engines roared, the wheels rumbled, the acceleration pushed us back into our seats, faster and faster we went until the plane tipped back and we lifted and climbed and climbed, and got that wonderful heavy swaying sensation as we rose and banked from side to side. Soon, from up high I saw the landscape below – well I saw it, Elly read her book – change from urban sprawl to towns connected by straight, straight roads, and farmland that wasn't like England's higgledy patchwork but was cut up like a massive parquet floor in a pattern probably unchanged since the first settler divvied it all out two centuries before in crisp uniform allotments. As we rose through clouds I could see through gaps below housing estates that panned out like epic doodles or fractals, like those paisley infinity posters on student walls. Little houses and their bright blue pools hung like leaves on twig-like avenues off branch-like roads off trunk roads off thick highways, all so samey and big. The conformity of it bored me into a long doze, and I woke up sweaty with a stiff neck, to see the clouds were now above us, and my ears were blocked and hurting.

We were descending, then over a massive stretch of sunlit deep blue-grey water we banked this way and that, then our side of the plane tipped down as if the captain were saying 'have a look at this' as a long man-made shoreline drew into view, lined by a vast crowd of epically tall buildings, standing in the sunshine alongside one another along the edge of the lake, like a gang of kids queuing to dive into the beautifully cool water.

Chicago!

What a skyline!

Just the name sounded like an explosion! ChiCAA-GOOooo!

A vast metropolis of skyscrapers, meat wagons, glamorous violence, gangsters with fabulous hats, fat lapelled pin stripe suits and long coats and roll-drummed machine guns drilling down those who *tried to cross 'em or ain't paid their dues, see! Nyahh! Nyahh! Wanna a piece a me, shee? Wois goi, huh?! Shee*! And all against a backdrop of police sirens.

'Look at that! That's it!' I said to Elly.

'It sure is!' she said, beaming. Our gaze met and our eyes agreed, this was brilliant!

We spied the Sears Tower – 'there's Ferris!' she squealed.

'If I'm a gangster do you want to be my moll? I'll get us some 8-liter Packard with goons with guns hanging off the massive running boards and crouched behind the spare wheels aside the engine.'

'And we never stop the car before opening the doors either,' she said, 'and we need a bloke in the boot to play sleazy saxophone jazz.'

'Yes, we always swoop to a stop with a squeal of tyres, tough guys already getting out, guns toting.'

'That's when I'm not at the speak easy, draped across the piano with my extended cigarette holder, and Martini.'

'With an olive in the glass.'

'Actually I don't like Martini.'

'Well whatever you want in a triangular cocktail glass thing.'

'Can you fit pints in them?'

'OK shweetheart, you and your cocktail pint, and boa, and extended cigarette holder, hanging around the car looking sultry, with one foot up on the running board, while I talk business with the boys you can make snipey comments out the side of your mouth.'

'I'd have to raise an eyebrow as well when I speak and look at you side on, *wrrr wwrr wrr*,' talking through clenched teeth in her best gangster-moll way.

'Yes, and you'd have to have your leg showing through your split dress and wobble your head when you say whatever it is.'

'Get me a Goddamn beer,' she said.

'Yeah, and I'd say "not now shweetheart, we godda take down the McDougalls' joint, dey're musclin' in on our toif," and you'd drawl, "that's a shame cos if that's a pistol in your pocket I gotta place you can holster it," and wobble your head again.'

We laughed, but as soon as I said it I felt bad, talking to her or about her in this sexy way. But when we got along like this, I just loved her to bits.

As the plane banked a row of sunlight spotlights arced along the cabin walls, then we levelled out and the wings extended backwards, arching like a bird's as the flaps were deployed, then as we descended the nose rose and the undercarriage whirred and locked down into position. Wherever we were landing it was away from Chicago's skyscrapers, and as we descended the roads and buildings beneath grew larger and the cars rushed faster, until pylons and trees zipped beneath us perilously close, then we were rushing above a massive field and then a rug of concrete slid under our plane and we had the teeth-jarring, seat-jolting *boff-d-boff* bounce of the wheels on the runway, the engines roaring in reverse and the plane lurching and swaying as our fellow passengers applauded! And rightly so, because we'd just landed in Chicago!

Brilliant!

O'Hare was bigger, cleaner and tidier than JFK. Elly again admonished me for getting out the guidebook, as if walking around an airport with massive rucksacks didn't mark as out as tourists already. Anyway to get to Shorewood we

21

needed to go from Chicago Union. From O'Hare we took a stainless steel train with chains draped in front of the driver's cab along a raised railway just like in *Running Scared*, while skyscrapers filled the sky with shadow as we approached the city.

Chicago seemed newer and more spacious than New York, the sky bluer and cooler, but we had no time to take it in. We changed trains to get to Chicago Union, and there had to not just find the Shorewood train, but specifically the Union Pacific Northwest train we bought tickets for, and not the Union Pacific Southeast or Pacific Union Southeast or Atlantic Union or any other stupidly named company thousands of miles from any ocean. Why not just have one company like British Rail, I said to Elly.

'You are so right!' she said.

'I always am.'

'It's incredible.'

'I know everything. What I don't know isn't knowledge.'

'Everybody should shut up and listen to you.'

'I could solve all the world's problems, but I'd rather be asked.'

'You're so modest.'

'I am Jesus.'

We nodded sagely.

We found the platform, or pavement as it was so low down next to the train wheels, and soon arrived our massive double-decker passenger train in gleaming steel, just like *The Silver Streak*, except this one was leaving Chicago station all nice and neat, instead of half smashing it down.

I wanted the platform guard to be a jolly little black man in a peaked cap with a throaty laugh who'd loudly shout 'ALLL a-BOOOOARD!' before blowing his whistle and a flurry of passengers would batter one another with leather suitcases down the platform, harried along by hissing jets of steam from under the long fat carriages, doors at the ends, and steps you had to climb, unlike London's blue trains with their dozen slam doors you could jump aboard even if the train was moving, and sweep everyone off the platform.

But no, no such platform guard. We boarded and our train eventually accelerated away to a ponderous trundle, as we rolled through a shaded canyon of office and apartment towers, then lower high-rise, then sunlit little blocks and homes, past factories and warehouses, functioning or smashed up, the buildings shrinking and spacing apart as the city petered out, and the sunshine reached right into the carriage, leaving no shade. We began to cook up and I began to niff. I was sitting on a different bench to Elly, and somehow I found myself crying, but she didn't notice, and I looked out at the flat, endless landscape. The railway tacked parallel to roads along which fat cars and long lorries overtook us, but everything was all so big and spacious that nothing seemed to move at any great speed, like the biggest aircraft that flies so slowly you wonder how it stays up, or what you'd do if they suddenly nosed out the sky and blew up on some distant town.

We passed railroad crossings with white X signs and alternating red lights, and others with lights like faces and thin metal arms raised up around them, as if telling cars 'for God's sake, STOP!', and that weird effect with the bell flipping from major to minor key, *deng-deng-deng-deng-DEEIIIING-ding-ding-ding-ding* as we approached and passed. There was scrubland, ponds, tall trees that gave glimpses of shade as their lush green leaves wrestled with the sunshine trying to mug its way through from beyond, gardens rammed with toys, or broken down pickups or boxy looking cars. So many clapperboard villas had swimming pools they simply weren't the luxury item of England. So much open space and grass, and people moseying around their verdant gardens, so inviting, if they'd stop the train and say '*hey Briddish people and yurr Briddish teeth,*' and we'd get along swell as they cooked up some burgers.

But the train kept moving further from Chicago, the stations growing further apart with less and less of anything between them. How far out were we going? I thought we were selling ice-cream in Chicago, parking our little glazed vans adorned with pictures of Mickey Mouse characters next to the Sears Tower, and in clean white shirts and Thunderbird-style hats on we'd smilingly coil ice-creams into cones, and stick in a Flake or Hershey bar to kids all bubbling with excitement at getting an ice-cream from the ice-cream man.

They jump up and down with glee when they see you coming, Christian said.

Then in the evening we'd all reconvene at the depot, a Victorian-era redbrick fire station, upstairs in the old fireman's hall we'd count up the day's takings, $100s and $100s, the avuncular Hank doling out beers, before adjourning to the balcony with its magnificent view of Chicago's skyscrapers, twinkling in the dusk, like a city in Space, and we'd swap stories of our day's daring dos. Then, bellies filled with beer and pockets with booty, we'd go delve into the City's grooviest clubs, get totally pissed, snog someone, before floating back to the apartment before the next day's gasoline and sugar-powered shenanigans.

So I'd thought. But now, an hour's train ride already out of the city, I couldn't even see Chicago proper. It was all houses and gardens and roads and low-rise and drive-in restaurants and big billboards, and space, space, space. The middle of anywhere.

Finally, the train slowed, and slowed, to walking speed, until it finally stopped, or maybe just nodded off and strolled into something, and we were at Shorewood. We dropped down onto the platform, unlike England where the three-foot drop between the carriage and the platform was only for pissheads to fall into.

The stout brick station building was like an attractive English village hall. If all Shorewood were like this, its main drag would likely have cafes and bars all with heavy polished woods, like in *Cheers!* or *Newhart*, along a long row of single-storey stores with vast plate glass windows, the drug store with a man in a white shirt and bowtie selling sweets and sodas, next to a mom and pop hardware

23

store, the barber shop, then at end of the row a massive diner with pastel-coloured convertible cars fanned out from its central burger house, topped by a revolving neon sign a la Arnolds from *Happy Days*, with server girls would be on roller skates, perching trays of burgers on car doors to a backing track of rock-n-roll piano chords as boys in leather or baseball jackets would preen and jostle around girls in ra-ra skirts, just like *Grease*. We'd eat there every night, spending the bucks we'd earned trawling the miles of roads lined by villas with huge lawns and picket fences and American flags and black and white dogs called Spot, and the kids who'd spent all day selling lemonade on the roadside like they do in *Peanuts* would come spend the proceeds on us!

Forget the city, Smalltown USA was the biz. We were going to be billeted in some apartment on Shorewood's main road, a basement bar below us with its downwards- pointing neon arrow sign flashing and buzzing all night right outside our apartment window through the Venetian blinds of the living room where as we'd sip Scotch in front of a fan with ribbons of tape billowing from it to bluesy saxophone music, like *Mike Hammer*.

OK - this was going to be great!

Newly buoyed and armed with quarters I went to call Penguin, and Hank told me Mrs Hank would be there in about an hour.

'An hour'? Elly said, wrinkling her nose, 'how far away are they?'

'Oh yeah ... I don't know if she's leaving right now, though.'

'No, maybe not,' said Elly, and got out her book.

She had a point, though. How far was Penguin from here?

We hung out. The Sun turned to a kinder mood, sitting squat behind the distant trees and casting a more golden, pink light upon the place, and there was nothing to do but smoke. After an hour a tall, strapping woman, a big head of curly hair flanking a long face, appeared and peered at me with sharp grey eyes.

'James Hopkins?' she said quietly, smiling lightly.

'Yes! You must be ...' shit, who was she? 'Err... Mrs Hank?' I said in my best bumbling foppish way, which she didn't buy.

'You may call me Jenny.' Her face was kind, but her tone was stern. I remembered that Christian had described her as the 'mom' of the place, the enforcer to Hank's benevolently loose-reined rule.

'And this is Elly.'

'Hello Elly, nice to meet you,' said Jenny. 'Is that short for Elaine?'

'Yes, but everyone calls me Elly.'

'OK. The van's out this way.'

We hastily picked up our stuff and were led across the car park to a massive Dodge van! Just like the *A-Team*! We piled into the front.

I tried to ask insightful questions about the area and ice-cream selling, but in the enclosed space I realised I ponged, while Elly sat quietly. Every minute we drove further from Shorewood along roads, then a highway, on and on, flanked not by houses but by dusty trees shielding scrubland with signs saying ''real estate opportunity – call Ted Beavis 09808093498795239485723495', and I felt anxious. Where the Hell were we going? After what seemed like a long time, miles from anywhere, we turned sharply off the highway onto a side road straight through a thick of dense trees, which cleared onto a grid of small roads lined with metal buildings, like aircraft hangers. It was an industrial estate. We turned into a large gravel-trap cul-de-sac with more hangers and a collection of white vans in rows, and parked up.

'OK – welcome to Penguin,' said Jenny.

The brick fire-station was in fact a metal shed, lit outside by a lovely blasting red, orange and pink sunset, but inside by dull blue-grey fluorescent lights, with a cold grey concrete floor and cold steel walls. There was a tarpaulin-covered car to the left, a pickup truck, boxes of tools, then row after row of long tables with half a dozen or so sweaty people counting money, chatting and drinking beer. On the right next to the entrance was a corral of filing cabinets and shabby desks, a computer, a fan (but no ribbons!), telephones and a huge wall map, eight by nine foot or so, of Chicago and Illinois. And amid this improvised office was a great big man, big belly, big strong arms, bushy grey beard covering his neck, leaning back in a wheeled chair that looked unhappy about its load.

Jenny announced our arrival and this Father Christmas stood up, revealing a surprisingly tall frame under the fat that contrasted with Jenny's leanness. But through his beard I could see he was smiling, and he looked like he smiled a lot. It was Hank.

'Very nice to finally meet you in the flesh, Jim!' with his fruity, low pitch voice, like the Swedish Chef, as he extended a big paw of a hand.

'Thank you yes, you too, thank you very much for having us,' I said, grinning.

'You must be Elly, or is it Elaine?'

'Elly!'

'Welcome to you, too, Elly. Well, this is Penguin HQ, this is where it all happens. Right now we're all pretty much done for the day. This is my son, Daryl, just counting up,'

He pointed a paw to a handsome but serious-looking man in his early 20s, and who looked nothing like Hank, counting through shrapnel opposite a very sweaty man in a t-shirt and baseball cap. Daryl nodded and smiled at us as he counted.

'Over there is Charlie, our trusted mechanical genius,' said Hank, pointing to a man in an oil-stained checked shirt, embedded deep into a collapsed armchair next to the tarpaulined car. He had a long drooping 1970s' style moustache, framing the craggiest face and wizened grey eyes, his hairy Popeye forearms alternately pulling on a whisky and a cigarette.

'How y'doin'? he doffed his forehead.

'And over there are the other drivers who'll you'll meet and get to know soon enough, some British, some native,' Hank pointed towards the long tables of drivers. 'And how was New York?' he asked.

'Great,' said Elly.

Lying cow.

'Yeah it was, er, good fun.'

'Did you see much?'

'Went up the Empire State, walked from there to Central Park,' said Elly.

'Then I tried to walk to the World Trade Centre but gave up. Oh I think I got mugged, that was exciting,' I said.

'What?' said Hank, so I told him and Jenny my mugging story, and my wondering whether it was a mugging or if I was just being aggressively begged at, but said it was brilliant either way because it was *Noo Yoik*, to which Hank laughed, 'So long as you had a good time!', while Jenny just looked baffled, and Elly looked appalled.

'Well,' Hank broke the awkward silence, 'I guess you know already from Christian, you're staying in the apartment with him and Ben? They'll be back soon, and will take you to the apartments. We'll do a full induction tomorrow and you go on the rounds, how does that sound?'

'Great!' I said.

'OK, great. I'll carry on here, take a seat, have a drink and we'll catch you later.'

'Great thanks!'

Jenny asked us if we wanted a beer, adding, 'I won't check you for ID,' possibly a joke, but said so dryly it just sounded like a concession, which it really was. She said things with the same quiet menace as Clint Eastwood. 'You think that's funny? Am I joking? You don't know do you? You feeling lucky, punk? Go ahead, laugh, make my day,' Magnum at my forehead, while I'm lying there trying not to laugh when you know you're going to get bollocked even more, for which he'd definitely kill me.

At uni there'd been this fat Sikh Brummie yob, doing dentistry 'for beer money' who bullied his saddo maths student flatmate, whose parents did a food shop for him every week so he was kind of asking for it. One day Brummie brandished a fork at him and said 'alloight, if you laff at this, I'm going to chuck a bucket of water over yous, alloight? Now - FORK OFF.' And the geek laughed. And he woke up later, very, very wet.

Clueless Nick had told me that. He was a posh hanger-on of Mark's, doing general studies, who only wanted was to have a good time but had no idea how to go about it. He even asked me permission to make a play for Elly, and I laughed, knowing he had no chance. None. Elly had the pick of the city.

'Jim! Elly!' a voice shouted. It was Christian! He came trotting in, all sweaty, his arms filled by empty water bottles and a massive water pistol, while he gingerly held a tray of money, and we both gave him very clumsy hugs, and we shouted with excitement, and he put his stuff down and shouted 'yay! Let's have another hug!' and we all went in together.

'How are you? How was your trip? When did you get here? How have you been? You look so well!'

26

It seemed longer than the three weeks we'd last seen him. He'd replaced his bob haircut with a crew cut that revealed his angular face, with its sloped down nose and a sharp chin, highlighted by a good tan, while his damp T-shirt showed off something of a six pack.

It was good to see him, he all excited and huggy like a big dog.

Ben appeared behind him.

'Yay! Ben's back!'

His mate Ben came in, tall and thin, with a mop of black hair and large eyes, like Paul McCartney. We didn't know him so well, but he was pleased to see us so we hugged him too.

'You got beers already?' Christian noted, 'Cool! You had a good day Ben?'

'I reckon. Maybe $130 for me.'

'Not bad, not bad, I'm sitting on something like that …' said Christian. 'Let's count up and get out of here.' Which they promptly did over beers, as we talked about what'd gone on since uni, the journey, New York, the mugging - Christian and Ben thought it was funny! - while Elly rolled her eyes. We got up to go.

'Just you wait 'til you see the car!' Christian said, then shouted 'yay!' again, and brought Elly and I in for another hug. 'This is going to be so much fun!'

Outside just lit by the hanger lights was a huge tan and brown estate car, a beast of angles and swoops, with wood panelling up the sides. It was a pure, American, 1970s station wagon, the family car from every TV show I'd ever seen.

'What … is this?' I said.

'This … is a 1972, Pontiac, Grand Safari,' said Ben.

'Woah,' I flicked my fingers in admiration.

'I know, right?' said Christian.

We stuck our rucksacks in the boot, or the *trunk*, and piled in.

Christian got behind the wheel. 'Get this. Charlie, right - '

'Who's Charlie?' asked Elly.

'He's the mechanic here. Vietnam Vet from Kentucky.'

'Charlie!' Ben screeched in a high-pitch hick-like way.

'Him in the armchair?' I said.

'Yeah! He replaced the original 6 litre engine with some 8-litre fucker out of a Cadillac. This car goes.'

'Gets through the gas, too,' said Ben, as we started away.

'And the fuel gauge is broke, but just keep it filled up.'

'The engine didn't even need replacing, he just did it for a laugh a couple of weeks ago. He said it "had no Goddamn torque!" And stuck in this engine he found,' said Ben.

At the junction with the highway Christian didn't wait but just floored it, the engine roared, the car reared up, and we felt the push back of acceleration as we shot across the road onto the opposite side. This car was great, maybe the apartment, which Ben said was only 20 minutes away, was as cool. It was obviously some large, open-plan studio affair, with a massive living room kitchen combo with exposed brick walls and jaunty-coloured wooden shelving units, parquet floors and big sofas with cool people on them – us – eating pizzas the size of dustbin lids, and a spiral staircase leading to the bedrooms and views across the city, above a street lined with cafes and bars and cool places and cool people talking loudly in cool American accents about cool things – of course it was! Brilliant!

We passed through a town with just such a high street, but didn't stop, instead going through to more highway, running parallel to a railroad over which we turned sharply, bounding over the tracks, onto more roads, past scrubland, then a large estate of wealthy villas.

Suddenly Christian shouted, 'that's home!' pointing to a dark building about a mile away, silhouetted against the brown sky of dusk. As we approached there was nothing around it except highway and scrubland and other large, lonely looking buildings, with neither town nor skyscrapers in sight. The building was five or six storeys high, but was 100 metres long easy, fronted by a vast car park. Only a few apartment lights were on, and it looked cold and foreboding, more like a prison, like our student res, their cold, white breeze-block rooms designed by a bloke who'd designed prisons, before he'd evidently gone and set up shop in Illinois.

Parking up, we entered the building through a heavy side door and went up a baking hot tower of steps, then onto a long corridor of doors like out of *The Shining*. Christian stopped at a door, stuck a key into the door handle, and entered the apartment with a joyful sitcom yell of 'Hi honey, I'm home!'

'Nyahh, go fuck yerself!' screeched Ben.

The front door opened into the living room. A massive long sofa and armchairs along the wall to the right, a smoked glass coffee table like something off Miami Vice, then a screen wall with shelves and a massive TV, behind which was a galley kitchen. The table had joint skins and roaches and tobacco on it, and all sat atop a thick, light-beige carpet. The room then double again to contain a dining room table and then French windows and a balcony. Ben took us right down a narrow hall to a bathroom and two bedrooms, ours being the larger room with en suite bathroom and walk-in closet - brilliant. It was all very warm and plush, but soulless. Not so much *Mike Hammer* as *Dick Spanner*.

'How did we get this place?'

'It comes with the job. Hank's got another two apartments in this block for other drivers,' said Christian. 'They're short-term rents for transients. The previous tenant was Japanese.'

'We found his panty magazines in the bathroom,' said Ben.

'No way!' I said.

'Nah,' said Christian, 'they were under the bed. Anyway, you two should freshen up. I'll put the pizzas on and when you're done we'll get seriously pissed and stoned.' We agreed this was an excellent plan, and once showered, fed, beered up some more and a spliff doing the rounds, things seemed a lot better.

'What else is there to do for fun around here?' I asked, 'not that this isn't fun!'

'I knew what you meant,' Christian said. 'There's a swimming pool next to the car park, so we can do that on Monday, our day off.'

'And go to the mall,' said Ben.

'There's a massive mall a couple of miles away, with an almighty Toys R Us nearby, which is great, you can try out all the stuff, last time we went we were playing roller hockey in the aisle,' Christian was genuinely enthused, although I worried we'd just get told off.

'Just up the road is Dooley's, our local bar, good for cocktails and line dancing,' said Ben.

'Oh yeah line dancing! They're classy like that around here,' said Christian, 'I don't line dance, not even for irony. You'd like line-dancing, Elly.'

She flicked a V-sign at him, and he laughed.

'When did yous both here?' Elly asked.

'June the ... fuck I'm not sure. When did I get here, Ben?'

'Let me just check the diary, cos that's my job,' said Ben.

'Haha, cunt. No - we came together - oops! Bit blue,' he said, looking at Elly impishly. 'June 8. I was thinking of leaving it until after Glastonbury, but I hadn't got a ticket and there was loads of money here.'

'When's Glastonbury?' asked Elly.

'June ... something, next week,' Christian said as if regretting not going. 'Do you know anyone who's going? It's supposed to be massive this year, it's the 25th anniversary. I'm so jealous!' he said.

'No', she said, 'I'd like to go though.' She'd never said that before. Most wankers I'd met who carped about Glastonbury didn't even know where it was. Several days on a rugby pitch full of hippies and cider piss, being deafened by crap bands, sounded like Hell. But Christian's enthusiasm made it sound fun and now Elly wanted to go. Shit. Maybe I should have gone sometime in my 20 years.

'Apparently it's Oasis headlining,' Ben said.

'Ahh, Oasis!' said Christian.

'And the Stone Roses!' said Elly.

'The Stone Roses!' said Christian, nodding.

'And Massive Attack!' said Elly.

'Massive Attack, they're good, they're good,' said Christian.

'And Pulp!'

'Really, Pulp?' said Ben.

'Now, Pulp are shit!' stated Christian.

'No, they're brilliant,' said Elly defensively.

'Pulp are fucking shit!' Christian replied, leveraging the rise out of Elly.

'They're great!'

'No. Oasis and the Stone Roses are great. Pulp couldn't fill a pub!'
Christian scoffed.

'No, not true!' said Elly.

'Britpop bollocks,' Ben almost yelled.

'Exactly, bollocks!' said Christian, jimmying away, 'Jarvis Cock is aptly named.'

'No!' cried Elly.

Was this a debate? Surely either you like a band or not? I took a big draw on the spliff. I'd never liked bands, just songs now and again, but even if I remembered the names of good songs on the radio, Our Price or Tower Records were sold out, so I never got any singles or tapes. I liked classical music because it was always there down the library and free, although someone said that was elitist and I was ignorant of all modern music, which was stupid as any fucker can turn on Radio 3, and as most people don't know most things, most people are ignorant. I didn't like classical stuff to be superior, I just liked it, because it made me dream … the spliff had fazed me out, and I saw Ben, Christian and Elly debating with some ferocity, him teasing, her saying 'no!' a lot, but laughing. They were getting on well, too well, and I got that strange feeling of falling backwards into my own isolation. How could people connect so easily about all this stuff? Beers seemed to flow into me as I had an ever growing sense of being forced to watch something I was not part of. I wasn't part of anything. My head hurt and I went to bed, Christian saying 'yeah, get some sleep, you've a long day tomorrow,' but I couldn't sleep. All I could hear was him and Elly bantering away in the living room, on and on about stuff about which I'd nothing to say.

Training Day

'Up! Come on! It's your first day!' Christian shouted as he hauled the duvet off me. 'It's Sunday, geddup, you're an ice-cream man – and woman,' he banged on the bathroom door, 'Elly, you in there?'

She shouted something over the noise of the shower.

'Whatever! We've got coffee and waffles on the go,' he replied, then pulled my leg, 'Up, up!'

I felt grotty as Hell, how could he be so chipper? Although Elly and I were sleeping in the same room (on separate beds), I'd not heard her come to bed. I staggered to the other bathroom and had the darkest piss of my life, then showered, dressed and went into the living room, where Christian and Ben were eating and watching telly.

'Stuff's on the table,' said Christian. I got some and sat with them on the sofa. The weather was on TV.

'What's it going to be?' I asked.

'Sunny,' said Christian. 'See all those sun symbols all over Illinois? That's a hint.'

All right, wanker. 'What's on after this?'

'The weather,' said Christian.

'This is the Weather Channel,' said Ben.

'Channel? Just weather? No way, really?'

'Way,' said Christian.

'It's a must watch for ice-cream men!' shouted Ben.

'Just had a piss the colour of old tea,' I said.

'Dehydration,' said Christian, 'Jet-lag. Water!'

The French windows were open and the breeze had taken away some of the previous night's stink. Outside the Sun had taken over the sky with its crisp blue army, not one cloud of resistance, and the order was heat. The view was of the car park, unhappy trees, highway, and Lego-like buildings randomly breaking up the horizon. Bit shit, basically.

Elly appeared. 'Elly! You look fresh and fragrant!', Christian said, to which she flicked a V and went for food. Coffee, nosh and fags all done, we followed Christian down to the car, which in broad daylight was simply magnificent. It was longer and wider than anything I'd ever seen, like a boat. Big headlights like Easter eggs in a box, indicators like bricks, a front grill like a plantation mansion portico, bent outwards like a plough. The bonnet and wings bowed up over fuck-off fat tyres, the lines of the car swooshing back before bouncing up again over the rear wheels. The windscreen and back window sloped like hillsides around a bunker-size cabin. Best was the wooden paneling along the sides, now all rotted as the lower halves of the doors had rusted. This car hadn't led some banal suburban life picking up groceries and kids, but had supporting roles in every 1970s US TV show and film, including *The Brady Bunch*, with a sideline as a passion wagon on hillsides overlooking LA, before blowing its fortune on drugs in the 1980s, then after rehab got this job ferrying ice-cream men.

Inside was a lot hotter than outside.

'And off we jolly,' said Christian, gunning the car, 'your first day. Are you nervous?'

'Kind of,' I said.

'Not really,' said Elly.

'All will be well, today you're being shown the ropes,' said Christian, 'then tomorrow we're all on a day off then you're back on the route!'

'I'll show you my rope! Ooer!' said Ben.

'I knew you'd say that!' said Christian.

We hit the long straight road flanked by those rich-looking, colonial-style villas, with lush lawns framed in water-sprinkler rainbows.

'Hank lives there,' said Christian, 'bought when times were good.'

'Hank Towers,' said Ben.

'We went round there once last summer, as a surprise, to say hello,' said Christian.

'He was not happy,' laughed Ben.

'No he was not! We picked up on that and vamoosed. He's a lovely laid back bloke, but business and home lives are *very* separate.'

'Is that the kind of place you'd sell a shitload of ice-cream?' I asked.

'More like the kind of place security guards would arrest you for trespass,' said Ben.

'We were chased to Hank's door by security in a golf-cart, Hank had to get them to leave us alone, you remember?'

'Two employees turn up on your doorstep with private security, no wonder he was pissed off.'

'I didn't think we looked like crooks.'

'We didn't, our old Dodge was the problem.'

'Hey, what the fuck's that castle thing?' I said, spying some enormous plastic battlements looming over trees ahead.

'Medieval Times, it's a theme restaurant, with jousting and banquets and pigs on spits,' said Christian.

'Brilliant! Let's go!' I said.

'No. It's shit,' said Christian.

'Have you been?'

'I don't have to, look at it.'

'Doesn't really appeal,' said Elly.

'There you go, Elly thinks it's shit too.'

But they'd never even been! I sulked for the rest of the drive. It was all highways, there was no real town, the odd dusty wind breaks of trees, like the industrial estate Penguin was behind. We bounded across the gravel as if in slow motion.

'There's the fleet,' said Ben, pointing to a herd of white vans lined up beyond the Penguin hanger, among which guys walked with large brown boxes.

'Our mounts. Our trusty ice-cream steeds,' said Christian.

I'd glimpsed the vans yesterday but not twigged they were our vans, I had expected goofily bulbous, glazed vans with large plastic Mr Whippies on top. These things were just big metal boxes, without even windows to serve out of, let alone dodgy paintings of Disney characters.

Over a dozen folks were milling around the vans and in the hanger, with Hank behind his desk.

'Hi Christian, Ben, Jim, Elly! You all good today?'

'Yes thanks.'

'OK ... training day! So Ben, you can take Elly, OK?'

'Sure!' said Ben, and Elly smiled.

'Aw!' said Christian, 'well ... see you later,' he said with theatrical disappointment.

'Christian, you take Jim and Mike here. This is Mike, everybody,' Hank turned to a gangly, gormless-looking sod with a ponytail.

'Mike is from Leeds.'

'Bleeds uni! Don't hold it against us!' he said, and we laughed. He looked old enough to be a mature student. Hopefully he'd shuddup while Christian and I talked, seeing as Christian was my mate, what gave me first dibs on witty banter. I was sad not to be with Elly but relieved she was with Ben and not Christian.

'OK, good luck!' said Hank.

'First. We go to Jess to get the float,' said Christian.

We went over to the stern young man we'd seen counting money the day before.

'Good morning Christian, Jim, Mike. Here is your float: $20 in quarters, dimes and nickels, check that and sign please.' The coins were in paper tubes like Polo mints that Christian broke open and put on slots on these plastic trays.

'All good,' he said, signing off, 'now, let's get one a stock list,' and off a table he picked up a small piece of paper, like those chits you get in bookies, with a grid of boxes and a long list of ice-creams, none I'd heard of, and he led us to the vans, the driver's side tiled like a bathroom with rows of blue stickers of ice-creams at jaunty angles. Close up, the vans were trimmed with red streaks of rust, yellow-grey petrol stains from the cap, loads of dents and scrapes shown up by the sunlight.

'This is my truck,' said Christian, opening the door to a larger van, almost a Luton, 'as they say, mine's a lot bigger.'

In the back, instead of a gleaming steel ice-cream dispenser and leaning towers of cones for coiling Mr Whippies into, was this massive metal box.

'Behold – the freezer.'

He opened the lid, as big as a dinner table, to this swirling cold mist atop soggy looking boxes. 'See in here all these different boxes of ice-cream. Now we check which ice-creams we're low on, and what we need more of we check on this list. You could do this at the end of the day when you've an idea of what's sold, although it can happen you don't have the same van the next day, but everyone does it in in the morning really.'

The freezer was like a sarcophagus, with dozens of boxes, the contents obscured by mist and box flaps.

'There's loads,' I said.

'At least 50 types on the list. Snowcones cost 50 cents, which is piss all, you can give them away. Choco Tacos are the most expensive at $1.50, which you never give away, that'll piss off Hank.'

'Do we sell Snowcones to get them hooked, then they progress to the high-end Tacos, the cocaine of ice-cream?' said Mike.

'Yes! Jim, tick off what I call out,' as he leaned into the freezer and started shouting names which I struggled to find on the list. Sour Towers. Snowcones, Popsicles. Choco Tacos. Fudgsicles. Strawberry Shortcakes, on and on, nothing I knew, not a FAB, a Funny Feet, a Lyons Maid in sight.

'These boxes are fucked,' I said.

'This is clean. See John's van. Now that is a pigsty. You do get a lot of wastage, though,' said Christian, 'you might as well just eat it.'

'Do you get to eat all the ice-cream you want and call it wastage?'

'You can do, but like in chocolate factories you eat all you like, then you throw it all up and eat no more.'

It wasn't the Mr Whippy machines I'd hoped for, we wouldn't be coiling them out, nor even scooping ice-cream out of great buckets with those blink-eye scoop-spoon things with the cog, like at Baskins, mashing one scoop atop another into some stupendously unwieldy tower which then avalanches all down the kid's T-shirt onto his shoes, making him cry and everyone else crease up. No. No Flakes. No 100s and 1,000s. No Ben & Jerry's. Just sodden, sticky, wilted brown boxes with SOUR TOWER stamped in black. All a bit shit, basically.

With the list done we went back to the hanger. Next to the main entrance were a half-dozen people queued up to a small window, through which a teenage lad in a thick fur-lined hooded coat and heavy gloves kept heaving brown boxes, saying 'Strawberry Shortcakes .... Popsicles ... Lick a Color ... Lemon Sharks,' while the guy at the front of the queue piled up as many as he could to take them to his van. Christian gave the fur-lined youth his list and we queued up. Hank was on his knees in front of the main entrance, chipping great chunks off this smoking white block the size of a portable telly, others coming to take away the chunks in towels.

'That's dry ice for your freezer. We don't need any because mine's electric,' said Christian. 'Be very careful handling that stuff, it's minus 40 C and will take your skin off. It also fills the freezer with carbon dioxide, which you forget as you lean right in to get an ice-cream stuck at the bottom, and take in a lungful of pure CO_2, and *whap*! You can't breathe, it's like you're stunned.'

'Wow.'

'It's quite a hit, a cheap one too.'

'Like the fainting trick'.

'Except you'd faint and fall into the freezer and be dead in the few minutes it takes for anyone to notice you're gone.'

'God, imagine that. Kids find the ice-cream man's not there so they try and raid the freezer and find a body, that'd fuck 'em up,' said Mike.

'Put them off stealing,' said Christian.

A young drawly voice said through the window, 'Christian!', then brown boxes smoking with cold were heaved through the window, with Christian taking a couple as more arrived.

'You gonna help him, retard?' said the voice from a face shrouded in fur, sharp blue-eyes … talking to me!

'Do what?'

'Carry his boxes, dumbass!' he said, then he disappeared back into the cold and dark.

I bristled and picked up the boxes.

'That's Daryl, the cheeky scamp,' said Christian. 'Just give him shit back, he loves it.'

In the van Christian showed us his kit. 'Get a radio tape, you can get one for $20.' He reached over onto the dashboard and picked up a massive bright-coloured water gun and pumped it, before firing a load of warm water in my face, making me gag.

'Jizz facial!' he grinned. 'You will need one of these guns. Kids ambush you with them, you've got to fight back, they love it.'

We handed the boxes to him as he distributed them into the freezer, while smaller vans rolled past on the gravel, their drivers hollering and cat-calling. Christian finally pulled a frozen bottle of water out of the freezer and stuck it on the dash.

'Another tip, fill up with water from Hank's cooler, put it in the freezer overnight then melt it on the dash for ice-cold water all day … So let's check. Loaded up. Float – check. Permit's in the window. Got maps.' Then he jumped out with the water pistols. 'Just going to load them up!', then when he came back he threw a cable into the back of the van.

'That's the freezer disconnected.' He started the van, the engine whined and farted into life, 'petrol… half a tank from yesterday, we'll fill up on the way,' he turned to us, 'we buy our own fuel by the way.'

'Really? Bollocks.'

'It's nowhere near as expensive as home. Anyway, let's go!' And off we went!

A couple of miles down the highway we stopped off at a massive petrol station – or *gas station* – with so many lanes and pumps, all under a huge orange ball with 76 written in blue.

'Seventy-six as in the 1776 declaration of independence. Petrol is freedom,' said Christian.

'What kind of petrol retailer associates their brand with a violent act of revolutionary democracy?' said Mike.

'Patriotic petrol,' said Christian, 'but no free tumblers.'

We drove on, Mike taking up position in the opposite door well, smoking with the door open, while Christian and I chatted.

'You were right about Hank, he is totally Father Christmas,' I said.

'He is, isn't he? Lovely bloke, never gets stressed, the worst he ever gets is when he says "murr, you guys"', sounding like a mild-mannered Chewbacca, and it takes a lot to get there. In fact the last time he stressed out was that time we dropped by at Hank Towers. "Murr you guys". They've got another massive place in Mexico for winter.'

'So they do good business?'

'Pretty good. Not as good as it was when they started. The competition's insane, and they're mostly former Penguin drivers who saw how much he was making and so they bogged off and set up their own businesses. Now the way Hank tells it, and give or take a bit of bullshit it's probably true, is he and Jenny were the first ice-cream vendors this side of Chicago in 1971, or '72 when they set up.'

'The height of the Nixon years. "*I did not secretly bomb Cambodia, the Cambodians knew about it all along*!"' I said.

'Nam!' said Mike.

'Did Hank not fight in Nam then? Carnage is Asia and he's at home selling ice-cream?'

'Hmm, good question! I don't know if he served. I struggle to see him on the front line sniping at gooks. That's one to ask him. If he did, he never mentions it.'

'Special ops! Sold ice-cream undercover in Saigon,' I said.

'Cuts down some Viet Cong ambush with his Gatling, *brhghghghghghghghghgh*! "Murr, you guys". Maybe I'll ask Charlie. Charlie definitely served, five years on the front line, that man's face is a war film … but we digress! So they made a fucking fortune through the 1970s they built up and up to about 40 regular drivers.'

'Shit.'

'Yeah, all in new vans, pretty much the monopoly, operating from this big base right near Chicago, way closer than now, and which got him his fuck off great big house, two other cars as well as the A-team van. Coining it from May through the summer, working half a year then going to their Mexican ranch for winter, also bought by this. Then some of his drivers wanted the same and become the competition. I mean you can replace drivers pretty easily, but there was one year when there was some mass defection and Hank didn't have *any* bloody drivers. And the competition is incredible. All these guys, Polar Bear,

Eskimo, Arctic, Iceberg, they're all ex Penguin. Hank's current location is a withdrawal, like I say he was practically in Chicago city itself, but he's moved out here where the land's cheap, permits are cheaper. There are endless little towns and estates being built, which Penguin can sell in, so there's growth of sorts. But he's out in the back of beyond with what, 15 second-hand postal vans converted to ice-cream trucks. Well I say converted, I mean they're vans with great big tomb-like freezers dumped in the back. It's a different world. Hank still makes a good living and keeps his gains, still got two sons through college and it'll do the next two.'

'O God, they have to pay for university here don't' they?'

'Fucking fortunes.'

'Horrible.'

'But none of that if he started up now. He's scaled down bigtime. And it was him that set it all up in the first place.'

'Bastard drivers.'

'Victim of his own success.'

We drove on for about 20 minutes, through junctions the size of football pitches, the road fanning out to four or five lanes each side and then thinning back to two. We turned off the highway and burrowed through a town, until we arrived at a long, wide, straight road, lined with big flat cars, heaving trees, strips of grass dividing the pavements from the kerb and houses set back up long lawns and drives. Like every suburban street seen in *Big* or *War Games*.

'OK, positions everyone. This is where the magic begins,' and just atop the dashboard he turned on a black box with two dials, and from right above the cabin came a synthesized glockenspiel version of *The Entertainer*, *bo bo bo bo, bo-bo, bo-bo ... bo bo bo bo-bo-bo bo bo booo*, at very slow speed.

'Turn the stereo volume to 11, drop the van speed to 5 mph,' the van's speedometer dropped to below 10 mph where no speed was recorded, 'down we go, nice and slow ... ooo, could be rude that!'

'Serious? We go around at this speed?'

'Yup.'

'This is literally kerb-crawling,' said Mike.

'Yup.'

'All fucking day?' I said, reaching for the fags on the dash.

'Yup. And no smoking! Looks bad for the kids. Serious. Don't light up.'

A few dozen yards away we saw three little bodies, two boys and a girl, jumping up and down, arms waving. 'Our first customers of the day! There she goes to get money,' said Christian, as the girl ran into the house.

We pulled up.

'Hey guys, how's it hanging?' said Christian, 'what can we do you for?'

'Hey ice-cream man!' said the smaller boy, before he stood and started to scan the side of the van, saying quietly, 'I want ... I want ... I want ...'

The bigger boy asked, 'Why's there three of you?'

'We're trainee ice-cream men,' said Mike.

'We want to be the new Christian,' I said.

'Wad?'

'Wad' he say?' said the bigger boy to the small one, still chanting, 'wad you say? I didn't get it.'

The girl reappeared.

'We're training to be ice-cream men. We're learning the ropes,' I said.

'Learning the *wad*?' asked the bigger boy.

'Where you all from?' asked the girl.

'Britain!' said Christian.

'London,' I said.

'Where?' said the girl.

'Wad?' said the boy. I looked at Mike as if to ask, 'are they retarded?'

'We are from far away, where Princess Diana lives,' said Christian.

'Oh, her!' said the girl, smiling.

'Right, what ice-cream would you like?'

'I want … I want …' the smaller boy was still chanting.

'Could we have … could we have … two Snowcones and a Sour Tower please ice-cream man?'

'Two Snowcones and a Sour Tower, Jim could you do the honours. That's $2 exactly please!'

I opened the freezer to see the identical brown boxes poking up through a low cold mist, like a wintery city of sugar, the ice-creams in identical compartments, their packaging all whited with frost. Which was which? What the or where the fuck was anything?

'Today would be good,' said Christian.

'Yes, yes, all right,' I snapped.

He swiveled his seat around and leapt over. 'Snowcones … are here, and Sour Towers are here.'

'I was finding them.'

'You did good, you did good,' he said, somehow simultaneously encouraging and patronizing. He took the kids' money, gave them the ice-creams, and they waved us off. 'I think Hank has too much choice, if we limited the choice we'd save loads of time, and probably less wastage of stock cos of higher turnover. Still, his company.'

'Did they really not understand what we were saying?' asked Mike.

'No they didn't,' said Christian. 'And always take the money first. I've had it where some little 6-year-old's come up and taken the ice-cream and licked it, then said, "hahaha, I've got no money, *fuck you* ice-cream man!", and run away.'

'Little shits!' I said.

'Yup. Mostly darlings though.'

'That's not provocation to back over them?'

'Unfortunately not.'

38

'Little cunts.'

'And never swear at the kids! Word spreads.'

'Never!' I said.

'Never!' Mike repeated.

'Never!' I said.

'Never!' said us all.

We rolled on, grinding along to each gaggle of jumping children that dotted the roadsides. A duo of jumping, waving boys, were ahead, one ran indoors, the other greeted us then stared at the stickers, 'I want ... I want.' And so it was for the next kids.

'Don't we just park up somewhere and they come to us? Isn't there a playground we can hang out at?' I said.

'No, not round here. See the distances we're looking at, just along these roads, just between the houses. Most of the kids play in their yards or in the street. Even if they were bothered to come to you, which they're not, you don't want them to in case they get run over.'

'You'd have a job running them over at this speed,' said Mike.

'Right, but they could dash out into the street and get run over by someone else.'

'That'll learn 'em.'

'*Ooo ho-ho, Solo*,' said Christian in a throaty Jabba-like way, 'anything, and I mean anything happens to a kid anywhere near your van, even if someone else runs them over, is your fault, because they were on their way to see you. That's what the lawyers say. You'll see later when some of the kids jump on the back of the van and hang on, they think it's really cute, but if you're driving and they fall off you are totally screwed. In fact, even if you were parked up, and they fell off somehow and hurt themselves, it's your fault.'

'So if some pig-shit stupid child gets mown down on their way to see us, it's our fault?'

'Basically. You're paying, or going to jail. Either way you're fucked.'

'Fucking Hell,' I said, partly in response to Christian's condescending tone, and that this ice-cream selling suddenly didn't sound like much fun.

'It could extend even, in theory, if a kid is on a some playground climbing frame and fell off while we're around, it's our fault for distracting him.'

'Presumably we'd be covered by insurance, but I guess in our case –' I closed off that avenue of thought, and Christian shot me a look to post guards on it. Mike didn't know our situation. He was here legit.

Christian carried on. 'Another reason we can't go faster is if they're out the back and hear us late, we might pass before they can get money off their moms and hammer down the drive, so you miss sales. Always check your mirrors for kids trying to catch up, because you don't want them to bomb along after you in case they get run over.'

'So, serve them as close to their own home as possible?'

'Pretty much, yeah.'

We turned at the end of the road, drove a block along, and lined up on another street parallel to the first. The map showed three more roads parallel to this one, and we spent the next hour and a half weaving along them, gangs of kids all excited when we arrived, then they'd flip into that hypnotic trance as they chose the ice-creams.

We did a few knots of streets and cul-de-sacs, then the houses thinned and we crossed through a commercial area with wider roads and sparse buildings. 'Next stop is a Mexican estate,' said Christian, which turned out to be a dense group of red-brick tenements, four or five stories tall, with loads of Mexican-looking people hanging around the cars, the balconies, playing basketball on the small court. We rolled in, the loud jingle echoing back before Christian turned it off – 'this is the whole place, it only needs a few second burst,' – with kids outside pointing to us and looking for adults for money, or fleetingly appearing at the balconies and doorways before darting back inside, then reappearing with notes.

'Contrary to my earlier statement, this is a place where it's easiest and safest just to park up, because everyone's within walking distance. They all queue up anyway.'

A stream of children approached, and a snaking line grew, each quickly choosing their ice-cream, some speaking English but many just jabbing the stickers and holding aloft as many fingers as ice-creams were wanted.

'Usually Snowcones or the cheapest ones,' said Christian. 'OK, how many? Que ...? Two, OK, but turn your hand around,' Christian laughed, gently turning a young boy's hand around. The boy shrugged and smiled. 'It'd be great if you could speak Spanish to find out when they're having their big BBQs and stuff.'

'Riba, Riba! It's el ice-creamo hombre!' I said.

'Shhh!'

After that we did a pit-stop at a park-up burger place, Christian grabbed some money out of the till, 'lunch is always on Hank,' and we got burgers and chips – *fries* – in cardboard trays. Then we took a straight road out of town towards estates that on the map looked like those paisley fractals seen from the plane. The Sun still monopolised the sky and demanded everything be hot. Either side of the road was empty brown real estate, heat shimmers rising from atop the tall, thin yellowy grass, then the gates of a housing estate appeared and we turned in to a vast island of neatly shorn, bright green grass beneath arced rainbows of hose water. The road demarked the border between scrubland and civilisation defined by green grass, fed by water drained from the empty land, civilisation based on theft.

Christian turned on *The Entertainer*, its dull notes now *bo-bo-bo-bo-*

boing excruciatingly into my head.

'Haven't you got any other jingle?'

'Trust me, this is by far the least annoying.'

'Can't we vamp it up a bit? Have some Prodigy or something?'

'No.'

He turned the nob, and tunes played in the style of a BBC computer played out, first *Popeye the sailor man*, then *Just one cornetto*, then something really jolly that jumped about.

'What's this one?'

'*Tie a yellow ribbon in your hair.*'

Then he turned it back to *The Entertainer*.

'Awww,' I said.

'Yeah I could have got down to that last one,' said Mike.

'My decks, my mix,' he said.

We passed a picture-perfect caricature of an American house, white picket fence, the prettiest flower beds, pastel-coloured garden ornaments, a swing seat on the porch, and a US flag sagging in the heat, with a tiny plaque on the fence that said 'winner of the inaugural best garden prize 1993'.

We crawled along perfectly smooth black roads, as sticky as melted cola cubes, without any bulged scars of old roadworks. The roads curved this way and that, all lined with large neo-colonial villas glittering white in the sunshine on banks and hillocks carved by bulldozers still loitering under tarpaulins. The estate wasn't even finished, some of these man-made hills were still open earthworks, half-clad with rolls of fresh turf, while the skinny trees speared into squares cut out of the *sidewalks* gave no shade. Between the houses were large fields with sculpted mounds, on which nobody frolicked. There was nobody around and we gradually picked up speed until just as we approached a road of unfinished houses, I saw in the mirror three kids, jumping and waving.

'Shit, Christian, we missed some. Back up!'

Christian checked the mirror. 'They're close enough, let 'em catch up.'

'Quicker to back up?'

'No, because you reverse over them.'

'And?'

'No…'

'I was joking.'

The kids caught up, breathless, did the chant, made their orders, then trotted back along the dazzling sidewalk.

'Nobody around, though,' said Mike.

'Does anybody live here yet?'

'No, there aren't many kids here, but take in all these building sites, builders *love* ice-cream, and they're all Italians for some reason.'

'Right … so where are they all?' I said.

'It's Sunday, fuckwit,' said Christian.

'Oi! Do we get weekends off ever?'

'Never. Weekends are when we make our money. If you chuck a sickie at the weekend, Hank will not be happy.'

He started to list potential selling sites to look out for. Builders were always up for ice-cream, so look for houses under construction or being renovated, piles of bricks, sand, planks, builders' vans, ladders, pots of paint. Gardeners too, so listen out for lawnmowers cos whoever's mowing's going to be hot. Kids' parties would always be good, look out for balloons on the gate or front door. Playgrounds were good. If you could see water sprinklers then someone was at home, probably the kids as well then. Some of the estates had big ponds where children went swimming, and there were known to be big water parks in some towns, and open air swimming pools, but there'd be a lot of competition.

You could make a fortune in a park, if you could get in without getting chucked out, especially if there was a little-league baseball game on, or a Mexican BBQ as they loved massive blow-out BBQs at weekends, 'the whole estate piles down the park, it's amazing!' said Christian, 'you park up and they just come, hordes of them, out of the trees, like an ambush.'

During the week look out for factories, picnic benches. Shopping centres could be a problem because you'd need a different permit to park near shops.

'What about schools? What time do they come in the morning and when's home time?'

'It's the holidays, fuckwit.'

'Oi!'

'Stop saying stupid things!' said Christian.

'Stop being a cunt!' I shouted.

'Don't say that word in the van! The kids will hear you!' he shouted.

'Hot isn't it?' said Mike, and we all laughed.

Christian carried on. Hospitals weren't much cop. Churches may be good on a Sunday or a wedding. Funeral homes and cemeteries were probably dead.

We exited the estate and were back on a highway.

'Isn't this the way we came in?' said Mike.

'No, this is the exit the other side.'

'You'd never bloody know it. It's all identical,' I said.

'It's pan-fucking-flat to the horizon, doesn't this landscape ever change?' said Mike.

'Not really,' said Christian.

We toddled along the road and Christian indicated we had time for a smoke, so we all lit up, before binning our ciggies out the door as we turned in through the gates of another estate, indistinguishable from the previous one, dropped to snail's pace and turned on *The Entertainer*. It was all large white clapperboard houses. Lego-like houses, with picket fences, American flags and lawns with visible turf roll lines, all made as if to a checklist.

But there were at least loads of children, dancing in the sprinkler rainbows and whose big bright toys littered the long, wide drives, or were hammering along the sidewalks on trikes and bikes festooned with ribbons and chrome. Every street we turned down we saw little people turn to us, start jumping and waving, and we'd pull up, Christian held court with the kids while Mike and I got the hang of the freezer, and sometimes a queue of passers-by grew. Slowly but surely the lines of quarters and dimes in the float grew longer, and the pile of green notes grew thicker.

'This is a great estate,' said Christian. 'I've played street hockey here with some of these kids.'

He grabbed a great clutch of notes, stuffed them into his burger bag and put it in the freezer.

'Prevent thefts,' he said.

'Do you get much thieving?' said Mike.

'It happens. Never to me. But if you weren't in that door well Mike I'd normally have that door locked shut.'

'Where do we go for a piss?'

'Carry a bottle in the back to piss in,' said Mike.

'Some drivers do that. Adam did that, he's gone now, great bloke. He had a piss bottle which he chucked at his competition on his last day, coming straight towards him and he leaned out and splashed it onto the bonnet of this guy's van then sped off. The other van was too big to catch up, he said.'

We spied a small copse of trees on the edge of the estate and took it in turns to go piss, two guarding the van and keeping look out, then we all lit up and drove on, when suddenly Christian shouted, 'put that fag out, someone's coming!'

Ahead was a little girl with her mother, and the girl came up to Christian with a colourful piece of paper.

'Hey ice-cream man,' she said so shyly, 'I did this picture of you.'

'Awwww!', said Christian, drawing it out so much even the little girl would think he'd over done it, 'that gets you a free ice-cream, whatever you want!'

We all said hello to the girl but she hid behind her mum's legs, making us laugh.

'Go on sweetie, choose your ice-cream,' said the mother, who was very good looking.

The girl peeked out from behind the mother, came and stared up along the row of blue stickers, a finger rubbing slowly over her lower lip, while Christian ostentatiously put the picture on the dashboard. Finally she chose something and with great ceremony Christian gave her the ice-cream, and they headed went back into her house. Then a boy appeared, slightly older, who just stood there eyes darting left and right, up and down the dozens of blue tiles, saying over and over, 'I want … I want … I want …'.

43

But then there was a problem.

'This costs a dollar, and you've only got 70 cents,' Christian said.

'Wad?'

'You need another 30 cents. You haven't got enough money. I can't give it to you.'

'But I want it.'

'You can't afford it.'

'Wad?'

Where do they come from? I glared at Mike who covered his face with his hands.

'Tell you what. Why not, instead, have a Snowcone for 50 cents, then you'll have an ice-cream – and, bonus, you'll have 20 cents to spend on something else!'

'So I can have a Snowcone?'

'A Snowcone – *and* 20 cents! You can buy some Bazooka Joes!'

'Wad?'

'Just buy a Snowcone!'

'OK ice-cream man!'

'Here you go, a Snowcone … yes, that's two quarters. Brilliant! Off you go sonny!' Christian smiled.

'I liked how you sold it as if he was getting 20 cents as well.'

'It's all in the pitch. Basically just sold that kid his own money,' Christian smiled, and Mike and I started to laugh.

We rolled away. 'But what a cretin,' I said.

'You have to be patient with them. It's their money, their ritual and if you hassle them they'll just wait for the next van. You have to go with it and get to know them, build their loyalty.'

'Oh. OK.'

'It can be difficult! Last week this kid was standing there 'I want … I want …' et-cete-fucking-ra, and I could just hear another ice-cream jingle coming closer and closer, and I'm thinking "come on you little shit, buy something for fuck's sake," but you don't want them to pick up on that especially if your competition's coming. Which that time was Freezer.'

'Is Freezer your arch-nemesis?'

'He is a cunt. I'd managed to get a long way ahead of him and was getting all the trade, right, but slowed me down, and I heard him coming – ooer – and knew if he saw me he'd overtake and steal the biz.'

'It'd be like the chariot race in *Ben Hur*!'

'He'd likely just cut ahead and do the next street before me. Or get out a baseball bat and just come at me.'

'No way!'

'Way!' he said, 'happened to Jake last week. He was stopped at a junction and his competition pulled alongside and got out with a bat and started banging the bonnet on Jake's van. Jake gunned it and sped off. Really, ask him.'

'Fucking Hell. Some wound-up Yank comes at me with a bat, I'd shit bricks,' said Mike.

'What kind of fucking name is Freezer?' I said.

We continued to crawl and weave the streets all day long in our *Big Trak* way, always arriving to heroes' welcomes. So it went til it was gone 7 pm, maybe closer to 8, the Sun now low and enlarged, glowering in our faces like it wanted a reaction.

'We're close to $450,' said Christian, '$150 for me, Hank'll give you a cut of the rest. We'll head back for 9. Hank doesn't really like it if you're back earlier than that.'

Cool. We were hot, and tired, it was oddly mesmerising job, but it was fun, and obviously good business. We arrived back at Penguin in good mood, and saw Ben and Elly happily chatting over beers. She saw us and smiled at me as I sat and Christian got beers, and we swapped notes with Mike while Ben and Christian counted up, and Hank indeed gave Mike and I a cut, we said it'd gone very well, and he seemed genuinely pleased we'd had fun, and he said on Tuesday we'd get our own vans, and so far, so good. Soon enough we were in the Pontiac, roaring along, singing away against the backdrop of the dying sunset of pink and brown, to go feed in a diner that was a classic study in orange and beige, with a pot of coffee on the go, big brown leather booths and a menu of massive salads, pizzas, and burgers. Elly and I chatted, she seemed happy, Christian and Ben were happy. I was happy. And we were all the happier for beer and spliff at the flat.

And tomorrow was a day off. This was looking like it might be fun.

Toy R Us

Our first day off and we hadn't even done any work! We woke to coffee, fags and bagels that Christian and Ben had gone and got from some 'brilliant bagels shop a couple of miles away,' as Ben said, unloading all these multi-coloured and speckled bagels onto the dining table, then Christian laid out the plan. 'First, breakfast. Then, I think we should attend the pool.'

'Swimming!' said Elly, like a child.

'Then we'll go to Toys R Us, and then the mall as I need some tapes for the van. And lunch at the mall.'

'The mall!' said Ben.

'The *malllll*,' continued Christian, 'where there's loads of places, then maybe kick around and chill … we could go to the cinema! Then get stuff for dinner this evening, as I'm going to cook,' to which Elly raised her eyebrows and smiled, and he added, 'and after that, Dooley's!'

'Our favourite bar!' said Ben.

'Our only bar!'

The pool did sound great. The countless pools I'd seen from all those miles up looked like bean-shaped blue flecks of paint on a wallpaper patterned by red roofs, green lawns and grey streets, so small you'd do about three strokes then hit a wall, before giving up with no idea how far you'd swum.

Obviously, the pool at this apartment block had to be massive, up on the roof with a panoramic view all round, the water dancing with sunlight, a long diving board, and ringed by beautiful people on sun loungers, chilling with drinks delivered from the Art Deco café bar by a sizzling, sexy bikinied lady slinking around like that girl at Caesar's Palace in *Father Christmas Goes on Holiday*. Yes! This would be so cool!

Instead the pool was around the back of the block, in cold shadow, its cracked concrete surrounded by a few tatty sunbeds, without sun, without people. The spring board had no board, just rust streaks from the ladders. But Elly looked pretty good in a swimsuit, so good that despite the cold water I got a stiff, so I just swam back and forth until it went away, which took a few lengths, although I didn't help myself by sneaking in a few looks at Elly as she dived in, swam about, climbed out and did it all over again. She kept throwing glances in Christian's direction, him upright on a sun-lounger, beer in hand, smiling while working hard to look uninterested.

But he was interested. They were both 'interested', he'd been interested in her since that very time they'd met, that night I took her out with all my flatmates, when I was very belatedly going in for the kill and she told me she'd lost interest and liked Mark. Christian didn't really speak to her, but said later, 'let's just say, I saw her.' She had that effect. And I had been that close.

Another horrible night some weeks later, we were at the student bar and Christian was gamely talking me up to her, although my chance had long expired, and being pissed, and pissed off, I said something stupid and she bit my head off and left me in bits, while she went upstairs and 'danced' with Christian

... although he said it really wasn't 'dancing'. Two girls from next door saw it all and said Elly 'was not dancing' in a shocked tone, without saying what exactly she'd been doing.

But Christian and Elly had been flirting ever since, simmering away, which was scalding to be around. He only lived in the flat upstairs with the boring 'mature' students who were mostly foreign, so he came down ours a lot to get stoned and drink and play cards and fuck about. Anyway one time it was just him and me and some other, we were all very stoned, and she came up in conversation, like she often did, as he fancied her too, and then he went quiet. And then he said in this weird way, 'I could rape her.' He was stoned, but it was weird.

Then later I'd already agreed with Christian to come to Chicago, and when she'd asked to come, I couldn't say no, and Christian said we'd all live in the same apartment and it'd be a non-stop party. And as uni for me tailed off into a black oblivion, missing all my exams, Chicago being all there was to look forward to as I'd get pissed with Elly, and she'd ask excitedly about Christian all the more.

Shit.

And here we were 1,000s of miles away, in Chicago, it'd all come off – *zz but they hadn't gotten off yet! Nor cum on one another!!* Not yet. They could still mess it all up – *zz they could make a mess.*

A few more lengths, then Elly said she'd had enough.

'OK, great! So now let's hit Toys R Us!'

A quick change and a few miles drive away along some highway we hit this vast shed in the middle of a massive car park, black tarmac heating up like a McDonalds hot plate, then we got the plunge pool effect of air-con pouring onto us at inside the entrance door, just inside which were a load of trike bikes, called 'my first chopper'.

'I think that could be misconstrued!' Christian grinned to Elly, and she laughed.

'So could the ball pit tent,' I said, pointing to a tent filled with balls and kids. 'Look at those kids playing with their balls,' I added, to which a passing mother said 'that's not appropriate!', leading Elly to smirk, 'you got told off.' Damn, why'd I get done and not him?

'You two need water guns for your vans!' said Ben.

'He's right,' said Christian. 'you need weapons, it's an arms race. Let's get you tooled up. And they're massive, they fire for miles.'

It wasn't a toy shop as such as just a massive warehouse of toys stacked up and up, the metal shelves went up forever as did the aisles. We came to an aisle with water guns, not those crappy 25p ones from the newsagent that crack in your hand, but great big chunky pump-action jobs, Christian brandishing one, saying 'I've got one just like this,' these thick sturdy plastic in bright yellows and oranges, racks and racks of them like the gun shop in *Commando*. I got one and pumped away.

'Looks like you're wanking,' said Elly.

Noting she said that to me but not Christian, I scowled as we continued to select.

'Has everybody chosen their weapon?' said Christian. 'OK! Let's go play hockey!'

'I'm going to find the models,' I said. Ooo, they had some lovely things, all these models, petrol engine, electric engine, wing spans feet in length, balsawood, polystyrene, mostly American things like B-29s but also Stukas and Lancasters. There was one Lanc with a 5-foot span which they had a picture of its beautiful skeleton before covered with tissue, it was magnificent engineering. All those balsawood models would take months to make, anticipation brewing and brewing, until the day you'd set them off on their maiden flight, and watch them fly all of 10 wonderful yards before they barrel-rolled into the ground and smashed to pieces.

Either way I had no money to buy these magnificent machines, beautiful toys I'd spent my youth playing with when I should have been out clubbing and partying, machines that I should have gone on to fly for real like Mark had. I got depressed and wandered around a bit and found a plastic bubble car, and tried to get in but got stuck instead and got seriously frowned at by a shop assistant who helped me out, so I went around and found the others had taken over an aisle, playing hockey on roller skates.

'He shoots, he scores!' said Christian. 'OK ... everyone got everything they want? Let's get these guns and go to the mall!'

All tooled up with water guns, we took the Pontiac, now a sauna, to the mall, which was insane to see emerge in the distance, as big as a housing estate made of knock-off Lego. The aisles were wide and high, lined with two floors of shops and disappeared into the distance, it was like flying into the Death Star in *Return of the Jedi*, massive open atriums of escalators and ludicrous fountains, like the reactor core, with gangs of boys in knee-length shorts and backwards baseball caps, milling around aimlessly.

I'd been to a horrible green mall in Bromley built in the 1980s, and the Arndale Centre before the IRA blew it up, although many thought the locals bombed it so it'd be rebuilt with government money, but this mall was epically, obscenely bigger than either. And the shoppers were fat like you would not believe, fat wasn't even a big enough word, where you couldn't fathom how their legs simply didn't collapse under the weight.

There were dozens of restaurants and cafés, everywhere sold coffee. The larger gaffs had forecourts and every one had a table in the middle annexed by a large gang of teenage girls, all drinking Coke or milkshakes, gossiping about fuck all, or looking ostentatiously bored, which was just stupid, or maybe the overwhelming soullessness of this palace of tat had sucked the life out of them. And stalls that sold only ice-cream, or just donuts, just bagels, just pretzels.

We found a clothes shop in which I idly looked at some shirts but the dummies had on at least two shirts and t-shirts underneath, 'a layered look' as

48

Elly called it. There was a big pile of those lovely broad flat caps, like a hexagonal flan, what Tintin wore in *Tintin in America*. I stuck one on and showed it off to Elly, but she said, 'you've got it on back to front.'

'No I haven't.'

'Yes, the peak should be at the back.'

'No it shouldn't, it's the peak. Do you know how to wear a hat?'

'Yes and yours is wrong.'

'A bloke I know from school wears one of these backwards, he looks like a fuckwit.'

'Because it's supposed to be that way around.'

'No it bloody isn't, it looks shit.'

'Suit yourself.'

Anyway at 20 dollars I wasn't going to buy it.

She wandered off, and a guy came over and said, 'hi there how are you today? Is there anything I can help you with at all?' Had I done something wrong? Was he trying to sell me something or chat me up, as he was camp as. But he was so friendly, and persistent, in a nice way, picking up on my accent and finding out where I came from, asked how long I was in the US and what was I doing, how long I'd be here, and he was genuinely enthralled, and where I was staying – without telling him exactly where – and how I liked it so far, diddler der. Before I knew it he'd found a long canvas-sand coloured linen shirt with a soft, lightly-padded collar, that I agreed looked great on me, and so did the green-striped shirt, yes this guy knew how to dress me, it did fit perfectly, and when he said the beige and pastel-green colours offset my dark hair, I'd never have seen that myself, and then I had to politely stop him from adding socks to the pile, although they were lovely quality socks, not any plain old socks, and the three-for-two offer was real value, and I would have bought them if I'd the money, but you know two very fine shirts were enough already, and he folded them in tissue paper and priced it up, and I paid, when he said at the end take care and have a nice day I thought yes I will thank you for all this!

Except now I was down to 20 something dollars on me.

In fact I thought that might be all I had.

Shit.

But I'd had a nice chat and had some lovely clothes. Well I thought they were lovely, then Elly came over.

'Show us what you bought,' said Elly. And hurrah, she agreed they were very nice, although I didn't tell her, I'd kind of been seduced into buying them.

Christian came bundling over. 'Come with me to the *Sesame Street* shop.'

This we had to see, and it was really an entire store stuffed with *Sesame Street* stuff, all the characters and Muppets in various sizes and guises from figures to soap to towels and books and board games. Then Christian said in this weirdly childish voice, 'Elmo...' and he bounded over to a shelf of boxed Elmos. 'I've got to get one for my niece,' he said, petting an Elmo like a kitten, 'she *loves* Elmo.' And Elly smiled away as he made this great show of what a great and wonderful uncle he was, so in touch with his inner child or whatever the fuck, and he's not too cool to coo and mew over all this childish stuff, o God he'd probably set up an orphanage just like the one Elly spent a day at in Colombia or whatever the fuck and she was now lapping it all up as he harped on – *zz he'll be lapping at her harp*. As horribly obvious as his great play was, and that's what it was, this was all one epic play, and it was going to last all day or as long as it took, she was going for it.

Feeling dread at what was unfolding I went out, and found a great shop next door rammed with telescopes and flying things and those swinging ball things that batter into one another, before we were hoicked out to find lunch at an 'amazing burger place' across the mall, and it was pretty good, but my dollars were rapidly dwindling.

'Right – now, why don't we while away the afternoon at the cinema,' said Christian.

I tried not to think about how that'd clean me out, but I suggested *Braveheart* nonetheless.

'Nah, Mel Gibson doing a Scots accent for two hours, bollocks,' said Christian.

'*Batman Returns*!' said Ben.

'Ooo Val Kilmer!' said Elly.

'Yay, Batman!' said Christian.

Yay, Batman, I said to myself in sarcasm.

Back to the Pontiac, now an oven, to drive to a cinema complex as big as a village amid a car park built on top of a village, with at least a dozen screens and tickets bought not from a piddle corner booth like the Streatham Odeon, but a whole bank of tills. The air-con was nice though, and the film was quite fun, better than the so-serious Michael Keaton crap, although the close-up of Kilmer's bum in its black-rubber suit was odd. Poor Riddler, a nice guy who'd only wanted to please, but was spurned and went mad as a result. It was so sad. Out of the cool dark of the cinema we re-entered the dazzling heat of the outside and drove to a 7-11 like shop near the apartment block for beer and food for the evening, the serving guy looked like a cocker Spaniel. I'd not money in my pockets, just moths.

We drove back to the apartment, Ben skinned up, Christian started doing a stir-fry, I flicked through the TV channels as Elly laid the table then read. Soon enough Christian shouted it was ready and we all sat down.

'This is very good,' I said.

'Yeah, nice one Christian.'

'Delicious,' said Elly coyly.

'Thank you,' he said with false modesty.

Oh the complete git. It was stir-fry, a bloody stir-fry, noodles and vegetables and soy piss, which he'd only cooked to impress her, her cooking skills limited to pasta-tuna-sweetcorn bake. He was like bloody Michael bloody Caine, in the *Ipcress File*, supposedly groundbreaking for showing a man cooking like a gourmet, in a sexy way and not like some poof, and for which he bagged this woman – yet, what had he cooked? A fucking omelet! And all Christian cooked was a fucking stir-fry – *zz fucking stir fry, it'll stir them into fucking!* – but he'd impressed her.

And I hadn't.

Then he said, 'And now! Dooley's!'

Total and utter piss. I thought we'd stay and drink the beer we'd bought. I'd no money at all.

'Can I ask a favour, Elly?'

'What?'

'Can I borrow $20?'

'You out of money already?' she said, wrinkling her nose.

Christian laughed, then said, 'look don't worry, I'll lend you $50 and you can pay me back Wednesday when you're working.'

'You sure?'

'Fine! BUT – put a tenner aside now for petrol cos you'll need to buy your own.' I couldn't say no, and was grateful, but already I felt like a parasite.

We left the building out the side door and walked along a sidewalk towards lights beyond some trees, until the sidewalk ended at a junction. With the traffic lights red we went to cross, but a driver leaned out and shouted, 'There's no crossing, you can't cross here.'

'OK, sorry,' said Christian as we carried on over.

'Were we jay-walking?' I said.

'Apparently. You get to the end of the pavement and then turn around and go home!' said Ben.

Then we were at Dooley's, this big, airy bar, glazed, light wood interior around a large oblong bar, bigger than most pubs I'd been in, and was cheerily light with a good hubbub of locals. We took up stools at the bar while Christian went to the bog. 'Who wants a beer? Ben, Elly, pints?' I said.

'Just get a pitcher, easier,' said Ben.

I stood and waited as the barmaid came over and was about to order when I heard Christian say 'you're here!', and Elly swiveled around on her stool to face him, legs edging apart as she said 'hey Christian'. He'd only gone a minute.

He smiled at her.

'Beer, Christian?' I asked.

'Nah! Let's have cocktails!'

'Yes!' said Elly. They ordered their cocktails, at $5 a punt, while I ordered a pitcher of beer, then sitting next to one another at the bar they turned in towards one another in conversation, while Ben on my right was talking to some other guy.

That left me alone with only the pitcher for company, and even that didn't last long.

'That barely touched the sides,' said Ben, laughing.

Then Elly appeared, asking, 'Where's that pitcher?'

'Beer?'

'Yes.'

'Er,' I felt like I was in trouble.

'Have you drunk it already?'

'Er, ' this wasn't going well.

'You only got it five minutes ago. Jesus!' she said.

'I thought you were having cocktails. I'll get another.'

'We had cocktails. Now we're on beer. That was a whole pitcher you drunk.'

'I bought it.'

'With other people's money,' she scoffed.

'You're useless,' she said, then she laughed, 'useless – you have no use.'

It was pretty funny, but soon enough everything went into a swirl and I don't remember a huge amount after that.

First day

Again, I awoke to Christian attacking me in bed.

'Get up!' he yelled, 'it's your first day!'

'Shit, so it is!' I leapt out of bed just as Elly came out the bathroom in a dressing gown, hair towelled up, as I subtly turned away as I passed her to obscure cover my morning rise.

'Looking good Elly!' said Christian, and she flicked him a V.

Breakfast was out on the living room table.

'Are you nervous?' said Christian.

'Kind of,' said Elly.

'I am, ish, but …' I said.

'A quick weather report, it's going to be sunny all day!' said Ben, 'you all set to rake it in?'

I laughed. What did we need? What could go wrong? Nothing! It'd be a piece of piss, hundreds of dollars from selling ice-cream to cute kids and hopefully girls galore! There had to be some summer romance to be had! I got a jack of adrenaline – this was it! All that planning and haggling, and here we were, our first day!

The drive in the Pontiac to Penguin was gloriously bright and sunny, and we were all in good spirits, me getting sudden little bursts of excitement as did Elly, and she looked at me and smiled, a proper smile, and said 'well arranged!'

Thanks! I glowed within.

In no time we were at Penguin, Hank greeted us as we got out the Pontiac and while Christian and Ben went off, Hank took Elly and I to the big wall map, pointed us to the towns we were to work, giving us permits and maps, mine was West Chicago, 40 minutes north. Then he said to take a stock list off the table, check the freezers for stock, come back to the freezer room for refill, get ice from him and the float off Jess. 'Any questions, ask anyone including me!' he beamed, then he got Kentucky Charlie over to take me to my van, an older van, one of the shittest looking ones. 'Number 13, unlucky for some,' Charlie said. Great.

Inside, I opened the freezer, but the layout of boxes was completely different to Christian's, the ice-creams obscured the frozen mist, the ice on the packets, the box flaps, then there was a long, tedious to and fro of me trying to judge whether a box was empty enough to warrant getting a new one, finding it on the stock list with its tiny writing, but after a while I got the list together and went to join the queue at the ice-room, when the guy in front asked if I'd put my list in and pointed out there was no point in queuing or they'd have nothing to give me by the time it reached the window. Oh yes, shit! It was getting pretty toasty out on the gravel, compared with the boys at the ice-room window in their arctic jackets, all red faced and blowing, chonking the boxes onto the sill and shouting names as drivers helped ferry each another's boxes away. A nice American girl helped me and reminded me, 'don't forget the ice and float.'

She was quite pretty and wondered if I'd ask her out at some point as I faffed about finding room to put the new boxes into the freezer, having to open them and put in the old stock on top of the sodden, mashed up boxes already in it.

Then as I went to get the float, I saw her again and thought she wasn't that pretty and I didn't fancy her. Jess counted out my float, then as I sat in my van wondering what to do next a bloke bounding across the gravel in another van drew alongside and said 'now you need ice!' – how come everyone else knew what I needed? Hank was on his knees out the front of the hanger, chiselling great chunks of dry ice off a block.

I queued up, he told me to put on gloves 'or it'll burn, and only carry as much as you can carry in your hands, don't pile it up or it'll roll back onto your forearms and burn. People have done it!'

We hoicked piles of this smoking salt to my van, and Hank opened the freezer. 'You gotta place it carefully all over the box, not quite on the bottom as the gas sinks,' deftly placing half a dozen chunks among the boxes, like firelighters on a frozen BBQ, 'don't breathe it in! It'll knock you out.'

'That'll last all day, but don't keep the lid up,' he said. He then asked if I'd driven an automatic and I said yes, but he showed me the gear stick anyway, then pointed towards the highway 'where you turn left, then right onto this road', pointing to the map, 'and 40 minutes later, you're there. Dead simple!' and back inside the hanger he went.

Just as I tried to back out, Charlie banged the side of the van.

'I ain't uncoupled your fridge,' he said, pulling this cable out the side. 'OK you're clear to go!' and I lurched back a few yards, braked too hard and made everything on the dash slide about, the coins on the float nearly spilling all over the floor, then I turned to go and lurched forward, whereupon Charlie came over and grabbed the door and said, 'you're driving with two feet.'

'Yes?'

'Well don't.'

Do what? 'How do I not, I've got two feet.'

'No, you use just one foot for the gas and the brake.'

'What was I doing?'

'One foot on each.'

'How did you know?'

'I could hear the brakes grinding those wheels!'

'Ahh… sorry, bad habit, I think there's a clutch.'

'It's an auto.'

'OK. Sorry!'

'OK. Don't burn out the brakes and see you later!'

I took off slowly without lurching, without realising that again I'd hit the gas but was using the brake like a clutch, making Charlie shout, 'no two feet!'

I took my foot off the brake and the van head-butted its way across the gravel straight towards one of the other business hangers, as I wrestled with the steering wheel which weighed a ton and the gravel made the steering so slushy! Someone shouted to look out as I just turned enough to avoid hitting the business opposite, then slurred the van to the lane towards the highway, finally driving in a straight line. At the edge of a highway, I had to go left, meaning I had to cross three lanes this side with enough speed to not get hit but slow enough to stop in the central reservation, then jack the van over the next three lanes to the slow lane, all in this shit heap van. It felt like waiting to swim across the Thames at high tide, while weighed down with bricks. Bollocks, this was horrible! Two trucks the size of a train engine howled past at about 60, the nearest one rocking my van with its slipstream, these things would take two miles to stop! It was like *Frogger*.

I gingerly pressed the accelerator then chickened out and braked, then someone beeped behind me, so I shouted 'fuck off!', then a few seconds later this young man from Penguin was standing next to my open door and said 'hey man, you're on the wrong side of the road,' and I was on the left-hand side, not the right.

'Shit! Sorry,' I said.

'Take care!' he said as he went back to his van.

Then something of a gap in the traffic appeared on my side and feeling flustered I floored it over to the reservation, although the van more like lurched dozily across while I could only see any number of massive things blasting towards me, but I was halfway over, and alive! Then another gap appeared on our side, or I thought it did, probably panicking I lurched over to the slow lane but fucked it and nearly went off into the ditch alongside the road, so corrected back into the lane by when a car screamed past, horn blasting, again that weird thing where it grows louder like 'EEEEE' then goes away 'OOOOWWWW', and then another one, and a shout of 'asshole', but I was too busy wrestling with the steering and gaining speed.

Done it!

I was on my way!

Towards West Chicago!

Hurrah!

But it took an age to drive to, and when I got there with no idea where to begin. I didn't know the place at all, didn't know what was where, it was just streets and things. Shit.

I tried to remember where would be good places to aim at, and remembered, look for parks full of Mexicans. On the map was a large park, so I trundled over and drove in, but it was a bit barren and very few people were about. I saw some diggers on a hill or some kind of man-made mound – *zz pubic mound zz* – with a fence around it – which had those yellow and black radiation wheel signs on it! – but also there were picnic benches, where a dozen builder types were having lunch, and as I neared one put his hand up and shouted at me to stop, and at first I thought I'd done something wrong like driven into a radioactive zone, but then they were all running over and I could see dollars in their hands and the orders piled in, big orders, but at the freezer I couldn't find anything through the thick carbon dioxide cloud bank over the boxes, so I had to lean in deep to see anything, then someone tapped the side of the van impatiently, I got this great lungful of CO2, which dazed me and slowed me down some more.

'Sorry for taking so long, it's my first day.'

'Yeah, sure seems like it,' said the first worker, looking at me like I was stupid. All right, wanker!

'Hey,' this woman said to him, 'he's new', or rather she said 'noo'.

'Thank you,' I said.

'You Briddish?' she said.

'Yes! Just here for the summer.'

She smiled and gave her order, then I asked about the radiation signs, and a bloke next to her with a massive moustache said, 'you seen that film *Silkwood*? About the nuclear plant, with Meryl Streep?'

'Yes!' I had seen it, late one night on BBC2, 'she worked at some plutonium plant that kept leaking everywhere and she was trying to expose it and they killed her.'

'Yep, exactly. This is one of the sites where waste from that plant got buried.'

'No way!'

'Yup. You got radium, you got thorium buried under there,' said a gravelly voiced man.

'Well … it's the same company that owned the plant where Silkwood worked,' the woman said, 'all that crap got mined here and it's now all one great big pile of radioactive garbage.'

'Which we're cleaning up. Too late for the houses built on top of it all though,' the man added.

'They did what?' I said.

He pointed over the hill, 'the site goes all the way down over there, and there's houses now.'

'Yeah … may see some three legged kids in a generation or two,' another man said.

I was too agog to say anything.

'Anyway ice-cream man,' said the moustache man, 'I'd like … mm … I want, I want...'

The rest of the day was a blur of long, long, long suburban streets, where even following the map I'd no idea where I was. I could have driven down the same street five times and not known it. A couple of times I'd follow straight roads like dyke roads flanked by scrubland to these big isolated estates, big green islands of houses dotted in seas of brown wasteland, and they were all just houses. No offices, no town squares, no shops, nowhere to go, but you'd need a car if you did. Massive places, so much space, so much unfinished and artificial prairies, the few bloody kids taking ages to choose the ickiest and priciest ice-creams, prices I'd have to get out and check against the side of the van, and while I learned some quickly, I was still scrabbling to locate them in the freezer and then trying not to faint when I forgot about the CO_2 gas.

A couple of kids actually gave up. They weren't as fun as I thought they'd be. Nearly always they'd see me, jump up and down with such excitement, I even heard a couple of times, 'it's the ice-cream man!' being shouted and a squeal of excitement, like going through those slatted doors in a saloon and everyone at the bar turns around and cheers, and the someone starts up on the piano, and the bartender starts hurling beers down the bar. But when I actually pulled up they didn't seem to care that much. I'd smile but they'd not look at me and just go into that trance, their eyes scanning back and forth and back and forth along all the pictures of ice-creams, saying, 'I want … I want …' which could expand out to 'I wanna … I wanna …' then to 'I wanna Sour …. I wanna Sour …'

A Sour Tower, I thought, remembering a name!

'A Sour Tower?' I suggested to a boy who just stopped and stared at me in confusion, said 'wad?', then continued the chant.

How much fucking time did it take? Then when I did say something, like to confirm their order, or argue about the change, they'd stare at me and say 'wad?' and I'd end up repeating myself, over and over. That and the slow speed driving down the endless, identical streets, the tune of *The Entertainer* hammering my head, the van like an oven under this brilliant Sun and blue sky, it was all surprisingly tiring, quite hypnotic.

I swiftly ditched the no smoking policy. None of the kids seemed to notice anyway, they didn't notice much if you asked me. As the hours wore on, I found myself increasingly unable to concentrate, with the heat, the sweat, never knowing where I was, being unable to talk to the kids.

As it passed 6 o'clock or something, I remembered Christian telling me not to be back 'til later, and the Sun was lowering and the shadows lengthening. I'd been at it pretty much non-stop, crawling along so slowly I'd inhaled as much exhaust as cigarette smoke. I passed a playground with only a couple of kids on it, parked up, took the money tray and went and sat in the sand pit to count up. The dollar bills alone hit over $270 that day, of which every third dollar was mine, a good haul. A very good haul. A strangely warm feeling of excitement and satisfaction rose up inside me as the sun warmed my face. The American dream! For a hard day's work, crawling the streets in an oven, high-tailing from estate to estate, but smiling all the way, so here's your instant reward, your wage.

I run away abroad from my fucked little English world, and now I was making it in the States, starting from scratch and learning fast about business in Chicago from the big boys. For all the heat and monotony and bollocks, the money and the adrenaline from scrapping it out every day to make more bucks was something I could see myself falling in love with. Would I stay on, learn business and make my life and fortune here, like so many millions had done before me? Would one of these fine white clapperboard houses, their eaves glinting with gold and pink from the falling Sun, one day be mine? Now I could understand why America was home to such battling commerce men, why would anyone spend their life working somewhere like *Glengarry Glen Ross*? Because it was all such a great game. And the balmy breeze vying for my feelings with the warm pink cloak of sunlight on me, it seemed everything was offering itself for me to take.

What need of the old, and constrained, here was the fabulous, limitless new country without a history, full of people escaping their pasts, people like me! No one knew me. I could be anyone I wanted to be! How free could that be? Could it free me from what I knew was about to happen?

I felt grand all the drive back to the depot, although I drove slowly, disorientated by taking the same road home but recognizing none of the towns or landmarks because everything was reversed, on opposite sides of the road, and the shadows were long and grey instead of short and dark, the colours drenched in soft pink instead of bright and stark.

Arriving at Penguin I saw Charlie wave at me, so I waved back and parked up behind a van, when Charlie ran over and shouted, 'I was waving at you to come park over there! Back up, follow me over,' and he guided me like a ground crew to an airplane towards a specific spot behind a row of vans, with a little power lead glowing on the gravel that he hooked up under my van's bonnet.

I walked into the hanger, Hank was there, feet on desk, 'hey Jim, how'd it go?'

'Yeah good, good,' I said, wide-eyed,

'Grab a beer and count up!'

Elly was there, Ben, Mike, and Christian, who was talking to some guy.

'Hey Jim, did you have a good one?' said Ben, thrusting a beer at me as I sat down.

'Yes!'

Christian introduced his friend, 'Jim, this is Paul, Paul, Jim.' He was like a heavier set version of Keanu Reeves – shit, would Elly fancy him? She'd gone to see *Speed* with Mark, and said how gorgeous Keanu looked

'Hey, good to meet yer,' said Paul, 'you just started here?'

'Yes, first day! A newbie!' I said.

'Rookie!' said Ben.

'Ahh, cool,' Paul drawled, and nodded slowly. 'I finish this week, you'll probably take over my round … you staying with Christian?' His drawl was so strung out, was he tired?

'Yes, me, Ben, Elly.'

'Cool,' he said, nodding. 'You all at college with Christian?' It was like he was talking in slow motion.

'Yes, I live downstairs from him.'

'Cool,' he said, nodding, 'and you're all here for the summer?'

If he knew all this, why was he asking? Maybe they were conversation starters, but all I could answer was 'yes'.

'Cool. You'll make loads of money.'

'Cool.'

'Probably. OK, I'm gonna chip, probably see you later.' He didn't say probably, but *pra-a-a-ably*. I wasn't sure about him, not least in case Elly thought he did look like Keanu. An image of her and Mark snogging on the back row of the cinema flashed into my head, then her and Paul doing the same.

I counted up again, slowly, cans of beer came and went, and we talked about our days, then I was pointed towards Jess who checked my counting and paid me the day's whack - $88.50! Yay!

'Good day's work,' he said, 'but don't drive with two feet, you burn out the brakes,' he chided me. God, everybody knows.

We piled into the Pontiac with Mike and headed back to the apartment, then when there Christian said, 'We've got no beer, Jim do you want to go get some?'

'Sure!' I said, and Mike said he'd come and buy a load as well, so everyone else got out and I moved into the driving seat.

'This is the first time I've driven this thing,' I said to Mike.

'Oh right,' he said, and I put my foot on the accelerator and the car grumbled, moving slowly forward. The steering was smooth but when I underestimated how much we'd need to turn to get out the car park, and we nearly hit the barrier.

'Big turning circle on this thing,' I said, to which Mike said 'it's like a barge.'

Fiddling with the gear to get it into reverse, I then turned again, and rolled towards the junction with the highway. 'Shop's right,' said Mike, and I found the indicator, then the lights turned green and I really didn't think I'd pressed the pedal hard but it launched off with a roar, the front rearing up like a horse.

'Woah!' I said, then Mike shouted, 'you're turning into the fucking traffic!', which I didn't get that at first as I was confused by this wall of cars that was on the wrong side of the road and which I was driving into, then I braked hard, the brakes worked so well they threw Mike forward off the back seat, but we'd stopped bang in the middle of the road and then the lights changed, so I floored the car to the right lane, throwing Mike back just as he'd recovered his

59

position, then he hit the door as I turned hard to realign the car, did so, then luckily realised we were only a few hundred yards from the shop, right next to Dooley's, and from where we got a massive box of beers out of a row of fridges that seemed to line the entire wall of the shop, and served by this smiley bloke with a hanging moustache and a balding head with side hangings of long hair that made him look like a spaniel.

Only in the dark on the way out of the car park I didn't see the central reservation, as high as a kerb, and twatted it with an almighty bang, like an uppercut to the car that forced me to over steer and fishtail while Mike hit the floor again.

'Shit. Sorry about that. Er, car's OK I think.' I thought it funny, but Mike didn't.

At the flat the others were chatting amid spliff, we beered up, and Mike poured forth about my bad driving. Mike really didn't sound like he was from Leeds or rather up north at all, while Christian said he'd heard Jess comment on my driving with two feet, which was all a bit picky, but then the spliff hit pretty quick, before I knew it I felt I was tipping back through the chair was staring at the ceiling and my feet were floating. Then Christian said something to Elly and she flicked a V at him, and he laughed, and she laughed, and they seemed to exchange some kind of glance, and I felt myself falling into the floor.

Solstice

I awoke fuggy, but found a clean t-shirt, and then found coffee, bagels, and Ben watching the weather on the telly, while the other two were still getting ready – zz – *getting ready for each other* – zz.

'Looks like another hot day,' I said.

'We're sure as Hell gonna cook, boy!' said Ben, like the Sheriff out of *Live and Let Die*.

'Quite surreal, every morning being parked in front of this,' I said.

'Yeah! Of all the good shit on TV this is what we watch. It's quite addictive, I wake up and think, "must see the Weather channel"'.

'Only in America would they dedicate an entire TV channel to what you can see out the window.'

'I wasn't sure if it was sunny outside, but the TV said so, so it must be true. Makes no sense to know really though cos even if it's shit there's fuck all we can do about it,' he said.

'Phone up the TV people and complain.'

'Obviously it's their fault. Although, if it's going to rain, and rain and rain, Hank can cancel a day's work. It doesn't happen often, he's still got to pay people on the minimum and overheads so we're talking monsoon level of rain or tornadoes or something. It'll fuck us on commission if we don't work but if we make no money while paying for gas and lunch, and Hank's wasted a load of dry ice, it's shit all round, so there is a point at which there is no point. Although Christian insists lunch is on Hank, which I ... kind of don't.'

Suddenly I heard Elly say 'oops!' from the bathroom, and she came into the lounge swiftly, looking flushed, then Christian came in with a grin and said, 'no it was my fault, I didn't lock the door.'

I gulped my coffee and asked Elly if she wanted one, but she just looked away.

At Penguin, people were chirping away busily, and Hank called me over to his desk, which with the map behind it more like a war office. He pointed to the map and said, 'today you're going to Woodstock.'

Oh my God, not *the* Woodstock?

He gave me a map, the permit and I got the stock list and pencil and went out to my trusty no. 13 van, put the map and permit in, then floundered into the freezer, gauging which boxes needed replacing, where they were on the list, some I couldn't find on the list, some on the list I couldn't find in the freezer – what a fag. Eventually I got it together and queued up to the ice-room, where this young lad with a long, thin face, eyes very close together, looked like his head had been caught in lift doors, was pushing boxes of stuff through the window. His Arctic clobber contrasted with the shorts and sandals of the ice-cream men standing in the Sun. I learned his name was Dylan, and he was Hank's son, although he didn't look like Hank at all.

Loaded with ice, I was about to leave, then remembered I was still plugged in, and Charlie undid it, then I slowly reversed out of my bay and went forward across the gravel, beeping and waving. Jess made some crack about my driving with two left feet, then he said something else but I thought nuts to him, drove off, and was soon lined up behind a trio of other trucks waiting to hit the highway, remembering as Hank had told me to turn right and not left, so I wasn't going to have to make some suicide leap across the lanes.

I pulled into the first gas station, filled up, paid and bought some Coke and smokes, then was back in the cab and about to go when I heard this loud slapping against the side and a young voice shouting 'hey Jim, you fucking dumbass!' Who the fuck here knew my name?

It was Dylan.

'Oh it's you! What's up?'

'You forgot your float, fucking retard.'

'What?'

'Your float! We just chased you down to give it you, asshole.'

He gave me the black tray with the Polo tubes of quarters and dimes. Ah shit!

'Oh right, thanks,' although I was somewhat fazed by his language, cheeky shit, but as I turned to go he said, 'sign for it, dumbass!'

'Oi! Leave it!' I said, signing, 'how did you find me?'

'Only one place you're gonna go, fucking retard like you,' he said, heading back towards the Penguin pickup with Jess at the wheel.

Pissed off by the little cunt, I carried on to Woodstock, quite a long drive, but this was where the greatest festival ever had been, the mother of all festivals, where all the hippies of the world met up and got stoned and fucked in the field, and shat among the trees. I decided to start from the town square, which was totally as it should have been, a great lawn overlooked by a lovely big classical portico city hall building, the square flanked all round by cute rows of shops, just like in *Back To The Future*, though no skateboarders. But it was so genteel and handsome and ordinary, so nice and well kept, dainty almost, but there were no music shops selling psychedelic stuff or old cafes with stoners outside. Where were all the hippies? I parked up next to the square but within a second a policeman with mirrored sunglasses asked me if I had a permit to sell there, so I showed him my permit, and he said 'that is not correct ordnance to sell in this zone,' or something, o fuck I'm in trouble, 'you gotta move buddy,' and I wondered whether I should show him my 'permit' in the form of a few greenbacks, but instead scooted off, stopping a few streets away to look at the map for residential areas, which they were, and I started the crawl into the suburbs, the roads long and interminable, just like those in West Chicago.

Still no Goddamn hippies! It was all so neat and middle class. I neared a house with scaffolding outside and men in hardhats on the roof, tacking down asphalt tiles, and one waved me to stop and they slid down the ladder like in navy films and queued up. One heard my accent, asked if I was Briddish, and we

62

got talking and I said I'd been in West Chicago the day before and this place looked just like it. It was all weirdly familiar, and he said 'You into films?' and I said yes, and he said 'you know they filmed *Planes, Trains and Automobiles* round here?'

'I did not!'

'Yeah and *Groundhog Day*, that was just last year or the year before.'

No way! I remembered *Planes* not least as I'd gone to see it with my parents and it was a 15 and my mum said two adults and a child as I was still 14, and my pa and I just made a face, but the cashier let us in anyway. I saw *Groundhog Day* at uni, and hated it. Just after Christmas, in the pub with Elly, she'd invited herself back to our flat, and Mark was there. He'd rented the film out on video, and I asked Elly if she wanted to stay to watch it, and she said she was there on Mark's invitation ... and together they sat on the sofa. Before Christmas, Elly had been pestering and pestering me to arrange evenings out with Mark so she could try it on with him, evenings that often ended with me absolutely shit-faced and upset, and Mark didn't want me hurt and said he was interested in some other girl. But something changed over the holidays. Since we got back, she'd been furtive, and our mate Val told me they'd met up, and *Groundhog Day* was when they chose to show me they were together. I felt sick throughout the film as I saw all Bill Murray's pathetic attempts to get her from *Greystoke*, then tried to kill himself over and over and couldn't even do that, and that was how I felt, while out the corner of my eye I saw Elly and Mark on the sofa, gradually enveloping one another. I had a bong off Dave, zoned out. Mark drove her home, took ages about it. I went into my bedroom and silently screamed.

Woodstock was a nice town, handsome, and with each sale I got to know the freezer better and count the change faster, and was making money pretty quickly. But there was nothing to suggest the world's biggest gig had ever been here, with the only music coming from the music box and the same conversations, over and over, and the chant, 'I want, ... I want', or the adults who'd ask, 'you Briddish?'.

And all they had to do was point, pay, piss off. One little boy just stood there and stood there, scanning away, finger to mouth, 'I want ... I want,' while I sat down to have a cig, but before I lit up he said, 'I wanna Choco Taco.' Which I knew cost $1.50, one of the most expensive things on the menu, but he might have had rich parents, so I got it and then he gave me the dollar in his hand, and as he reached out to grab the Taco I held it aloft.

'Wait, stop,' I said, 'this isn't enough money.'

Momentary bafflement. 'Wad?' he said sharply, hands and eyes wavering towards the ice-cream, now tantalisingly out of reach.

'It's a dollar twenty-five for a Choco Taco, and you've only given me a dollar.'

Pause.

'Wad?' he spat again.

What the fuck did I have to say? 'Choco Tacos cost $1.50. Here's only a dollar. There, see the problem now?', but no response. Was this kid innumerate as well as unable to understand basic English?

He looked puzzled. 'I don't understand you ice-cream man,' he finally said, 'you're talkin' weird.'

'It costs a dollar twenty-five and you've only given me a dollar.'

'Wad?

Oh Christ.

But it wasn't the maths, or the *math*, it was the language, or rather my English accent, he didn't get. None of them did, all having been born and bred on pure American voices, whereas I'd been brought up on the same programs as him, so this wasn't a problem. Then I realized the solution lay with *Sesame St.* I felt corrupted just at the idea of warping my speech for the sake of a few cents, but still I did it, deploying my best *Sesame St.* accent, I said, 'go ask your mom forra kwarder.'

As if the clouds had parted, to pool him in a spotlight of Godly sunlight to a chorus of angels singing 'Aaaaaaaaah!', his face lit up in comprehension. 'OK, ice-cream man!' he said, and off inside his house he sprinted.

KWARder. KWARder. Five nickels make a KWARder. Four KWARders make a DAHler, don't dey, Elmo?

Fucking Elmo.

As the day wore on and my mood went up and down, thinking of Elly and Mark, Elly and Richard, how I'd messed it up for me, then fucked up the year at uni, fucked up my whole life.

Sometime around 5, along a lush street of green, the road more like a track and the trees tall and strong, a woman in a sarong flagged me down. She was standing in the uncut grass of a long front yard with two towering birch trees, shimmering dark green and silver in the sunlight. She had a colourful wispy shroud around her shoulders, like something from Camden market, slightly worn, like her sarong. She had long hair and crow's feet, but was strikingly pretty. Behind her were three children spinning around and around, and then there was her broad-fronted house which its peeling white paint revealed greyed wood, but it wasn't rotting, just lazily succumbing to the fingering embraces of the grass and vines now exploring its frame. With Christmas tree baubles, tiny mirrors in five-pointed stars and fairy lights dangling from the porch, it seemed like a jolly, happy house, which it had to be, what other state could it be in?

'Hey ice-cream man, are you here to celebrate?' asked the woman.

Ooh, she had nice eyes.

'Celebrate what?' I said distractedly, suddenly aware of having held her gaze too long.

'Don't you know, it's the Summer Solstice?' she said, cocking her head to look at me.

64

Behind her the children were twirling around, repeating in sync, almost like a backing group, 'it's the summer solstice, it's the summer solstice,' as if it were the most wonderful thing in the world, spinning with their arms out like how we used play *Wonder Woman* in the back garden, which didn't really involve much beyond saying 'Wonder Woman!' and spinning around. Their hair was as long as hers, but they looked healthy and handsome.

'That sounds nice, are you going to have a party?' I asked, still unsure if the Solstice mattered.

'Sure,' she said, 'we'll be having a BBQ, friends and neighbours around, bringing their guitars and accordion and play music the night long until the Sun sets late, drink beer and smoke and party out here, and sleep where … we fall,' the last words going up and down as her eyes rolled before she looked at me again, her face so amused, her eyes saying, 'isn't this fun? Isn't it magnificent enough just to be?'

She was pretty big, in her late 30s and I'd've normally not looked at her twice, but there was something incredibly sexy about her, like she'd always known how to have a good time, and done it well. And she knew it.

'Do you wanna come?'

Just the invitation made me blush. 'O well um, no … um. .. I have to get the van back, er, and things.' No matter how nice she seemed, an evening with a room full of strangers made me flinch with shyness. 'But it does sound fun, thank you very much for asking!'

'Oh my Gahd, you're like that Hugh Grant,' her eyes widened.

Hugh Grant – well I never did! Do what you like, woman, take me!

I couldn't help but laugh.

'Well if you're passing, just drop by, the offer's there. And another time, stop by, we can sit and just talk about things,' she smiled. Just to talk about things, would have been lovely. Jesus it was all so lovely, I wouldn't have talked about anything, there would have been no need for words.

She ordered three Sour Towers for them for now, and five Choco Tacos for later, a good sale for me.

But for all that, all I got was dollars.

It was late but so light, I was selling well past 8 o'clock before heading back to Penguin, with the Sun, fat and low in the sky, tinged people with gold and buildings in pink, and it was a beautifully warm drive back. It was still light at base, as Charlie guided me in like an airport groundsman, waving planes into position, and I was still one of the first. Hank was behind his desk and said 'you forgot your float. I'm sorry I should have reminded you, but we got you anyway.'

'Yes, sorry about that,' I said, remembering Dylan's colourful language. Little arsehole.

The others started coming into the hanger all loud and jolly. We counted up, swapped stories and drank, I told about the float and Dylan's rudeness, to which Ben said, 'just tell him to fuck off, he loves it.' Then I told about the

65

woman, her strangely sexual mystery, her offer to party, to which Christian said, 'take her up on it and fuck her.'

Goddamn. He had to debase everything.

And I only wanted Elly. I could live off her fumes, and I was, as she sat counting her money, glancing up now and again at Christian, looking at him from beneath her brow.

'I was surprised though, it being Woodstock, there were no signs or anything to say this is where the greatest festival ever was.'

'That's because the Woodstock you're thinking of is in New York, fuckwit,' said Christian.

Oh. Well that answered that.

'Did you have a good day Elly?' I asked.

'Yes, made quite a bit. Some really sweet kids. There was one bit though where I sold a load to these Italian builders, and then one climbed onto the van and one came in the other door and they wouldn't get out. '

'Shit!'

'They were just teasing, but I was telling them I had to go and they were like, "no, no we keep you here and eat your ice-cream all day," "we come with you, we help you".

'Proper Italian ice-cream sellers, were they all called Toni?' said Christian, which I didn't think was funny as Elly seemed a bit ruffled, but she laughed, adding, 'it was insane ... but they were nice. And the kids were cute. Although they didn't understand me a lot. They all say "what" all the time, which is rude.'

'Wad?' I said, looking at her like it was her fault I didn't understand her stupid accent, or *stoopid* accent.

'Wad?' said Christian.

'Wad?' I said, as did he, then Ben cut his chat with some other and said, 'wad?'.

'Wad?' the other guy said, then everyone was saying 'wad?' at everyone else.

'Fucking "wad" me one more time, you little cocksuckers!' said a black-haired bloke, although he said 'lirral cockshuckersh,' and he introduced himself as Aidan from Halifax, and his mate brown-mop-haired mate Jason from Bradford. Halifax and Bradford, northern towns I only knew the Saturday teatime football results. Bradford! Oh no, the stadium fire killed all those people!

The guy Ben was talking to looked a lot like Jeff Bridges, and funnily enough was called Jeff. He had a very friendly smile, a strong handshake and when he stood up to leave he was bloody tall as well.

Then Christian said, 'There's a plan for a few of us to go into town. Let's go spend our winnings!'

Me, Christian, Greg, Ben, Elly, Aidan and some of the others got in the Pontiac and others in this A-Team style Dodge van. I talked with Aidan, who said 'cockshuckersh,' a lot and was doing economics at Nottingham, where

Jason was doing engineering, and both were on the fifth floor of our apartment block. Jason didn't say much else, and I was worried in case I mentioned the Bradford City fire and upset him.

In town proper, we came across a bar, large and airy inside, with a long, long light-coloured bar in the centre and a vibe like the one in *St. Elmo's Fire* or *Class*, which both had Rob Lowe and that wet McCarthy guy. We pushed two tables together and deployed pitchers of beer. I poured myself a glass, then another and another, whereupon Elly said, 'where's that pitcher I just bought?'.

And I realised the pitcher was finished, and she was standing there staring at me.

'Do you mean this one?'

'The finished one. You've drunk it haven't you? God you're useless,' and she stalked off to go sit next to Christian, patting his arm. Damn. I felt a bit sick. Jeff started talking to me, I found out he was a high school teacher, but I was tired and pissed and sad and quickly ran out of chat, left to watch Christian and Elly getting on very well.

A woman who looked like Ally McSheedy walked in, brilliantly, as she was in *St. Elmo's Fire*, and a crush blew through me, but what could I do to go chat her up? Stuck on the end of the table, my head clouded up, all alone.

St. Elmo's Fire.

Elmo again.

Sesame St.

Elmo.

Fucking Sesame St.

Fucking Elmo.

Zz - Christian using Elmo to fuck Elly – zz

Appalling Paul

When we got to Penguin Hank told me I was going back to West Chicago, which was a shame as Woodstock was fun, but he said it'd be good to settle into a place.

I liked Hank, and his fat reasonableness contrasted with his spindly son Dylan, who proved his wankerliness again as he stacked boxes out of the freezer-room window, saying, 'don't forget your float, fucktard.'

'Fuck you, mate, really, fuck you mate', I thought, and went into one of those modes of mood where you can almost hear a turbine in your head fire up and start whining faster and faster, but I loaded the ice-cream into the freezer in 13, and which was becoming quite orderly, got the dry ice, float, permits, map, filled a big Coke bottle from yesterday with water, detached the power line and drove off – with one foot! I was learning.

Down in West Chicago, things were slow. I tried the radioactive park but there were no workers there, probably all died of gamma radiation, then I aimed at a new part of town on the map but got caught at a rail crossing where this train of trucks about a mile long took like a day to pass, so I did a U-turn and went to find other places. I aimed at a high school before I remembered they were all on summer holidays, or *vacation*, and then found a park with a baseball game being played by a load of eight-year-olds, but couldn't get anywhere near it to sell anything.

With only a couple more sales cranked out in the next hour I headed back to town. Bollocks. It was radiantly hot, where the Hell was everyone? Shambling through town, into a park, then in the distance I saw a tower and a slide and children in swim suits – a water park! So I set course for that. As I cruised through the car park towards the entrance with all its turnstiles, flanked by a hotdog stall and a guy with balloons, the sounds of children squealing in the park grew louder and I could see clearly through the chicken mesh fence these wonderfully blue pools of water with kids jumping in, everywhere glistening with sunlight. It looked so inviting, I wanted to go dive in, and be out before anyone noticed, but there were surely shitloads of sales to be made.

Then before I'd been parked up a minute, a fat guy in a police uniform appeared from nowhere and said, 'you got five minutes, buddy.' Jesus, I needed a permit to be here, too? I sold two ice-creams to a woman and her child, when fatty reappeared and banged on the bonnet, 'time to go!'

'That wasn't five minutes,' I said, but he just stared at me, so I drove off, trawling the streets, full of sunshine but empty of business.

One kid said, 'no thanks ice-cream man, we had one already just an hour ago.'

Crawling, trawling, from one identical street to another. It was all so random yet monotonous.

In the later afternoon I found an estate with a really weird, psychedelic layout on the map, and only one entrance and one exit to the highway. Somewhere in there a robust teenage girl with brown hair and brown eyes flagged me down, her baggy t-shirt doing nothing to control her large boobs as she jumped about, but there was something bouncy and fun about her, and when I told her I was Briddish she got really excited.

'Wad? Oh God that's so cool! Have you moved over here?'

'Just the summer, I've got to go back to uni.'

'Wad?'

'University. College.'

'College, right! What are you doing at college?' and I told her, and instead of saying 'o what?' she said 'o wow!'. And we chatted and she said, 'ice-cream man, can I ride with you on your truck? I promise I won't misbehave. I promise, I'm not stupid.'

So I said sure, and opened the other door and she got on the footplate, and we drove down the road, and she suddenly said, 'o, pull over, pull over!' as we passed a large patch of open grass with a group of girls all about 15 or 16 just relaxing in the sun, and she called them over and a queue formed, her at the head next to me, telling her friends to hurry up as I didn't have masses of time, which was very considerate, and she bragged about how she'd ridden on the van, and I thought o shit they'll all want it, but nobody seemed bothered. Those with ice-creams circled around while the others queued, then this other girl, 16-ish, blond hair ponytail, gave her order, but also waved her hand at me as if to get me in close, was she going to ask me out or something? She had pretty, narrow blue eyes, and she got in quite close as I crouched on the driver footplate, then she said, 'if you let that fat girl onto your van she will never leave you alone. Believe me, she's an idiot. Don't put up with her at all.'

'Ah ... right, OK.'

I looked to the brown-eyed girl but she was walking away with her friends, and she spun around and said, 'he's Briddish,' a popsicle thing in her mouth. She shot me one last glance, waved and turned away.

Could I have asked her out? Should I chase her, get her name, or was she a total fuckwit? Why did I listen to that other girl? I could have asked her name and ... she seemed old enough to me.

Back at the hanger I told the others about the girls.

'You've got to look out for kids hanging onto the van,' said Christian.

'It was fine, I said she could.'

'No it is not fine, if she'd fallen off you'd have been fucking sued to pieces.'

'He's right, Jim. They think it's cute, it's not,' said Ben.

'That or you get every kid on the estate trying to get on the van and you're fucked again.'

Fuck! 'OK I'll tell 'em to piss off.'

'Never swear at the kids. I don't like swearing at kids, even if they've sworn at me,' said Christian.

I wasn't sure what was worse, the fuck-up or being patronised about it. Fuck your moral high ground, Christian, we're kids too!

'If some little shit's being a little shit he's got to be told, or he'll never know it and never change,' I said.

'No, you're wrong.'

'No, I think you mean you disagree.'

'I disagree because you're wrong.'

Oh fuck this guy.

'It's bad for business,' he went on, 'word gets round. The kids don't like you, you don't sell. Never get angry with the kids, no matter what they do.'

Him telling me off to not to tell the kids to fuck off made me want to tell him to fuck off. That and that, shit, he was right.

'What else can they do?' said Elly.

'I've heard them getting into the van and running riot, that's never happened to me,' he said. No, nothing bad *ever* happens to him! 'But keep that other door closed at all times, Jim, locked at all times. You don't want kids getting in the van.'

'All right, I get it, OK. I get it.'

'Never let them in, even if they say they want to help.'

'I said I got it!'

'It's tempting to leave it open so you can see out better and get a better draught, but they'll sneak in while you're serving and nick the float.'

'Do they do that?'

'It's happened. That and anything that happens to them in the van is entirely your fault. And they could say anything.'

'Like what?'

'Like you touched them up.'

'What? No way.'

'Seriously, you hear this shit. John, last week had this girl get into his van and she wouldn't get out, and he was being patient, but getting pissed off, and she was saying "I'm staying here as long as I like and if you come near me I'll scream and say you molested me." She was like, ten or something, and he was just, "what the fuck". Luckily her mum came and told her to "get the fuck back in the house," and said sorry to him. He was lucky. He's not going down that street again.'

Then Paul came and said hi, or 'hiiiiiiiii', not really talking so much as words falling from his mouth as he yawned, then he said, 'OK Christian, catch yer later, 1030, probably,' although really he said 'praaaably'.

'1030, yes, probably,' said Christian.

'What we doing?' said Elly.

Christian glanced around, then said hushedly, 'we're going around his gaff later.'

'Praaaaably,' said Ben.

'Praaaaaably,' replied Christian, 'I'll tell you in the car.'

70

On the way to a diner, he told us our spliff supply was low and we were buying some off Paul.

'Who is he?' I said.

'Paul! We met him earlier.'

'No I know that –'

'I know,' said Christian, 'Paul, or *Paullllll*', creaking it out like an old door, 'is a Brit. Cleans Swiss ski chalets and instructs in winter and sells ice-cream and dope in summer.'

'Fucking Hell. That's quite a circuit,' I said.

'His dad is loaded,' said Ben, 'loaded.'

'City banker,' said Christian.

'He sounded American,' said Elly.

'He makes out he's American, but he's Brit, actually quite posh. Went to Westminster. Turns out I played his brother at hockey once,' said Christian.

'Winter it's slopes, summer it's dope,' I said, which got an 'ahahaha!' from Ben and a 'nice one' from Christian. Elly beamed at me.

We cruised along the highway, the windows right down for maximum breeze, then we were blasted by the loudest horn ever and we saw this massive black pick-up jostling alongside us, the guy at the wheel in a baseball cap shouted, 'Hey assholes! Get that shit heap off the road!'

It was Jeff!

'Fuck off!' shouted Christian, and he flicked his cigarette at the pick-up, it ricocheted in sparks off the back, while we all shouted and flipped birdies. Jeff swung a couple of yards out then swept closer in, in a real hick drawl he shouted at Elly, 'Hey girl! You wanna good time? Ditch these pricks and take a ride with me!'

Elly leaned far out the window and arms up, waving her bust at Jeff shouted, 'yeah baby! Come on!' Jeff laughed, his truck roared forward, dropped back, then did it again, then he beeped his horn and swung off at the next junction.

The diner we hit was called Denny's, all plastic leather booths, massive menus with massive salads and burgers, and it was busy, and groups of youths, or *kids* filling out the larger booths. Then we cruised on through quiet suburban streets lined with houses like out of *Back To The Future* by day and *Halloween* by night. We pulled up at the bottom of a long drive leading to a large one-storey house, a swarm of moths rioting around a dingy porch light.

'This is it,' said Christian.

'Sure? I thought there was a wrecked pick-up on the front lawn,' said Ben.

'Sold it for scrap.'

'Don't get the wrong door at this time of night, you'll get shot,' said Ben.

I worried that'd happen anyway, Paul as a dealer would know some shady types, who were probably all inside, strung out on crack. What if they were all

71

armed and robbed us, or one of the addicts shot us out of paranoia, or some neighbour came out and shot us, or called the police, who'd come raid the police and we'd all be shot.

All these thoughts swirled as we walked up the drive and huddled under the porch light, my face gave me away as Elly asked, 'what's wrong?'

'Dealers.'

'Tsk, man, calm down,' she said, scathing.

On the drive there was in the darkness a silver Chevrolet, like an Austin Montego, mashed up with rust and lighter coloured patches from dents filled and sprayed, unfinished repairs from when its owner realised there was no fucking point.

Paul eventually opened the door, a waft of dope floating out.

'Hey, come on in.'

Inside was spacious, but sparsely decorated, there were two massive, cheap looking sofas, the white painted walls with stains instead of pictures, the ceiling light without a shade. Bloody grotty.

'Take a seat ... Do y'all want beer?', he drawled, like W C Fields, 'ran oudda whiskey, hadda make do with food and water.'

We deployed on the sofas, a spliff started to go around, and went to my head pretty quick. Christian and Ben and Paul chatted about the dope market, Elly looked like she was listening intently. I didn't get much of it but heard Paul say 'probably', or '*praaaaa-a-ab-ly*', again and again, as he and Christian haggled, then gathered notes from us all as Paul weighed out the weed on some scales.

It struck me, Paul wasn't some kind of drugs king pin, or cool on any level. He was boring and seedy and his house was a mess. It was all a big fat fucking so what.

But maybe Elly fancied him? The thought lodged in my mind as my head lifted and I felt myself tipping into the floor.

Jeff

Next morning in the Pontiac I sat behind Christian in the front passenger seat, Elly next to me, her big sunglasses making her look like a bee. I asked her what she thought of Paul, and she grimaced, as did I. Phew, she didn't fancy him. I got a drag off her cig.

Christian put a hand up behind his head, and I pretended to lick the back of it just as he unwittingly moved it out the way, making Elly laugh. He put his other hand back and I went to lick that, only to be repelled by this massive black pen mark all over it, and Elly laughed again.

Penguin was bustling, but Paul wasn't at the hanger, maybe he'd been busted after we'd left.

'Back to West Chicago, Hank?' I asked.

'Sure are,' he said.

I was getting used to the routine. With trusty No. 13, I checked the freezer, put my khaki rucksack with smokes, snack and licence on the dash, gave in the list, got the float, put a bottle of water in the freezer and loaded my water gun, queued up for the boxes of ice-creams, got the dry ice, unplugged and off I went – then smarted at a shout of 'two feet!' from Charlie, which pissed me off as I was sure I'd got out the habit, then made the suicide leap over the highway and aimed for Westy, Ol' Westy, *my kinda town*, *shee*, *with broads*, *dames and molls*.

Where would I start today? I saw down a road to my left a railway crossing, which the map showed as a rail line beyond which I'd never explored. Had I been on the wrong side of the tracks all along? I had to go see! In the distance I saw red lights begin to flash and heard the ding-ding-ding of a bell, so I gunned it to the level crossing, but just a few yards shy the barriers fell and I screeched to a halt, although there was no sign of a train for ages, until this massive freighter engine came through at walking speed with a caravan of trucks that went right back around the corner out of sight. Bloody Jesus, how come I'm always getting caught by these things? I got out and walked to the barrier, saw a few cars had lined up behind my van, and one beeped as I walked back, he waved me over, and ordered two ice-creams! Others followed suit, and I did a quick $10 of business before the barrier raised.

The houses on the other side were handsome and large, brick and wood, some with hexagonal, well-glazed towers on the corners, where you could read all day or snog your girlfriend, and the trees were tall and overgrown. It was all a shade rundown and shabby, maybe a classy part of town once but fallen on hard times, like Liverpool's amazing Georgian merchants' houses housing shitty students. But it was handsome and laid back for it.

Along a long road appeared a clearing, like a green, and I saw a group of boys on the grass, they saw me, all jumped up and down, one threw down a baseball bat, another his *Peanuts* baseball glove, one ran to a house for money, and they did the 'I want ... I want,' but they seemed nice and I remembered what

73

Christian said about getting to know them, so I asked, 'are you playing baseball?'

One said 'Wad?' – but another said, 'no, it's softball.'

The first lad asked, 'wad he say?' and the second boy replied, 'he asked if we were playing baseball,' and the first boy turned to me and said helpfully, 'no, it's softball.'

'Softball's not the same as baseball,' said the second boy.

Yes, yes, we've established that, I thought, then asked, 'can I play?'

They looked baffled.

'Wad?' said the boy who'd even understood me.

'Can I play?'

'No.'

'Oh.'

'It'd be weird,' he said.

My eyes opened wide. 'Weird? Why?'

'We're young. You're twenny or something,' he said.

I was going to say twenty-something year-olds could play baseball too, or softball, or whatever the fuck it was, but most of the group were already heading off, except the biggest one, not up to my shoulder in height, but looking at me as if making sure I stayed there and didn't follow them.

'Oh, OK. See you later then,' I said, and went to drive off. I wasn't massively upset but was pissed off with this biggest boy, the arrogant little cunt.

I trolled around, before finding myself back at the playground where I'd counted up a few days before, and parked up, putting the map on the van bonnet and smoking a cig like a cigar. It was easily hitting the mid-80s now, and the Sun was beginning its long afternoon march across the sky, keeping the temperature up in the unbearables.

I needed a strategy. A system. A rhythm, for best use of time and fuel. When would people be in the parks? In their homes?

I did some streets but they were quiet, so I aimed for a park, did some business, then in a cluster of shops just outside the park entrance was a tacky little store bedecked with slivers of bark and rustically hewn slices of wood, like a forest version of stone cladding, so I pulled over for more smokes and Coke.

Walking into the shop it felt like a bucket of cold air tip over me from the air-con above the door. I went around, gathering random things, 'til I got to the till where a tall young shop assistant with a blond mullet said with a smile, 'how's business, man?'

'Fucking shit,' I said, then said 'sorry,' and he laughed. 'Everyone's staying indoors, I'd have thought everyone would be running up for ice-cream, but no-one's buying a thing.'

'Yup.'

I liked that he liked that the ice-cream man swore. We grinned at one another, in mutual appreciation of our shitty existences. Behind him were top-shelf mags, and I saw one titled *Shaved Snizz*. The only porn mags I'd usually encountered before were rain-soaked ones found under hedges. I'd never actually gone into a shop and got them off the top shelf myself, like certain men did, let alone asked for one.

But then I realized, I was an adult, a man. I could do what I wanted! And flushed with manliness I dared myself to ask him, 'right, excuse me, sorry, would you mind passing me that copy of *Shaved Snizz*?' and smiled, thinking, 'yes – I asked you for that magazine without a flinch of embarrassment!'.

'Sure!' he said, and passed it over! Brilliant! I put the magazine on the counter, and flicked through the pages, carefully so as not to tear them or even leave thumbprints on the printed pictures. The pictures were strange, all of these women with shaved fannies in various poses as this muscular chap fucked them with this aggressive look on his face. Having perused, I returned the mag, said 'thank you very much,' paid for the Cokes and smokes and left.

Trouble was the magazine gave me a massive boner that just wouldn't go away, meaning spending an hour selling shit with the driver door closed and leaning awkwardly through the window while my frustration peaked. I worried a kid might see the closed door as a chance to take an ice-cream without paying, and if I was seen chasing a child down the road with a raging boner I'd be shot, but it didn't happen.

So the afternoon passed selling to morons. Just off the highway I saw a large group of well-dressed people spilling out of a large, 60s' looking building, with stone cladding and a tall chimney piling out smoke, and they stood around in this car park. I did a quick U-turn to sell a load of ice-cream, then saw they were all dressed in black and a sign saying. CREMATORIUM, so I U-turned and bogged off.

With somewhere over $180, I was ready to roll back to base, but passed through a nice, hilly green area, quite lush with tall birch trees, and decided it'd be the last road before heading back to Penguin. I stopped for a sale – then the engine wouldn't start. I lifted up the bonnet in the hope of seeing something obvious but there was nothing. The van was fucking dead as.

Then this little man appeared next to me and asked, 'What seems to be the problem?'

I said it wouldn't start and was going to try giving it a push, but he said that wouldn't work, then looked and poked a bit, before declaring, 'this can't be fixed. You got someone you can call?'

'My boss.'

'Do you want to use our phone?'

'Really? Can I?'

'Sure, no problem. Come on over,' and he led me towards this big, wide house, with colourful flowers in the beds on the neatly-mowed front lawn, then the very warm inside was rammed with pottery dogs, cats, vases, ships in bottles, and framed pictures of family on every table, sideboard and wall. He took me through to this massive, olde wood style kitchen, just like the ones on any sitcom, and this kind old lady introduced herself, remarking, 'oh you're Briddish?' while the husband said something mechanical about the van and pointed to the phone, on the wall, with a massive long flex – brilliant!

I called Hank and he said be an hour, leaving a lot of time to chat, so I asked this old man, 'so, are you retired?'

The man looked in surprise to his wife, who looked back with equal surprise, then he turned to me, 'no, I run my own store, a hardware store on the main street.'

A mom-and-pop store! Brilliant! Although what should I ask next, do you sell things? Not much mileage in this chat, so I asked what she did and she said something about a school, only then I realised their surprise was me apparently thinking they were ancient enough to no longer be working but waiting to die. Great, I've come into the home of this lovely helpful couple and offended them. I wanted to cover my face with my hands but thought, sod it, it's fucked already.

So an awkward hour passed before Hank and Charlie turned up, I said thanks and bye to the not-that-old couple as the men hitched up the van, me in pick-up, I told them my faux pas and they laughed.

As I counted up at the hanger Jess scolded me for driving with two feet, saying it was that that bust the van, although I was pretty bloody sure it was the carburettor as Charlie the Mechanic had said.

'I've realised I drive with two feet, cos I've been using the brake like a clutch,' I told the others.

'Your driving is too sophisticated,' said Elly.

'Spasticated,' said Mike, 'remember you tried to kill us both the other night.'

Coming from Christian, I've have been pissed off, but for Mike I thought that was funny.

'It's all about clutch control, they all drive automatics, great big go-karts, "stop" or "go". They don't understand what a clutch is, it goes over their heads.'

'Bloody everything goes over their heads,' said Mike, 'these kids understand shit. I now see why it says SLOW CHILDREN on the van.'

'That and *what* all the time? *Wad? Wad?*' said Ben.

'Yeah! *Wad?*' I said.

'Some horrible kid ran off without paying,' Elly said, 'but I chased him back to his house and his mother was so apologetic.'

That reminded me of my raging boner angst, but didn't tell them, it'd take too much explaining, while talk turned to the Pontiac being bust or something, then Jeff said, 'I can give you all a ride home in my pick-up!'

'Oh cool, yeah. Come for a smoke!' said Christian.

Ben and I piled into the back of Jeff's big black pick up, with Christian and Elly in the cab, and we had the most glorious open air ride back to the flat, though I wondered what they were talking about in the cab.

Elly gave Jeff a quick tour of the flat, then we roosted on the sofas, divvied out beers, Christian lined up a trio of fat spliffs and sent the first one on its way, and as we chatted about the flat, selling ice-cream, Jeff's job as a teacher, the differences between British and US universities, or 'college', and all the debts American students have, and I remembered my student loan that I'd spent all on beer in the first term. Then Jeff saw under the table a copy of *On The Road* and picked it up, saying, 'o wow, who's reading this? This is awesome, you know Kerouac?'

'I brought it in order to understand the *real* America, so I could do America *properly*,' Ben said sardonically, making Jeff chuckle.

'It's well thumbed,' he said.

I remembered a copy of *On The Road* at school, the cover picture of a long road across a desert, tapering towards the horizon. It looked boring as Hell. But Jeff started talking about it, Elly said she'd read it, and Ben got enthused, as Jeff flicked through the book, 'lemme find a good piece,' as Ben suggested good bits and Jeff nodding, saying, 'o yes! And then he goes on about ...', Ben and Elly joining in, but it all went over my head. Then Jeff found a page and started reading aloud:

'"I woke up as the sun was reddening; and that was the one distinct time in my life, the strangest moment of all, when I didn't know who I was – I was far away from home, haunted and tired with travel, in a cheap hotel room I'd never seen, hearing the hiss of steam outside, and the creak of the old wood of the hotel, and footsteps upstairs, and all the sad sounds, and I looked at the cracked high ceiling and really didn't know who I was for about fifteen strange seconds. I wasn't scared; I was just somebody else, some stranger, and my whole life was a haunted life, the life of a ghost." It's beautiful, he's a genius.'

Elly hanged on every word, and Jeff read more, about some guy called Sal talking about Coke machines. What the fuck was interesting about that?

Jeff read on: '"Sal, we gotta go and never stop going 'til we get there."

"Where we going, man?"

"I don't know but we gotta go." That is Jack Kerouac!' he enthralled.

It all sailed past me, but I noticed how as he read out the excerpts, the tone of his voice fell at the end of every sentence, like these actors at uni had done for this terrible play set in New York that I'd got into (then bailed out of). They were all doing, or trying to do American accents, not even New York accents but shitty generic 'American' accents, where everything they said started loud then dropped down some flat scale of notes before ending low. It's weird, anyone who can't do American accents does American accents like that, and yet it was how Jeff was reading out – but he was a real American. An American acting badly as an American sounds like a Brit acting badly as an American?

Like that strange voice people use when reading out the Bible. This fucking berk Ben Levalle did the Bible reading in chapel at the end of Lent term, about some fool nitpicking Jesus with doubts, to which Jesus answered, 'it was then I carried you,' or some incredibly humbling statement, Levalle read it out with that exact soft-spoken, Godly pious way everyone everywhere reads out Jesus' knockout one-liners of wisdom. What the fuck the crappy Godless arsehole Levalle who everyone hated knew about Jesus was anyone's guess, but I knew he was a bad actor because I'd acted with him – yet that one time we both auditioned for a school play that would be touring the US, including New York, that fucker stole the lead role off me! *Stole*, as his folks had invited the director around for dinner before the audition, so I was told. I got fuck all. And yet there that piece of thieving bad actor shit was dishing it from the pulpit. Fucking boatload.

Meanwhile Jeff and all were now talking about other Beat and twentieth century writers, until Christian said something authoritatively that caused Jeff to argue back, Elly chipped in agreeing with Jeff, and I got this pang of panic, o shit does she fancy Jeff?,. then panicked about how everyone could see Kerouac's genius but I couldn't. Maybe I should have read it better. There was so much I should have read. I thought of arguing that people actually hated it and only pretended to like it because they were being ironic, but my feet were floating, I felt I was falling through the floor, felt too stoned to speak, but also couldn't leave without falling through the coffee table. I was trapped.

Jeff looked at me and said 'are you OK?' but as I didn't reply, Christian said, 'he's partied out. Does it a lot'.

I caught Elly's eye, she stuck her tongue out at me, then looked at Christian.

Eventually with enough planning I cobbled together enough energy to get up, not fall over, and get to bed, lying there for an hour hearing the banter and the laughter.

Airborne

Next day I woke groggy, but got on clean clothes and on the table were cheese rolls, coffee and fruit juice.

'Some spread! Nice one.'

'We got it early,' said Christian.

Both the Weather Channel and the view out the French windows agreed, it was another beautiful day of bright sunshine and blue skies, the air clear and fresh. With the Pontiac bust or something we all managed to pile into the A-team van the other flats shared, and while it was a working day, there was the excitement of it being a Saturday. Everyone at Penguin was in a better mood, and I was whistling as I sorted the freezer, loaded up with ice-creams, deployed the dry ice, congratulated myself for having so speedily and neatly got my van primed, treated myself to a cig, and fucked off. Taxiing across the gravel, wheels bounding, I felt so grand, even Charlie's waspish shout of 'how's your *two*-foot driving going, Jim?!' pinged off the armour of my good mood, not least cos it wasn't true, as I said 'it isn't, I'm using one foot! HA!', and I gunned toward the highway, for the 40-minute hammer to West Chicago.

Having pit-stopped for fuel and fags, West Chicago neared. I felt I was getting a handle on the layout, at least I knew some good stretches, places not to bother with, and mulled where best to begin my attacking run.

But over the sound of the other traffic, and the air billowing through the van's open doors, I heard a rumbling sound of engines far too low and throaty to be cars or lorries. They could only be aero engines! Something pretty big was flying pretty low, pretty close, and I scanned the sky, craning my head out the door, or ducking forward to see up through the windscreen, until suddenly something flashed above the treetops – and there it was, a B-17 bomber! Its magnificent dazzling polished metal fuselage, tapered to its tail like a long, frozen raindrop of mercury, that unmistakable, massive tailfin swooping like a rollercoaster onto its back, those thick, thick wings with its four fat radial engines, thousands of horsepower churning away. What a machine! Its thumping great wheels were down, it was lining up to land somewhere. But where? If I could just get a bead on its direction, relative to mine ... I was going north, so it was going north-east-ish? I pulled in at a gas station to scour the map, where I spied a county airport just a few miles away, no mere air sock and grass job, it had runways, taxiing routes, all sorts. Wasn't O'Hare big enough for the state? Then I heard a horrible howling and saw three A-10 Thunderbolts going over in formation, their massive dust-bin jets at the back and Mauser guns jabbing out the front like some weird insect mandibles, and flying the same direction as the B-17. Right, it had to be an airshow – and I'd have to go, because if I could get in I could park up all day and make an absolute killing, all while watching America's finest flyers have an almighty meet-and-greet. Ooh, what a piece of piss this Saturday would be, a feast of flying machines for me and a freezer full of Greenbacks for Hank.

Traffic on the road and in the air thickened towards the airfield. The B-17 was such a stylish, beautifully curved aircraft, designed by people who seemed to hold to higher ideals than just war and blowing things up, people who understood aesthetic beauty and put that above the unfortunate secondary task to which the plane was put, bombing people. So elegant, but over 50 years old and now in semi-retirement, still showing off. A-10s meanwhile were just ugly. With their bomb racks protruding from their arced wings, and overly large rear ends, and ugly, insect-like faces, they were like flying tarantulas, and with as much ability to reason. They were built to drop napalm on children, and if they weren't doing that they were at a loss as what to do. A pure killing machine, that was the plane of our times.

I heard another throbbing wave of noise coming closer, and as I glanced to my right I saw an old Lockheed Constellation banking around to land – ooh what a plane! The lovely dolphin-like fuselage, those four great radial engines, the romance of air travel! I juggled glancing at it with looking at the road, swerving when too carried away. Then a distant growling heralded the appearance of F-4 Phantoms at treetop height, threatening to head-butt everyone who looked up at them. Such chunky planes, built as jet fighters, not as dogfighters with cannon but as missile-platforms. Flying one of those was apparently like driving a truck.

At the airport's main entrance the guard person said traders like me would have to go to the main tower way around the other side, just follow the perimeter road, which I did, my head screwed left to see the dozens of landing, taxiing and parked aircraft just the other side of the chicken wire. F-86 Sabre jets! A P-38 Lightning! What a show already!

Two miles later I hit the entrance and parked up amid a load of jeeps, khaki Humvees, and Army-green A-team vans, and asked a man in camouflage who I had to ask for permission to park up and sell ice-cream. He pointed me to the tower, up the external flight of metal stairs I went, at the top in the full-round glazed office were a half dozen men in camouflaged army kit milling around, talking on radios, pointing out the window, checking check lists and handing them to the one seated man, also in camo gear, stashed behind a desk. They were proper military, serious people doing serious things. The desk man said, 'OK you three please,' pointing at me and two other men dressed like rocks, who promptly lined up and introduced themselves by shooting out their names, *rat-ata-t-atat*:

'Captain Jonathan Wilbur, pilot, 442 Squadron, Marine Corps.'

'Lieutenant David Smith, navigator, 88 Squadron, USAF.'

Holy rubbish, what had I walked into? Then the desk man looked at me, so I blurted out, 'Errr... Jim Hopkins, ice-cream man, Penguin,' I hoped he didn't think I was taking the piss.

'OK. I'll deal with you first, Mr Hopkins. How can I help you?' Fortunately he didn't seem narked.

'I … have … an ice-cream truck. And I saw the show was on. And I wondered if I could sell a load of ice-cream!'

'OK. Do you have a permit for this event?'

'Ummm….. no! I just turned up on spec.'

'On what, sorry sir?'

Sir? Me? 'On spec. Um. I just thought – I was just passing, but I don't have a permit.'

'OK. As a private vendor you would need a permit to sell ice-cream or any other ordnance at this event, and such a permit would need to be applied for and granted in advance, and unfortunately we cannot issue one for you today on the day. So, I'm sorry I'm going to have to say no, but thank you for asking,' he said, firmly, but gently, more gently than I'd expected from this man in combats who otherwise might have yelled *'HOLY DOGSHIT! GEDDOWN AND DO TWENNY, ASSHOLE!'*, which I would have done, had he asked.

'Right, OK, fair dos. How would I apply for one in future, or rather, my boss?'

He reeled off some departments and job titles and permit numbers, that'd all take seven to 10 working days and would involve a fee, 'how much I could not say for certain right now, but if you got your employer to contact the offices as outlined, after this event, they would be more than happy to help.' He smiled.

'Brill! I'll get him to do that,' hoping I'd remember who he'd mentioned. I wasn't going to waste his time repeating himself.

'That's great sir, and you take care and have a good day now.'

'Thank you, nice one. Would anybody like to buy an ice-cream before I go?'

'No, thank you very much, sir.'

'OK great thanks! Cheers bye,' and I scuttled off.

These guys were combat veterans, they had to have been in the Gulf War, the war that'd put me off joining the RAF, and give up on being a pilot. While Mark had gone and joined, and could fly on those wonderful machines, and Elly had loved him in his uniform, looked at him in that dreamy way, then fucked him for it, fucked him, fucked him, fucked him, entrusted him with her secrets. What chances I'd missed. That night he'd taken her to the officer cadets ball, she'd been so excited, hired a ball gown, but for once she spared me details, so instead Mark went on about how stunning she looked, and how they ended up outside on the grass in the dark.

In a pub, when it was just us two, she did tell me how she'd almost been in tears at the stunningly decorated dinner table, lined all around with such handsome young men in their beautiful mess uniforms, who might all get killed defending us, including Mark, and that made her heart swell and her eyes well up, but she also noted how much she fancied half of them and had to tell herself 'no Elly, stop it, you're here with Mark,' at which I laughed at the time, but all of which seared my mind like acid that night and the days after.

81

Another time, another pub, our mutual friend Val asked her in this sultry, 'so there much going on down there with Mark?' and Elly grinned and said 'it's sizeable' and other secrets I could hear but I couldn't move away from the chat without looking like I was, and more acid scorched my mind.

Instead of lining up a supersonic bomber to land on a runway, I was grinding along a runway-straight road to the horizon, sweating in this metal box with my bomb load of sugar. As I stopped to let two kids stare and drool, I looked up and saw in the blasting blue sky two parallel white vapour trails, so clean and straight, following this tiny metal arrow, flying at untold speed, at freezing altitude, somewhere else, somewhere fine, somewhere free. To London?

'That plane's high, ice-cream man,' said one of the kids.

I'd given up the chance to fly, the uniform, the order, all that Mark had, all that Elly fell for. So I tortured myself all afternoon trawling around West fucking Chicago, selling ice-cream. Surely to fucking Christ this was too simple a job to fail at. The buyer points, the ice-cream's served, the money's handed over. But even then these fuckers couldn't understand shit. They couldn't count, and when I told them they'd got it wrong they didn't understand me.

'I'm talking the Queen's English, asshole!'

'Wad?' they'd say.

'You're innumerate!'

'Wad?'

My mood lasted all the way back to the hanger. A spliff in the back of the Pontiac lifted me slightly into a haze, as we rolled towards town, but the breeze through the windows as we flew along the highway was refreshing, and the bright lights of Chicago proper were as astounding and romantic as ever.

Along the heated pavements we scuffed, until Christian led us to some club where the entrance led into a dark, twisting tunnel that opened into a large, dark room, with a bar with a glowing surface, the walls covered with bad graffiti in terrible, 1980s' style fluorescent graffiti and a lowered dance floor surrounded by a raised ring of booths that were mostly empty. It was hardly heaving. The music wasn't good enough to dance to but was loud enough to wreck conversation except for tennis conversations where you alternately turn your head to shout into an ear or be shouted at, or be so in one another's face that you had to be in some shagging relationship, as I was sure Elly and Christian were about to be, so my mood slumped again into a total 'just fuck off' zone. I wanted to be left alone, get pissed, zone out, but the beers were over-priced bottles and I was shortly running out of money. This was lining up to be one tedious evening.

In our booth the music was too loud to chat, but there was Christian, arms across the back off the booth, Elly getting in closer to him, seemingly engrossed in conversation with him as he'd laugh and knock back a beer, his arm relaxing, gently dropping around her shoulder. Damn it.

But there were a few women around, single women, and unless I was fooling myself I'd got two repeated glances of interest from two girls. With enough Dutch courage maybe I could chat one up. And getting into my fourth and final beer, unless I could scrounge one, I spied a good-looking woman at the bar who was definitely giving me the eye, and who smiled when she caught me looking at her. Twice in fact! Definitely! I told Ben I thought my luck was in and was about to have a go chatting her up, to which Ben said 'that's a bloke.'

'Fuck off is it.'

'Seriously, this is a transvestite bar.'

I was open-mouthed as he said, 'some of them are women. Fuck knows who though.'

Oh for God's sake! Did I look like *Crocodile Dundee*? I couldn't go around feeling them all up until I find a normal one. What the fuck. What was I doing in a fucking transvestite bar in Chicago? Any other time or place this might be funny, but not tonight. Who organized this? Bastard.

Fuck night

The next day ground along. Sales weren't bad, but my thoughts were, kerb-crawling through my mind between self-hate, lust, worry, and 'why didn't I ...' questions, all compounded by the throbbing monotony of the jingle and the stupid children.

When my forearms felt as red as the glowering Sun, it was time to head back. The few glowing clouds at the sky's sunset party were heading for the door, with the red streamers being brushed under the dark carpet on the horizon.

On the last straight stretch of highway, a pair of headlights blinked out of the dull mauve horizon, growing wider and brighter as they neared, before going boss-eyed and disappearing into the trees towards the hanger. A following pair of headlights did the same. My van followed them in, I saw a pair of red rear lights ahead, then close together, then disappear around a corner, and then the hanger came into view.

So precise was Hank's operation, we all left at the same time, and returned at the same time, laden with money and stories, and sometimes more stories than money, especially to explain our moth-eaten money-boxes, told as we put bills into piles, coins into slots, then took our takings to be checked by Jess. Cigarette smoke covered the smell of sweat and beer masked the shit of the day.

Except this evening, neither Elly nor Christian were on the beer. In fact, whereas the last couple of days, they'd both been pretending to casually catch the end of the other's conversations and casually tossing in quips or anecdotes they'd actually been sitting on for ages – this evening they were quiet, as if ignoring one another. It felt like that strange unease one gets when looking of the front of the house and sees blistering sunshine, but something's just not right, and when you look out the back it's a gun-metal grey mountain scape of clouds, surfed by shimmering rainbows, rolling towards you.

Then it struck me. Tonight was the night they were going to fuck. All the flirting and pussyfooting of the last few days, weeks, months, would finally end, and tonight would be when they'd consummate their lust. A night to remember.

Over the days, they'd stuck with their gangs as they played in the snow, building the snowmen, throwing snowballs, kicking up the snow as they all so innocently and playfully pulled their sleighs to the top of the hill. But they were just using me and Ben and Mike and others to stalk one another. So helplessly would one 'fall' and become trapped in a snow drift, so so eagerly would the other help them out, giving their need to touch in public so innocent a veneer. But they were here to sleigh, and they were so near the top of the hill, their faces bright and cheeks red with energy, hardy exercise and excitement in anticipation of the great, long slide down.

For all the heat in Chicago, watching them stalk one another, it felt freezing. Them and their trendy, hi-tech skiing outfits that could probably be zipped together, and they no doubt would in some apres-ski aw-he-haw-he-haw in front of the fire, while I looked in through the snowed up window from outside, standing in a blizzard in my scraggy, holed, long-coat.

Oh for fuck's sake. A sense of dread was growing from within as my mind cleared out of all the funny things that'd happened that day and the prospect of what was to come. I sank a beer in a minute, then a second, a third, blaming tiredness for being quiet as we drove the Pontiac home. There was no doubt, tonight was the night.

'Why don't we go out clubbing,' said Christian, to which Ben vaguely agreed, Elly said 'yes! Sounds good!', and with the vote already carried I gave token agreement, although I said not some bloody tranny bar, please. Christian avoided stopping off at any time-consuming diners and we went straight back to the apartment, where he rolled up a spliff while Elly showered and changed. I showered, half-heartedly searched for some vaguely cool clothes, wondering if I could somehow hold them up at all, delay things until their lust blew out uncontrollably, they'd be over-eager and wrong-foot themselves in the final dance, one of them would drop the ball, stall the car on the grid. Somehow would of them would fuck it up enough.

But all my trendiest Top Shop garb stunk out, even my fine shirts. I couldn't go. Anyway, why go? Why force yourself to watch the inevitable, final, macabre dance unfold, while not crying into expensive beer?

In the living room Christian was flicking through club listings, with Ben on the spliff, and then he announced his retirement. I went back into the bedroom whereupon a vision beheld me. Elly was dressed, stunningly. Dark leather sandals, thin crepe light pink ankle-length skirt, that draped up to the base of her bum, them shaped up over her arse so smoothly, up to her waist. It was a tad translucent in the dim bedroom lighting, so illuminating an agonisingly warm little world within. On top, a tight, buff cardigan cut with flower shapes in the design, semi-concealing a crisp white T-shirt and her fabulous breasts. Pure, elegant. Sexy. And all for Christian's benefit.

'You look lovely,' I got out, trying to be gracious in defeat, but instead sounding sarcastic.

'Thanks,' she replied, caustically.

Christian walked in, and stopped in his tracks.

'You look ... lovely,' he said, as if searching for the most innocuous adjective in a barrage of suppressed wonder.

'Thanks,' she replied, blushing.

Great. Same comment, and she responds as if on different planets. Well that's it. There's no turning back. Please, before you fuck each other, can I just say, fuck the both of you.

With Ben now gone to bed, we took final drags off the spliff in the living room, then I said it, 'you know, I can't be arsed. You go, I'm shattered.'

Elly looked surprised and, for a second, sad, 'aw come on, man.' Did she want a chaperone?

But Christian jumped in. 'Yeah, an evening in would do you good, put your feet up and relax.'

85

The stage was set, it was just him and Elly, and they were heading out the door before even finishing the spliff. How could such a bastard so effortlessly come across so sincere?

I went for another beer, but my mind was clouding over. I'd lost, and Christian was taking what was mine. Why? How had I thrown it away? What did he have that I didn't? Verve? Joi de vivre? Being suave? Where had he gone in life, what paths had he trodden that learned him the petty trivia, tricks and wisdoms that'd make the split-second difference in getting Elly interested? Why was nothing I'd done right? All I wanted was vested in that girl, and she was off with Christian.

Why?

Why?

Why?

The cold cloud of doubt in my head descended into a freezing fog. Every thought of her was warm, and wistful. Every thought and action of mine was cold, futile, dead. Every facet of Christian's existence made him the better man. They couldn't rub my face in it if they wanted to, they were out, somewhere, having their own sprightly conversation that somehow, somehow filled the time and followed the path they both knew so inexorably would lead to bed, a path I'd somehow never charted on my maps. For them it was all so easy, they were both so well practised in the dark sensuous arts that they could both pleasure each other from first glance to final fuck with neither's feet touching the ground, whereas I would be drunkenly offering snogs from the end of the bar. That's why they liked each other so much and I liked myself so little. Then I heard a voice.

Such self loathing imagery. Can't even fight back, can you? See what happens, you fuckwit? Not only do you lose, but you rub your own face in it afterwards. That's the sign of a real cunt.

Demon number one had made his first statement. I felt sick, and slumped heavily into the sofa, eyes darting, unable to focus on anything. I had to get to bed. Maybe there I could hide under the duvet and my mind would go away. At least there Ben wouldn't walk in and have to ask what was wrong and be baffled by my panicky incoherence before he worked out the stupid story and then laughed at me. But what if I drank myself into oblivion in bed, and left the cans everywhere?

That's right. Hide. Hide. You wanted to fuck her, didn't you? And you failed. And she knows. That's why she hates you. Really, deep down, she needs you, to protect her and to torture you. Vengeance on you for wanting to soil her. You're disgusting.

Demon number two.

You know full well she needs you to protect her, but you have black thoughts all the same. She can't trust you. She doesn't trust you. You don't deserve it. You're evil but incompetent with it ... fancy that.

It would be laughable if it wasn't so fucking true. My mind had split in two within my aching skull. On one half lay the gas-stinking trenches of my life, where above floated grey clouds that formed into images of me.

Go on. Over exaggerate. Wax lyrical about yourself, please, we really want to hear it, and so does she - not. You're such a dramatist, you've concocted this epic melodrama over what, a fuck? Geez, that's why she's going to fuck him and not you. That's why she's wearing what's she's wearing, to please him, and not you. That's why she's responding so well to whatever crap one-liners he throws up, and she'll reward him tonight. Him, not you. That's why they're out together lining up how they're going to their experiences to explosive use all over each other later on, and not you. And you're not there. You'd only bore them if you were.

Demon innumerable. I lay on the bed, smoking my larynx raw, while my mind disintegrated. Maybe I was truly mad, and my best hope in life would involve years of therapy and pills to stave off meltdowns while others happily fucked and fucked. Could sexual frustration get one locked up in a padded cell, where you'd be doomed to stay in as the condition only worsened? Suicide would be preferable.

And you didn't have the guts for that either. Imagine if you had, how many people you'd hurt. But you're considering it, when you promised yourself never to contemplate such an idea. And, well, well, you failed on that too. Who are you? Why are you alive? What for?

Escape. Maybe I could escape. With what? Steal the money from the drawer, take my passport and the Pontiac and just drive off.

And get everyone worried? Do you think they'll respect that? You're on your knees already, begging them to like you. And the best you can come up with is to betray their trust further by stealing. And when? Now? They've got the Pontiac! That's great, that really is ...

How many hours the 'World of Jim as Abridged by His Demons' went on, I don't know. I was just paralysed with self-hate and dread, and my throat was hurting like Hell from smoking.

Sometime around two, a low, distinctive rumble could be heard outside. The Pontiac was growling home to its car park stable. *Oh my God, they're back!* The demons shushed themselves noisily, excitedly telling themselves, No talking. Let him see for himself. Then there was silent, deafening laughter.

I went to the drawn blinds, two fingers prising them apart like some bad detective film. Would I see the car in the car park, bounding up and down to their rhythm on the back seat? Or would he be taking her over the bonnet?

There they were! Getting out. Her first, then she glanced back to Christian as he got out, him grinning broadly, as she began to trot towards the apartment block. My fingers flinched back from the blinds in case they looked up and saw me, but Christian's focus was on her as he ran after her. Damn.

What can I do?

What did I do wrong?

How did I get here?

Shush, shhhhh. You'll see.

In no time the apartment door opened and closed, and she said, 'I'm not going to do it,' as if determined, but also excited. But there was some ruffling, muffled sounds of contact. Footsteps padded further into the living room, towards the French windows and the massive sofa. Thumping. Rolling. Now what were they doing? Wrestling? A minute passed and she said, 'get off!', not loud enough to wake anyone, but loud enough for anyone awake to hear - insomniacs and perverts like me. Then something chinked, like glasses clashing, and something like a chair falling over?

'NO!' she said.

My heart pounding, was this rape? If so I had to intervene, I'd have to step in and save her from his evil clutches.

But I was paralysed with fear, having to face his wrath and maybe hers?

But I couldn't stay here and listen to a crime going on.

But was she really saying this so that someone would come rescue her?

But it didn't make sense, not after all the build up of the previous weeks, days, hours.

There was a wrestling, and a loud squelch. God, was this ferocious kissing? I couldn't bring myself to go see something I'd wanted so much myself but missed. I was transfixed in an apoplexy of lust and self-hatred, fear.

But what if it's rape? The struggling noises had stopped. She wasn't saying no again. She wasn't crying out. Had he muffled her?

Go on, it's a fucking crime, you chicken shit. Rescue her!

And if it isn't? What if she's well up for it? Then I'll see …

Fuck that, idiot! Go and see!

I don't want to see it.

Are you ever, ever going to forgive yourself for not intervening?

And what if I see them at it. Crime or no, I don't want to see them, see her … I …

That's right. Think of you. Only you. Do you think they're thinking of you now?

I had to see. Stepping down the narrow corridor to the living room was like walking on the thinnest ice, with every step delivering that agonising little sound of a crack, like an electric shock. Every nerve on my soles felt out every fibre in the carpet. The sounds from the living room became more clear. Were they writhing? Was she resisting? But not crying out?

Where were they in the room? Near to the dining table? The sofa? The floor? Which way were they looking? Would they see me coming? *zz - you'll see them cumming - zz*. They might easily see me, and it would be innocent enough, but my cock had overtaken my conscience, this wasn't intervention, or an innocent trip to get a beer, this was pure bloody voyeurism.

The only light in the living room came from the dull blue light coming from the car park outside. I scanned the room in its darkness. They weren't near the kitchen, not in front of the TV, were they on the sofa? I lowered into a crawl, feeling as if the noise of every crushed carpet fibre would wake the dead. It must have felt like this when escaping from *Colditz*. The slowness of my crawling made every muscle scream as this dog's-eye panoramic of the room panned into view. The coffee table … the dining table … a chair …. If Ben came out for a piss he'd trip over me and I'd be truly rumbled.

But look! There they were. Half-under the dining table, where we'd eaten the stir-fry Christian had cooked solely to impart that je ne sais quoi sexiness of the man who can cook, what he'd read about in some men's mag about how to fuck women, and it'd fucking worked!

Under the pale blue light slicing through the semi-drawn curtains, I could see him on top of her, one leg straightened behind, the other bent up, as if mid crawl, shorts on, moreorless. Getting grip. Keeping her down. Her skirt hitched up to her waist, and her arms around his back, I saw her near leg, staggeringly smooth and so light in the dark, was raised around his midriff. With a shuffle, the other knee appeared the other side, and her knees gently rocked back and forth. A small light cloth lay next to them, o fuck they're her pants. Then her furthest leg lifted up so a naked calf and foot came into view, and then her thighs raised up through vertical and her legs straightened so her feet ebbed towards the table top.

They were fucking, and by God they were so damn fucking quiet. What felt like ice maggots of denial and loathing gnawed into my mind. Retreating with glacial speed out of view, pushing myself up with a hundredweight on my back, I retraced my steps to bed, crawling onto the mattress and laying my weight down spring by spring. No way was I going to sleep. Then a wet fart sounded in the living room, luring me back. Were they spent? I knew I'd hear that sound in my mind a thousand times before dying. I had to go see, and an eternity later, having crawled through the corridor that felt laden with trip wires, sentries, microphones and mines, I was watching again. This time, Christian was on his back, his hands seemingly behind his head, with her on top, skirt discarded and her large, perfectly shaped arse, like two boiled eggs in a silken moon blue handkerchief, rising and falling over his thighs. O God if she went high enough I'd probably see his veiny cock appear and disappear into her. She hadn't even a goose-bump on either cheek, instead were two slightly darker little patches… carpet burn?

I could feel these images forge stamp onto my mind. I'd never forget this and this vision would recur at any moment. My mind would make puns from the most innocuous things and electrically connect across my conscious with the imagery of these two fucking the daylights out of each other in the crisp yellow light and blue tints of midnight Chicago.

Suddenly she slowed and stopped, upped herself, and shuffled her knees back and went down on all fours, her head level with his groin. Then she lowered her face and I could hear kissing sounds. As she established herself, got into a well-practised stride, her back arched from convex to concave, and her arse hoisted high on her thighs, knees aligned with Christian's shins. And there it was. Her arse crack blurred by her splayed cheeks, an indistinct line followed down to a two tidy trims of glistening black fur, surrounding two white, bowed, lips around a narrow black ellipse. As she rocked gently back and forth, going down deep enough where she must have almost kissed his torso, that black ellipse was beckoning me over. The eye of my storm, the epicentre of a year of Hell and sometimes near-criminally desperate hankering, was there, just a few feet away, luring me in. Ready and waiting. I could just walk over and take her from behind and be done before she could have her mouth free to complain.

But … *too chicken to spontaneously join in though, aren't you?*

Instead, I hoisted myself up and silently retreated to the bedroom. By now the Sun was awakening from its hangover and was moving to take the day shift from the Moon, drawing its pink limbs out from under the deep blue cover of the night sky, and the bedroom began to warm in the light, killing off any chance of sleep as I buried my head in the pillows. Then I heard the creak of the bed next to mine, and I guessed it was her but I couldn't turn to see in case she saw me looking which would prove I'd been awake all along. By now I was so guilty in every thought and action that just a glance from her would have had me confessing to everything from having watched it all to Kennedy's assassination. My head turned towards the window, although I just make out a narrowed view of her reflected in the brass poles of the bed-stead. Then Christian padded rushedly into the room, he grabbed some part of her and rucked up her clothing. 'get off,' she said almost as a token, which accompanied the sound of the bed-springs grinding under his extra weight. There was more ruffling of cloth and then the slapping ping of elastic and cotton things rubbing down much skin, until something small and light impacted floppily onto the carpet. A joint cracked. Bodies manoeuvred and slapped lightly, there was a farty squelch and they both laughed, an ooh from her and an aah from him, then quiet puffing started rhythmically and accelerated over a couple of minutes (but seemed like hours to me). I looked hard at the reflection of the bed behind me. He was taking her from behind. Eventually there was a final judder of the bed and skin slapping, she gave a little oooh, and soon a sound like a heavy, heavy wet kiss. They whispered something and laughed, and he went to his bedroom. Only now I dared look over to her, her back towards me, and in the warm, pink light as the sun appeared drowsily over the car park, she heaved with knackered ecstasy as a damp stain appeared and grew where her modestly replaced skirt tucked in where her legs reached her bum.

Somehow I got to sleep, but those scenes had locked themselves into my sub-conscience and lay stockpiled to wreak havoc in the weeks and months to come. Somehow, hours later, with the husk of my ego lying in smoking agony like my raw throat, I got up, got washed, dressed and fed, found myself in the Pontiac. Christian was in the front passenger seat, hands again clasped behind his head. Elly was next to me, Ben, and some others in the boot. Like me, she'd showered, and like me she was still wearing yesterday's work clothes as she sat languidly, relaxed as if totally overdosed on a cocktail of adrenaline and lust. Which they both were. And now they were ignoring each other again, no need to flirt or bait one another anymore. They'd both cashed in all over each other, and now they could play the best game of all, keeping a secret, being so exclusively in on the know about their wicked act. She'd covered him with her, he'd filled her with him.

Two more pointers about her appearance had the manners to haul me from my pit of self-loathing and into the trashed garden of frustrated rage, which is in fact a pleasanter place to be, if Hell has different levels of unpleasantness. Her mouth had the tiniest of grins pulling at it, and her blue eyes had two perfect little sachets of pale blue colouring beneath them.

Whatever sluttery you could accuse her of, she was guilty as Hell, and the court of public opinion knew full well. It had to be staggeringly obvious to everybody. Only the blind or those unable to smell would not see what'd been going on, and I could sense all the other drivers preparing their lewd comments and sniggers until, confronted, Christian and Elly would faux begrudgingly announce their sins before the court of public opinion.

Court of Penguin in session, all rise! Judge Hank presiding. Elly stood accused of all night sluttery, all night they've been at it, and loving it. The jury of ice-cream men were reaching their verdict already, 'We find the girl guilty of fucking all night long, loving every bit of it, and sentence her to repeat said acts for all our benefit for the whole summer.

'And what say you for the defendant, Christian?' would boom Judge Hank.

WAY-HAY! the jury would roar.

Meanwhile charges of voyeurism and perversion would be levelled at me as the public gallery would scream with laughter and I'd be punished with watching them at it again and again.

'No, just let him be him! That's punishment enough, the pathetic little fuck!' Elly would shout from the benches, and Hank would bang his gavel.

But at Penguin no such things unfurled, no-one commented, nudged, winked, raised an eyebrow, rolled an eye, even squinted suspiciously. It was all only obvious to me, who'd seen a live sex show. Well fair enough, as I'd had to sit through the auditions and rehearsals, I'd be there on opening night with a front row view, to give flowers and a standing ovation.

Whatever else happened that day, fuck knows. I saw a church emptying of people, but that's all I remember. I don't remember the evening, which must have involved a heaving plate of food at some cheap restaurant, gallons of beer, dope. I just turned off. The next day I was more aware, but it was another day off, a hot day, 80 degrees or so, and every waking moment I seemed to be with them, watching them watch each other for secret signs in glances, tone of voice, nods and winks to show it wasn't a one-off and arrange another clandestine tryst, with all the excitement of lust and secrecy waiting for another gorgeous, explosive, fluid filled session of sweating spiced by the fact no-one else knew!

91

The day off, some vague plan about going into Chicago proper was replaced by going to the mall to not buy things. They didn't notice my quiet. I think my first reengagement with them was some barely cynical comment about something. Every response to their questions carried the slightest tinge of superiority, the twinge of mock surprise, tone lade with the sentiment of, 'Oh you must tell me. Well, I never did. How could it be so?' Or so I told myself in quieter moments while convincing myself of my cunning, the sole enjoyment I had was thinking, 'no, I know your secret'. Yet the demons were quiet. Suspiciously so. Maybe they thought they couldn't possibly cap or add to the living nightmare already endured. Had the demons been trumped? Were they themselves now wracked with doubt? Or maybe, if I was worried that the voices in my head were hearing voices, shouldn't I turn myself in now? Maybe they were waiting for darkness. They mostly came at night.

It's amazing how paranoid you can be when you're wracked with guilt. I battled to convey a perfectly normal tone, maybe a tad more tired and miserable, or just hung over, partied out, which was what they'd expect. I could see the questions lingering around them both, however, well for us all in this cumbersome trio, namely 'when do we start again, and when do we tell everyone?'

I was numb. Catapulted straight into a rock-face. Feeling my whole body buzzing malignly, waiting for the broken-bone pain to manifest, while their bodies ached for more hard, hot, long, slow fucking, which I would be in attendance of, willingly or not, officially or not. Still my demons were eerily quiet. What foul offensive were they plotting? Caught in the suspense between their next assault and Christian and Elly's next fuck, I began to feel true ire. Christian and Elly's tip-toeing around one another and everyone else, they seriously thought no-one knew, that I didn't know. This was actually just insulting. That was it. I was mortally insulted, you two total cunts.

At Dooley's I got pissed, just about remembered Christian buying me a pitcher, then then he wasn't there any more, nor was Elly. I was so pissed I don't remember even getting back to the apartment block.

Monkey boy

Waking for work, my mind was a mash of mental Hell.

Elly wasn't in the room.

My clothes stank.

At breakfast, on the drive in, at work, Elly and Christian were paying each other more and more attention, little nuggets of chat, bumps, touches, open interest in one another. They were clearly becoming less coy, and another tryst was inevitable. Fuck's sake, they'd obviously done something the night before.

Christian said something about a possible new arrival in the flat, but I was too out of it to care. All I thought of was those two, thinking they were at it every second they were out of sight, beneath the veneer of being oh-so-partied-out, my mood swung between shock, rage and frustration. What were they waiting for? Were they wondering if they could handle a relationship, or would they admit it was just lust and they were just animals – except they were mature adults who could deal either in meaningful relationships, or just hard-core sex.

Fuck first.

Questions later.

Kill myself now.

Somehow though, for all I'd dreaded seeing, and seen, I was somehow still alive, and I hadn't run, although images of their fucking filled my mind all day out on the job, a Hell in my own mind, with no salvation. A couple of times rage coursed through me such that as I delved deep into the freezer to find whatever frozen sugary shit the kids wanted, I took in a great lungful of the freezing carbon dioxide, knowing just a few breaths would knock me out, and I'd fall into the freezer, not knowing a thing, and be dead in minutes. I tried twice, but my body freaked out and I jerked back out the freezer. Couldn't even kill myself properly.

Along a road I'd not traversed before, the houses all still big and the lawns huge, but there was something a bit run down about it all. Under a tree in the distance stood a fat woman and her two kids waving at me, and I pulled up, and so they started, 'I want ... I want ...' and the mother just stood there and let them piss up my entire day. Oh for fucking crying out loud you little fuckers!, and I said, 'come on, come on.'

The kids stopped chanting, and the mother simply stared me.

'Well?' I said.

Then she stepped back and pulled her two in to her and said 'er, you know we don't want any ice cream now.'

'What?'

'It's fine. We don't want anything, thank you.' Quite terse. I looked at her quizzically, her kids looked bewildered too, then she said. 'No thank you ice-cream man. We don't want anything from you. You can go now.'

I was going to ask why they'd pulled me over but thought I can't be bothered, but still drove off perplexed and pissed off, then all the more pissed off as I thought of those two fucking and I got a rager with which nothing could be done. Smashing one out in the van had prison written all over it, but it meant serving with the door closed. A litre of Diet Coke guzzled and thrown in the back then me off for an hour.

Eventually the rage subsided, and back to serving one little girl asked me why I looked sad.

'Do I?' Her boldness and concern surprised me. She was no older than seven, but she gave a shit.

'Yes you do. Are you OK?'

I wasn't going to tell her, but didn't know what to say, but that she asked was enough though to make me nearly cry, so I smiled and said, 'OK, well, now you've asked, that's made everything fine,' and gave her an ice-cream for free.

The day began to die, and I went past a house with a long lawn out front and a birch tree shimmering green and pink and gold, and as I kerb-crawled by I saw a little girl playing on the lawn and she looked up and ran about, but turned around, and turned around again, and turned around again, and I thought, 'sod it' and drove on. Another kid was about 30 yards ahead, and I served him then saw back up the road a large man in a baseball cap, waving his arm at me, so I U-turned the van back to him and there he was, holding the little girl up in his arms, and I got closer and saw tears streaming down her face, and he said 'you sure near broke my little girl's heart, mister!', somewhat joshing, but I put my hands to my face in guilt and said 'I'm soooo sorry! Sorry! I didn't think you were coming over.'

He said, 'she was turning around looking for me for money.' Again, free ice-cream seemed to make it all better.

At the hanger my take-home worked out at about $60, which wasn't completely shit. Ben was in a good mood and bantering with Jeff, and Paul, and some new guys, while Elly and Christian were making some silent communications, the fuckers.

I hammered a few beers to steady my nerves, while Christian was over talking with Hank, came back looking slightly surprised, and brought over this shorter guy in standard sweaty ice-cream man garb.

'Right everyone, this is Adrian,' said Christian, 'he's being moved into our flat, he'll be in the room with me and Ben.'

'Hi Adrian,' I said, outstretching my hand.

'Oiiii.' he said, looking around vacantly.

Oi?

He was stocky, with a very round head, like a light bulb, and very short black hair. His chest hair sprouted out from his T-shirt collar, his mouth had a kissy look to it, his ears stuck out, his eyes were dead round, brown. He looked like a chimp, and not a fun PG Tips one but one that'd rip the arm off some poor toddler.

We asked Adrian some questions but he gave one-word answers. Maybe he was shy. Maybe he was a nice guy. I was too hot and pissed off to care right now. Part of me wanted him to be a great bloke to distract me from all this shit, part of me didn't give a fuck. And he was ugly.

The car was like an oven from baking all day, but I'd not noticed how hot it still as outside and how sweaty we all were until we walked through the diner door and were drenched in cold air from the air conditioning over the doorway, like going from a sauna to a plunge pool. We took one of those big semi-circular booths, where the people in the middle are trapped and have to push past everyone else to piss.

Adrian seemed to perk up when his drink arrived, although he still said 'oiii' when starting to say something. He was doing medicine at Guy's, and so started talking with Christian, while Ben and I chatted across them, then the burgers and massive salads arrived, but Elly, on the opposite end to me, was quiet, looking down and away.

Then Adrian, 'Oiii ... Jim, pass the pepper.'

I gave him one of the small shakers out of the condiment box. He said, 'I asked for the pepper, not chilli spice.'

'Eh? Oh, sorry.'

'Idiot'.

I did a double take at him: 'Oi!'

He smiled when he said it, but it was a bit bloody much too soon, mate.

We carried on eating and chatting, 'til he swivelled to me and just stared.

'What?'

'I need to get out for the toilet,' he said, in a tone like I was an idiot.

'Oh sorry,' I said, moving out of the booth, 'you could have just said ...'

He shifted off to the loo without a word.

'Wurrr!' I said, 'I don't like him. Something really ... really like, presumptively arrogant about him.'

'Yes. I know what you mean,' said Christian.

'He's a medical student?' Ben said.

'Yep. Paediatrics. I would not let that fucker within a mile of my kids.'

Elly looked aghast.

'What's up?'

'I don't like him, there's something about him. How he looks at me.'

We all sat a moment in silence.

'Right. I'll talk to Hank, we'll get him moved upstairs,' said Christian.

'He's that bad already?' I said, almost laughing.

'He's that bad already,' said Christian.

'Their flat's bigger anyway isn't it?' said Ben.

'Yeah.'

Then Ben tipped his head at me, I said 'what?' then saw him looking past me and I turned to see inches from my face, Adrian's crotch, back from the loo.

'Oh sorry mate, you want to get in?'

'No, I want to stand here all night,'

I got out, let him slide in, flipping two raging birdies behind his head.

Back at the flat, Christian showed him the room and he hauled his rucksack in, Ben got beer out the fridge, Elly plonked onto the sofa, then, with all the rest of the sofa and chairs free, Adrian sat down right next to her.

'OK to sit here?' he said.

She didn't hide her discomfort, then Ben, seeing all from the kitchen doorframe, said 'Elly, shall we go to the shop to get some beer?'

She jumped up to go.

'Is that the shop where the guy looks like a spaniel?' I said.

'Yes!' said Ben, 'Dogface! You think so too?'

'Ha. Here's $5.'

Then Christian said 'we need to do some washing, get your stuff, Jim, come and help me.'

Elly gave me hers all wrapped in a ball, 'don't you go sniffing through it,' she said, just to piss me off, then went out with Ben for beer, leaving Chimp to hang out alone. It was already well late by the time Christian had led me up to the top floor where the laundry was, this large room rammed all lined around the walls by large 1970s' washing machines. It was like a furnace. Whatever it was outside, at the top of the building in this windowless washing room it was another 20 degrees hotter. We loaded up a machine with clothes and bed-sheets, (ZZ - *look, look, where are the stains*, Demon no 1 shouted at me in a drive-by. *Is it only the carpet that needs unpicking?* asked Demon no 2, adding, *now's your chance for a good deep sniff* ... Yeah hi guys, you weren't missed.).

Christian eventually murmured confidentially, 'There's something you probably ought to know about Elly and I.'

Gosh. Finally. Now he was going to tell me, and now I had to act surprised. Just hitting him would have felt so much better, but I had to pretend I didn't know, because if he knew I knew he'd wonder how I knew, and I'd be damned, and just being that one step ahead of him was the thinnest slither of satisfaction I had amid all this Hell. I'm one step ahead, and, I'm going to out act you, I thought, leaning back slowly against a machine with my most innocent, quizzical facial expression of, 'why Christian, what on Earth could you have to tell me?'.

'Well, I don't know if you'd noticed recently, but ...' he began with the most patronising tone. Could you insult my intelligence more? But keep it covered, out act him! He obviously thinks you're an idiot, and isn't sorry for it.

'Elly and I have been ...'

What, Christian what? Fucking? Again? How many times? Where? Tell me please, so I won't have to tread in anything when I'm in the living room.

'Having a ... thing type thing.'

I creaked my eyebrows up in full Roger Moore mode. Off he went with the blurb, while I felt rage flood through me. My God, I hate you enough already, but now you're right there taking me for a total fool. How much am I going to hate you for this one day, I wondered, looking all cool and 'do what?'

all the while.

'She's been giving me the come on for some time, you know, things, signals, you just know them.'

Yes, Christian, we are so men of the world.

'Err,' he began, with a tired, world weariness of a man who couldn't beat them off with a shitty stick. No, don't chicken out now! Don't spare me the gore! Go on, pour it all over my tongue! Watch me fry it up later! But Christian's revelation was a carefully constructed, beautifully scripted concoction of abashed ums and ahs that would take time. 'Things the other night after the club, just, well, boiled over and ... we did stuff.'

Maybe it was brave to tell me this. Maybe it took guts.

ZZ!- maybe he'd taken her up the guts – ZZ

'You slept with her?' I said, after a cool pause, sweat dripping from my nose.

'Yeah.'

'Ha ha, you dirty bugger. Nice one,' I scarcely got out.

Damn! No blunt instruments to hand – *ZZ! Except his great blunt cock as her hand steers it home! – ZZ.* Two evil puns already, the first salvo of many searing quips the demons would be churning out over weeks. Normality restored ... what kind of mind did I have? Why wasn't I dead? Somehow all this rage and chaos behind my eyes manifested for Christian as a blink. He looked at me sincerely, fairly paralysing me with incredulousness.

'So, you're all right with it?'

'Mmm, yeah. Sure.' I'm cool with you having fucked the girl who you know is she of my dreams on the bed next to mine. Tell me, Christian, what fucking good is it to ask me that now? Please, tell me, what are you getting out of this? *Big cocked Christian baffles pissed young failure*, ran the headline.

'Because knowing how you've felt before, well, I thought it could be a bit difficult, I mean I'd thought for some time there was a serious probability at uni of us two making a thing of it, but back then it was difficult, claustrophobic,' he said.

Now he's considering my feelings – *zz what was she feeling as he lanced his cock into her? – zz* He didn't see any resemblance to our living now and being trapped on that fart-can, Sky-lab. Maybe he could have woken me up the other night to check if I was OK then with where he was burying his bone. But no, he has to come ask me days later if I'm OK with it all. God.

'No, Christian, it's fine, really. Don't worry about it. To be honest, I had guessed that this could happen. So there. She's not my girlfriend, never was.' I smiled. I'd never acted so intensely for an audience of one, and never without a script. These two fucking six-form amateurs couldn't even audition for jack shit *... ZZ and their undress rehearsal! Opening legs night! Accolades of deflowering! Standing ovation against the wall! zz.* The madness. A migraine clouded in. I screwed my face up, features slowly crinkling in to the nose. Christian asked, 'Are you sure you're all right?'

97

'Yeah, yes...it's not that, just really tired. And I knew about yous anyway.' Oops. Character lapse. Prompt! *Zz pumped zz*!

Christian pursed his lips. 'You knew...?' but didn't take it further, as the talk drowned itself in the gale of noise being whipped by the washing machines, and we packed up our detergents and headed down to watch the Weather Channel for tomorrow, which promised thunder and lightning storms, non-stop rain.

As we walked in we heard Ben and Elly were already back, unloading beer into the fridge, while Adrian said 'oiiiii....you didn't need to get beer there was already some in there, didn't you fucking see it?'

Now at least I didn't want to kill myself so soon, I had to kill Christian first. Or maybe this baboon boy. We had a stilted evening of beer, Elly sitting tight close next to Christian the whole time. Bastards.

Racing the train

After Christian's laboured confession, I'd stayed up drinking until I passed out. Next morning I drove the Pontiac auto pilot to Penguin, hangover disguised by hat and sunglasses, moreorless walking in a straight line, loaded up, float, gas, cigs, vault onto the highway to West Chicago, erection screaming all through lunch.

The sky was overcast but the day got hotter, as if building up to a storm, but the ice-creams were going out and dollars were coming in amid the usual fuckwit conversations with illiterate and innumerate children, all barely serving to distract me from images of Elly and Christian fucking. At some point in the early afternoon I began to crawl along Sherman Avenue, one of the nicer streets with well-kept houses and trees tall and heavy with dark green leaves, while halfway along the road dipped and rose as did all the land around it in a large circle, like some kind of massive shallow pit, probably a large pond long since drained. On the one side was a patch of open grass, a sloped village green, on which three young boys were playing baseball. They'd seen me from a distance and I saw one cross the road - carefully mind, despite the lack of traffic he stopped and looked both ways like the Green Cross Code man had taught him well - and into his house, reappearing with some notes just as I pulled up and he and his two friends converged on the van.

Two of them started the chant, while the one with the notes, a slender boy with blond hair and blue eyes, said 'Hello ice-cream man, how are you?'

Well thanks for asking, I thought for a second, the girl I'm in love with is fucking my best mate and my best mate is fucking her, in my face. I'm actually feeling kind of suicidal most hours of the day, including now, meaning I'm going to stick my head in the freezer and end it fucking all. So you better get your order in quick. But, obviously, this lad of all of 10 years or so didn't know about that, nor did he care, why the fucking fuck should he care, so I stuck with, 'great, yeah, thank you for asking. How are you?'

'I'm very well thank you,' and he smiled at me warmly, like he meant it, then turned to choose his ice-cream. I took the orders, took the money, gave out the ice-creams and counted out the change into the blond boy's hand, who now looked at me intensely, 'where are you from, ice-cream man?'

'From? Britain. London.'

'Ahh. I thought you sounded different.' Sounded different, but he'd understood what I'd said. A rare one! 'What's your name?'

'Jim. What's your name?'

'Joly. I live just over there with my mom. My dad's away on business and my sister's at camp. We play here a lot.' Which was a lot of information.

'Why aren't you at camp?'

'I've got a week in a month's time,' he said.

'O really, where's that?'

And he told me, and I asked if he was looking forward to it, and he said kinda, and he talked about the fun activities they got to do at camp, and the

99

location, and the log cabins next to a lake, and the daily tasks and outings and songs, and it was all real neat fun, but also sometimes you get crappy other people you don't know, and it's all a mix, and you meet new people and that's exciting, but the other people aren't always so nice, but because of there always being fun stuff to do it OK and nice people outnumber nasty ones and the camp is so big you can always get away from them, and at night they could sleep outside and last year they saw so many shooting stars, and so on. Sounded like a real summer.

As he and his friends ate their ice-cream Joly and I talked, and carried on after his friends finished and they went back to the baseball stuff, and one put on the big Charlie Brown glove, another threw a ball at him, then one yelled, 'Joly! Come on!' and Joly said, 'sorry ice-cream man, Jim sorry, sorry Jim! See you again!', waved and turned.

As I drove off I realised he was one of the first kids ever to have asked my name. In fact he was the first. He saw me as more than the man who drove a truck of frozen fat and sugar through the neighbourhood. And he seemed like a very nice, friendly boy, naturally friendly which was all the remarkable for its normality, who hadn't done the gormless mantra, 'I want, I want ..' but had asked questions as if I existed, and, and, very exceptionally for this part of the world, he'd understood everything I said. Not once had he asked, 'Wad?'

That cheered me up no end. A few streets later of course two boys pissed on my bonfire when I gave them their ice-creams which they opened and licked, and then one said 'we ain't got no money ice-cream man! Aahh hahahaha!' and off they went, and I called them little wankers which didn't bother them because they didn't understand, so I told them they were too young to wank, which bothered them even less, and I was about to tell them to fuck off but some man came to buy an ice-cream so I thought better not, but he saw I was pissed off and asked what was wrong, so I said those damn kids scammed me. And he turned around and called them assholes and told them to fuck off, and they ran off, which was great, and made me laugh the rest of the afternoon.

Counting up over beer at Penguin, others all around, Elly patted me on the shoulder and gave me a beer, which was strangely nice of her, before she went and sat next to Christian and they plotted among themselves. Christian then told us Hank and Mike had agreed for Adrian to go live upstairs from tonight, he just had to get his stuff out from ours, and that was sorted. Elly kissed him. It was really weird. I'd never hated them both so much, and been so fucked. But I wasn't dead and I didn't feel like dying – *zz* – *no but it felt fucking good for them* – *zz*.

I didn't know what to say or do, but we got into the Pontiac and drove for home, everyone in a good mood, me too, before I turned from watching the highway to see those two petting, and the rage surged and I wondered if I just threw myself out the car onto the highway, would I be killed outright or would I need be run over a few times?

We were hammering along tracing parallel to a steep embankment, atop which was a railway, or *rail road*, and we heard a train's horn, and looking up we could just see the tops of one of those epically long freight trains, with huge, dirty, painted box wagons going way, way back out of sight, and bit by bit we gained on the train as bit by bit the embankment fell in height, such that when we passed the engine we were near level with it, the engine we could see through the flitting bushes was one of those massive unpainted steel jobs, with a sad-eyed cabin and a light for a nose, just like out of the *Silver Streak*, and we carried on, the train giving like a farewell blast of its atonal horn.

'There's got to be hobos on that train!' I declared.

'Will it beat us to the junction?' said Christian.

'Put your foot down!' shouted Ben.

'OK Ponty, do your stuff!', and he floored it, the engine roared, and even at this speed the front lifted and we felt it pull away.

Hundreds of yards ahead we could see the road junction where we had to turn right and then almost immediately hit the rail crossing, and the junction traffic lights were just flipping from green to yellow, then to red.

'We'll never make it!', I said.

'Shit!', said Ben.

'Change … change … change …' said Christian.

The train's tonal horn wailed again behind us.

'Change … change … change …' Christian carried on.

We could see cars at the junction bouncing left to right as the lights remained stubbornly against us.

'Come on and change, you fuckers!' I said.

'Change, Goddamn!' said Ben.

'Change … change … change …' Christian continued.

The train wailed again, demanding the crossing be closed.

The Pontiac roared along, we were now just a 100 yards from the lights.

Red lights.

Very red lights.

Not an orange among them.

'Change. … change … CHANGE … CHANGE' we all joined in.

'Come on and fucking change!' squealed Elly.

The train wailed again.

'CHANGE for FUCK'S – SAKE!' shouted Christian.

We would have to slam on the brakes almost like now unless something happened sooner, and Christian began to lift off the gas – then orange lights appeared beneath the red ones!

'COME ON!'

Then green!

'Hold on!' Christian said, gunning again to take the corner at maximum speed, swinging right hard enough to tip us all over one another to the left, but then we heard the bells of the crossing and just as the car lined up straight we saw the crossing lights flashing red.

Either slam on the brakes – or gun it – and Christian floored it again!

'Too late! Fucking Hell!' shouted Ben.

'Fuck it! Aagh!' I said.

The bells rang in our ears, the lights flashed angrily at our defiance as if shouting 'STOP YOU FUCKWITS', but the barriers still hadn't fallen and Christian aimed straight for the rails, the front wheels going *d-dsh* over the first rail and the car bounced! Glancing right we saw the white light of the train coming with another wail.

Elly squealed, as the car went *d-dsh d-dsh* over the rails and the barrier to the left began to fall.

'Hahah, eat that, sucker!' I said as the back wheels *d-dshed* over the final rail, the back of the car bounced down. We were clear and we cheered.

Back at the flat, Elly installed herself on the sofa in front of the TV. She'd somehow stolen a few ice-creams including one called a White Shark, a lemon tasting thing, quite nice, but large, it had quite a girth, and was smooth and rounded and ended in a rounded tip, and as she watched TV she licked it, sucked it, and pulled it back and forth into her mouth. Adrian appeared at the door, and I handed him his rucksack without him coming in, a clear hint in itself, and he just took the bag and fucked off without a thank you anyway.

Then Christian said from the little corridor, 'quick Jim, come see this,' but it was another one of his fucking meetings – *zz another meeting about fucking zz*.

'Following on from last night, what I said about Elly, well we've got this thing going on,' he said, which was great because it confirmed they'd been fucking loads since, I just had to imagine when and where. 'So ... it makes sense that we change bedrooms, and I sleep in your room with Elly, and so ... do you mind sharing with Ben?'

Oh, er, no, but do you mind if I just kick you to death in the meantime, Christian? So instead of course I said: 'Makes sense. What, change now?'

'Yeah, tonight's good.'

I switched our stuff from room to room, and by that switched rooms. Then I got pissed while those two went to bed early, and the demons came out to keep me company.

Eskimo

Ben had raised the blinds, but still drunk from the previous night I didn't get up until I was broiling with sweat under the duvet. Christian and Elly were tiptoeing around one another with sly grins on their faces, but that was all I noticed. Everything was a haze, nothing registered until I found myself bombing along to West Chicago. I didn't really notice our side of the highway narrow down to one lane, road works having turned the other lane into a trench, some feet deep, though I was hypnotised by the queue of cones lining the edge of the trench, which, with my mind and cock both on a different planet, meant I never noticed the traffic in front had totally stopped until this voice in my head said in a deadpan way, 'crash imminent ... stop ... now ... stop now, stop now. Now, now', like one of those autopilot voice-siren things on airliners that so demurely insist, 'pull up' *woo-woo* 'pull up' *woo-woo*, when you're about to nose into a field and kill 100s of innocent people. Or careen into the back of a halted car, as I was.

I slammed on the brakes, locking the wheels to that horrendous screaming when tyres are being erased on tarmac, but the van started drifting towards the trench, so I had to let the brakes off to steer, and continue hurtling towards the stopped cars in front! Brakes slammed again, tyres screaming, again, the van skidding back to the trench, brakes off, steer again as the convertible car ahead was now just yards from getting a van load of free ice-cream, then as its trunk seemed about to go out of sight under my bonnet it was foot-through the floor brakes, a final screech, and – STOP! I nearly head-butted the steering wheel, and the sound of screeching tyres was replaced by a horrid, rapidly loudening sound of scraping metal, as the freezer in the back slammed into my seat, whiplashing my head back and jumping the van forward just half of the last foot between us and the car, winding me on the steering wheel. But, still pissed, and with the luck of the drunk, none of it hurt, and I was so elated I started laughing, maniacally, such that the driver of the car in front, who looked like he might be about to come and have a go at my near miss, swiftly sat back down. Don't fuck with the ice-cream man in kamikaze mode, I said, lit a cig, sniggered, snotted uncontrollably all over the cig and laughed even more.

That was a bright spot in a day that passed in a haze all the way through. I was dead to the world, even the shitty kids I just waved away without losing my rag, but the takings were low and around 3 or so I thought, this is just shit. My takings are a joke. Everything's a fucking joke. My life's a joke. It's all fucking over. This job is shit, this summer is shit. I've fucked everything. I've never done anything in my life that mattered, and never will. And this Demon in my head just said *'yep, it's all your fault.'*

I trundled along, three kids in a front yard waved, I slowed, and the mom came out with them to pay and as they chanted she said 'only today cos it's so hot are you getting two ice-creams.'

Double sales I thought, but when I got two of each of their orders the mom looked confused.

'Didn't you say double?' I said.

'Ooh! No. Yes. But I meant they'd had ice-cream already off another guy.'

'Another guy?'

'This morning just before lunch. Drives a light blue van, big guy.'

'Eskimo,' said one of the boys.

'He's fat cos he eats all his ice-cream,' said his sister.

Another van. I'd thought I'd seen one, and it was light blue, and I'd heard the name Eskimo from other punters, but stupidly had never made the connection that we basically covered the same ground. Yes of course, an obese bastard in a blue greenhouse on wheels, windows steamed up with his sweat, his bulge jammed against the steering wheel, I'd seen him on a flyover some day previous. Aha, that's Eskimo.

Selling ice-creams.

On my turf.

What a fat ass.

This somehow galvanised me into doing something, so I scoured the map for new roads to try, but there were none in close range.

Ah fuck. Course I had competition, everyone else spoke about theirs all the time. I'd just not met mine yet.

Bollocks. So instead of creaking along some shitty new roads for a few hours, I thought stuff it, go big, and looked at nearby towns, with one called Bartlett not far away, so I headed there. It had a few large, new estates, winding, widdly streets and lots of little cul-de-sacs, quite hard steering but fun to explore, and the kids seemed nice. Good money made for a good mood, but then I saw it – on one of those swing benches on the porch of a house, were two teenagers snogging, in the loveliest embrace of lust. I thought of Elly and Christian. My head hurt, I felt really tired again, and though a couple of gaggles of kids were coming towards me, I thought fucked it and drove off, heading back to Penguin, or wherever, wherever away from there.

Driving back my mind filled with all the instances of when Elly and Christian had met before we all come out here, all those times at uni, each time I was there, as they'd met through me. That night of 'dancing', all those looks and comments between them since, through which like so many times before my mind trawled for the hideously obvious clues about what was going to happen. A Demon had appeared to interrogate me about each memory.

You didn't notice then – were you blind? Remember when he said this and she responded in that way, was that not obvious?

What were those things he said and did that won her where you didn't?

I knew at the fucking time! But what was I supposed to do?

Oho! It's them who's having the fucking time! Great, so you knew, what did you do to stop it?

Stop what? How was I to stop anything?

Oh yeah, sorry, forgot, you couldn't even start it.

The worst came last. As I drove along, the red rays of the sunset filling the cabin, an image appeared that filled the windscreen and all beyond, her with her arms around Richard's neck, the horizon of Illinois turned into some Colombian vista, and she was looking into his eyes with such happiness and love ... but that was then, this was now, and he changed to Christian, and the steaming jungle hills became the skyscrapers of Chicago, its towers twinkling all golden red in the sunset, they were smiling lightly at one another, what they had together, how they found one another, and how this could be the beginning of something incredible, something eternal, their faces half lit by the sunset, the light breeze from Lake Michigan fondling their hair as they so tenderly kissed, with all those profound things to do together in their lives, all those things that were theirs for the taking, an eternity of a journey so mind-blowingly beautiful they might as well be flying past the rings of Saturn, and all to the *Song of The Indian Guest*.

I wondered where I was, lurking in the shadow of this scene, and a Demon said, *'it could have been you, but you blew it. What did you do wrong? Anyway stop ruining it with your presence.'*

My mind felt as cold as the cirrus clouds of Neptune.

There was a loud horn, then another and a third jacked me out of this reverie. The lights I hadn't realised I had stopped at had changed to green. I fumbled to start off when I got beeped again and heard some hollering, and without thinking I found myself swing out the door onto the footplate just in time to see a saloon edge out from behind the van and roll past, as I hung off the wing mirror and arced a foot at the car, shouting 'GO FUCK YOURSELF' as it passed, the driver of the following car looking as surprised as his kids in the back. I got back in and drove off, gripping the steering wheel 'til it hurt, thinking that with every oncoming car, bus, or truck, just one slew of the wheel would slam me head on into them, I'd go through the windscreen and plant face first into their engine, and die. Fuck everybody and go out with a bang! Just one great yank to the left - *Zz –she's yanking him off – zz*

I pulled into the next gas station, parked up next to this verge at the rear of the place, punched the side of the van until my hand hurt, head-butted it until that hurt too, then sat down and cried.

Sometime later I drove back to Penguin, hoping I didn't look upset, which I did but there was nothing I could do about it. I sat down and Elly came in, and sat next to Christian, and he turned and smiled at her and patted her forearm, and asked quietly if she'd had a good day, and she smiled and said yes, and she sat and he got her a beer, and for the first time they looked like a couple, which was quite sweet, but also sent this great pang of something cold through me, but what could I do? Maybe accept they were right together.

Yeah, accept that. That's the mature thing to do, you can do that, no?

Maybe I could. I knocked down two beers and now seeing them in the

105

flesh – *ZZ did that the other night – zz* ... in the real, it didn't seem so horrendous.

'You all right Jim?' said Ben.

'Yeah!' I smiled.

'Your eyes all right?'

Balls. 'Wind in the van. Hay fever. Oh yeah, guess what, fucking Hell, I found out about my competition today.'

'What did you find out?' said Ben.

'That he exists. He's called Eskimo and he's a fat fucking cunt.'

'You only just found out you got other trucks? I've counted three others down my way,' said Christian.

'Do you see many fat people when you're out? I'm amazed by the number of fat people there aren't,' said Ben. 'I expected to see way more fat people.'

'I had one on my round today who was massive, o God it was quite horrible,' said Elly, 'she was huge.'

'Probably unemployed.'

'Why can't they work? Get a job as a road block,' said Ben.

'Job going in the small ads – "wanted – boulder",' said Elly.

'Yeah, train on the job,' said Ben, 'I should have suggested that to this bloke today, came out of his house down the drive to a backing track of tuba music. Took him ages to get down the drive but thought it worth the wait as he'd clean out half the freezer. Well I didn't want to hurry him anyway in case he fell over and took me out like something off *Raiders of the Lost Ark*.'

'Was it worth the wait?' said I.

'Eh? Oh no, sod only had a Strawberry short-shit before going back in.'

'Did he leave a trail of dinosaur footprints in the asphalt?'

'Bloody fat people fuck everything up,' said Jason. 'They need bigger cars to ferry them and their shopping around, more fuel in the cars, bigger planes and everything, it's all energy, all sends petrol prices through the roof.'

'You say petrol instead of gas?' said Jeff.

'Petrol? Wad? Wad? Petrol?' said Ben.

'Wad?' I said.

'Wad?' Ben said, scowling with incomprehension.

'Wad?' I said, teeth gritted as my irritation with the kids boiled up.

'Yeah, gas is that stuff that comes out your arse,' said Ben.

'Ass!' said Jeff.

'Arse! ARSE!' said Ben.

'Ass!'

'Gas from gasoline.'

'Gas comes out your ass. Not, *garse-o-leen* comes out your *arrse*,' said Jeff.

'I like the word gasoline. It just sounds like something's going to blow up. People say gasoline, I get this image of someone with a can of it, slewing all over something before blowing it up,' said Christian.

Mike came in. 'Thanks for giving monkey boy to us,' he said.

I was mid pull on my beer and choked it back out.

'Oh God, has he pissed you off already?' said Ben.

'Not pissed us off. But he's a freak,' he said, pulling up a chair, 'like a fucking chimpanzee, and the way he goes "oiiiiiiii". It's like, "what, mate, we're right here, talk to us normally if you like. We have evolved." Well he hasn't, but hey ho, see the scabs on the back of his knuckles as they scrape the floor.'

We all went and ate at a *Wendy's*, the same crowds of screaming teenage girls filling out booths, again these great big menus with great big salads and burgers, then home, spliff, Dooley's, where we took a long table, and Elly put her arm around Christian's shoulders and kissed him before she drifted off to the bog, that shot of warm affection like a slither of ice in my mind.

'I can't believe you're being so cool about this, Jim,' Christian said.

I smiled at him, took a long pull of beer, and wondered he didn't know I wanted to kill him, rape her, kill myself. Well no, I didn't really. I'd cut out the rape and murder bits and go straight to doing myself in.

But if he thought I was taking it well then my acting skills hadn't completely left me.

I went to the bar to order another pitcher with my crappy doctored student ID, which had worked already enough times for beer and cigs, but knowing it was dodgy made it feel like buying smokes as an under-aged kid, your friends outside the newsagents who'd put you up for the job, and you steeled up, said 'Twenty B&H' in a casual low voice that'd disguise being 5' 5" with no facial hair, 'B&H', not 'a packet of Benson & Hedges, please,' because that was the giveaway, but anyway they'd tell you to get out, and you'd come out empty-handed to a tirade of abuse for being uncool.

So it was I was at the bar, prepping the nonchalant delivery of my line, 'pitcher of beer, please,' ID ready, but not too ready in case it looked like I was over-eagerly showing it, as if expecting to be disbelieved. The barmaid handed the change to the last customer, she turned and pointed to me but just as I was about to say my line she pointed quizzically to the guy next to me, I gagged a second, stumbling over my cue, but the other guy pointed back at me to go first, I said 'ta', I steadied to say in my manliest voice, 'pitcher of beer, please,' when someone said 'woops!' and my shorts were yanked down to my ankles. Christian – the bastard! As I tried to pull them back up he laughed and hugged me so I couldn't do it. The barmaid looked surprised, the other guy laughed, and then she served him anyway. Elly had seen it all walking back from the bog and she was also laughing.

I fucking wasn't.

'Oh come on Jim! It was a joke.'

'Get us a pitcher,' I said, and sat at the end of the table. He got one, then sat with Elly, and they were soon all over each other. Ah go fuck yourselves, as they would soon as they got back, and I got this sick feeling. Yep, we got back, they went straight to bed, and I turned on the telly to drown out the noise of their fucking.

Then I got curious and went to listen at the door, but as I put my ear to the door it went ajar by a slither, making me freeze in case they heard the door latch, but they carried on, panting. Through the gap I could only see shadows, but she was on top, panting away, riding up and down, *uh uh uh uh uh*. I remembered Christian saying how much it turned him on when a girl went on top and rubbed her own tits, which she was probably doing as well. Bastards.

Eskimo II

Next morning the Weather Channel predicted the usual, it was Sun, Sun, Sun. I was in one bitch of a mood, not helped by those two emerging from their bedroom all pleased with themselves, but I decided to be pro-active. I showered, my first in days, put on clean clothes, ate something for breakfast instead of just jacking up on coffee and fags, and was ready before anybody else. I was stoked, and as we approached the car I remembered all the snipes about my driving over previous days. 'I'll drive,', I said, and if I say so myself, it was a class performance, smoother than Damon Hill, so smooth you'd never know we'd even turned a corner or once stopped at the lights. So fucking good that Ben actually said as we got out, 'woah, beautifully driven,' and I saw Elly's eyebrows arched above her sunglasses in tribute, and said 'very smooth'.

'Not that you'd know,' I nearly said, but I really didn't like saying stuff like that to her. Instead I flexed my shoulders and got on with shit. I checked the freezer, then noted all the rubbish piled up at the back of the van, bottles and cig packs and bollockery that I and others built up over weeks, like under the King's Cross escalators. I hoyed up the rear roll-door and all this shit poured out, like a kid being sick, I scooped it into a box, quoting the *Battle of Britain*, 'muck and filth everywhere, Mr Warwick. Place is like a pigsty!', then cleared up the cockpit.

I got the float and as I sat there with Hank, Mrs Hank just a couple of feet away, Dylan went past. 'Oi, oi Dylan! Dylan!' I said loudly, 'What was it you said the other day? "Fucking retard!" Say it again, it's really funny. Go on.'

He stopped and looked at me, eyes wide with surprise, but only said 'err...'

'Go on! "*Fucking retard*!" It's hilarious.'

'Er, no, no, I don't want to say it,' and off he slouched.

'Awwww.' But no dice, he hastened away. 'Well, I thought it was hilarious.'

Hank rolled his eyes.

Aidan went past, 'morning,' he said, to which I replied, 'morning, cockshuckersh!' and thrust a fist aloft.

Up in Westie, I was about to begin what I'd found to be a nicely profitable run, half dozen roads around Maple Avenue. All were at least a mile in length, running parallel to one another, house numbers reaching the high hundreds, and crossed by another set of shorter parallel roads, creating a stretched grid of oblongs. It was utterly, mind-numbingly, soul-destroyingly identical, all these clapperboard houses all along the roads that dipped and rose to the horizon, like that infinity effect of two opposing mirrors in a changing room, the only distinguishing bits being how rusted the cars and trikes were on the drives, or how much more one listless flag on the lawn had bleached from years of glaring sunlight.

But it was good money, and the van auto-piloted itself as I scanned down the roads. A lot of kids, a lot of time, very little shelter from the Sun, the big trees that gave their names to the streets were set apart, and with no ponds to help cool any breeze, everyone around here would be hot and hungry and only ice cream could cool their souls.

The jingle was on, here I was. But where was everyone? No-one was coming up or jumping with glee. I stopped a couple of times and turned off the jingle and could hear kids somewhere, in their backyards, but they weren't coming out front. Why the fuck not? Not until the middle of the next street did anyone buy anything, a young woman who said 'you're all busy today,' then went in. Busy? Was I fuck. I ground along to the end, then along again.

Nothing.

An hour of crawling, a gallon of fuel, three cigs, and only two sales to show for it as I, gritting my teeth, rounded around yet another end-of-street to the last lane. Then as I hit the first cross-over road I heard it, another jingle. I stopped and jumped out to look up and down the road, and then he appeared - a curvy blue van, with glazed cabin and badly rendered Disney-like paintings on the sides. It was Eskimo! That fat fuck! Turning towards me it was clear. He'd just finished the whole area. He slowed as he passed me, right fucking close, grinned, and chugged away, having cleaned up at least $40 of the day's takings.

What a cunt! Outraged, I sped off to some other part of town he couldn't find me. I blazed towards a massive junction, eight lanes across, and although the light had already gone amber I wasn't stopping now. I floored it, turning left in a long, sweeping curve, the road easily wide enough to take my speed – except it wasn't as the van started to drift further out, to the right, and I was rapidly in a big flat skid, heading straight towards the pavement. A sickening vision came to me of hitting the kerb side on and flipping over. I desperately turned into the skid and braked, to little effect, turned again, and was just, just about to swoop past inches shy of the kerb, when a horrible scratching metal sound led to this *WHAM* behind me and the van shoulder-barged another yard right, back at the kerb. We were going to flip. With the strength that comes with sheer terror, I yanked the wheel again just that much to the right so the front wheel slammed the kerb at an angle rather than side on, the jolt almost knocked me off of my seat as the other wheels nutted the kerb and the van rampaged onto the pavement with a series of horrible bangs, fishtailing along as I fought to retake control, only then I saw 20 yards ahead two girls jumping up and down in excitement. I desperately decelerated, rolled off the pavement, and stopped.

I guessed that getting run over by the ice-cream man could be pretty exciting, but I was dazed. Only when I went to get their order I found the freezer had slid right up against the right side of the van, that was the WHAM! during the skid that had so nearly thrown us completely over the kerb.

As I drove away, a voice in my head said, *'can't even drive an ice-cream truck without trying to kill yourself and everyone else? Some fucking driver.'*

Then I said aloud, 'yeah, actually, I am some fucking driver,' and then all was quiet.

I found myself in a lovely, leafy part of the town, lots of open space, houses set back from the road. I pulled up, closed the door, lit up, and sat and stared, and stared. At nothing. My mind wandered back to the previous March, back home, one day, driving to Croydon to get some arty materials. The road, flanked by vast mock-Tudor and Victorian villas, was wide enough for some good speed but had testing twists and troughs. My mind went off on some romp, as usual dominated by how I'd get Elly to love me, get her into bed, where we'd make love forever. She was the one. Exactly what I was plotting I don't know, and much of my mental chatter was around 'why wasn't it me' and 'how did you you're your chance?', as I'd been berating myself for months already.

Then a voice like mine, but icier, stronger, said, *'In the end, it's just a shag, a fuck's a fuck, so just lock her in a room and rape her. She'll get over it.'*

I mulled over that point as another voice said, *'you can't do that. If you do that, she'll go to the police, and you'll be finished.'*

'Right, fine. Kill her.'

'If you kill her you'll have to kill yourself. You can't rape and murder your supposed Goddess and expect to be able to live with yourself. Indeed, raping her would be enough to do yourself in. What a betrayal. She wouldn't have to go to the Police. You'd do yourself in. That's how you're built.

Possibly. If that's how it goes. It will. Fine. Thems the breaks.

Whereupon I came round and feeling unsafe at driving the car at all, at everything, unseen hands yanked my car over, tyres squealing, and bounded onto the pavement.

Then I'd thought: *'Here's the plan – don't' harm her, just do yourself in. If you're thinking shit like this, it's better just to end it now, and you'll be the only one hurt.'*

OK. Kill myself before I end up doing something to her. Sounds best. Death with honour. One life lost instead of two.

I sat on the bonnet and smoked for an hour, staring at the floor, stunned by the enormity of the cold-hearted clarity of what I'd just concluded. What monster was I becoming? Is this my destiny? Do some men grow up to be rapists and murderers in this way, and am I joining them? I couldn't be with her and be like this. I couldn't trust myself. She couldn't trust me. But then life without her was unimaginable. So yeah, better just to do myself in before anyone got hurt.

The memory of that day stunned me this day, sitting in the van, outside someone's house, before I suddenly thought, this is ridiculous. Get up. Get the fuck up and do something. Go and sell some ice-cream. Which I would have if the van started. I got out and opened the bonnet, but then couldn't even be bothered to pretend to know what was wrong with it. Then this old man came out of his house and asked if all was OK and he had a look and said he didn't know either, and very nicely invited me in so I could call Hank. His wife made me tea, and they were lovely and calm, and talked about England and my plans, without me telling them everything, and I remembered not to ask if they were retired. Hank and Charlie turned up, fixed some loose connections and were done in 15 minutes. The couple refused ice-cream as thanks, then I was off up the road to Bartlett for the last two hours, wiggling along the winding streets and took $60, before heading back to Penguin.

Cashed up and beered up, I saw Elly looking sad.
'What's up?' I asked.
'I really don't like the idea of

'What do we want for dinner? Tacos!' said Christian, 'Taco Bell!'
I didn't like Mexican but the decision was made and that's where we went, by which time my mood was in some hideous place of total rage. Queuing at Taco Bell, Elly turned and smiled at me. 'Fuck off,' I said.
She looked at me, surprised.
'No, really, just fuck off.'
'Just standing here,' she mumbled, and looked sad, looked away. I felt bad for a moment, but over-ridingly, I wanted to kill someone. Christian, mainly.
The tacos looked like some great crispy vagina. As Christian tucked into his I sat and seethed, picking at the food. Elly gave me a sideways glance, something like fear in her eyes. I glared back and she looked down.
Ben started up, 'Mike was telling me, apparently Adrian's chatted up some girl on the round and is going to meet up with her, she's only 16 or something, and he's 21, but he's going on about how she's so hot and it's going to be a hot date and she really wants him and he'll give it to her, all this shit.'
'Sixteen, that's a bit young,' Christian said.
'Oh God, no!' Elly said, 'He'll do something!'
'Sixteen ... hmm, that's statutory rape if they do cop off,' said Christian.
All a bit uncomfortable.

At home, I remembered there was a spare Great White lolly in the freezer that Elly had pinched, but it was gone. Then I saw Christian on the sofa with it.
'Where did you get that Great White?'
'Freezer.'
'Fuck.'
'There was only one.'
I nearly screamed but instead just stormed off to the bedroom and hurled myself into the darkness, onto the bed. Christian appeared in the doorway and asked 'what's wrong?'
'Nothing! Fuck off!', I said, wrestling with the pillow.
'What did I do?' he seemed genuinely shocked like he'd really fucked up.
'Nothing! Just fuck off!'
'Please tell me what I did!'
Course I couldn't because it was bloody ridiculous, so ridiculous he

112

didn't connect it to how I'd left the living room.

'Nothing! I'm just tired, leave me alone.'

'Tell me what I did!'

'FUCK OFF!'

And he went, and I felt bad for shouting, but I thought he was a cunt. They both were. I wanted that ice-cream.

Eskimo III

From the moment I woke up, I determined, I would beat Eskimo. I hit that same grid of roads 45 minutes earlier than I had before. Jingle on dead low, just as I finished the first road, turning at the end for the next, I saw out the side a little blue blob shimmering through the watery mirage of heat waves right back up the road. Eskimo. Right on time and best part of a street's length behind me. All he had to do was keep that distance, and I'd clean up. Of course he could catch up each time I stopped for a sale, a sale denied to him, but he didn't, I guessed maybe because he ended up going slower and slower just to grind out a dime for every other dollar I took in.

All he had to do though was see me, take one of the cross roads and steal the lead on the roads I'd not yet plundered.

But he didn't. I'd seen he wore glasses, he had to be short sighted. He just didn't see me, in the distance, or on the cross roads as I threaded back and forth, as if a loom. Still, it would have been lucky timing for him to see me across these short roads, me going the other way, and anyway at these crossings I turned off my jingle, then having checked the coast was clear I'd bomb over them.

And I made some half decent money for once. The fat fuck would have to live off his fat for a day.

Having cleaned up, I then drove on to the Mexican estates and did some tidy business, then pulled up for a smoke and a think. I'd have another go over the wrong side of the tracks, and luckily made the crossing just before a half-mile freight train snaked through, which would have eaten up 10 minutes, although I could have sold ice-creams to any waiting cars. Anyway, I hit those streets, and by mid-afternoon in the boiling heat the takings were already over $180.

I was thinking of going up to Bartlett for the final blast of good money, as I was trundling in some industrial wasteland through walled in by a raised rail-line, and beyond which were nice looking houses, shaded by tall trees, back on the right side of the tracks. The crossing over the rails was like a humped-back bridge, and *The Dukes of Hazzard* sprang to mind. I drove at it at full tilt and took off, yelling *Yehaa!* in flight, but the landing was all wrong, the front wheels really crashed and my forearms banged on the steering wheel and there was this horrendous fuck off great big bang from under the bonnet, then this terrible clattering sound. I hadn't landed like the Dukes who'd always then fishtail their escape into a dust cloud, so much as Deputy Roscoe who always nosed his cop car into something hard, like the road.

This horrible *tacca-tacca-tacca-tacca-tacca* noise, hard and loud, was coming from the engine, but as I was still going I went on hoping it'd go away, which it didn't. I pulled over and opened the bonnet, saw nothing, so drove on another 50 yards, but the *tacca-tacca-tacca-tacca-tacca* carried on, and I pulled up. A passing man asked if the van was OK, offered to look at the engine, and immediately saw the engine fan was scything away at some thick metal cable things deep below the engine.

'Your engine looks like it's at a weird angle. I don't think you can drive this.'

'Oh. Ah. Bollocks.' I had a sinking feeling.

'Nope. It's like your engine has dropped, fallen or something,' he said, giving a grimace of defeat.

The sinking feeling turned to feeling sick. I'd truly fucked the van.

'Do you want an ice-cream for your trouble?' I said.

'No thanks,' he laughed, 'have a good day now.'

I rolled the van on a few more yards into the shade of the lovely tall trees that provided a cathedral-vault of heavy green all down the road, then with my map I went to the phone box back near the crossing to call Hank, tell him I'd broken down, but I didn't tell him how I'd done it, and the pretence was the hard bit, like making a sickie call to work, you know they can see through the croaky voice and you know they know it's bollocks.

He said he'd be down in an hour so I'd just have to hang on and relax.

Except I was nowhere near a park, playground nor anything, and as a great day of sales stuffed, I couldn't relax.

Only after 20 minutes or so did two boys, no older than eight or nine, came trundling along the pavement on BMXs.

'Hey ice-cream man. We don't have any money, can we have free ice-creams?'

Oh God. 'Umm, no. You need money.'

'Awwwwwww ...'

'No, look, I've broken down. I can't go anywhere, I can't afford to give you free ice-cream.'

'Awwwwwwww ...'

'No, it's not "awwwwww", I wouldn't normally just give you free ones, and now I've busted the van you really can't have any.'

'Awwwwwwwwwwww ...'

For fuck's sake.

'It's really hot,' said one.

'Yes it is.'

'And you're so nice,' said the other.

I chortled at that.

'Pleaaaaaaaase ice-cream man, you're so nice, it's so hot, pleeeeeeeasssssssse ...'

I was too defeated to argue and they were quite cute in their silly boy way.

'OK ... you can have one each –'

'Hooray! Thanks ice-cream man!'

'- but no more than 75 cents worth.'

'Awwww ... '

'OK, fine, nothing.'

'OK, OK, thanks ice-cream man.'

They then went into the ritual of staring at the array of blue stickers, 'I want ... I want ... I want ...' and I could see their gaze was going all along the $1, $1.25 ice-creams, and not the 75c and 50c jobs at the bottom they could afford.

'Can I have a Sour Tower?'

'No, that's a dollar.'

'Awww ...'

'Can I have a Choco Tacco?'

'No. They're even more.'

'Awwww ...'

'I said 75c max each. Do you kids understand anything?' These little bastards actually did understand me, so I got out and pointed at the cheap ones they could have.

'Now, you can any of these here.'

'Can't we have one of those?' pointing to something that cost a dollar.

'Between you? Yeah.' I went and got one and gave it to them.

'Where's the other one?' said one.

'You only get one to share.'

'We don't want to share,' said the other.

'I want one, too,' said the first.

'No. I've said you can have an ice-cream each, yes, at 75 cents. That one costs a dollar, so you have that between you. Do you see what's happening here?'

'We're just kids and we don't understand what you say or math 'cos we're young.'

'What the f-, what the frig? You've understood everything I've said. Jesus. Go and learn something, got get your *Speak and Spell* or whatever it is you have.'

'A what?' said the first, while his friend started again with 'Awwwww ... I want one.'

'I'm so generous, you've still got 50 cents left. That'll buy you a Snowcone. Do you want a Snowcone?'

'I want ...'

'Snowcone or nothing,' I snapped.

'I want a Snowcone.'

I gave him one and he started hacking at it.

'So what you two doing the rest of the day?'

'We don't know. We got nothing to do.'

'It's Sunday, it's a gorgeous day, why aren't you at the pool?' I said.

'Pool's boring.'

'So you're just going to play around here? That could be fun?'

'Nah, it's stupid,' he said, although he really said '*stoopid*', then they went off and talked among themselves, then came back.

'Can we have another ice-cream?'

'No.'

'Awwwwwwww ...'

'I said no.'

'Awwwwww, you're bad ice-cream man.'

'What? That's not fair!'

'Yeah you're bad. We just want another ice-cream. Please ...'

'Give us another ice-cream, bad man.'

'I said no, Damnit. I'm not bad I gave you one already'

'You're nasty, nasty ice-cream man and your truck's bust up.'

'We don't like you, we're not going to buy any ice-cream off you,'

'You didn't buy anything anyway. Stop asking.'

'Awwww ...'

'Leave me alone. I gave you a free one already. Go away.'

'You're mean and stoopid. We can stay here if we want.'

Then I lost it. I stood up, walked over to the nearest one, grabbed him by the T-shirt and said in a quiet voice, 'I'll tell you what you can both do. You can both piss off. I gave you free ones, and now you just want more cos you're greedy little shits. Well piss off.'

He looked surprised. 'Ice-cream man's cursing!'

'Yeah! Piss off.'

'I'm gonna tell my mom.'

'Tell your fucking mom. Go on. Piss off and tell your mom and I'll tell her what shits you are. Geddit? Go!'

They looked at one another with worried expressions, turned and began to trot off.

'You're really nasty,' said one over his shoulder, a tearful tone replacing his cheeky tone.

'Yep.'

I sat down and lit up. The trouble was I'd no idea when Hank would get here and there was enough time for these kids to go get their dads and come have a go at me, but I thought of the kid's smirking face, then Elly's smirking face, then her and Christian fucking. I felt like sticking my head in the freezer but instead just sat on the step of the truck and chained through a fistful of ciggies and contemplated where my life was going. Absolutely nowhere. The one fucking day I'm making good money, I outfox fatso, then I go fuck the van, for which I'll be bollocked.

This is just Hell.

I was also nervous of angry dads coming back to do me in, but in the next hour only one person passed, a lady who looked at me so I stared at her until she stopped looking and I was free to go back to my thoughts of death. Finally, a pick-up truck with a crane on the back slowly rose up over the crossing and down again. I saw Hank in the cabin, pointing towards me, Charlie next to him. From the way the truck gingerly scaled up and over the crossing I was sure they'd guessed what I'd done, and I stood nervously waiting for the bollocking to come.

117

But it didn't.

They looked under the bonnet, said the motor clips had snapped and the engine had just dropped.

'Shit. Can you fix it?'

'Nope. Gotta take the whole engine out. There's an afternoon's work in that, gotta get back to Penguin,' said Hank.

With the speed of men who were very well practised at this sort of thing, they'd chained up and hoisted the van and I joined them back in the cabin for the drive back to Shorewood. We were quiet. I was mired in guilt and frustration and worry about being bollocked, if not fired for wrecking the van. Surely it was obvious what I'd done. But it never came. Instead Hank asked a couple of pleasantries and how much money I'd already made that day, I told him, and he said he'd double what my take would have been to make up for the lost earnings.

I did a double-take. 'you ... really? No. Oh. Um.' I didn't know what to say, it didn't seem right, but I wasn't going to turn down free money.

'It's only fair. You were doing a very good day's takings.'

I nearly cried. What a nice man.

Back at the hanger, with nothing to do I sat with a chair at the hanger door, watching Charlie work on my van. With this great block and tackle pulley hoist thing, he attached chains to the van engine, and hoicked it up high. Charlie was something else. He was like Jon Voight in *Midnight Cowboy*, but his looks pulverized by years of hard living. Hank came and joined me, giving me a beer. I told him who I thought Charlie looked like. 'He can keep that whole fleet of trucks goin' on spit and gum,' said Hank. He told me Charlie was born and raised on a Kentucky farm, spent his youth tinkering on his dad's tractors and getting his father's rusted sedans roadworthy, but when he got them back on the road, the furthest he'd drove was his local town, 5,000 folks, ten miles up the road. That was all, and he didn't even hit the bars there. Instead his pa let them drink corn liquor at home. He was about to expand on that, when he had to answer the phone. 'Sorry Jim, got an issue with the supplier, talk, to you later and you just take it easy' and he squeezed my knee, which made me laugh. Then it made me want to cry.

Ben was the first one in and I told him about my day, and what Hank said about Charlie. 'Yeah, Charlie drinks like a fucking fish and sometimes fucks off for weeks on end, but he's on a retainer of tens of thousands of dollars cos he's a genius. He went on a bender a couple of years ago that closed down Penguin for the beginning of summer. Hank wasn't happy.'

'Your engine fell out?' said Jeff. 'That's too bad. Worst I've had was a flat. Last year Riccardo was heading to the gas station down the road, and as he slowed to the lights just before them he thought the van was drivin' kinda funny, and as he stopped he saw this wheel roll past, and realised it was his.'

Mike, Christian, Jason, traipsed in, then others who I'd seen around, but not really met. Mike introduced me to two blokes in their 30s, Addy, a stocky,

118

balding Yorkshireman, and his mate Ali, tall and thin, small chin and round penny glasses.

'What's the seat like in your van?', Addy asked.

Strange question. 'What do you mean?'

'Is it fabric covered or vinyl?'

'Oh. Huh! Vinyl, I think.'

'Right, so's Ali's here. Mine's fabric, 'ickle me's going to have to bring a towel in to sit on so I'm not soaking up years of arse sweat soaked into it.'

'Ah. Right, yes, I see your point.'

'And who's the lovely lady?' he said towards Elly, who I introduced, and was in a good mood, then this gangly, very young looking chap, boggly eyes and full of enthusiasm, introduced himself as Adrian. Another Adrian!

Ben ended up talking with Adrian chimp and one of the others, while we all chatted, then Christian came over from talking to Hank. 'OK, Hank's told me we've got another guy coming to stay in our flat.'

Oh fuck, not another freak. I failed to look happy and Elly looked forlorn.

'Here they come,' Christian said, pointing behind me and Ben. We turned in our chairs and saw Hank approaching with this beefy bloke.

'Ok y'all, this is Greg, we're trying him out here, so he's going to be staying on the spare bed if that's OK,' said Hank, tilting his big bearded head, and that great smile. I sniggered to myself, no-one can refuse Uncle Hank.

'Hi nice to meet yous all,' this guy said in a Glaswegian brogue, and he shook all our hands vigourously. Christ, what a grip. He looked like a beefed-up David Coulthard, close-shaved hair, grey eyes, and underneath his torn, damp T-shirt was a great chest and sixpack, beating Christian's easily. Ah shit, would Elly fancy him?

On the way to a diner Greg said how he'd been doing painting and decorating in Illinois for a few months, and following on doing jobs for Hank took up the offer to sell ice-cream.

'Oh cool. So have you got a green card?' I asked.

'Green card? No! Not even a work visa. Just cash in hand stuff.'

'Ah, like us,' Ben said.

'Aye, Hank said we were on commission.'

'Yeah, the legit lot all get a basic, we're all on commission,' Ben said. 'So where you from originally?'

'Paisley. It's a shite hole. Junkies and jakeys, real problem with skag and shite. Nay work, and that and fighting fuckers like that all the time I just came oot here.'

'So you've had a few skirmishes?'

'Oh aye. Got done a couple of times too, which wasna fair, self-defence, some diseased jakey shite comes at yer with a bottle, yer gonna deck him hard, but his eyes are like this' – he prised his eyelids as wide as he could as this energy flowed into him, 'and getting back up, "yer fuckin' stayin' down there

119

mate!"', and his face contorted into rage as he raised a fist and pounded it towards the floor of the car, repeatedly, as if back in the fight.

'I got a bit of a rep as a bad boy. I wasn't a bad boy, I was naughty, just defended mysel', but hey ho.'

Right, he's got a temper and is quick with his hands. Elly and I looked at one another, then saw Greg looking surprised, putting his hands up, 'it's all right, I'm a nice guy!'

'Didn't say you weren't'! I said defensively, but he laughed.

We got a box of beer and went to install Greg in the room with Ben and I, then we got stoned. Greg seemed a pretty nice guy, just not one you'd want to piss off.

Batman

I woke up. Not being dead, I had no real excuse not to get up and put a face on it all. Greg, sleeping in our room, emerged bleary like coming out of hyper sleep in *Alien*, and after brushing up we all went down to the Pontiac, me in the front while Ben drove, Elaine and Christian behind us and Greg as rear gunner in the boot. I could hear Christian and Elaine being all touchy, pinching, lunging, sounds of 'stoppit' and shite.

'What you two kids doing in the back there? Don't make me turn around!' Ben said.

'Nothing, dad!' said Christian.

I had the window down and was leaning out now and again as if something interesting were outside, anything to look at with the wind blasting in my ears than put up with those two.

Christian said something but I couldn't hear him, then Ben leaned over and touched my arm, 'careful with that door, Rob, remember the locks are knacked'.

'Eh?'

'The locks are fucked. You'll fall out,' shouted Christian.

I looked back at the outside of the door and noticed the deadbolt holding it shut. If it opened I'd spill onto the road and it'd be all over.

'So don't lean on it, fuckwit!' said Christian.

I turned and stared at him, and he pursed his lips mockingly, turning to Elaine for backup, which she duly gave him with a beaming smile.

Fucking wankers. I hope you catch fire. 'Kill them, kill myself, whichever's easier,' I felt all through bombing up and the drive to Westie.

Another day, another dollar. Or lack of.

After hours traipsing around West Chicago, I didn't see Eskimo but I didn't see many kids. It was dull and I was bored, then I saw my water gun on the dash, and realised I'd never used it. Right. I saw a boy and a girl, seven or so years old, jumping up and down, hands aloft. I pulled over, up they came, quite nice they said 'hello ice-cream man', and instead of going 'I want .. I want ...', the boy immediately asked for two Sour Towers.

'What? Can you Heck! I'll give you something !' I said with faux rage, got out the water gun and fired at their faces and bellies. They squealed, but not with delight, 'it went it my eye, it went in my eye, it hurts it hurts' said the boy, while the girl stood, stared in shock, her bottom lip beginning to wobble before she turned on her heel and ran back to her house, crying.

'Oh fuck.'

I hastily gave the boy two Sour Towers, having to put them in his hands as he couldn't see, said 'OK kid they're for free!' then drove off to the sound of a mom 'hey ice-cream man, ice-cream man! Get back here, asshole', myself hunched over the steering wheel as if bullets were whizzing over from behind.

Christian said they loved this kind of shit. Lying bastard.

Business was dead anyway so I trundled to Bartlett, and was trolling around one of the new estates with massive white wooden houses, even the hillocks all newly sculpted and carpeted with turf, like some massive model kit, populated by model families. Plastic people that all bleached white in the Sun.

Through the rainbow of a lawn sprinkler I saw a girl and a boy look towards me and then trot to the pavement, or *sidewalk*. A sale! She was 9-ish, he a bit younger, both neatly dressed and the toys in the garden unbroken, tidily arranged and hadn't lost any colour from being left outside. As they perused the ice-creams, hypnotically chanting, 'I want … I want …,' I noticed the girl had on a finger a beautiful blue bird, bright blue, hopping back and forth along the finger.

'Ooo, what's that?' I asked.

'What's a what? O this? It's a parakeet,' said the girl.

'It's so pretty.'

'My brother's got one too,' she said, offhand, and she returned to the stickers, ignoring the bird as it scrabbled to keep its footing.

'It's so tame. Why doesn't it fly away?'

'They can't fly. They had their wings clipped,' said the girl, 'anyway I'd like to order now.'

Oh no. They'd clipped its wings? It's a bird. All they can do is fly, that's what they're born to do, and they clipped its fucking wings?

I must have looked aghast, as the girl asked, 'are you OK ice-cream man?' – not out of concern though, more, 'are you doing your job?'

They ordered two Choco Tacos each, one for now, one for after dinner, a quick $6 deal which would normally be great, but showed they were rich kids, and I had this vision of mutilated birds, treated like toys until the kids bored of them and flushed them down the loo, or flicked them off the upstairs windowsill.

They might as well have killed it, and it's totally at their mercy. If that bird fell off her finger it couldn't glide to safety, it'd just smack onto its head, and hopefully die instead of living life as a shitty toy at the mercy of these kids. Could I see the pain in the bird's eyes?

This was so depressing I felt a bit sick. This beautiful little bird, now just a plaything. What kind of fucking parents bought their children mutilated pets? What kind of bastard sold them? What did they cut the wings with, secateurs? Maybe the children weren't evil and gave these pets the best life, but they'd already cut their fucking wings! Maybe the little boy could work out a way to fix them, he'd get into model planes and use balsa or some Airfix bit to reattach the broken wing spars. But it'd be hopeless.

'Bye, ice-cream man,' said the girl, but I was too sad to reply as I remembered my own maltreated hamster, which I neglected until it got sick and weak, and somehow a fly laid maggots up its bum and my pa put it out of its misery one night. Poor little thing. Why don't children value anything?

The lane to the estate exit sloped up sharply to the main road and had a no left turn sign, the way I wanted to turn. There was no-one behind me and I looked up and down the road in both directions, running absolutely straight to the horizon about a mile each way, its distant surfaces like mercury beneath the heat shimmers. Ah fuck it, I went to turn left, the van crawling up the slope and tottering like an old man over the road onto the far lane. Just as I straightened up, far far ahead on the horizon I saw a tiny sliver of reflected sunlight, and the shape of a vehicle slowly wobbled into focus. Wouldn't it be Sod's law if that was a police car, I thought, but I couldn't tell.

As I slowly built up to cruising speed, the distance between me and this other vehicle closed, it shaking steadily through the shimmer, until I saw it was a car. With a large roof rack. More yards closed, and the roof rack became a rack of lights. Fuck. Oh yes it was a police car, a white police car. I stared ahead, driving as straight and steadily as I could, a precise 3 mph below the speed limit, nice and safe officer, while my fingers gripped the wheel a bit tight and sweaty, until this bright white and shiny saloon with red and blue lights on the roof and a gold stripe up the side floated past me, and I stole a glance at the driver, a tubby policeman with mirrored shades and moustache. He passed without slowing, and as I checked my wing mirror, it kept going. And going, and going, and going, past the junction I'd come out, and beyond, and seemed to disappear into the shimmer, and I calmed down a bit, lit a cig and thought about which estate to attack next.

Then as I threw the lighter onto the tray I glimpsed in the far wing mirror another silvery flash of sunlight way back up the road behind me, on the horizon. I carried on, driving straight and steady, but for sure I could see something gaining on me, slowly, but steadily. It was a car, with not a roof rack but lights, a white car, that damn police car, had turned around and was gaining on me, reeling me in as the furlongs passed, with all the time in the world. I drove as straight as I could, but I was getting decidedly nervous.

Like during the Blitz on London in winter 1940, British fighters called Defiants, instead of forward facing guns in the wings, instead had a turret behind the pilot that face rearwards, which surprised German day-fighters at first, but they just switched to attacking from the front and shot them all down. Defiants were switched to night-fighting against bombers, but they were slow, and to catch a Junkers 88 involved a long stern chase over many miles before the Defiant could pull alongside and let rip. But then a long burst of tracer fire would briefly light up the frozen black of the night sky as an engine got drilled off and the Junkers and its crew evaporated in flames.

What this guy was doing. The police car was now positioned right on my tail, just a car's length behind, where it sat for another quarter mile as I brewed, and brewed, feeling a bit sick, wondering if he wanted me, and if he did why didn't he do something?

Finally, the lights flashed once and the siren gave the laziest 'w'YOo'. Oh bollocks, I said, rolling to a halt.

I got out the van.

123

'Stay there, son,' said the police man.

'Hello,' I said cheerily. 'everything all right?'

'Do you know why I've stopped you?'

'Err....'

'You turned left out of a no-left turn.'

Oh balls.

'Oh. Erm, yes I did. I didn't want to have to come down and turn around.' There was no point in denying it or pretending I'd not seen the sign.

'Wad?' he said. Oh God. 'Did you see the sign?'

'Yes.'

'Why didn't you obey it?'

I paused, not wanting to say, like a child to a teacher telling me off, but I thought there's really no point in trying to lie at this point. I'm fucked already.

'Laziness.'

'Laziness! Right,' I was sure I saw his eyebrows arch up above his shades. Oh fucking fuck. 'Where you from?'

'Britain.'

'Ah, OK. Well Briddish guy I want to see your driving licence.'

'Yes. I do have a driving licence, I've got an international one.'

'Present me with it please.'

'Ermmm....I scoured the dashboard in panic. Where the hell was it? I started rifling through everything.

Then I remembered, I'd stuck it under the elastic of the sun visor which I flipped down, and there it was wedged in with some papers stuck in a plastic envelope.

'Found it! I said in triumph and gave it to him.

'I don't know about any international licence, I need to see a state driving licence.

'I don't have one, just an international one.'

He looked at it like it was toilet paper.

'It's valid,' I said.

He looked at my picture at the back and the name, 'James ... Jim ... Hopkins, Jim that's a nice name, uhuh, barely old enough to drive, sure ain't old enough to drink!' he said.

'What me? Tee total.'

'Uhuh,' he said, totally disbelieving me but giving the licence back. 'I'm sure it's you but it's still not a valid state driving licence, which you need on you. Add that to you pulling left out of a no-left turn.'

He pointed to a small disc on the windscreen.

'That's your permit, and it says West Chicago.'

Permit? What the fuck was he looking at?

'But this is Bartlett. Where is your permit for Bartlett?'

'Um ... errr... I thought the permit was a permit to sell ice-cream, I didn't know it was er, specific to somewhere, er ...' Bad lying.

'Who do you work for?'

'Penguin.'

'The Penguin! Ha! Definitely criminal,' he said, 'Where are you insurance papers?'

What the fuck insurance. 'I must be insured but I don't know about papers,' oh this was just going wrong, wrong, wrong – fuck fuck fuck!!

He inhaled deep, then started, 'OK – so you deliberately take a wrong turn out of an estate you've got no permit for, and no valid insurance papers to show me, this is enough to put you before a judge,' he said, as I took in a sharp gasp of breath, 'fraid' so. OK, Penguin-man, looks like you're going to have to follow Batman here down to the station!' he said, laughing.

I was in real trouble. On top of the untold fines, they'd find out I had no visa, I'd be fucked, then Hank would be fucked, then we'd all be fucked, and we'd all be deported or go to jail. I imagined myself in half an hour's time at the sergeant's desk, him laughing cruelly as the facts spilled out, the little cell with ceiling-to-floor bars just behind him where I'd be put as they sent squad cars to raid Hank's. Oh no ... oh no ... before sundown it'd be all over and we'd all be in so much trouble. We were doomed. Oh no ... oh no... My nerve broke and I laughingly blubbed, and said in this painfully tearful voice, 'o God how much is this all going to cost?'

'A few hundred dollars,' he said, 'I'm not sure,' but his tone was suddenly soft.

'I really didn't know about the permit thing. Sorry, I'll definitely stick to West Chicago. I thought this was West Chicago.'

'It's called Bartlett.'

'Right. Yes. Um. I mean I just thought it was part of West Chicago in general, or something. I didn't know it was different.'

'It is. And if you don't have a permit, you can't sell here. You can sell in West Chicago, and only in West Chicago, not in Bartlett, not in no place. Clear?'

'Yes.'

'But I still gotta see insurance, I can't let you go without it.'

I got into the cabin and started scrabbling about, then he got in behind me and poked as well, pulling down the sun visor where I'd put my licence, and immediately he pulled out a plastic envelope and said, 'these are them! Why didn't you show me these before?'

'I didn't know.'

'Who the hell is your boss? Doesn't he tell you anything?'

'Not really.'

He harrumphed. 'Obey the road signs, they're there for a reason. It might seem to you like a waste of time but there's been accidents on this road, people driving fast and they turn left. Man got killed just this winter gone. That sign's there to stop them. You don't know better.'

'No you're right. Sorry.'

'Just you stay out of trouble. I don't want to have to chase you down in the Batmobile again.'

I high-tailed back to West Chicago and traipsed the streets again, too excited to do much tactical aplomb. Counting up at the hanger, I'd still made a third off $190, and hit the beer, but now I was worried because Bartlett was good money and made West Chicago less shit.

'All the permits for the others are taken,' Hank said when I asked about other routes, 'but you're doing a real good job down there, Jim, your takings from West are higher than what we often get,' and he gave my arm a pat. Shit, I couldn't tell him why.

'Did you have a good day Greg?'

'Took me fucking ages to find all the fucking ice-creams, the freezer's a nightmare! And ah nearly died when I was in there, ferreting away to find some shite, panicking for some fuckin reason, and took in a breath and that freezing fucking carbon dioxide near knocked me out, shite!'

'Horrible isn't it!'

'And I got a call in about dangerous driving.'

'What? How'd they know who'd to call?'

'The number's on the back.'

'Is it? Never seen it.'

'Probably rusted off,' said Elly.

Ben had had to chase kids who'd got ice-creams but then said they'd no money and ran off. We all agreed we'd demand cash up front from here in. I told the others my story, except the bit about being in Bartlett, and they all found it funny, although Christian called me a fuckwit for the wrong turn and Elly agreed.

In the car, Ben started. 'Fucking get this. Mike was talking to Adrian about his impending 'date' with this girl,' Elaine grimaced, 'and I was there, and Adrian's getting all "she's going to suck me dry" and "I'm gonna fuck her arse off," stuff like this,' and he asked what would happen if his charms didn't work and she didn't get excited, and he said "I'll spit up her".'

'Oh God!' Elaine exclaimed, as did I.

'Cunt!' said Christian.

'I know, when I heard that I wanted to hit him,' Ben said. 'Mike was like, "mate, you can't do that, that's just so not on," but he told him he didn't care.'

'Fucking hell.'

'Shite. He sounds like a real piss of work,' said Greg.

We ate at a diner and I worked out that after dinner, beer, then tomorrow's petrol and fags, lunch, I'd have fuck all left. This was going on every day. We hit Dooley's, drank, talked shit, and Greg engrossed with a couple of the others. Then suddenly Elaine got up and walked out the bar. Ben looked at me somewhat surprised, and mouthed, 'she all right?' I pulled a baffled face and then went outside to find her pulling hard on a cig, looking at the gravel, turning this way and that, all flustered basically.

'I'm really scared about this girl with Adrian, he's disgusting.'

'He is, but what are we supposed to do?'

'I don't know! But it's statutory rape for one.'

'It is, but what do we do? Find out where they're going and call the police?'

She just shook her head and looked away, sadly.

'But what? What do we do?'

She said nothing.

'You all right?'

'No! I've just fucking told you. You don't listen'.

'I do! I'm out here, Jesus bloody!'

'All right, sorry. But he's a freak!' She tutted, heeled her cig into the tarmac and went back inside.

I felt a bit sick. I hated seeing her upset like this. We went back in. Christian was talking with a few of the others about going to Six Flags the next day, I'd forgot, it was our day off. A fuck-off great big rollercoaster park it'd definitely be fun. Back home, got stoned, everyone else went to bed while Ben and I watched a bit of *Mystery Science Theater 3000* before he sloped off. I stayed up on beer, then as I went to the bog I heard them fucking, and as I came out I heard her cum.

Six Flags

The shitty clouds of self-hate I woke up under evaporated the second I heard Ben say something about Six Flags and we should be off already to have a fuck-off great time.

Elly didn't look excited though.

I asked if she was coming – *zzz she'd been cumming*.

'No, I don't really like rollercoasters. They scare me.'

'Not even the scenic railways?'

'Nah. I've never liked them.'

'Elly loves to ride,' said Christian, and I was grateful he'd saved me having to conjure up my own pun to torture myself with.

'You all right?' I asked her.

'Yeah, fine,' but she seemed kind of distant.

'She's fine,' said Christian, busy putting his shoes on.

'What you going to do instead then?'

'Have my own space.'

'That sounds very nice.'

She smiled.

I was disappointed, things weren't as fun when she wasn't around, as if her presence just made things legit. But a fabulously sunny day at the funfair would be such a good adrenaline jag. And it was a proper big American theme park, not some touring gypo enterprise back home, rides put up in the local park with bits of 2 x 4 by blokes with pints in hand, and no added thrill of a ride collapsing or being stabbed by kids off the estate. This was proper, the kind of stuff we'd seen on *Jim'll Fix It* or *Blue Peter* as kids, seared into our young minds, 'I – have – got – to – go – there!'

I just didn't want her to miss out.

But Christian, Ben were all ready to go, Greg too, then Aidan and Mike and Jason arrived – the whole gang was going, yay! And down we went to the Pontiac.

'I've brought a couple of newspapers and magazines for the journey,' said Aidan, which was surprisingly nice for him, before he added, 'only so I don't have to talk to you cocksuckers!'

'Do ... do you ever say anything apart from cocksuckers?' I said.

'Yeah – fuck off!' he replied.

In the front Ben and Christian conferred over the map, muttering about distances and roads, travel times this way or that, then Christian announced in his drawliest US accent, 'we've got a tank of gas – no, we've got half a tank of gas, half a packet of cigarettes and an hour to get to Six Flags.'

'Hurrah!' we shouted as we rolled away.

'I looked at Six Flags as one of the job options,' said Mike, 'anyone know anyone who went for them?'

'Yeah we've got a mate working there,' I said.

'Oo, can she get us in for free?'

Fuck, I hadn't thought of that, then I remembered, 'oh no hang on, she's in Missouri. So, no. Shit, sorry.'

'Ahh.'

'Is that what Val's doing?' said Christian.

'Yeah, but she's not at Six Flags, she's at some other place.'

'Elly was talking to her the other night on the phone and there's a chance she'll come visit, for a day or two. Which would be nice, she's got a great arse,' said Christian. And a boyfriend, I thought.

'So what made you choose ice-cream over rollercoasters, Mike?' I asked.

'Money.'

'You see more and meet more people doing ice-cream, and aren't stuck in some park all day dealing with randoms,' said Ben.

'Good point,' said Mike, 'although we spend all day in a van dealing with morons.'

'Good point!' said Ben.

Aidan surrendered the *National Enquirer* to me, saying 'there you go, cocksucker', and I expected to read all about UFOs and bombers crashed on the Moon, but there was a story about JR Ewing, or rather Larry Hagman, at home with his family, as the poor bugger was recovering from a liver transplant following cirrhosis of the liver. I read some of it aloud, 'it says, some reporter asked him once if it was true that he drank three bottles of champagne a day when on the Dallas set, and he said no, it was actually five bottles a day, and he was just floating around the place.'

'Jesus,' said Ben.

'There's a picture of the operation scar, fucking look at that,' I showed the others.

'Fucking Hell. Absolutely opened him up,' said Greg. 'A lot of shite like that in Pais, jakies and alchies, they never hit 50.'

'The liver is the only organ that can regenerate itself, so to smash it up like that you have to drink a lot, and I mean, a lot,' said Christian.

'He says him and Bobby, all the shots where they were drinking, take after take, they were getting pissed,' I said.

'Sue Ellen as well,' said Aidan, 'they were all just pissed, arguing and throwing bottles at one another. It wasn't a soap, it was a fly-on-the-wall documentary.'

'Were they really drunk on set?' said Ben.

'Yeah, look,' I gave the mag to Ben.

'Wad?' he said.

'Wad?' I replied, then everyone in the car went 'wad? Wad?' at each other.

'So all those episodes ending with him going "Meh! Heheheh!" and knocking back a massive whiskey were real!' said Mike, 'That's why they ended the episode then, cos he was too wankered to continue! Hahaha!'

129

'God, he looks like death,' said Ben.

'Linda Grey was fit,' said Christian. 'I'd definitely fuck her. We were all supposed to fancy Victoria Principle, but I didn't. I wanted Linda Grey.'

'I loved the theme tune!' said I.

'Hit it!' shouted Christian, and we all sang the theme song, everyone picking out a part, lead trumpets, bass guitar, drums, and it went so well we sang it through several times.

I started the theme from *Dynasty* but that didn't take off, but everyone knew the *Colbys'* theme, although no-one watched it. Greg launched with *CHiPs*, which we agreed was brilliant and yet totally gay, followed by *Hawaii 5-0*, for which somehow the drums involved everyone in the back slapping each other's legs, then we belted out the *A-Team*, and the *Fall Guy* although we'd forgotten the words, and then the sad song at the end of the *Hulk* when Bill Bixby hitchhikes off towards his next meltdown.

Onto the highway, 10 lanes wide, and finally signs appeared for Six Flags, the miles dwindling like a countdown as we filled the air with banter and ciggy smoke, until on the horizon we could see amazing loops and curves and towers emerging, like an array of rocket launch pads on acid, their bright colours greyed by the haze.

'Look at those fuckers!' said Greg.

The arrows on the signs pivoted from straight on to left, very left, then EXIT, which we all started shouting at Christian just to piss him off. The park now seemed surrounded by one wooden massive rollercoaster, like a parabolic curve on graph paper, but all of the rides were huge, stupidly big, acknowledged with comments like 'oh my god', 'look at the size of that!'

'I hear that a lot,' said Christian.

'I'm not going on that,' said Aidan.

'I don't hear that so much,' said Christian. An image of him and Elly fucking came and went through my mind like a Kodak holiday slide. Bastard. But I was quickly carried along by the excitement, as we approached what America was best at – fuck off great big rollercoasters.

The car park was a like a huge metal lake of sunlight rippling off cars, and Ben told us to remember our parking location, 2.6, or it'd be days before we found the car again. Even this close, the park was so big that the roar of carriages and screams were out of sync with what we could see of rollercoasters diving and hurtling around. We corralled beyond the turnstiles with the maps to argue about where to start - the Python? The Exterminator? The Candelabra? Or in the zones, named like Yukon or Southwest Territory. Ultimately we opted to start in the middle and spiral out like a snail shell.

The first ride we hit wasn't a train of cars on rails, but rows of seats hanging from a single rail and from which people dangled. The snaking queue was massive, but it evaporated quickly, and we took up our places, hoicking onto the hanging seats, legs swinging free as this great padded yoke-like thing *pssshhhd* down onto our chests so tight it was almost hard to breathe.

Then the long, long climb with our seats hanging from this weedy, twisted looking track, and we jabbered to one another that if anything was going to go wrong please would it go wrong now. 'Fuck this', said Mike, and Aidan said 'this is too much, I want to get out', but too late, *clack, clack, clack*, up and up and up, me wondering if in fact I'd made my last mistake, would this be my end, and then the ride topped out, going so slowly, with such deliberation before we all get killed, then it banked sharply to the edge of a precipice, then just ... waited on the edge, as our eyes and mouths opened wide to let our hearts leap up and our stomachs empty, and we – were – OFF – DOWN DOWN DOWN into the depths!

It was so fast and turned so tightly, jack-knifing and throwing my head everywhere as it careened so close to all those spindly concrete legs, shafts and girders, straight and twisted like badly cooked spaghetti that each one I thought I'd obliterate my knees into, and then almost as fast as it'd started it was over and we had a whiplashing halt back at the boarding platform.

What a rush!

What a start!

We followed on with rides that did enormous loops where the change in your pockets felt it'd fall out and rain down on us passing below, but best were the traditional up-and-down scenic railways where everyone throws their arms up for every hill, beautiful wooden structures hundreds of yards long and scores high, built from entire forests. The best by far was the one with a plaque near the queue dating it to the 1930s, all designed with slide rules on plans covering a football pitch if drawn to scale. Even a 1:72 scale model of this would fill your bedroom, cost a fortune in balsa wood and take months to build, I thought, remembering the one-metre wide B-36 model I got for my 16th birthday but never built, to some guilt.

Like with the other rides, we took the end car to maximise the whiplash, the *clack-clack* ascent hurting my neck from leaning back so long, then tootling around the top we got a magnificent panoramic view of the park and the pan-flat state as the land rolled away forever, the people down below so small, then the train approached the cliff edge, slowing just enough to give us time to get upset, then resign ourselves, and then it hurled itself and us straight on and down, down, and down, us all screaming until it bottomed out and the Gs silenced us as we were pushed down into our seats, before it reared up, vaulted a hillock to make us weightless, our arms flung aloft and screaming again, over and over.

And that's what we did, all bloody beautifully blue-sky day, the rollercoasters we'd seen on TV we were now riding for real, until all sunburnt around our collars and sleeve hems, our feet fat from padding around the tarmac and rammed with blood from the G forces, we decided to go. The drive back was quiet, some of us dozed and sweated onto the vinyl car seats as the Sun glowered in front of us, buttering our sweaty toasted faces on this golden road of cars and lorries.

131

We stopped off for fuel, my noting that the needle was right down causing Christian-git to snap, 'it's always down, it's bust.' Then we cruised into the apartment car park, arranging vaguely to meet the others in Dooley's later, and lolloped indoors.

Opening the apartment door we heard Elly's voice, then another in a northern accent said, 'is that them?' It was Val!

'Sure is,' said Elly, sounding chipper.

'Val! You came!' I shouted, giving her a big hug.

'Hi Jimbo! How are you? Oop – you're a bit sweaty, aren't yer, luv!'

'Val!', cooed Christian, but they didn't embrace, then he introduced Ben and Greg.

'This is brilliant,' I said, 'Elly said you might come but wasn't sure, you up for a couple of days then?'

'Erm ... well, there's been a bit of a development on that front,' said Val.

'How many days did you get off work?' said Christian.

'A few.' She looked a bit sheepish, then said, 'I was wondering if I could stay a few days, um, while I work out what I'm doing next.'

'Or where,' said Elly.

'What to do next, and where, right,' said Christian, clocking as we all had, something was awry.

'Hmmm ... doesn't sound like you're going back, Val,' I said.

'I've left,' she said, biting her lip.

'Uhuh,' said Christian.

'Quit.'

'Uhuh,' Christian, Ben and I said.

'It – was – shit.'

'Uhuh,' we said again, nodding.

'Worst fucking job I ever 'ad,' really saying *fooking*, and then *ever* with real aplomb.

We all nodded, then burst out laughing.

'They treated us like shit. Like idiots,' she said.

'So hang on,' said Christian, 'Elly – did you know this morning that she'd left her job?', but Val cut in:

'I'll only be here a couple of days if that's all right, as soon as I get myself sorted I'll be out. I'm really sorry to just turn up like this.'

'No, no, don't worry,' I started, but she spoke over me:

'Honestly I won't be any trouble.'

'Oh it's fine, fine, I mean you were coming for a couple of days anyway, what difference does a couple more make?' said Christian, 'it's all right, we get it, it's cool! Right guys?'

'Yeah fine!' Ben said.

'No! I'm not having some unemployed layabout stink out the flat!' I said, smiling, but Val didn't appreciate it. 'Joke! It'll be fun.'

'I fucking hope so ... I'll work out what I'm doing and all that. Thing is I've still got my work visa.'

'Is it not tied to your work?' said Christian.

'Don't think so. They didn't cancel it or owt. Well they didn't have time to get it off us. I quit last night and left this morning. It were a bastard journey getting here, well long, train, bus, bus, even hitched a bit, taxi, but long and stinky.'

'Have you eaten? What we going to do for dinner?' Ben asked, 'should we go to Denny's?' but Val had eaten and no-one was that hungry, so we agreed to graze on what was in the fridge, where Ben found a load of beer.

'Oh I got you a load of beer, by way of thank you for havin' us,' said Val. A lot of planning had gone into this.

'You're more than welcome now!' Ben said.

Beers were divvied out as Christian skinned up, and I asked, 'so what was so shit about it?'

'Everyfink, and I mean, *everyfink*. Start with the pay, which was shit. At uni, right, when we signed up to this, we were promised, right, $4.75 an hour.'

'Not bad.'

'Fucking great if we'd got it, but we didn't get anywhere near that. Nowhere near, we got below minimum wage.'

'There is no minimum wage,' said Christian.

'Yes there is.'

'No, this is a free-market economy.'

'There is a minimum wage, Christian, believe me, right, it's $4.25 an hour, I've checked it, that's the recommendation –'

'Recommendation – it's not statutory –'

'Fine, that's what it should be and' she replied, talking louder, 'don't cut me off Christian cos I've had this bloody argument enough times already, right,' and he raised in hands in surrender, 'in any case, they promised us $4.75 an hour back home, friggin' minimum wage or not, before I even left Britain. But guess what we got?'

'Less,' Ben said.

'A lot fucking less! $3.48! Over a dollar twenty five less, that's like a quarter less than what we were told, what's that in pounds?'

'Mmm, the rate's what, 1 to 1.55, 1.60?' said Ben.

'Summink like that, so we're getting, about £2.30 an hour, not even that. It's shit,' said Val.

'That is shit. I was getting over three pounds an hour at McDonalds, what, three years ago,' I said.

'Yet but the $3.48 must be post-tax though, $4.75 gross,' said Christian.

'No it isn't! What makes it even more weird, $3.48, I mean 48 cents, random, but at first look y'know I thought that's right, cos that's post tax, like yer say Christian, although fucking hell, if you're on fuck all and a quarter of your wage goes on tax that's worse than Britain, but anyways, right, no don't interrupt, it's $3.48 gross, not net. So then there's tax off that, so it ends up, we're earning, like, 20 shitting quid a day, a whole day. You'd get that on a fucking evening pub shift.'

'We don't get a minimum per hour,' said Ben.

'We're all on commission,' said Christian, 'we can earn fuck all.'

'No, but you knew that before you came,' Val retorted, 'whereas what we got was not what we signed up to, and what we got was shit. Can I ask what you do take home?'

'A good day, about $70 to $90, not a bad day at any rate,' said Ben, 'about average $80 on the down side.'

'Mebbe it's not secure but we're 'secure' on twenty pissing quid and even $50 is still about £35, almost double what we're on,' Val said.

'Yeah, yeah, I see that,' said Ben, 'I've never had as bad even as $50.'

'I bloody have!' I said. 'What's your average Christian?'

He just silently raised his eyebrows as he lit the spliff. He was obviously on a lot more, probably the amounts he'd told us in uni we'd all earn, but, in the event, weren't. Well, we weren't. He was fucking coining it, for all his false fucking modesty of possibly earning nothing.

Val continued, 'and we said all this to the manager and then another manager, and him, and her, and him over there, fucking blah, and they were like, "we don't know what you were told in England or what you agreed to, and it doesn't matter now anyway," and we're like, "it's the same bloody company, are you telling us you don't know what they're saying, these guys who are recruiting us on your behalf, you don't know on what conditions of pay or anything else?" And they're just like, "whatever".'

'And it'd be the same rig every year, it's not like it's new to them,' said Ben.

'No it's not new to them, but it's new to us and that's why they take the piss!'

The first spliff began its journey around.

'You would not fucking believe what slave-drivers they are. I've been here over four weeks now and in that time I've had two days off. Two! And you're supposed to do 10-hour shifts, they're a fucking joke, they're always longer, and there's no overtime for 'em either, but there are two shifts a day and they alternate, and the morning shifts you have to be up at the crack of dawn and work right well beyond lunchtime to late afternoon, then some lot take over and sometimes they don't get finish until 10 or 11 or some ungodly hours. But you're doing the late shift one day and the morning one the next, so you come back and flake out and then lie there stressed knowing you've got four pissing hours sleep, and then they switch the shifts back again the next day. It's a joke!'

As she really got into gear her talking began to speed up.

'And they're really sly! Get this right, they told us you get a meal with whatever shift you're on, cos there are two shifts. But it's not like you turn up and get breakfast or lunch at the canteen, cos there ain't no canteen. Instead you 'earn' your lunch with points for every hour worked – one point an hour –'

Ben's eyes widened as he mouthed, 'one', which Val caught, 'yeah, right, fookin' one – but the points are only valid at a couple of the burger bars on site, right, so it's not some range of food but junk food so you get fat and spots, for which if you pay cash we don't even get a discount, we pay punter rates. Points though, you get 10 shitty points per shift, but you can't cash in all 10 points at lunch if it's halfway through a shift, you get five points or worrever you've earned to that point, which doesn't get jack. You could wait 'til the end of the shift, whenever that is, for the whole 10 points, but you'd starve to death, so halfway through the day you end up half paying for shit lunch out of your own shit wages.'

I'd taken a few tokes and passed the spliff to Elly, and caught Ben's gaze, he was looking spellbound as Val cantered on.

'Ten points whether you worked 10 hours or 13. And cos there were only a couple of places you could eat, you had to get to those places from wherever you're working, and the site is massive, a mile across, and you only get half an hour for lunch so you spend 10 minutes getting to the shitty burger bar where you then queue up, then try and get back without being seen running or throwing up your shit lunch because that's against regulations to run, but they're really arsey if you're late and can dock pay.'

She finished her beer and crushed the can and waved away the spliff as she got into a gallop.

'They dock time for bog breaks, for fuck's sake. So with all these shit shift times you're all jacked on coffee, so you get dehydrated and drink loads of water, luckily that's free from the fountains, but then you're forever busting for a piss and hopping from foot to foot while serving people who can see you want to go to the loo but you can't for the sake of losing 50 cents. And you can't operate machinery when you're tired and hungry, that's fucking dangerous, but that's what they're doing, they're operating real bloody great machines with dozens of people on board.'

Ben laughed, 'shit, you should see the state we arrive at work in!'

I laughed. Luckily the long drive to West Chicago gave me a chance to sober up most days.

'No fucking shops either to get food from for our flat, or make lunch, like, the nearest one is like five miles away and you gorra walk to it,' Val raced on. 'There's some decent restaurants nearby, as in not a hundred fucking miles away like everything else, but still gorra walk all the way there and back, and you can't eat out every night, specially not on our pittance earnings. And you can't drink at the bar on the site even when off duty and you can't bring your own drink to the apartment, if you're caught with alcohol you're fucked. We can go to a bar some nights and come back totally off our faces and be up five hours' later running rollercoasters, still pissed, but that's OK, but no drink where we sleep and shit. Honestly it's like being in some fucking nunnery. One of the girls was caught with beer she'd had to get back from the shop by hitching there and back so she's basically going out to get raped and left in a ditch for the sake of a few beers, so, right, so get this, they confiscated her booze and docked her pay, and we're like "you total cunts!" But it's also "if it's such a fucking crime, why don't you sack her?" and they're saying they were cutting her some slack, and it's like no it's not, obviously it's cos you'd then have to go hire someone else, and they can't hire anyone else cos all the locals know what a fucking shit place it is to work so they come to Britain and hire idiots like me.'

All this came out at such speed, with such passion, we just stared at her, this northern girl who'd come out of the blue. I failed to stifle a snigger and she glared at me. 'Sorry Val,' I said, 'it's not funny, it's just that your righteousness is great, carry on.'

'Shurrup Hopkins!' she tried not to laugh, 'and you would not catch me going on one of those rides, any of those rides, they're death traps. See how decrepit and bust up they are in the machinery rooms, like ancient stuff, ancient. No, over the years there've been *lurrds* of deaths, one of the park hands was telling us one night.'

'What, at Montana?' said Christian.

'No not in that park, not all in that park – Montana? Missouri!'

'Oh yeah, sorry.'

'Everywhere, they're fucking dangerous. People getting flung off rollercoasters and smashing into the ground, trains getting jammed upside down, brakes not working and cars crashing into one another or brakes working too hard and everyone gets whiplash, kids getting their legs caught between the train and the platform or trying to get out at the top and falling 100s of feet. There was one kid who panicked at the top of a water slide and tried to get out, well he did he reached of the railing and held on and the log thing went anyway so he was left dangling until he fell off and smashed onto the rocks at the bottom. In front of all his family.'

'Jesus. Shit,' said Ben.

'Hope they got a refund,' said Christian, sending another spliff on the rounds.

'Sky ride cars falling off cables. This bloke' – or *blurrk* as she said – 'was telling us how often someone gets killed or hurt and the ride gets investigated and the report comes back saying, what were it, it's "operationally and mechanically sound", or the park gets fined like $1,000 under state law and the ride opens up a week later and no-one knows what's happened. $1,000 is just fuck all.'

'It's not like that, they get sued for millions,' said Christian.

'Yeah but still have to sue them, you've still got to get a lawyer who's prepared to take on this fuck off great big company. Anyway this bloke right, aw God he was tellin' us about some haunted house thing that burned down and killed eight people.'

'Probably is haunted now,' I said.

'Well no cos there's only a pile of fucking smoking bricks left to haunt. People falling off rollercoasters cos the barrier thing's not locked properly and no-one's checked and the coaster hits 5G at the first corner and sends someone flying out, throwing them across the park ... until they land on some poor muggins vendor like me. I go splat under some fat fucking bastard. That's a fun summer.'

'Ah yeah, I've read about that, or some case where a woman fell out because she was so fat the barrier didn't lock,' said Ben.

'I'm surprised she wasn't wedged in,' said Elly, 'but surely she'd have bounced on impact.'

'Just part of the ride,' said Ben.

'It's usually human error, they have multiple safety features to stop these things, they have to for insurance,' said Christian.

'But they don't always work! One time a kid got thrown out and died cos the barrier fucked up, but there was this green light system that said he was locked in. I felt really bad for the operator when I heard that. Some other park worker was in this rollercoaster and it jumped off the track and he smashed his head on a rock.'

I had a toke on the spliff and it hit me about the same time as Christian's joke about the refund and I started to snigger.

'Another bloke drowned cos the water was so cold it gave him a heart attack. It's crazy, it all goes on all the time and no-one knows about it!'

'That's just ill health.'

'O for fuck's sake Christian! I know that! Another time this bloke went in and stabbed two people and then shot a load more.'

'That's hardly the park's fault!' Ben laughed, as did Val.

'What ride was that? *The Weirdo*,' Elly said.

'Snot funny!', said Val, laughing, 'well it is. Just goes to show, parks do that to people.'

'He probably got sick of queuing up and just did one.'

'Probably got sick of working there more like!'

'Supposed to be a fun day out and you end up taking your life in your hands.'

'Good name for a ride, "take your life in your hands".

'"Don't expect to live."'

'And the toys you can win, those massive teddy bear things at the shooting gallery and hoopla, they're shit 'n all, made by the tiny hands of Chinese children.'

'Orphans of Tiananmen.'

'Shame we didn't win a teddy bear at Six Flags today,' said Christian, 'instead we got a Val.'

'And it's all so petty, no-one's having a good time, everyone's pissed off and feeling scammed, and I thought I just can't spend my whole summer dealing with this petty crap for the sake of wankers, so I quit. All those teenagers you see in the malls could be working there, but they won't, cos they know what it's like, so they ship us out to do it on lies! It's a joke! That fucking bloke at the job fair telling us all what fun it was, I'm going to kill him when I get back, I'm going to go to the next fair and tell everyone not to come!'

The more stoked she got, and the more stoned we got, the harder it got not to laugh. Luckily Christian erupted just as Ben and I couldn't help ourselves, and Elly joined in, and Val.

'Anyway so's if you can put up with us ... I could get a job around here. I've done bar work and waitressing and like I say I've still got me work permit,' which was more than anyone else in the room had.

'Should be all right, shouldn't it?' I said.

'Yeah, fine! We'll have to scout out if it's a problem with Hank or the landlords, but do it subtly in case it is a problem. We don't want to tip them off.'

Which was ironic, as Val was the only one in the flat with a legit working visa.

'We still going to Dooley's?' said Ben.

'We got loads of beer here ... fuck it, let's show Val Dooley's, and she can meet the others!'

Still all sweaty but too stoned to care, we all shuffled up the road to Dooley's, where Aidan laughed at our red eyes and stink and called us 'stoner cocksuckers', but it wasn't irritating.

Independence Day

'Wake up you British bastard! It's Independence Day!' Ben shouted me awake.

I was still murky, but managed to say 'great'.

'It is, and Hank wants us at work by 9:30. Sharp.'

No bagels or spread for breakfast, though, nothing laid out at all, except Val, slumbering on the sofa, not waking up, or pretending not to wake up until we'd necked some coffee and were about to leave.

'Awright Jimbobs,' she said.

'Laters Val. We, who still have jobs, have to go to work.'

'Fuck off, you're not funny.'

'Yes-I-am!'

Maybe we didn't have time today, but it seemed the breakfasts weren't like they had been before Christian and Elly first fucked, and certainly Christian hadn't cooked an evening meal since then, either. Well he'd no need to try anymore. But now I realized as we drove to work that on top most of our money going on petrol, cigarettes, beer and general pissing about, we were spending loads on diners, and I wasn't saving anything. Meanwhile neither Elly nor I had plane tickets to go home. Hmm. I'd have to start squirreling notes away somehow.

Early as it was, work was humming with activity, then Hank went and stood at the hanger door, and shouted for everyone to come into the hanger, be quiet a second, and then he said with mock solemnity that today was Independence Day, which got a cheer from the Yanks and a boo from the Brits, and a laugh all round as we pointed, jeered and jostled. Then he told us there would be street parties and parades, and fireworks in the evenings, so we should home in on those and business would be good, that we should stay out 'til past sundown, 'and when you come back we'll have burgers on the go here 'til midnight.' Whereupon we all cheered, then went back about our business with renewed vigour. One way or another it was going to be exciting, and as we crossed in and out the hanger we'd say to one another, 'parties, parades and fireworks', and nod conspiratorially.

This was grand enough a mission for Hank to wave us all off. Our beleaguered by jovially defiant Commander Hank, with his ragtag bomber squadron of Yanks and Brits, an Atlantic Alliance of rookies, mercenaries, and battle-hardened veterans back for second tours, bringing freedom in the form of ice-cream to oppressed and uncivilized children across Illinois. Each day down at the hanger, Hank would direct his pilots, already briefed on the weather, by pointing to the targets on his huge wall map, little markers for who was going where, as they sortied out every day from his great metal hanger, with its massive, folding screen doors.

The drivers got their maps, permits and ammunition as tubes of quarters before going to their neatly-lined up mounts, loading the bomb-bay-like freezers with ice-cream and placing dry ice among the ordnance gingerly, as if setting the

139

fuses. The freezer doors slammed, the back roll-doors whirred down. Charlie the War Vet mechanic had already tweaked and busted any gremlins, leaving the pilots to do their flight deck checks on fuel, bottles of frozen water thawing on the dash, water guns loaded, maps and ammo on the tray. The battery-charger was disconnected, the pilot fired the engine, then taxied his van across the gravel, maybe in a packet of two, three or four other vans, converging at the highway where they gave final salutes before taking off for their long solo flights to their targets.

There, one spent hours battling countless enemies identified by their markings and makes of mounts, countering their tactics and deployments. Some routes were worse than others, and a pilot might groan in anticipation of being sent to some far-flung target, known to be swarming with enemies heavily armed with baseball bats or selling ice-cream at least a quarter cheaper, all helping to deliver low returns and even lower morale. But then pilots would be rotated onto safer, nearer routes, with key intelligence used to concentrate on areas or days of high activity – like July 4, a day when Penguin could make a killing and reassert itself as an ice-cream power to be reckoned with.

We could be lost in enemy territory, have to make forced landings if the engine fell out and glide to the roadside, Hank's rescue jig taking hours to lumber into view, and if they couldn't get the van airworthy they'd tow it home. But mostly we made it back after a good day's bombing, sunburnt and sweaty, tired but pumped, counted up the shrapnel over tales of run-ins, lucky escapes, tactical victories and other tips, over beers instead of bacon butties.

And while on the job we were all fighting for ourselves, for some reason we were also all loyal to Hank and thought of ourselves as Penguin, and would work for no other unit.

Yeah.

Cool.

So I thought as the wind whistled through the cockpit, before I remembered pilots could also come home to. Hell. I'd no home in England, the family home where I'd grown up had been sold months before, the same day ma and pa split up prior to divorce. One day in which everything was wiped out. But I was an adult, as an adult, and a Brit, you saddle up and press on, to find new Hell, to come back from months of touring that Hell to find another man's kitbag hanging behind the front door.

Like finding Christian and Elly fucking.

War is Hell.

I started my normal run but there was nobody about. Loads of American flags, but no people. An hour's trawl threw up $15 of sales. It was dead as. This was shit. Where the fuck had everyone pissed off to? Where were the takings? No office workers in the middle of town, even my favourite shop was shut. Oh for God's sake, idiot, I thought, it's July 4, nobody's working.

I scoured the parks, but there were no more people than usual. 'Parties,

140

parades, fireworks.' No parties yet, no fireworks, they had to be at a parade, or the parade, but that'd be, fuck – where would that be?

I saw one family wobbling along a road of big houses.

'Hello,' I called out.

'Hi ice-cream man, thanks but no thanks,' said the dad.

'Yeah OK, but where are you all going?'

'To the parade! It's on Main Street.'

Main Street! Shit, of course, that's where everyone would be as well. I looked at the map, and through town there really was a 'Main Street', so I aimed there, but some way from it was a road block of ropes between cones, and a fat woman on a camping seat. Neither she nor the seat looked happy.

'Can I get through?' I said.

'You driving in the parade?' she asked sarcastically.

'I doubt it.'

'No can do,' and she pointed back up the street.

Okay, Tubs, you're so clever, I thought amid an efforted eight-point turn. All the roads were blocked off blocks away from the main drag of Main Street. But more and more people were appearing and heading in its direction, I'd never seen the pavements so busy, all with garlands and balloons and flags, but with every turning towards Main Street closed, as I bombed along roads against tides of families and kids I began to panic as I knew I was missing the party and all the sales that went with it, but all the kerbsides were so chocker with parked cars there was nowhere to park up and serve.

Down a road lined with tall trees and fat houses I finally got close enough to see the main drag some 100 yards or so further away, where I could make out a cordon of people watching big, big floats, covered in glitter, trundle past to the catty sounds of distant brass bands and the *womph-womph* of music beats, and I got a strange twinge of excitement, but again rope and cones blocked the way. A man in shades and baseball cap came over and confirmed I wasn't getting any closer, so I U-turned and began bombing back up the road, 'slow down!' shouted one man. Eventually, eventually, I found a place to park, netted a quick $60 in business, but most people were heading straight past me for the parade. I gave up and decided to just go watch the show.

And it was incredible.

The procession of vehicles, acts, floats, all sorts, went as far as could be seen up and down the road, hundreds of yards each way, with the crowds five people thick lining the road. Everybody in the town was either in the parade or watching it.

Fire trucks festooned with waving fire men rolled past, great butch blokes in T-shirts and braces and getting admiring comments from women of all ages. Then there was a marching band, teenagers in elaborate gaudy outfits and epaulettes, towering hats with colourful plumes, and all wearing white gloves, somehow playing the music while marching in time and formation while boiling away in their satin uniforms. Fuck, just marching in formation was hard enough,

141

I remembered from the cadets. And they must have been *sweltering*, who does this? Who joins parade-ground suffragettes anyway?

Then there was an assortment of old cars from the 1940s and 1950s, all in good nick, painted in bright pinks and blues, the convertibles with busty women sitting up high on the back seat in racy old-time outfits. Then there was a massive 4x4 with bunting on the bonnet and red-white-and-blue ribbons on the wing-mirrors and a sign, 'Everson Motors Sponsors the Fourth of July', or some such endorsement.

Then a Cadillac convertible with a woman dressed as the Statue of Liberty perched on the back seat, then a quadrant of horses with cowboy-looking men on their backs, holding flags, then some children in little electric jeeps with tasseled cowboy hats, then a brass band on a big boxy float with a 10-foot polystyrene figurine of someone in 18th century dress on the back. A large group of large men on stupidly small mopeds appeared and drove around one another in figures-of-8. They were all wearing fezzes, were they part of some local Masonic lodge as I'd seen in an episode of *Happy Days*.

What was all this stuff? Anyone with wheels and a Stars and Stripes flag it seemed could join the parade, and the US flag was everywhere. Every surface, every car, every lawn, every person had a flag, or bunting, or something red white and blue with bunting, or tassels, or tasseled bunting, and so many people were red with sunburn. So many fat people as well.

It was a long, conveyor belt of stuff that meant everything to everyone watching and waving flags, a belt that kept stopping and starting. It was spectacular and obviously very good fun, all just like out of *Ferris Bueller*, just a bit smaller. But none of it meant much to me, and I wondered, Jesus Christ, is this culture round here? Then I thought, come on, don't sneer, just cos you don't get it. But if I moved here, would I have to buy into this? Is this what these people do for a good time?

Without selling owt I couldn't hang out for long, so I went back to the van, sold some Sour Towers and Choco Tacos and then headed on to Bartlett, which lacking a main drag, duly lacked a parade. But there were a lot of hot children in their front gardens, some rioting while others water-cannoned them with hoses, while families barbecued in others, and adults and youths trolled along the baking pavements, with impromptu vendors selling hot dogs, corn on the cob, burgers, watermelon, cold drinks – and me selling ice-cream! I did a very, very good few hours, business descended as did the Sun, then revived a shade as someone pointed me to the park where there were fireworks due at 8. I got as close as I could, within sight of two other ice-cream trucks but too far to identify them, with so much business from many people all over the pavements and open ground the enemy didn't matter. Some mother, while her kids scanned the blue stickers all open-mouthed, said, 'you know, I think the ice-cream man comes round so often and just sees us and his eyes just go "ker-*ching*", and he just can't help come back for more,' and she was kind of joking, but there was an edge to her voice, like it's my fault it gets so hot that people actually want the crap I have to sell. Yes, you've rumbled my evil plot where I force you to give your kids money to buy my crap, and yet that's exactly what you're doing! Stupid cow.

Next in the queue was a boy as round and sun-burnt red as his father, like tomato and son, I wondered if I touched either my finger would go *psshhhh!* as it burned against their skin.

The boy started with the 'I want … I want …', chant, before his father rabbit punched hard in the back, and spat: 'Get a fucking ice-cream, Mac!'

This outburst surprised me into a nervous laugh, while the boy was only partly distracted by his father's thwack. Poor bastard.

Sales carried on as the Sun went down, the rockets went up, and I was almost sad to leave this outdoor party that taken over the town, rockets blowing up all over the place all the way home, in fact the entire state, the country was out blowing itself up.

Back at Penguin, the hanger door was up and people were crowded out on the gravel. Charlie waved me to my parking place with some excitement, and as I got out Hank put a beer in my hand and said 'count up quick! Do you want a burger?', and I saw a massive BBQ set made of an oil drum split in half on which lay something like a mattress of burgers and sausages, hissing and spitting away.

I counted up over $480 – what a day's work! Then remembered a chunk of that would have to go to one side – yes it would, no no, not beer, not dope, I argued with myself.

All his family were there, Jenny, Dylan, Jess, the two other boys, and all the other drivers, Jeff, the girl I thought was pretty but wasn't, Christian was with Elly – and Val!

'Elly picked us up from the apartment,' she said, 'thought I'd come and introduce mesel' to Hank and see if he needed a driver, but I'm not sure I want to do it.'

'Did you do some of the round?'

'Yeah I picked her up this afternoon,' said Elly.

'I said 'ello to Hank anyway to ask if it were OK to stay in his apartment and he said "yer".'

I went over to Ben and Jason.

'You had a good one?' I said.

'Yeah – bloody good money,' said Ben, 'though some random leaned out the window, so I stopped, and he just shouted, "you limey bastard!" and slammed the window.'

'I had a guy come out his house the other day, shouting at me, but I couldn't hear him because of the jingle,' said Jason, 'so I turned it off and said "what?" and he said, "I said TURN THAT SHIT OFF."'

I saw Charlie wielding knocking back from his own bottle of Wild Turkey, while Hank's kids let off small rockets and roman candles in the middle of the gravel. Then Charlie muscled over with larger rockets, bringing the action

143

closer to the hanger until he was standing almost at the entrance, a rocket in a tube in one hand, and using his cigarette to light them, as he revolved around his *Turkey* bottle now nestled neatly in the gravel like a redundant launch tower. In the sharp hanger light his face was so seriously haggard and ragged, the skin heavily lined from years of searing sunlight, so many pock-marks and lines but obscured by his big whiskers that also shrouded his mouth and its missing teeth. But with his shirt hanging loose, unbuttoned all the way down and sleeves rolled up, he didn't have an ounce of fat on his tall, commanding frame, his well ripped body, all highlighted by sweat.

'Jesus, look at Charlie partying,' Ben said, "that's' finest moonshine corn liquor, boy! None of that goddamn hippy shit,"' he said in another terrible southern accent, flourished with a mock spit, '*Bt-ding!*'

As each rocket got bigger and so did the kickback, Charlie seemed to get drunker, reeling more with each launch. He lit a banger the size of a dynamite stick, stood holding onto it for a frightening couple of seconds, before lobbing it skyward, it blowing up a yard above his head. Hank appeared behind me and I said, 'Oh Hank, sorry we didn't say about Val, she only turned up last night, it is definitely OK if she stays a few days?'

'No problem with me, she seems nice.'

'Phew. Thanks, sorry again. Charlie's having, er, a good time.'

'That's how Nam Vets party.'

'God, so he is. Wow.'

'Yep. You seen *Platoon*?'

'Yes.'

'That was his life for four years. He's what Charlie Sheen would be in the real world. He joined up at 17, went straight to Nam and spent four years on the front-line keeping the tanks and jeeps going.'

Seventeen, so diddler der, that made him … bollocks. 'How old is he now?'

'Forty-two.'

My face must have said it all, as Hank added, 'yeah, he's, er, younger than he looks.'

Four years that must have taken him from being a wonderfully youthful genius mechanic from the sticks of Kentucky, into a battle-hardened, soul-destroyed drinker, sinking a gallon of spirits a week to stay sane. His face looked like a warzone of trench warfare, battered and chiseled and bombed by life and booze. Yet he had the six-pack of a fine, strong man.

I asked Hank about the mammoth, inter-state benders that Charlie sometimes disappeared on, that shut down the company until he could be brought back. 'He don't go on benders so much these days,' he said, 'There are only a few numbers on my mobile phone - here, home, and Charlie. He's good because if he's on his travels, he always phones to let me know where he is and if I need to come after him. If he's going to Kentucky that's easy, but sometimes he just goes off any old where. Sometimes I get him before he gets out of the

144

state before he turns around and we meet up on the way. Couple of times he's got the other side of Iowa before I either get to catch him up or he's turning for home. Once though he got to Arizona. Every time I'd get to where he was, he'd phone, "*Hank I'm in Wichita now*", or '*Hank I'm in Albuquerque*". Endless.'

'Brilliant! Did you pursue him on a Harley Davidson, Stars & Stripes bandana on your head?'

'Heck no. I take the campervan out the back. He lives like a free bird, trapped in the cage of his mind. But with autos he knows more than a tree full of owls, and he's family. So I keep him on.'

Charlie had gone into the hanger, then re-emerged onto the gravel with another arsenal of rockets wedged under one arm, massive things, warheads like ketchup bottles atop launch sticks like broom handles, using one hand to load the launch tube before kissing the fuse with his cigarette, his boozy state now inuring him to the ferocious backfire from the rockets as they screamed up and up and up into the sky before erupting into enormous chandeliers of fire. A cordon had emerged around him, except for Hank's two smallest who were too young to pick up on the danger until Hank yelled at them to come to him. Charlie let off a half-dozen rockets until Jenny told him he was riding his luck.

'Good for Jen, he'd listen to no-one else in this mood,' said Hank.

Jen thanked Charlie for his work and said she'd take over, he needed a break, upon which he staggered over to Elly and said he was really sorry, but he had to just say she had a body for which he'd pursue her all round the world, which led to a strange quiet, but he added, 'but I don't think I'm alone in thinkin' that, so for that reason lemme tell you got the best truck, no. 8 won't ever break down cos I don't want you stuck alone somewhere.' Luckily it hadn't gone all totally quiet like it normally does when someone says something totally embarrassing so everyone can hear, but Elly looked at him in a way that was ... kind, and said 'thank you' very quietly, and touched his hand, and he went awkward, like he was blushing, and staggered off, presumably to find something else to drink, or blow up.

'Strangely ... chivalrous,' said Ben to her, and she was about to say something when Jeff came over, all tanked up, and said, 'this is the day we celebrate our Independence from you Goddamn limey bastards and your Goddamn asshole King,' which got a big 'oo hooo!' from us, as he continued, standing there swaying with a bottle, 'no representation, no taxation, and this country's thrived ever since,' saying 'thrived' in a thick redneck accent, and getting a 'YEAH!' from the Yanks, just as Charlie reappeared defiantly with another rocket, 'but you shitty li'l brainwashed Brits and your shitty teeth, wouldn't understand!' said Jeff, obviously trying to wind us up but in fact doing more to wind Charlie up.

'Wouldn't understand shit!' said Charlie, flapping his hand in pain from the shower of sparks as the rocket that had just *phhssshed* into the sky, as Jen came over and said 'God damn, put that hand under water, have a rest will you?'

'We *let* you go independent, cos you all stunk,' replied Christian.

'All you bloody colonists, running away from your non-problems in Britain, come over here and fuck it all up, and we said, "all right, enough already, these people are hicks, they always were. Fuck 'em!" And still we trashed the place as we left,' I said.

'This country's a fucking disaster. Look at Canada, lovely, as rich as here, nowhere near as violent. Why? Cos the Queen's in charge!' said Mike.

'Yeah, what the fuck is it with you lot and your Queen? No seriously, what the fuck?' said Jeff, 'and don't forget we bailed you in two world wars! Weren't for us you'd all be speaking German!'

To which Elly lashed back, 'Not as if you lot bloody understand English!' to cheers from us.

'Yeah! And if we did speak German at least, we'd speak it properly and understand the fuck we're saying to one another!' said Christian.

'Yeah!' went the Brits.

'Wad?' said Ben.

'Wad?' said I, and Elly, and Jason, and soon the whole place was going 'Wad? Wad? Wad wad wad?' like a horde of angry ducks.

'And on that, that all kicked off in '39, you lot didn't bother showing up 'til 41 when all the real fighting had been done!' Ben said. Jeff was laughing.

'Yeah Jeff, tell us, why is the White House white?' I said, to which all he could just about say, was 'aww, man!' but he was in fits.

Then Elly asked me, 'why is the White House white?'

'Cos we burned it down in 1812.'

And Jason asked, 'Did we? Cool! What did we do that for?'

'For a laugh.'

To which they both laughed, so I said, 'see, it's still funny even now,' and they laughed some more.

146

Kangaroo car

The Sun was out again, like it thought we couldn't get enough of it. I wasn't particularly fucked the morning after Independence Day, Hank had said it'd be a slow start for all so we could come in a couple of hours late. I showered, found a T-shirt that didn't completely stink, and made it into the living room where the others were milling around, Val on the sofa, having a smoke.

'What you going to do today, Val?' said Ben.

'Eee ... Look for work.'

Elly did a trumpet tune like something off a Hovis ad.

'Eck ee thump, life's tough in Illinois after t'mine closed,' I said.

She scowled amusement. 'Well first I've gorra get me CV copied and stuff, but ...'

'Anyway it's nice to have you around, Val!' said Ben.

'Ee, thanks!'

We got in the Pontiac, its vinyl seats already searingly hot. Steve swore as he started it up, 'I'm getting sick of this car. We're supposed to be swapping the car for the A-Team van this week, but Addy's being a dick.'

'Which one's Addy?'

'He's the Yorkshire guy, the older one. Looks like Brian Glover.'

'Oh, yes, I think I know. His mate looks like Himmler.'

'Yes!'

'They're both like, what, 30?'

'Yeah.'

'Bit old to do this shit surely?'

'Money's money.'

'But they're students?'

'Yeah.'

Mature students are weird.

We cruised to the depot. I started checking and loading, failed to ignore the silent signals and strokes between Christian and Elly, got my stock, float, water bottle and guns loaded, fags, map and coins on the dash, then started for West Chicago where I hit Maple Street, same earlier time now, with neither a sound nor sign of Eskimo. At a few junctions I'd stop and turn off my jingle to listen out for Esky-fucker, but there was nothing.

But there was little business, either. This was all bafflingly unprofitable, until suddenly I spied this blue blob limping round a corner, a quarter mile ahead. Nuts! Counter punch from Eskimo! Cutting right, maybe I could finish the remaining roads before he did, but in the end there was only twenty dollars to be had. Our vans converged on a junction, and we scowled at one another. He was fat, folds of fat, and ugly, balding with a pelmet of black hair around his head, he couldn't have been that old but a life of shit food had made him a pig.

For all the scowling though neither of us reached for a baseball bat or even seemed to mouth anything at one another.

This was silly. What was I doing in this stupid country, stupid job, battling over kids' dimes and nickels with cardiac cases like him? He probably had kids to feed, or give pocket money to, who'd spend it on other ice-cream men, for which he'd beat them, and his wife.

Aw fuck this. Eventually he turned in one direction and I went another, finding myself soon enough at the weird wooden store, where I bought Coke, a cheap cigar and had another flick through *Shaved Snizz*, funnily enough the guy behind the till handed it to me before I asked. After that I went and did around Joly's way and lo and behold he was there, on the green, with his *Peanuts* gang, and I pulled up and we had a really nice chat in this shaded enclave of sanity.

A few bucks on the Mexican estates and then some, then cruised back to the hanger around 8, everyone there already, but quieter as they recovered still from the night before. Christian and Elly were having some close chat between themselves, so I grabbed a beer and counted up.

'I made a good few off the Mexicans today, they really bloody love their ice-cream. Turn up and they all flock to the van!' Jason said.

'Eez ze ice-creamo hombre! Caramba!' said Ben,

'Yeah I was sorry to see them all come out all orderly and queue up, I thought they'd be piling around in sombreros on horseback.'

'Firing pistols into the air! One of those whatsit bands with trumpets hailing your arrival!'

'I need a white suit, like the man from Del Monte'.

'Were there young girls with maracas and things leaning over the balcony of some bordello?' I said.

'I can't believe I'm hearing this, even as a joke,' said Jeff, looked painfully amused, 'I mean these are stereotypes bordering on racist.' We were taken aback for about a second and then laughed some more, firing imaginary pistols in the air again while bucking off our chairs.

'Everything you ever learned about Mexico you learned from *the Three Amigos*,' said Jeff.

'Well yeah, how we supposed to learn otherwise' said Ben, mockingly, so I backed him up, 'Yeah Jeff. Shuddup!' then turned to my float and beer before glancing back at him, 'cunt'. Roar of laughter, even from him. Then I saw Greg at the end of the table, looking a bit pissed off.

'What's up?' I asked.

'I got a ticket for speeding,' he said.

'Shit!'

'Hank covered half the ticket though, which was great. little bastard kids all over the van though, one of them I nearly picked up by the throat,' and he mimed picking up a boy and pinning him against the van, his other hand cocked back like he was about punch this kid in the head.

Elly looked shocked, and he saw her.

'I widna actually do that, I just felt like it. Ach, yer silly girl.'

She raised an eyebrow at him and took a drag on her cig. He looked bashful, then like he was pleased. Pleased at being told off by Elly?

After counting up at the hanger my takings were about $60, and we adjourned to a diner, where Christian suggested some big bar he'd heard about. Elly was quiet in the car though, and I asked what was wrong.

'I really don't like the idea of Adrian meeting that girl,' she said.

'Really? Could it be that bad?' I said.

'He's just ... there's something so freaky about him.'

'Oh God,' I said.

'We have to stop him,' she said.

'But how? What are we supposed to do? Surely it won't be that bad,' Ben said, 'but he is a fucking freak.'

Elly stared out the window and an eerie silence fell. It could be that bad.

Back at the flat to change, Val shouted from the sofa as we walked in, 'Hey everyone! Get this - I've gorra job!'

'Class! Where?' I said.

'In a diner literally one fucking mile up the road, you know where the bar and the shop is, there's a shopping business courtyard thing beyond that?

'Is that where we've got bagels from?' said Elly.

'Oo I dunno, not seen a bagel shop.'

'Yes,' said Christian. How did he know?

'Anyway, there's a diner there. Good basic plus tips and they're giving us 10-hour shifts. Piss easy work. Just got to get me head around the fucking menu. Oh and the servings are huge 'cos they're all fucking fat bastards, the manager were like "no offence but you're quite small, the meals are heavy." Oh he was patronizing, but he seemed all right.'

'Wicked! When do you start?'

'Tomorrow!'

'Fucking Hell, that was all very quick.'

'No slackin' with me, Jimbobs. No fucking money, either. So it's waitressing or going on the game.'

'I'd be up for that,' said Christian.

'Fuck off Christian, no amount of money, nothing on this planet, would *ever* make us fuck you.' To which he had no reply.

'That's you told,' I said.

'And it's walking distance. So long as I don't get run over crossing the highway.'

Christian rolled up a fat one in which we all indulged to celebrate Val's amazing news, then Mike and Jason came down, and the spliff passed around. Christian said he was OK to drive, and it was better that he did as he knew where we were going but couldn't explain it.

We loaded ourselves into the Ponty and Christian stuck on a dance tape, but as he unparked he managed to stall the car.

'You definitely good to drive, Christian?' I asked.

'Yeah, yeah!' he laughed, and gunned it so the Ponty's front reared up, possibly with a little too much bravado, but we were soon bombing along jollily, until we turned towards the railway crossing, where the red lights and bells were already going off, but Christian gunned it and we crossed, just, just evading the descending barriers.

'That was a bit close, Christian,' exclaimed Ben, but we were already at the box junction, with the traffic lights now turning against us as well. It all combined to overload Christian, who didn't know whether to stop or floor it, so somehow he went for both options and fucked it all up, kangarooing our automatic car right across the junction, to a chorus of 'woooahhs' and 'what the fuck', and 'shit!' from us all. The wall of cars that should have been crossing our path and smashing into us luckily held back and patiently watched this rusted fuckwagon slap across like a fish out of water – patiently, bar one car, which just as we reached the other side swung out behind us, stuck on its red and blue lights and said loudly, 'WeeeoOOOOooo'.

We pulled over. Christian stared ahead as it sank in for all of us, shit, it's the police, now we're fucked. Two cars slowly drove past, one with a child in the back, mouth agape at the trouble we were now in with the squad car parked behind us.

'Yep, here comes plod, no, shit there's two of them,' said Mike, tail-gunning from the boot.

Torchlight started jiggling onto both wing mirrors and then onto the steering wheel and dash, with the sound of boots clumping coming towards us in stereo with an officer either side.

I moved to open my window, but a voice shouted, 'keep your hands where I can see 'em! Put 'em on the dash!'

The cop next to Christian leaned down, torch full on Christian's face, and asked with a hint of amusement: 'Pardon me sir, could you explain that feat of driving we just witnessed?'

'I'm extremely sorry officer, extremely, my foot slipped on the accelerator.' Christian sounded surprisingly sober.

'Your what? Licence please.'

'And yours!' the cop on my side said to me, briskly.

Mine? I wondered, but said, 'it's in my left pocket,' I said, reaching down, knowing a false move could have me shot.

'What is *this*?' said Christian's cop, as did mine with more bite as we presented our grey cardboard AA licences.

'It's an international driving licence.'

'You guys are British? Uhuh. Is that how you drive back there in that Britain?' said Christian's cop. Mine leafed through my slightly sodden licence, 'confirm your name', which I did, then he gave it back, and said, 'OK Jim, get out the car. '

'I wasn't even driving.'

'But you may be intoxicated,' he said, which I didn't see was relevant. Was he going to shoot me and claim I'd tried to run off? I got out anyway and followed him to the middle of the road, which didn't seem the best place to do anything.

'Now stand straight. Put your feet together, stand straight, like on parade.' Which I did.

'Hold one arm fully stretched out to one side like this, close your eyes, and try to touch your nose.'

'My nose?'

'Your nose. ... *Keep your arm straight bend at the elbow!*' This would have been quite fun if he hadn't been such a dick.

'Now say the alphabet.'

'ABCDEFGHIJKLMNOPQRSTWXYZ.'

'XY – wat?'

'Z.'

'Zed? What'd you say?'

'Zed! Oh, sorry, Zee. We say Zed.'

'Now say it backwards.'

Ummm... 'Dez. Eez.'

'Wat?'

'Oh I see, shit, um, Zee.. YXW..VUTS ... RQP O .. no! mm. no that's right. O M *N*M LKJI ... H GFED C .. B ... A.'

'You had to think about that, huh?'

'Yes?!' like that's unreasonable.

'Now I want you to walk the line.'

'Do what?'

'Walk down this centre line, putting one foot in front of the other, right up. Heel to toe.'

'This is difficult anyway.'

'Just do it.'

As I walked down two stretches of white centre line, I saw Christian sat half out the car, torchlight in his face as his cop bollocked him.

'OK Jim ... you passed the test, you can get back in the car now,' while the other one said something to Christian, who put his hand up and swivelled his feet into the foot well. Were we being let go? No.

'I can smell dope in the back of that car. You got dope in there? Everybody out.'

'No there's no dope in the car, officer,' said Ben, to which the cop replied, 'I'm not talking to you.' Everyone got out.

'You all line up on the verge,' said one, while the other leaned in and poked the car about.

'I can certainly smell dope. I ain't gonna do ya, I just want you to admit you've been smoking dope.'

'We haven't smoked dope in here, we've got no dope,' said Ben, in exasperation, as it was true.

'Maybe. But it smells of it, you been smoking it somewhere. Just admit it.'

Ben looked utterly pissed off, was this just a power trip or a trap?

'I'm not going to arrest you, I just want you to admit you've been smoking dope.' He was focussed on Ben.

'I promise I'm not going to arrest you. Just admit you've had a little weed.'

Poor Ben.

'All right. Yes. I've had some this evening,' beads of sweat rolling down Ben's face, more out of anger than fear.

'There you go. I knew it and don't conceal stuff from me. That's all I wanted to know. See I ask you something and you tell me the truth, and that's how it is. Because I knew already. So don't you try and lie.'

Ben's face was as calm as it could be, but by God he was furious.

And then the cop handed back Christian's licence, and we were sent on our way with a warning to be careful and stay clean and don't come around here messing up again, as he wouldn't go so easy next time.

For the rest of the drive, only a few minutes, the atmosphere in the car was charged, and didn't improve at the bar, which was really a big field with some big tents attached to a large tatty shed, with lots of plastic picnic chairs and tables with puddles of beer on them. Somebody got some rounds in while we put two tables together, but thereafter we didn't do much apart from pick over the incident, and seethe.

'That cop. That fucking power tripping cop,' said Ben.

'Yeah why was he having a go at you? If we smell of it, we all do,' said Jason.

'Fuck me ... *fuck* me ... what a cunt,' Ben replied, revving up, looking like he was going to smash the plastic pint in his hand.

Christian and Elly at the end of the table, Christian bent over, looking cartoonishly sorry for himself, like he had a right to feel that way, while Elly ... seemed to be commiserating with him, her body language was all conciliatory, which made me sick with incredulousness, that bastard nearly got us all killed *and* busted – could she at least have a go at him?

'So how's your day been otherwise, Jim?' asked Mike, dryly, which made me laugh, but I couldn't answer beyond that. I was too angry to focus on anything.

'Sorry man, bit frazzled.'

'Yeah. Don't worry about it.'

After a round we decided the evening was bust and we went back to the apartments, Elly driving, but I was feeling increasingly dazed with anger. As I went to the fridge to get a beer, Christian appeared, and I just turned to him, stared at him, and said quite calmly, 'Christian ... don't ever do that again.'

'What?'

'That stoned driving. Don't ever do that again. Really. Fucking Hell.'

He looked surprised. 'You're serious.'

'Oh yeah.'

The others were all over the sofa trying to watch TV, but there was a buzz of ill-temper, Ben still exclaiming, 'why did that cunt have a go at me?' until he said, 'fuck this, I'm going to bed.'

I tried to watch what was on, but couldn't, and turned to Christian and said 'you nearly fucking killed us.'

'Sorry. It wasn't a good one.'

'Don't ever fucking do that again.'

He didn't reply but looked sullen.

A couple of minutes later I said it again, and he said quietly, 'I know, I know, I'm sorry,' but I was too stoned with anger to care. Then he got up and said sheepishly, 'right ... um... it's been a bit of an evening ... I'll see you tomorrow.'

On some kind of auto-pilot I followed him to his bedroom and shouted from the doorway, 'you nearly fucking killed us, and got us fucking busted, Jesus fucking Christ!'.

He was already on the bed and writhed on his pillows, 'all right, all right, I'm sorry, I fucked up, sorry!'

'Fuck-ing Hell!' I said and steamed back into the living room, where Val had now appeared from work and Elly was filling her in.

'An exciting evening I hear, Jimbo?' said Val, biting her lip.

'Yeah. So Elly, did you have a go at Christian about it?' I spat at her, who looked at me wide-eyed in fear.

'I didn't, I didn't say anything.' she said.

'Yeah I know. That fucking told him. Good work.' She didn't reply but looked miserable, then left for the bedroom with Christian, leaving me to tell Val the story and calm down. Which, countless cans and some hours later, I did.

Domestic abuse

At the hanger next morning, I was told I was no longer on van 13, but today would have van no. 9 and probably tomorrow, with 13 going to one of the new guys. Charlie told me 9 was a better van and more reliable, so I said could I have it every day, but he was non-committal. This was strange. Why give me a shit-heap if there's something half decent to drive, so you won't have to come pick me up all the fucking time? But whoever the lucky sod was to get 13 he was welcome to it.

So I thought on the drive down, quite sober this morning, had a shower but my clothes stunk out my clean smell. I did the Maple streets. I didn't see Eskimo around. But no-one was buying much today. It was overcast and muggy, and they all just stayed where they were, doing whatever they were doing. At a Mexican estate a couple of kids came over and stared and muttered, but only one wanted a Snowcone, and the youthful ones made weird finger signs and gesticulations. Then I did both sides of the tracks, up Joly's way.

His house was on a road that had a sharp incline into a large basin, maybe a dried up lake, around which were a dozen houses shaded by heavily laden trees, lush with leaves. All the cool air in the area rolled into the basin and stayed, and it was in this large grassy pool that Joly and his friends were playing baseball like they always did, in this oasis of normal.

I parked up and served ice-creams, then one of the kids asked for a free one, and I said no, but this kid kept hassling, until Joly said 'no leave him alone, he can't give us all free ice-cream all the time.'

What a dude.

Joly had enough innocence for a ten-year-old, and chatting to him and his mates was mentally and physically refreshing, being able to talk to children without feeling the need to stop myself screaming at them.

Joly didn't seem mean and didn't talk about mean stuff, and if I did seem a little cooked from driving an oven all day, distracted by thoughts of my mate's stuffing this Goddess, just that he asked made me feel better without having to burden him with inappropriate details. And when I did ask to join in the game of ball, a suggestion of Christian's to win over children on the routes, they'd been delighted, instead of growling to one another that the ice-cream man was trying too hard to be cool.

Although I was shit at baseball. Today's game went like all the others, I'd vengefully swing a bat over or under the ball that would sail past me into the trees. STRIKE! one of the boys shouted, three times in a row.

'You don't hit so good, ice-cream man,' one said.

'You're darn' tootin'. Why don't you play cricket?' I replied.

'Wad?'

'It's a Briddish game,' Joly said.

Certainly is, young feller me lad. And a fine game at that.

I thanked them for the game then got on my way to streets I didn't normally hit, then passing some identical house on some identical estate, stood a woman who flagged me down for what I thought was ice-cream. She was quite old, forties, a bit overweight and fat in the face, but she was nice and when she heard my accent she asked where I was from and I said Britain and she said that was interesting, and we got talking, and then she said: 'What's your star sign?'

And I thought this was odd but I said 'Cancer.'

And she said 'Cancer! Isn't that interesting ... see we're in sales of supplies, office supplies. It's good business. Would you want to come and work for us?'

Eh? 'A job?'

'Yeah. We had another guy, from Canada, like you, just came here, with nothing I might say, and we gave him a job, and he's doing well, really well if I say so. One of our star performers. And I think you could look very nice and presentable, and be charming, and do very well.'

What the fuck? 'Where, here? In Chicago?'

'In Chicago, in Milwaukee, all the towns not just the cities.'

'Selling what, sorry?' I was too surprised and baffled, but she forgave that.

'Office supplies. We give the catalogues and the products and a car, and you go do, presentations and all. I think you'd be good. You don't need to worry about the paperwork for visas and stuff, we can sort that.'

'I can't say yes now!'

'Wouldn't want you to, go think about it.'

What the Hell, offers of jobs falling out the sky on me? I didn't know what to say, but it threw me for the rest of the afternoon. Me? Sales? Office supplies? Why me? Could someone just turn up and do it? Was I that person? If she thought so, why not? I didn't have anything else going for me, either.

But would it win Elly? Would it make her swoon? Sales, money, in Chicago! And think of the nice suits you'd get, all the light wooded bars you could go to, loads of fit women in them, the cool apartment like you'd dreamed. Make a success of it, make loads of money, then she might love you.

But I'd be away for months, years. She'd go out with someone else. I might come back with shitloads of money and find she's gone.

The Sun arced through the sky, whatever jingle was on blurred out of my mind, the van ground the kerbs, kids here and there jumped around while others belted indoors. The afternoon passed.

I turned into a cul-de-sac, the road looping round a single tree, and it was oddly depressing. A woman holding a young child to her chest came out and flagged me down. I said hello and asked what they wanted and she replied quickly she wanted this and that, but the way she spoke was, kind of meek, and then I flinched as I noticed she had a massive blue swelling over one eye. She'd hit something hard, or been hit hard.

I first thought oh God I hope my flinch wasn't obvious, but it was obvious because as soon as she'd said her order, she looked sad and turned her face away.

With false jolly-dee I zipped back into the freezer, and handed over the ice-creams, exchanging notes and change, and I was light in voice and stuff, but it was all total cack, and avoiding her gaze, which probably made her feel worse. She said thank you and went back in to a well-kempt house but with some peeling paint, the yard tidy, if a little overgrown. Maybe the overcast weather, the sky like a big dirty duvet keeping the humidity in, made it all so much sadder than it was, and with no-one else around, all so much lonelier. I felt so, so sorry for her as I drove away, wondering what I could have said or should have said, before realising I'm just an ice-cream man. What the fuck was I supposed to say or do?

My peeled upon my back with sweat chilled with the breeze. I couldn't think about anything except that poor woman the rest of the day.

Slewing back across the crunchy gravel at the hanger, Charlie waving me in with torches in the dimming light, I saw Hank standing outside talking with Greg, who had his hands up to his head, then he threw them down, turned this way and that, then chopping his hands up and down while Hank stood, hands on hips, and shook his head.

Greg didn't look happy.

I cashed up over beers, chatted with the others, then Mike came over.

'Oh yeah, let me fill you in before monkey boy comes back, last night was Weird Adrian's date night with that girl off his round.'

Elly flinched, which Mike picked up on, and said, 'no, no, it wasn't that bad –'

'Did she stand him up?' I asked, then said, 'wait, what did you call him?'

'Weird Adrian. Cos he is. As opposed to other Adrian who's nice but a bit rubbish. Anyway she didn't stand him up. We all went bowling at the mall and they came with us, well we met her there, in fact it was my idea to have her come there, right, because he was getting arsey about demanding the van to take her out, "oiiiii I need it as a passion wagon", yeah right, fuck off, whereas we all wanted to go bowling, so I said "look, just bring her along, bowl with us or talk to her at the bar or whatever the fuck, then after drop us off and you can drive her home," which he kind of went along with, but for me this also means we could keep an eye on the freak, right, sort of arms' length chaperone.'

'Right,' Ben said, and I nodded to Elly and made a face to say 'good thinking', and she nodded back, as Mike went on:

'So she came, he mum dropped her off, and she was a really nice girl in fact, more grown up than you'd think for only being 16, I mean obviously fuck knows what she saw in Adrian, what with him being weird and all, but she happily joined in the bowling, chatted with everyone, nice lass! And pretty. Weird Adrian though – ha! Right, get this, totally overcome with shyness, he sits there the whole night, barely said a word to anyone, right, but least of all her, can't even look at her, just looking, scared,' and he did an impression of someone sitting in the corner, shoulders hunched, eyes rattling down at the floor.

'Rubbish lad, for all his talk. She was nice, deserved better than him. Anybody does. Anyway she had a nice enough time, and then we all took her home.'

'Is he going to see her again?'

'Don't think so. He said something afterwards about like them "not getting on so well", but it's just bollocks. I said, "how do you not get on with someone you don't even talk to?" and he just shuttup. He was shitting himself the whole evening. Actually anyway I said to her, really not to bother with him, and that he was weird, and she just made this face and said, "yeah". She was onto him.'

'Nice one Mike!' Ben said. Elly smiled in relief.

'Yeah, cool,' he guzzled the rest of his beer, 'Oiiiiiiiiiii!' then let out this appalling belch.

Whereupon Weird Adrian monkey-boy walked in and everyone started laughing.

'Oiiiiiii, what's so funny?' he said.

It was then that Greg came in, red-faced and sweaty went to a far table, hauled a chair out too hard and set it skidding into the hanger wall, then he sat down, back to us, head bent down into his hands.

'It's all over for Greg,' said Christian.

'Really? No shit, why?'

'Crashed a van today. With the speeding ticket and that call about driving, I mean, no. Hank said 'enough already'.

'Shit.'

Greg looked blown out. Ben handed him a beer, as he sat, one hand massaging his temple, occasionally tutting aloud or banging the table. We gingerly got him to the car and went home, then Dooley's, where he seemed a bit chirpier.

'Hey Greg, you not on the vans anymore?' I asked innocently.

'Ah no, (he really said 'ach, noo'),one of my decorator friends called, got some work lined up for the next couple of weeks so I thought "shit, steady money, better than Hank's, why not"'.

'Ah OK. Fair enough.'

'Yeah...' he looked at his beer then back at me with a glance like he wasn't sure about something.

'What?' he said with a suspicious chuckle.

'Nothing.'

'What?'

'Nothing!' I was trying not to laugh.

He moved swiftly at me with his arm up like he was going to thump us – in jest, I think, but I squealed anyway as he growled 'What's so fuckin' funny ye wee cunt ah'll fuck yers –'

'Did you crash the van?'

'Ah ...' and he held himself back – just – and his stare softened, and he started laughing. 'That too, aye. And the wee kids, there little shits, Jesus I coulda' throttled them.'

'You pissed off about it?'

'Nahh. I got this other work, but I'm driving fast to earn him money, that's why I got the ticket and all, but he has a go at us?'

'He did pay some of that though, you said,' I felt a bit edgy saying that.

'Aye! He did! And...' he snapped, eyes wide in rage and I thought oh shit he's going to do something, then he suddenly looked away, 'Ah fuck, I got a ticket, then crashed it anyway and some other shite, you're right, I fucked it up.'

'I know, I feel terrible really. Sorry man, didn't mean to have a go.'

'S'all right.'

'Nah, I fucked it. Hank's actually all right, I'd've fucking fired me too, probably.'

'Hired. Fired. Easy come, easy go. I'll get another pitcher and fill you up.'

'Thanks mate, gez a bez.'

Later, Elly asided to me, 'Is he staying in the flat?'

'Well yeah.'

'No, I mean permanently.'

'I think so.'

'Ah OK,' she trilled, and turned away.

No no no no, please please please no.

We went back, spliffed, then I drifted to bed, to the sound of fucking.

Jobs

Surfacing out of my stink, I watched the Weather Channel which predicted rain later that day. Then, near leaving time, Val invited me outside for a smoke. It was humid as Hell outside.

'I've been having a good chat with Elly these last couple of days,' she said, 'she's really been a bit lonely, she said she's not had really anyone to talk to.'

I was quite hurt by that, but tried not to show it although I said, 'She could talk to me?'

'Not really Jimbobs, she was tellin' us about her and Christian, I don't think she would want to tell you about that,' not that she needed to, I thought, I practically smelt the whole fucking show.

Zz - hole-fucking show - ZZ

'She said the first night they didn't use a condom as they got just so carried away.'

I took a drag on my cig. Again I wanted to leave but there was no way of leaving without looking like I wanted to fuck off.

'She said it's cleaner than most she's had, and not quite as purple.' Val looked at me, waiting for my response to learning this about Christian's tackle. I couldn't even think, 'for Fuck's sake'.

'Val ... I don't care. I don't want to know. Too much fucking detail.' *zz - too much fucking detail indeed! - zz*

'All right Jim, don't bite me head off, just making conversation!'

Yes, quite. *ZZ – meanwhile Elly won't bite his head so much as suck it - zz* . FUCK off.

Bombed up and bombed off to Westie.

I hit the streets, the sales started.

But now thanks to Val, everything with purple on it reminded me of those two. And there was a lot in the freezer with purple on it, column shaped things people stuck in their mouths and sucked on.

That was the backdrop to the day. The jingle throbbing my head, the kids with their 'I want ... I want ...' and, 'wad? Wad? Wad?' and reminders of him cumming in her, both ends.

I think I saw a couple of other ice-cream vans, but far away, following routes that wouldn't overlap mine for a couple of hours at least. Then mid-afternoon it began to fucking chuck it down, binned it almighty, time and again there were these epic flashes, and booms of thunder that made me cow in the cabin as I drove along, the door closed against the spray off the road. Again and again, God took another crack at the heavens with his lightning hammer and the black horizon would fleetingly shatter into a thousand brilliant cracks.

The Sun did come out, late in the day, and I toured Bartlett for so-so takings. I thought I saw another white van, but only a glimpse, and I scraped a little over $170 all day.

159

A diner, then the flat, where I was trying to watch TV while Elly was talking to Val about something and she suddenly exclaimed 'it's like jizz!'

Oh God why are you talking like him?

Christian asided to Ben, 'she loves cock. Especially oral.'

Then I got a boner which had to be dealt with. There were two bathrooms in the apartment, one in the big bedroom Elly and I had slept in, now with Elly and Christian fucking in it, and the other on the corridor.

I needed a dump as well so out of habit headed for the bathroom of what was once my bedroom, but it was engaged – they're in there, fucking! Then I remembered they were in the living room. But the slobs had strewn the clothing all over the bed and floor, all discarded with such hasty lust, amid which I saw a pair of Elly's knickers.

Knickers she'd sniped at me not to 'have a sniff of, pervert' or something. What a shitty thing to say.

So to spite her, I did. They were a white pair, and had been worn but weren't dirty, I held them to my nose and niffed.

They smelt ... interesting.

I smelt again. There was a light, light pungent mix of something sweet and something salty, sweat but not acrid. It smelt lush. Whether it was the smell or the naughtiness of it all, and it was her idea, my boner was raging. I had to smash one out.

With the corridor bathroom free, and everyone watching TV or doing stuff in the kitchen, there was enough background noise to cover a quick bishop throttle. The toilet seat didn't waddle, the lid didn't batter back against the cistern, the floor was tiled, not wooden, so there shouldn't be any creaking or reverberations into another room, the sound of slapping wasn't that loud, although if you get carried away you become oblivious to the noise you make.

All was going well, until suddenly the door opened and I caught half the face of Greg around the door, and I said 'oi!', and he said 'oh, ah, oops! Sorry,' and back out he went, then there was a muffled snigger. Fuck. Had he actually seen me, what I was doing? I was frozen, cock going limp in my hand.

The mood gone, I cleaned up and adjourned to the living room, Greg looked up at me and said 'sorry man, didn't mean to barge in',

'I thought I'd locked the door, shit, no problem,' as if all was well. Had I just been shitting he'd have looked the fool, but smashing one out put me on the back foot. Still, as the minutes passed with no further mention, I realised I'd got away with it.

'Fuck this!' Christian suddenly shouted, 'let's go to Dooley's.' It was busy, with a few from the other flat there. We got chatting to this bloke at the bar, in his 40s maybe, in a pretty tired looking suit, who when he found out we were British doing this ice-cream job said in this loud camp way, 'Wow! You guys are great! You guys are terrific!' his bright white teeth gleaming away. He actually seemed like a nice guy in some dead end sales job, but we didn't get any beer off him.

Then there was this chap from England, sounded cockney almost, done up in smart-casual, like a professional football hooligan, and he was with a woman, blonde, very nice eyes, slim, pretty really, but her skin was pocked like she'd had terrible acne. A shame. But he was saying, almost tenderly, 'ain't she beautiful? I could look at her all day,' and she had a smile of sorts on her. Then suddenly the background music turned up in volume, and half of the bar cleared to reveal a dance floor that I'd not clocked before, this music came on and 20 people hit the floor, blokes in Stetsons – for line dancing! Brilliant! It was hilarious, round after round, punctuating each turn with a clap and a step here, forward, back, sideways, twirl, clap, something like that, one half of the bar had been cleared of all tables and chairs and there were five lines of five people, manoeuvring away all in sync, it was great. I was the only one dancing for a while the others crowded around one of the high tables, but I didn't care, then Val joined me, then Elly, oh it was such fun, sweat pouring down us.

Then I went to reload on beer, asked Mike if he was dancing and he said if it wasn't big-box little-box he wasn't interested, but then suddenly I saw the woman with the pockmarked face at the bar, and she whirled around, her face twisted with anger, or sadness, she was shouting something at that cockney bloke whose hands were up as if to calm her down, his expression one of, what, sorry? Then she burst into tears, covered her face and shoved through everyone to the door, and he followed, shouting her name.

I couldn't work it out.

So I carried on dancing.

Then we went home.

And then they fucked.

Who's been in my van?

Next morning everyone was ready when I walked into the living room, and they stopped talking.

'Hey wanker,' said Elly, and laughed.

'Yep, busted!' said Christian. Val's mouth was agape in mock shock. Greg was there looking embarrassed, but he wasn't at all, and started laughing.

'Now, now, nothing wrong with a hand shandy,' said Christian.

'We say having a chug,' said Greg.

'Polishing the bishop,' said Ben.

I absolutely could not get myself in the mood for this, not even smile ironically.

'Ah, come on, man, I'm sorry, it was funny,' said Greg.

'Leave the boy alone,' said Christian in his best patronizing way.

I lit up, then Val said, 'I'm on a late this evening, so come by the diner and meet the guys I told you about, then drive us home.'

'What you doing work wise, Greg?'

'Oh I called my mate yesterday, painting work already, starting tomorrow. Still stay here though if that's all right?'

'No problem!' said Christian. Now there were six of us in the apartment.

Due to the wanker shit, I sulked all the way to Penguin, where Charlie told me 'You're back in truck number 13.'

Aw fuck.

'I like truck number 9. It's nippier,' I said, not a rusting ball of shit.

'Nope. You only had 9 while that young man trained on 13, but he's changing route.'

But I'm no longer training, but didn't bother to question it and went to No. 13 where I noticed Elly's van parked alongside, and she walked came over, staggered really, and started rolling herself against my van, then said with lusty exhaustion, 'I am knackered.'

I so, so, so did not want to know. 'I'm ... a bit busy.' I said, expecting her to say 'you're just jealous!' but she just looked a bit sad, and walked off to her own van.

Zz – sauntered off legs wide like a cowboy, his jizz flowing down her legs – zz.

I refrained from punching anything and calmly opened the door and got in. 'This is my van, this is where I work. This is my domain. All is calm,' I told myself. Then I opened the freezer and glared in horror. Whoever the fuck had used this van the day before must have dropped a basket of grenades into it, it was a fucking tip. Not even close to the mess I'd cleared up, it was like someone had carried out an airstrike, the entire freezer strewn with the corpses of slain ice-creams blasted out of their homes, crushed under ripped cardboard.

'Who did this?' I said, quietly.

'Who did this?' I said again, louder.

162

'Who the fuck did this?' I said, louder still, and started saying it again and again as I jumped out the van, shouting, 'WHO THE FUCK HAS BEEN IN MY VAN? WHO – FUCKED – MY – FREEZER?'

I stormed past other vans bombing up, and stood facing the queues to the freezer room and the dry ice, shouted again, everybody looked at me, but nobody answered. Dylan stuck his head through the freezer room window and said 'what's going on? What are you – '

'SHUDDUP!' and he flinched back inside.

'SOME CUNT FUCKED MY FREEZER - WHO WAS IT?' Again, no reply.

'SHIT!' I said.

I steamed back to the van and tried to take a stock check, but it was a joke, then Elly appeared and was trying to help sort it but I told her to get out.

'WHO'S BEEN IN HERE, THE FUCKING PLO? WHO DOES THIS?!' I shouted, 'WHO THE FUCK FUCKED MY VAN?', then there was this almighty bang, the van rocked, and I saw Aidan in his van through the back window backing away then turn to go, 'SHURRUP, COCKSHUCKER!' he yelled and floored it before I could board him and give him some, spraying my legs with gravel, stinging like Hell.

'FUCK OFF!'

'You OK Jim?' Hank had appeared. I was about to go off on one but he stood there, a paw towards me to signal, 'mellow ...' and I just sat in the seat. Nearly cried. Hank said, 'sorry about the freezer, that was the new guy, Adrian, I'll have a word with him. You take care of yourself.' And off he plodded.

Hours passed. I did a Mexican estate and got some intel to come back in a few hours when a party would be on. So I went off to do Maple Street and all, for pretty pissy takings, then set course for another Mexican estate. The flat, featureless Illinois landscape means with a very small gain in height you can see a fair distance, and as I approached a critical flyover, I saw the blue blob of Eskimo farting along towards the same destination. Had he just done beaten me all around Maple? Mother fucker. Ah, fuck him, I thought, he's probably driving to hospital with another heart attack.

I went cruising around Joly's, and was sure I heard a jingle in the distance. Then from a high point I fleetingly saw a white van far, far away, and again heard a jingle come and go. In wondered who the fuck that was, but didn't find out. I stopped off for *Shaved Snizz* for Diet Coke, smokes, the tiller knowing I was never going to buy the magazine. As usual, it was a bad idea and I got a headache. Frustrated enough, the afternoon passed with as many kids telling me to go away as were buying, which was piss.

Ground through more streets and estates like strange fortified enclaves, with so many houses around so many little roads, but only ever one entry point and one exit point onto the arrow-straight highways.

Late in the afternoon I turned into something of an island of a couple dozen houses looped around a road, all backed by scrubland and unhappy trees, in the middle of nowhere. But I'd been here before and made a quick $10 with nice kids.

Children were making noise somewhere but no sign of them, until a girl, 10 or so, ran down a sloping driveway. She didn't look familiar, as I pulled over instead of the usual 'I want, I want,' crap she quickly said, 'I'd like a Lemon Calippo please!'

Great! 'Good choice,' I said, burrowing into the freezer, 'that's a dollar please'.

She proffered the single dollar note in her hand, and I went to take it, but she snapped it back.

'Ha! No! Give me the Calippo first!' she said.

'No. Money first, then ice-cream.'

'Ice-cream then money,' she said.

I smiled at her from side on, said calmly, firmly, 'no, money first. It's not cos of you, but it's money first.'

She offered the note, which I reached for, then again she snapped it back, 'hahahaha!' and she skipped around.

Aw fuck. 'Umm, do you want the ice-cream or not, because if not, I'll go.'

'OK, OK, I'm sorry,' she said, offered the note ... then snapped it back.

'Right that's it, I'm going.'

'Oh please ice-cream man!'

'Money first.'

She offered again, pulled it back, then said curtly, 'I want my ice-cream'.

'It's not yours til you pay for it,' I said, then, 'look, forget it, I'm going,' and pressed the accelerator to go, but she hopped in front of the van and stood arms out, face all of mocking.

'What are you doing?'

'Give me the ice-cream!'

'We've done this already, get out of the road.'

'I ordered an ice-cream where is it?' The Calippo was on the dash, but I said, 'We're done, I'm said already, get out the road please.'

'I want my ice-cream!' she grabbed the wing mirror and swung around to my door.

'Let go of the van please.'

'Not until I get my ice-cream!'

'No. I gave you a chance, you messed about, and now I'm going. No ice-cream. Let go of the van, OK? I'm going.'

'Give me my ice-cream!' she said.

'I said no! Now, just go away, now? OK? Now.'

But she was still holding the mirror so I couldn't drive off in case she fell or went under the van, or just pretended to do so, so someone else would come and have a go.

She had this smirk, 'ahahaha, I've got the ice-cream man's attention now!'

I was getting jacked up in a fucking stand-off with a 10-year old over a fucking buck. I lost it, threw the Calippo out over her head onto the pavement, 'there's your ice-cream, go get it, get out of here,' figuring she'd go get it and I'd be gone.

Oho, no! Like that, her face flipped from smirk to rage. Like a cobra she vaulted up onto the footplate, leaned into the cabin, shouting right in my face, 'You apologise to me! You apologise right now!' this fucking 10-year-old, such anger, such arrogance.

'Get out of my van,' I said, taken aback.

'No I will not, you and apologise to me now or I'll get my father out here, ice-cream man!' she said, rigidly tall, eyes wide, eyebrows arched right up, jabbing her finger at me.

'Right now. ice-cream man!'

'Get out of my van,' I repeated.

'You apologise now!'

She was actually scary, and fearing she'd freak out if her dad didn't, I found myself saying, 'all right I'm sorry. You got me mad. Now can you step off the van, please.'

She did step down, but said with this creepy mom like voice, 'I don't like your attitude,' her arms folded.

'I'm going to go now,' I said, and began a gentle U-turn in the road, slow in case she jumped back at me, then I pootled a few yards further, saw her turn to go back to her house, whereupon I stopped, leaned out and yelled, 'hey!' She turned. I pointed at her, twirled the finger at my forehead, mouthed, 'you're fucking mental' at her. Then she started running towards me, brow down, staring right at me, face set with concentrated rage. Oh my God it was like *Terminator II*! I floored it, didn't quite squeal the tyres to get away, but suddenly the van felt so heavy, as if running on sand in a bad dream, anyway I hacked out without stopping onto the main road, her still in pursuit, so I flipped a finger and bombed off, seeing her still running after me in the wing mirror.

About a mile away I pulled over to calm down, have a smoke, then got the map out and drew black lines through that estate. A quick $10 wasn't worth that nasty piece of work.

I told the others about it back at the hanger, 'I was just waiting for her steel hook arms to smash into the van.' Then how angry I felt, had had to pull over. 'Couldn't believe I apologised.'

'You shouldn't have, you should have called her bluff and got her dad out,' said Christian.

165

'Yeah, I just wanted out,' and was about to add, 'who do you think he'd believe?' but he cut in:

'Never apologise.'

'OK, it got her off the van, then I told her to fuck off and left.'

'Never apologise.'

I was about to say 'do you want to fuck off?', and glanced at Ben who shook his head lightly in sympathy, then the gangly, boggle-eyed Adrian appeared, 'hi everyone!'

'Hi Adrian' someone replied, or groaned.

Then he said 'hello Elly' in this pathetic silky voice, to which she politely sighed, 'hello Adrian'. Mike took a deep, slow drag off his fag and tried not to laugh. Oh God, has he got a crush on her?

'Sorry about the mess in your van, Jim,' he said.

Oh! Nice of him to apologise.

'It's all right. Was a mess though.'

Cunt.

We cashed up and pissed off, inviting Mike to get stoned at ours.

'Well if I must!'

Round he came, and round the spliff went.

'So, Elly, how you can resist young Adrian's charms?' Ben said.

'Fuck off man!', she laughed.

'"Young Adrian"', said Mike. 'Ha! We call him "crap Adrian". You see when he came in, 'hi everyone', no response, he's like Cliff Claven. Well they do, but it's more someone'll mutter "aw, fuck."'

'I'm sure Jason said that today,' Ben said, 'I was amazed Adrian didn't pick up on it.'

'No but he wouldn't, that's the problem, he's totally immersed in his own rubbish little world,' said Mike, 'Honestly the guys in the flat think he's a complete joke.'

'It's kind of sad, really,' Elly said.

'No, no it's not, because he just doesn't get it. If he was in any way affected by it, yeah, it'd be sad, but he's not. This is why he can come in every day "hi everyone!", oblivious to the tumbleweed blowing past, or when he says "Hi Elly" like he's Leslie Phillips peddling a bottle of Black Tower, and practically the whole depot's cringing. Doesn't stop him in the slightest.'

'Awww,' said Elly , 'he's not that bad.'

'No, he's not bad, we don't hate him, he's just crap. At first I felt sorry for him, well not sorry really but you know he stands out a bit, he's kind of, you know, "young",' he continued.

'Yeah,' said Ben, and started sniggering.

'And you want to be friendly with everyone first off, so we had a couple of chats over beers, although he doesn't drink, but –'

'What, he never drinks?' said Elly.

'No. I think he did once in his life, and threw up or something, I'm not even sure that happened, he probably said it to impress us, anyway we don't care, and I've tried chatting with him and ... there's nothing there. It's just rubbish – thanks mate', he said, taking the spliff off Christian, taking a great drag before sending it along. 'He's just the most gormless bastard. Like just the other day, he came back eyes all agog and excited, about how some bloke had shouted at him because he'd been driving too fast down a road, and then suddenly he saw kids wanting ice-cream so he jams on the brakes but loses control, freezer shifted on him,' at which I spluttered, 'then he clatters onto the pavement, nearly took out these kids, avoided them by way of going onto this guy's lawn, and it's been raining so the van gouges the lawn to shit, throwing up grass and mud all over, he even showed us the van later with the mud still streaked up the sides, Charlie was like "what did you do, motherfucker?", and he's telling us as if he still couldn't understand why this guy was pissed off with him for nearly killing his kids and destroying his lawn, like he's the victim. Shit like that all the time.'

'OK, he is crap,' said Ben. Everyone went quiet for a moment, then we were all absolutely pissing ourselves.

Downhill

I was hauled out of bed, found clothes, found coffee, found fags, found myself in the car park with Ben and the other flat going into the van.

'Where's Christian, where's Elly?'

'They had to go somewhere,' said Ben.

The chaps bantered away in the van, but my head was clouded and I felt something was awry. At the hanger I bombed up, bounded across the gravel for the highway behind Aidan and Jeff. We perched up at the highway, ready for take off. I beeped and yelled, 'move asshole!', to which Aidan shouted fuck off. Then Jeff pumped his fist up out the door, and vaulted his van right, followed swiftly by Aidan.

I rolled forward, a few cars went past and a lorry like some ICBM, a gap appeared, so I staggered the van over to the central reservation, just fast enough to avoid getting wiped out this side but not so fast I couldn't stop in the middle. Then I saw an on-coming car was a big brown station wagon. I peered and saw it was the Pontiac, then clocked Elly and Christian in the front seats. Christian saw me and waved, Elly's mouth wide open in apparent joy, I guessed at having been seriously fucked over the last hour.

I felt sick, and as they slew out of sight up the lane to the hanger, distracted with anger I nearly floored it out in front of a lorry hammering along, its deep horn blasting right in my ear, the van shaking from the lorry's shock wave. A voice in me said 'for fuck's sake Jim, don't get killed,' but bloody Hell.

What a load of shit this all was. Where was my life going? Fuck, why was I born middle-class? All that meant was I had expectations to fulfill, needing a stressful high-paid job that needed brainpower and concentration to get the clothes, the car, the house and all the trimmings. Fuck all that. All I wanted was to loll about, have a laugh and get totaled. But nope, I was part of someone else's grand vision, and here I was failing spectacularly and being taunted by my 'friends'.

Elly was the girl who could disengage your mind from all reality. Her allure was insane. She had that power. I'd envisaged myself chained up next to her bed as a sex slave, there wasn't one part of her body I wasn't prepared to worship and lick for sustenance for all eternity. I could live off her fumes, sitting next to her was like a meal in itself, breathing in her aroma, her breath, just a whiff would catapult my mind onto this radiant plane of tranquility and beauty. Like hearing something like Stravinsky's Firebird for the first time, and realizing such beauty could exist, and you're amazed and exultant, because the world's actually more incredible than you ever knew.

Every time I smelled her.

One kiss from her could hydrate me to march across a desert.

So I thought as again I had to brake so sharply the freezer hit my seat again, then sharp braking on a corner caused me to fishtail, the freezer sending me right again, although all this woke me up for the day ahead.

I crossed the first junction of Maple Avenue, saying in Jimmy Savile style, 'now then, now then, wu-wu-wu-wu, next up pop-pickers, is *Can you tie a yellow ribbon*. Wu-wu-wu-wu!' I glanced to my left and saw Eskimo coming the other way two junctions down. The bastard had cleaned up already. Sexual frustration boiled over as I baked alive in my metal box, then this infliction of financial pain from Eskimo, and I thought, 'after all I've done to stay ahead, you go and do that. Well *fuck* you. No. Not today, you don't get me, not today. You disgusting fuck.' I saw one of those silver-arched phone boxes, and went over and dialled 911, and in my best American accent I said, 'Hello, police please, I've just seen an ice-cream man drahving like a maniac,' and then thought tone it down, this is Chicago, not New Orleans, then told the dispatcher it was a light blue ice-cream truck, with Eskimo written on the side, the driver was obese and wore glasses, and I'd seen 'him headin' for the Juan Pablos estate but he was takin' corners on two wheels, my Gahd afficah, my Gahd, he'll kill us ahll!'

She thanked me for the call, and I applauded my good citizenry, then went and drove after Eskimo, and passed him a few minutes later pulled over with a white, chrome and gold cruiser parked behind him, talking to an equally fat officer, Eskimo's dimpled underarm fat jiggling in the sunlight as he squawked his innocence. I sped past (within the law) and took over $35 at the next estate, meanwhile telling anyone who understood I'd just seen Eskimo under arrest, and the kids should stay away from him.

Only later I realized I'd not only cost him those takings and slandered him, but if he'd been fined that would have wiped out his day's earnings at least. 'Ice-cream war is Hell,' I thought, then, 'I love it when a plan comes together.'

Good old No. 13 delivered Karma by breaking down yet a-fucking-gain, somewhere between the water park, the *Shaved Snizz* shop, and a closed high school. The fucking van stopped then wouldn't start. I managed to push it a couple of times almost to start, but putting it in 'drive' just juddered it to a halt.

It was dead as a doornail.

Two tubby youths were plodding along the sidewalk, one with a baseball bat, the other had a glove, suggesting they were going to play ball and not rob me of my pissy $50.

'Hey you two, come here,' I said.

They plodded over.

'Help us push start this thing, and I'll give you free ice-cream.'

'That's a good deal, mister.'

They pushed and shoved, and heaved the van down a shallow hill, to no avail.

'OK, try again,' as they plodded up. They readied themselves and, being on the flat, I helped push from the driver's door. With some effort, we got the van up to brisk walking speed in neutral, until I hopped in and wracked it into gear. The engine crunched and the van juddered uncomfortably to a standstill.

Still no dice.

Then one of the kids said, 'mister, this is an automatic. You can't push start an automatic.'

I was hot and hot tempered.

'Course you fucking can. What's the difference? Come on, push!', thinking, don't lecture me on mechanics, fatso, I'm twice your age.

'Won't work, mister.'

'Just push!'

And they did. With them at the back, I put the van into neutral, jumped out, yelled at them to push while I heaved against the door frame, got some momentum, then I jumped in, jammed it into first gear, and it jolted to a halt, again.

'Ain't workin', mister.'

'Let's try it again!'

They shrugged and tried again, and again, a bit of bickering, until all sweaty and puffed out we gave up.

'Can we have our ice-creams?'

'What for? Is the van going yet? No. So no ice-creams.'

'You said push the van, nothin' about getting it started. Didn't work cos it's an automatic. Ain't our fault.'

Damn these legal minded kids. Fuck them for being right. I gave them ice-creams.

'I'd say it was the battery that's dead.'

'All right. Do you know where I can get some jump leads?'

They looked at one another, then, 'wad?

'You know, jump leads, to charge the van.'

'Wad?'

'Jump leads!'

With a little shake of his head, one said, 'don't know them, mister.'

'They go from one battery to another. This battery's fucked, right, so you get another battery, and attach them together with jump leads.'

'Wad? Err ... Oh! Oh! Battery cables!' cried one.

'Yes! Battery cables, them's the fuckers!'

'Ice-cream man, you swear *real* bad.'

'How come you can understand that?'

One of the boys then said 'I think my pop's got some, I'll go get him.' And off he went. About 15 minutes later a pick-up truck pulled up, out got the boy and his dad, who was also fat, but his forearms were solid, with man's strength, not pissy boy strength, and he had a big drooping moustache and a baseball cap.

'Hi man, my son says your battery's dead.'

'Hi. Um, yes, I think so, can you charge it up?'

'I can try,' he said. 'Heard you tried pushing it,' and he chuckled.

'Yeah ... fixing engines ain't my thing,' I said. Well fuck it, it wasn't.

He nosed his truck to mine, opened the hood and then attacked these stonking great black and red cables from his battery to that on my van. After a few minutes and a couple of tries of the engine, it started and kept going, and he told me to keep the engine running for a while. I offered them both two ice-creams each and they accepted, then with a friendly wave off they went. Nice people, nice thing to do, and it saved the afternoon which earned me another $80.

Back at the hanger someone was getting excited about a kid who climbed onto his van and wouldn't get off. I caught Ben's gaze and we agreed that neither of us was impressed. In the Pontiac he said, 'Ha, newbies, letting the kids clamber into the vans, all so excited when they meet their competition for the first time. We've been talking about this stuff for weeks.'

'Yeah, these new boys, they know nothing,' said Christian.

'We're battle hardened veterans, nothing left to surprise us.'

'Veterans, yeah!'

'Yeah!

Veterans!

Val was already back at the flat. As I sat on the sofa to read, she came over and told me, 'Fucking Hell, right, I came back to the flat this morning cos I forgot summink on the way to work, found those two crawling all over one another. "Oh, hi Val". Yeah right, don't mind me.'

Please don't tell me this.

'She's a screamer, Jim, Jesus you could hear her from the bloody corridor.'

Shuttup Val. Shuttup. Just shuttup.

In the saddle

It was a day off, and the plan was to go to a horse track.

'I'm not going,' said Elly, 'horse racing is cruel.'

'I'd have thought you'd love it,' said Christian. 'You spend a lot of time in the saddle,' then he said to the room, 'she loves a ride in the morning,' and smirked. She didn't.

Mike came in with Aidan and Jason, 'come on cockshuckers!' he said, followed by two stout dudes, Glen and Dave as he introduced them. We all got up to go, except Elly, and Christian.

Aidan told us Addy had the van so we'd need the Pontiac, then we were down in the car-park where some others waited.

'We all going to fit in?' I said as we piled into the Pontiac.

'Suppose so,' said Ben, 'yeah, two in the boot, it'll work,' but added, 'we've got to sort this van situation, it's getting silly. Christian said we were supposed to get the van two days ago, and now he says Addy's avoiding him. I don't think I like Addy,' he asided to me.

Outside was overcast, and horribly muggy. Sweat patches appeared in the armpits, chests and backs of our T-shirts in no time. But the race track would have to be a huge expanse of lush green grass with a massive ring of white railings, a grand stadium rammed with people dressed in their finest, trilbies for the men and fine hats for the ladies, all clutching tight their racing papers, betting slips and opera glasses as the *thrub-thrub-thrub* of the horses' hooves loudened and loudened on the final straight, the voice of the commentator over the Tannoy accelerating and rising with excitement as the horses loomed larger and louder as they jostled towards the finish line, the ridiculous list of odd names, Grease Paint, Purple Turkey, Flannigan's Folly, Red Lorry Yellow Lorry battering off his tongue until the race in the last 200 yards was clearly down to just two horses with silly names, *two horses with two silly names*, it's TWO HORSES WITH SILLY NAMES, TWO HORSES WITH SILLY NAMES, the crowd roaring louder, the ground vibrating from hammering hooves, clods of soil hoofing up, 'AND THEN THE VOICE CLIMAXES AS ONE HORSE NOSES AHEAD AND IT'S ONE HORSE WITH A SILLY NAME! ONE horse with a silly name,' the voice slacks off and slows and the jockeys and the horses the roar of the crowd turns into a mass 'phew' of spent excitement, and the jockeys slow the horses to a canter, then a trot, sweat pouring off them, like everything seen in *Champions*, or *National Velvet*, with young Elizabeth Taylor, in her jodhpurs and boots, riding hat, close cut blazer.

Then I realised she looked just like Elly, and I thought of her hopping off a horse onto the ground, patting the horse's neck, entering the stables and leading the horse into a stall, taking off her hat, when a stable hand suddenly appears from behind and comes up right close and grabs her, and she's caught unawares but knows who it is, leers to herself as she turns into his embrace and they fall into the straw and he pulls down her jodhpurs and she's ...

'Jim. Are you all right?'

'What?'

Ben, next to me in the car, was looking at me oddly.

'You had a strange expression on your face.'

'Oh.'

We pulled into the race course car park. The next race line-up was announced over the Tannoy, but the overcast sky had annulled my sunshine blasted image. The stadium was dirty whitewashed structure with flaking concrete walls. The grass was brown scrubland, troughed with rainwater. The punters wore T-shirts, jeans, baseball caps. Still, the jockeys had such wonderful colours, white, royal blues in bold chevrons, bright green and pinks spots, red and yellow checks, in this satin fabric, but ... it was all a bit shit.

For my first bet, my horse led up to the line, then lost by a nose. As my horse came back, the jockey caked with clods of the sandy clay, I said aloud 'dog meat'. I think he heard and I suddenly felt really guilty. No other punt got closed. Fucking Hell. Story of my life. I thought of Elly and the other girls I'd somehow missed out on.

On the highway on the way back the Pontiac broke down. Ben sat smiling at the wheel while Glen, quite a fat fellah who looked like he liked chips and beer and not much else of interest, and the others poked about under the bonnet, Glen getting a shock, I shouldn't have laughed. He said something about a filter being fucked, and pointed to this fist-sized thing that jiggled and made a gurgly electric noise. The mugginess and the heat off the engine, the frustration got sweat pouring down our T-shirts and everyone got snappy, before the Sun came out and we got that acrid smell of drying tarmac.

They fixed the car and we carried on. Back at the apartment, Elly and Christian were looking strangely refreshed and smiley, then Val came in with some crap from the local shop. I suggested we go into Chicago proper, go up the Sears Tower, but it was decided to kill the rest of the afternoon at the mall, to spend money I had, but couldn't spend if I wanted to get the fuck out of here.

We couldn't park closer than 80 yards from the Death Star of consumerist shit and got soaked by rain. Inside, Val and Elly wanted their own girly shopping trip as they had girly things to talk about – I couldn't *guess* what – so that left us Christian, Ben and I to hit some bagel place.

He bit into a bagel, melted butter oozed out of the hole, and he laid a conversational gambit, starting with a stalking horse of matters of sex, then tacked with the breeze to his real port of call.

'So, has anyone received their brown wings yet?'

What?

'Buggered a girl,' Christian explained seemingly for my sole benefit, not that Ben knew either. I said no, and he magnanimously admitted that he didn't have his either. Then he paused, pursed his lips and looked to me conspiratorially for a second. The bastard! Guess what he and Elly would do next. Son of a bitch!

Eventually we all met up again I suggested seeing *Apollo 13* at the flicks,

173

but no-one wanted to go, rather Christian didn't want to go so Elly didn't want to go and the other two were 'easy' so none of us went. We found an arcade and ended up playing air hockey, before deciding just to get pissed at home. By now it was getting dark, and we stopped off for Christian and Ben to get beer from this massive supermarket while we three sat in the car. They came out with a box of beer each, and as I started the engine Christian shoved his box through my open window.

'Oi! Wanker!' I shouted.

'Fuck you!' he drawled, pretending to be pissed, and then instead of getting in the back, he went and lay across the bonnet of the car.

'You wanna piece of me, asshole?!' I yelled, jolting the car forward.

'Yeah!' he shouted through the windscreen.

I flicked the accelerator and we lurched a foot forward.

'Oh yeah?' I shouted.

'Yeah!' he shouted back.

I put my foot down and the car reared and roared across the empty car park. I started to throw the wheel left and right, making his raised feet billow left and right.

'God, be careful!' said Elly, but Christian was laughing, and I realised he could be thrown off and go under the wheel, but I was so stewed with heat and anger at him I thought, 'yeah, good'.

I had his life in my hands. If I slammed on the brakes he'd fly off and I could run him over. I clenched my teeth, I could actually kill him, and I wanted to, and I could, and that made me feel ... powerful. A voice in my head said 'just do the cunt.'

But before I could do anything else, suddenly headlights flared from a parked car 50 yards off the left, and then lights flashed on its roof, it hovered rapidly towards us and the dreaded *wyooOOOooo* of a police car siren wooed.

'Oh for fuck's sake,' said Ben, as I hissed 'shit', adrenaline drowning it. We were in trouble. Christian glanced toward the cop car, then at me with this pained expression, before he slumped his forehead against the windscreen as I gently slowed us to a halt.

'They've been sitting there, in the dark, all this time?' said Elly. 'For what? For us?'

The window already down, I put my hands on the wheel, licence in one hand, as Christian peeled himself off the bonnet as the cops pulled into our path and got out, brandishing torches.

One came over, 'keep your hands on the wheel,' he said aloud as he came to my window. They're there already! Despite it being dark, he still had his shades on, and stood with hands on hips.

'Licence' he said, curtly, and I gave him it. 'What the? You call this a licence?'

'It's an international driving licence,' I said.

'It's a piece of crap,' he replied, then shone his torch into the back of the car.

'Explain what you were doing,' he said sharply.

'I was riding on the bo – I was riding on the hood, officer,' said Christian, with some obsequiousness.

'That is idiotic behaviour.'

'Idiotic is apt, officer,' said Christian.

'Wad did you say?'

'Idiotic is apt, officer.'

'Idiotic is wad? *Ap*? Wad?'

O shit. They don't know what apt means. But we couldn't explain it without it looking like they were idiots. Which they were.

Shit. Oh double shit. I'm going to laugh.

Do not laugh. Do not even look like you're trying not to laugh, or you will be totally done.

'Yes … apt,' said Christian, his tone on a tightrope between sarcasm and exasperation, me unable to speak as stifled mirth quivered through me. I felt for Christian, having to deal with this, knowing if he fell, we were all fucked.

'Apt? What is this shit word?'

'It means appropriate,' said Ben, adding in his poshest Brit voice, 'it's a very British word, it's very appropriate to call us idiots. Because we are.'

'Yes, you are!' said the cop, pleased to escape that jam as well.

'Everyone out!' his mate said. We got out, they lined us up to pat us down, shone their torches in the boot, the foot wells, the glove compartment, under the seats.

'Any open beer or liquor in here?'

'No officer.'

'Better not be.'

Ben looked weary.

'You been drinking?' he asked me.

'I haven't.'

He checked the boxes of beer, they were unopened.

'Well I don't know if we can do you for stupidity,' said one cop.

'We're genuinely sorry officer, just high jinks,' I said.

'High wad? You high?'

I groaned within.

Then his radio came on, he spoke into it, turned to us and said: 'You kids, you go home, you go to bed, you hear? And don't let me catch you here again.'

And off they sped.

Back at the flat Elly went for a shower, Christian went off to the shop for something, I opened some beers, Ben put on some music, then rolled one up. Meanwhile Val asided to me that Elly had said her and Christian weren't so hot at the mo, they were still doing it – *oh really no shit you think?* - but he seemed to be being distant.

Why was she telling me this? To see what I could tell her about Christian, and she'd feed it feed back to Elly, I realised. Fucking wankers.

I suspected they'd been getting 'closer', but Christian had only just before the summer finished with his girlfriend of years, so he wasn't going to be into anything heavy, but Elly was probably getting heavy, and he just couldn't be bothered.

Fuck that. She'd had a go at me enough times for being 'heavy', though we were never together.

I told Val he was probably still getting over his ex.

'Has he not said owt to you about it?' she asked.

Definitely fishing for info. Cow.

'We've not talked about it at all, really.'

The beer and the spliff seeped into my mind and I remembered what Christian was on about at the bagel place. He'd try it anyway and if she thought it'd keep them together she'd definitely go for it.

It was a bastard, sweaty night, and there was some strange huffing from their room. Her oohs were not the rapid ughs of scarcely satiated pleasure, but shorter, higher, almost eeks or gulps, with long intervals between. He took some time to cum and only he came.

Next morning though she bore this languid air of knackerdom, little blue sachets of all-night-lust under her eyes, with her triumphant 'I've been fucking, I've been fucked,' smile was the same as ever.

176

Near miss

The Weather Channel said it'd be hot, hotter than the day before, illustrating its dire prediction with psychedelic colours.

Val joined me at the Pontiac for a quick smoke, the car park, with its black tarmac and great grid of white lines, was like some massive grill, cars as steaks, us as sizzling gristle.

Then Val started, 'Me and Elly were talking the other day and we think you should go back home.'

'Why?'

'Cos you're not enjoying it.'

'What? Yes I am.'

'Are you sure? Cos you don't seem to be.'

'It's all fine. I'm pulling it back.'

'Well we don't think so.'

'Why do you think this?'

'Cos you're not getting in to everything, you're not your usual vibrant self so much, like you are at uni. I reckon it's cos of Elly being with Christian and shit, but a few times you seem to be set back, not getting on with others. Quiet, like you hate it.'

'It's not great all the time, but I'm having a laugh. What do you want me to do?'

Yeah I was bloody pissed off about Christian and Elly, what the fuck am I supposed to do about it? They fuck on the bed next to mine, then sneak about and take the piss, and then when I am pissed off they talk about it amongst themselves and decide it's me who should leave. Thanks, guys. Feel free to go fuck yourselves. *ZZ – fuck each other, more like – oh look, they already did - zz.*

At work I asked Charlie to have a proper look at the Pontiac, but having bombed up and fucked off, I stoked up about what Val'd said, I couldn't even mind my own business without someone having a fucking go at us.

And so was set the tone of the morning, shitty thoughts about here and home, heavy smoking, road rage. Go home in failure, like everything ever, or stay with fuckheads. Fuck this for a game of cards.

About halfway through the round, I was cruising along a wide, quiet street, one side with houses, the other a broad stretch of grass. There was a road junction about 50 yards away, each corner a large pocket of grass and trees, then the road stretched away, dipping and rising into the midday shimmer with houses either side and tapering into heavy tree cover. I had the jingle on full blast, my focus went from the kerb to the junction, where cars were sailing over from left and right. Then glimpsing beyond the junction I saw something, a small blob of white, right in the middle of the road. This blob moved as it neared, a little head appearing atop a torso with little arms pumping. Oh holy fucking Hell it was some kid right down the middle of the road, right for me – except there was this fast road right between us that he'd hit first. I floored it for the lights, red against me, and I begged them to turn green, green, green.

This child, a big toddler, a boy, was running, weaving in the shimmer.

Green, green, green.

He was far closer to the junction than I was, and he hadn't slowed an iota.

Green, green, green, I was saying aloud, accelerating, cars still bounding right to left over the junction, and if any of them now turned into that road they'd likely run him down. I had to get there, even if I caused an accident that would stop the traffic, as I shouted, GREEN, GREEN, GREEN, stuck on the jingle full blast and hit the horn, while someone on the sidewalk said 'hey, slow down …'

On red-amber my van practically vaulted over the junction, with the child just a few yards away, now at risk of being run over by me. Oh God! I slammed on the brakes, the tyres screamed, the back fishtailed, which luckily stopped the freezer dislocating my back but sent it into the side of the van, jolting me sideways another foot. I swung out the door, ran and picked up this two-foot suicide buyer of ice-cream and hopped onto the pavement. Just then I saw a lady run into the street, looking this way and that, face twisted in panic, shouting a name, hands flailing. I shouted 'Oi!' at her, and she ran to us.

'Thank you, thank you!' she said, an east Asian lady, as I handed the boy over, who she hugged, chided, then carried back to the house.

Could have bought a bloody ice-cream love!

There were impressive black streaks snaking from the rear of the van, all skew-whiff across the road, so I parked up properly, lit up, and pondered that the boy might have died coming to see me, but I'd saved him. The latter won out and buoyed a day of shit trade. Even a late assault on Bartlett hauled piss all, some bloke saying another truck like mine had passed only 20 minutes before.

Back at the hanger, others were talking about the turning from onto the highway. 'I saw Bill nearly get wiped out yesterday,' said Jeff, 'he was ahead of me and must have looked the wrong way, pulled out and this semi was going full bore at him, horn blasting, and missed Bill by nothing, I was like "Oh my God no", covered my face, but then I saw he'd reappeared in the reservation. I thought he was wiped out.'

'First hazard of the day – get onto the highway without dying,' Ben said.

'That's a point, is the car OK?' I asked.

'Charlie fixed it,' said Christian.

The Pontiac was fixed and it was so warm we all stuck to the seats. At home Christian said, 'I'm going for a shower,' and down the corridor he went, followed a second later by Elly, at a trot. I distracted myself with a beer mission from the shop and the spaniel-faced tiller, getting back just in time to find them both red faced and filmed with damp. But I was inured and with enough spliff we had a fun evening of jokes.

Endless

Another day, another blurry start. Shat, showered, hand shandy, unstinking T-shirt, coffee and fags, and there'd be sunshine all day, said the telly.

'Well that's a fucking surprise,' said Ben, 'I don't know why we bother with this shit, might as well just leave the telly off and paint a fucking great sunshine on the screen, "there you go, assholes, today you're gonna fry".'

I spurted coffee down my light coloured T-shirt.

'Know what I mean though?' he said.

'Elly spurted last night,' Christian slithered.

In came Val.

'How's the diner?' I asked.

'It's all right, yer, yer, not bad at all. Some of the people are a bit dim, but not offensive. Gets pretty busy, but worse is when it's not and you're just standing around. The manager's not a dick as in comin' along expecting you to be doing shit if there's nothing to do, the tables are cleared and clean, coffee's loaded all that bollocking malarkey.'

'Customers nice?'

'I tell yers, there's some interesting people come in, a lot of stupid girls talking total shit and thinking they're it, but fuck them. There's a lad comes in called Bobby, he's got a mate as well, Sandy, anyway I've chatted with him a couple of times and he seems pretty canny, told him about yers all and I think he's like to meet up if you wanted to come along?'

'Sure!'

We drove to work, bombed up, hit the road, refuelled with gasoline and fags, and I began the drive north.

ZZ - Christian went south on Elly -zz.

The Sun was out and had full reign of the sky. At one point I pulled up and saw a plane 30,000 feet above, this little glint of its silver fuselage ploughing arrow-straight vapour trails spreading back for dozens of miles, gradually blurring, becoming jagged by the high winds, then fading. Watching this plane gave me a pang of homesickness, just as a young lad asked his order, then repeated it to my distraction.

'Wad?' I said in response.

'Sour Tower. Where you from, mister?'

'Britain.'

'When you going home?'

I looked up at the plane, now heading out of sight, and felt so sad. I didn't want to be here, but I didn't want to be there.

'Some time.'

It was getting hot, the jingles were thrubbing away at my mind, but the takings were trundling in, every street a handful of kids jumping up and down, hands high, or occasionally a group of workmen hoying off roofs or downing their shovels onto dunes of earth and running over to me.

I saw a couple of white vans, in the distance. The heat was such, so tiring, I wasn't really bothered about the competition, or anything much. It was just too damn hot, and even driving faster only got more hot air breezing into the van faster.

I couldn't stop thinking about those parakeets. How I'd thought they were tame, but in fact they couldn't fly away, they couldn't even glide to safety if they fell off that girl's finger, scrabbling for footing as she did the whole 'I want ... I want ...' shit. They'd just fall on their heads and die while she loaded up on sugar.

It was so depressing, why would anyone mutilate a bird like that, just so kids could maul them? What is the point of being alive in that way? You've clipped the damn things' wings, they have absolutely no reason to live. I was the girl looked after them as best she could, she wasn't intrinsically evil, but the very idea was warped.

Oh God.

Why don't these children value anything?

It was a long day driving around in this wheeled oven, and despite the heat, the takings were crappy.

A couple of beers cooled us at the hanger, then spirits revived we were off in the Pontiac, chatting and laughing as I drove, til the junction where we beat the train was only a mile ahead, when suddenly the throaty roar of the engine quietened, choked, then stopped. I put my foot down and for a second it revived, the nose lifting a tad, then died again for good.

'Fuck, the engine's died.'

I kept footing the accelerator but nothing.

'It's dead!'

'Better pull over,' said Ben.

'Yeah, sure,' but then, 'God, the steering's gone stiff.'

It was getting stiffer, and I was only edging towards the hard shoulder. The brake pedal had also depressed.

'The brakes have gone shit as well,' I said, confused and panicked, 'the fucking brake pedal, it's gone into the floor.'

Even with my foot hard on the brake pedal, this massive car's momentum propelled it scores of yards further, and with this part of the highway being so badly lit, we were lucky there was nothing to hit.

'Jesus, this car's a fucking missile. Why would it die like that?' I said.

'No gas,' said Christian.

'Yeah, but what about the steering and brakes? Something's totally fucked it.'

'Yeah – no gas. It's all power steering and brakes,' he said condescendingly, then he said, 'I put in a load only two days ago.'

'Gee, one of the dangers of a busted petrol gauge,' said Ben.

'I put in five gallons. There's no way we've burned through that.'

'Did Charlie drain the tank or something when he fixed it?' I said.

'Oh yeah. Shit. Must have. Then he didn't tell us,' said Christian.

'Fuck. That's a class move, pisshead,' said Ben, then squealed like an angry cat in response to his own anger.

Balls.

We found a petrol can in the boot and went and stood lined along the hard shoulder in the semi-dark, Ben waving the petrol can aloft as we shouted 'gas, gas' at passing cars, a couple of dozen cars lighting us up with their headlights then roaring past without blinking an indicator, except for one pick-up from which we got a single loud horn and a lot of laughs, our shouts of 'gas, gas' turning to 'fucking wankers!'.

The side of the road was such an alien landscape of concrete and scrub, everything tinged gold and brown from the road lights, the tarmac and earth all still warm from the day and we sweated sheets.

'Why aren't these cunts stopping?' I said.

'Not like we look dodgy or anything,' said Ben.

Then Elly said, 'give us the can, man, get in the car.' We all did. She stood out in the lane and only the second car to pass us pulled over 30 yards ahead, whereupon Elly banged on our car, I hopped out and we approached this VW Golf, or Rabbit, me a few yards behind her to stay out of sight. There was a long-haired young man behind the wheel who was smilingly chatting with her, then was less enthralled to see me, but kindly enough let us both get in, me smearing his car seat with sweat. He took us to a gas station a couple of miles away, and back, and we thanked him on his way with a spare can of beer.

Then we applauded Elly, which she accepted like a diva, the car choked into life, we filled up proper at the same gas station, then went and filled up with beer.

ZZ-Then Christian stuck his nozzle in Elly's tank and filled her up-ZZ.

181

The Devil's son

The colours on the Weather Channel map were trippy as, as it predicted Sun, Sun, Sun, and the mercury was rising, rising, rising.

'We'll be sweating a ton today,' said Ben.

'I've got no clean T-shirts,' I said.

'Sweat's good,' said Christian, and looked at Elly, who blushed.

Val trilled in. 'Actually I'm on a late tonight, so if you want come by the diner and meet the blokes I was telling you about, then drive us home, that'd be great.'

At the hanger Christian asked Charlie again if he could fix the petrol gauge, to which he said we should be all right if we watched how much we put in. So it was 'no', basically.

'We did that already. That's great, thanks for fucking nothing Charlie,' said Ben, 'especially as we fucking ran out of fuel last night cos he fucking drained the tank.'

'Trouble is this thing does about 5 mpg,' said Christian.

'On economy. Five fucking gallons per mile.'

We scattered to the far corners of our shitty bit of Illinois, the flat bit with empty land considered valuable for having nothing on it, a dead brown sea of needly grass surrounding prison islands of houses for white people, all lush green from stolen water, while the small Mexican estates were covered in tarmac, so they fried all day long.

The sunshine was searing, the heat rising, not a cloud in the sky nor a child on the lawn, except as mirages.

Until at last I saw a real one.

There on the little slither of grass stood a boy, eight or so, standing stock still, one arm outstretched with the fingers of the hand clawed upwards like he was about to catch something, presumably a flying ice-cream. But he didn't move or speak, he just stared at me. Was he retarded? Was he allowed out? I spoke *Sesame*: 'You awright?'

He didn't even blink. Was he devoid of manners or senses?

'Err, you wanna ice-cream?'

He nodded thin grey eyes seared at me from under his blond mop. He was creepy. Then his eyes flicked away to scan the selection list, tracking up and down, up and down.

'How much money you got?', I said, saving time by limiting his choices, but if it was just a piddly Snowcone I'd kill him. He ignored me though, still scanning up-down, up-down.

'Kid. How much money do you have?' Silence, scanning, but I saw his open hand was empty, as was his other hand.

'Do you actually have any money?' Those little dark grey slits stopped and flitted back to me. His face pinched. I'd found a fatal flaw in his plan.

'Do-you-have-any-money?'

He blinked, then, very slowly shook his head.

'No?'

Those grey slits narrowed.

'Then piss off', I said, and drove off. In my wing mirror I saw his face slowly turn to follow my departure, his body motionless, his hand still out, waiting for something to fall into his open mitt. Like fucking Damien. I had to speed off in case I got decapitated or suddenly felt the need to hang myself.

That was the highlight of the day and I felt sick and dizzy on getting back, which Christian said was dehydration, the treatment being beer, and by the third I felt normalish.

Elly was counting up, but looked forlorn. No, she looked stressed, like she had when Weird Adrian was in our flat.

I got more beers and gave her one.

'What's up?'

She spoke quietly, still counting. 'There's a bloke on my round, he's got a crush on me and he won't leave me alone.'

'What does he do?'

'He always comes out and comes up really close and talks and talks. I liked him at first, when he was just chatty, but he's asked me out a couple of times now and I say no, and he's getting kind of tiring, he has this look to him. I don't like it.'

'Why don't you just not serve him?'

'He always buys stuff.'

'But is it worth it?'

'It's a good part of the street, I've stopped stopping outside his house but he'll always come further down. And with other people around, I don't want to make a scene.'

'Aw. Shit.' I didn't know what to say, but felt a bit sick for her.

Everyone else was talking of low takings, very low takings. Then we overheard young Jess say 'aw man, what the Hell?', as Crap Adrian sat with him, ridiculously damp with sweat, delicately unpeeling wads of sodden notes.

'He saw these kids playing on a water hydrant,' said Mike.

'I've seen that!' said Elly.

'Cool, like *Sesame Street*!' said Ben, 'I saw at least two ambulances.'

'Yeah, I saw a few,' I said.

'Yeah ...' said Mike, 'anyway he sees these kids playing at the fire hydrant, fuck off great big arc of water going all over the road, and Adrian,' and he started laughing, 'and so he goes over to sell them some ice-cream,' and laughed some more, 'and like we all do, his doors are open and shit –'

I started laughing.

'And he somehow doesn't connect if you drive into the water it's going to go somewhere, so he drives right up at this hydrant, all this water starts blasting into the van,' now Elly and Ben were laughing, 'to which any normal person would drive off, or just close the fucking door, although any normal person wouldn't have driven into it in the first place, but this is him we're talking about, anyway, the water's blasting in soaking the whole van, right, so he panics,' and he started flapping his hands at an imaginary blast of water, 'like this'll stop the water cannon flooding out the van,' ... whereupon he couldn't talk any more. Jason laughed until he went silent, like he was unable to breathe.

'Meanwhile all these kids are jumping about pissed off cos ice-cream man's parked in their waterfall, and he's still soaked through despite it being a fucking oven out there, with this paper-mache blob of bank notes, so Hank's pissed off.'

'Could have been worse,' I said, "I saw all these kids playing next to a hydrant – so I ran 'em over!"'

The heat was still hideous as we drove to Val's diner, where she took us to a booth where sat two lads who she introduced, Bobby and Sandy. Bobby had these striking, deep blue eyes, and thin but dense black eyebrows. A grown man with a hairless chin, he had a granddad shirt and waistcoat, and one of those soft padded velvet hats you could get as a jester's hat, or a Cat-In-The-Hat top hat, his more like a crown ringed with shallow triangles. His mate Sandy was like Shaggy, with a longer beard and a Goth T-shirt. Amazingly, in front of Bobby on the table was a cell phone.

'He's got a cell phone,' Ben mouthed at me, I arched my eyebrows at him.

'So you're in the business of keeping our children distracted on sugar til they get fat and have to pay massive health premiums,' said Bobby.

'Nah. They're l'il bastards,' I said.

Bobby said he was working in software development but did a bit of hacking too, refusing to say what exactly, just 'political' places, and we got onto the government and Clinton, he said Gore was a far more effective and sounder guy, but Clinton won out through his sexily ruthless edge.

'I wouldn't say no to Bill,' said Elly.

'Hillary wasn't bad looking either,' Christian said.

'And Gore's behind building the Internet,' Bobby said.

'Oh yeah we've got email at uni,' I said.

'Email's not the same as the Internet.'

'Isn't it?' I didn't use either so didn't care.

'But you gotta watch out for it. The Pentagon first built the Internet to withstand a nuclear attack. Imagine the US as a series of military centres, right? Factories and bases all across the US, all linked by Eisenhower's highways – oh yeah, all that freedom-of-the-open-road Kerouac crap, *On The Road*, you read that?

'Been told about it,' I said.

'That's just oil industry goddamn propaganda, Kerouac did all that driving on a stipend for Standard Oil as they wanted him to write a book promoting cars as 'freedom' and all that crap to get the younger generation to back it all, ultimately to stop them joining the hippies and the environmentalist movement.'

'But. Hang on, Kerouac wrote it in the 1940s, hippies weren't 'til the 60s?' said Ben.

'Yeah, but it was promoted big time in the 1960s. Thing you gotta understand was post-war US had massive over capacity for tanks and trucks and steel, so they converted to making massive cars, which needed highways instead of crappy country roads, but the highways were really all about moving the new missiles around quickly instead of keeping them in single bases you could bomb in one go. The Internet is the same idea, but instead of missiles on roads you have information flowing all over that no one single attack can destroy the system.'

Eh? It made sense but I was trying to unpack it all as Bobby jabbered on.

'And all those highways were paid for by people fooled into thinking cars and roads mean freedom, hippies driving all over the country in their Dormobiles, tying them into the system. It's the same for the Internet. Sell it as a new frontier and get the civilians to fund what is essentially a military enterprise.'

I didn't know what to say. Nor did Ben, nor Christian, for once.

'And you selling sugar to kids, keeps them fat, they need heavier transportation and more oil to move around, all benefiting the oil and steel industries while keeping people's minds rotted on total shit.'

This was … great. Sandy had said nothing but he looked somewhere between skeptical, intrigued, or all-knowing? Inscrutable.

'We eat total shit in this country, that's what the government wants. I don't even eat meat.'

'I'm a vegetarian,' said Elly.

'You eat meat!' Christian grinned lasciviously. I thought of his cock firing his jizz into her mouth, then the jizz strafed my brain, steaming like acid from a punctured battery.

They started talking about vegetarianism, where I lost interest as it was as this self-righteous student phase was as interesting as the 'which kebab shop is the best', debate, about which otherwise bright, interesting people get ludicrously passionate. Saying 'that dead animal you're cooking smells good', saved no animal's life ever but did piss off the hungry cunt eating it. But those arguments always went down badly so I usually held my tongue.

ZZ - Christian went down with his tongue - ZZ

It was a fun evening and good chat, but all soured at the flat, with everyone hot, red faced, Val and Elly on the balcony talking about what a load of shit this all was.

'There's nothing for me here. Nothing. In Colombia we had the most amazing time. And the kids were beautiful, they had nothing, but they were so full of life, I mean they had nothing. The kids here are shits. This job is shit, it's so constrained, I feel like I'm stuck,' said Elly.

'Even if Missouri had worked out, it'd've been shit really, for fuck's sake what's that about, a summer working in a theme park? Now I'm waiting tables? I could do that at home, fuck am I doing it here for? Aaron's having a shit time 'n' all. Twelve hours a day banging on doors to sell some pants picture they never asked for, he's making no money and says all he gets are burned feet and people telling him to fuck off.'

'I feel trapped, I don't like it.'

'At least you're getting some action.'

Elly smiled meekly.

This was all depressing as Hell. This was supposed to be a summer of fun and making loads of money but no-one was enjoying it. I felt like it was my fault. I downed my can. Another failure to chalk up. And tomorrow was my birthday.

Gay times

Twenty-one at last! Legally able to drink and I wouldn't have to use my crappy fake student card, I could present legit ID, still a pain though, presenting a passport for every bloody round. Christ. In England you blagged it and got the beer, or they stared you down and that was that. Here it was ID bloody everything.

After a day of hot weather that stood out as hot even among a series of hot days, we got back to the flat, I showered, shaved, put on my best shirt and trousers and reappeared in the room to shouts of 'happy birthday' from all, a beer and a spliff from a beaming Ben, and a small pile of presents, no horrible plastic silver key in a box but cool stuff, including a children's book, 'the story of farts', as I farted a lot.

I even got a peck from Elly.

Bliss!

Then Christian wrecked it: 'Maybe she'll give you a birthday blow-job.' My cock tingled in vain. Christian, you smug git, if looks could kill, please interpret my expression now to mean, I'm-going-to-cut-your-balls-off-and-stuff-them-down-your-throat-before-I-burn-your-ghetto. And why did she let him talk about her like that, but she said, 'I'm not touching it.' Christian grinned triumphantly. Cah.

A load of us piled into the A-Team van for 'a great place' Christian said he knew in town. Him, Elly and Greg occupied the front while I boiled in the back with the others, catching any fresh air from the front, that came with snippets like Elly saying, 'I always swallow.'

'Ah bet you do,' Greg replied, like a randy bumpkin on the cider.

'She does as well,' said Christian.

Elly, why do you say these things? And that's some boyfriend Christian is.

'Would you ever take crack?'

'What about heroin?'

'Nah'.

'Poppers?'

'I've done poppers,' I said, happy to be able to contribute something cool, 'they fucking stink but then you feel like you're floating five foot above everyone else.'

'I've never heard of them,' Elly said.

'I've never done them,' Christian said, hinting at some darker, medically-based reason why he wouldn't do something that stupid (although he'd done everything else) or because he didn't need drugs, eh? Something knowledgeable, anyway.

'Gays use them,' Christian said, and Greg took the bait: 'You some kind of poof boy, Jim? Ha ha!'

'If you ever go to Soho in London, loads of porn shops sell it,' I said, 'I've never bought them, just tried it at a party.'

'We know what kind of party!' Greg laughed, as did everyone else.

'It facilitates buggery,' said Christian, 'loosen the anal muscles and ease penetration,' he grinned broadly, and slyly glanced at Elly, who didn't respond, then Greg said something but I heard Christian mutter, 'they might have helped the other night, actually'. Agh! A spontaneous screaming cock swell seemed hideously imminent and I blinked hard. Aren't private asides just the very flaming best? You and your in-jokes *ZZ in pokes his cock in her arse, sliding it in deep as he takes her through some truly awesome sexual barrier-zz*

Great.

Swallowing and buggery.

Thanks, Christian, what an arsehole! *Zz – oh yes! Let me tell you* - oh don't bother.

As we cruised the highway I could see the skyscrapers of Chicago emerging on the horizon, growing taller, more numerous and defined. I smiled, what a place to be, and what a day for it, to finally come of age, just running into a club shouting 'It's my birthday, I'm 21,' should be enough to get you laid. Maybe we'd hit some whore-house or find a classy street-walker? We were tourists after all. Gee.

We tucked the van in an alley near an overhead metro line, and we walked along the sidewalks and tall buildings that still glowered with heat, although the Sun had set hours before, leaving a dark pink-blue sky in its wake. It was like strolling among the fins of giant radiators, but it was an empowering warmth, us in Chicago, on my birthday, the mood good enough to get drunk and maybe pull.

Where was Christian taking us? Suddenly he stopped outside a venue with a long front of blacked-out windows, 'here it is!' he said. The bouncers were friendly instead of goons, and in we went. The place was rammed with guys, many shaven headed, with earrings, many with heavy moustaches.

I felt dozens of pairs of eyes looking me up and down, undressing me. Men's eyes.

'Chicago's greatest gay venue!' yelled Christian, over a cacophony of chatter.

Yes my chances of getting laid here were very high indeed.

Ha. Fucking. Ha.

But once the first couple of rounds of Guinness had been downed, it was great. Fascinating. On the dance-floor men were whirling and dancing in a wild, sensuous sway, which I'd remembered from the Al Pacino film *Cruising*, and now was seeing for real, with blokes snogging off the sides! Meanwhile up on a platform was a brick shithouse of a man, amazingly sculpted and toned, with blond hair and blue eyes. He could have been an SS officer by day, then evenings spent dancing in just a hard-hat, tool-belt and skimpy denim shorts, which he occasionally pulled down so punters could poke his very taut bum, glistening with baby oil, as Ben pointed out.

With ABBA, Wham!, the Bee Gees playing, a great evening's entertainment was in store.

Ben and Greg playfully chatted and flirted with some types at the bar while I got a round in. But, as I turned away with a trio of Guinness pints clasped together, I felt something spidery dallying around my groin.

Shit – some bloke's touching me up while laden with pints I can't spill. Bastard!

But it was Elly, her hands cupping under my bits and weighing them in her palm. She looked at Val, mouth agape, like she was impressed, and Val's eyebrows arched up in approval.

I'd seen and heard all about what those pouting lips, slightly puppy-fat cheeks and rolling tongue could do and a blast of lust fuelled into my mind like someone was frying sugar in my head and its bitter-sweet magma swirled behind my eyes.

Name of God, girl, either do it or don't tease me to death. Do you want me to try it on?

No Jim, don't go there. It's her sense of fun. It's what she does because she's free.

Val's hand replaced Elly's and she gave her a similar look of wonder. I exploded, verbally, half-laughing with excitement and frustration, 'Look, is there a point to this?' and put down the drinks on the nearest table. Elly smiled such a warm smile and wrapped her arms around my shoulders, hugging me close, her smell intoxicating me like nothing else ever.

'Happy Birthday!' she said, adding, 'I love you,' words I'd have killed to hear. And I mean mass murdered.

'I love you,' I replied, free just this once to say it without a backlash of accusations of emotional blackmail.

So marry me, I didn't add.

Some pints later, I went for a slash, and while I saw a few blokes hanging around in the loos I concluded that gay bogs really were for pissing and not necessarily cottaging or whatever else the papers said went on. Safely spaced between two empty pissers, I was slashing away, when, suddenly, from behind, a whiny voice yelled, 'You've got a defective cock!'

Who on Earth said that? Who the fuck would go into a men's toilet and break the Golden Rule, that you Do Not Act Gay - let alone comment about other men's cocks!

Then I remembered, this is a gay club, it's OK to be gay. In fact did that mean it was worse not to act gay? This was a puzzler for the pisser.

But the real question remained, this defective cock – who had it, and what was defective about it? What does a defective cock look like? Then I realised, being in a gay club was the best chance to find all that out, *without* getting beaten up. I looked around, but saw three sets of eyes looking at me. *Me!*

189

'You've got a defective cock!' said a blond to me, bits still untidied away. All this attention, I must have looked like a rabbit in headlights. I wondered whether to run for it, but the more pressing matter in hand was he'd just told a gang of guys my cock was defective – a charge no man would really walk away from.

'What do you mean, defective?' I said in a manly manner, although I wasn't sure that was appropriate or whether it'd incite something, although what gay men do when incited I'd no idea either was curious to find out. How do gay men sound butch, or how should a straight man defend his honour in a gay club, or indeed act gay to fit in, but manly gay to repel boarders? Too many subtleties going on for my drunken mind.

'It's defective!' said the blond.

A bloke with a shaved head next to him piped up, 'Yeah man, that ain't natural'.

Indignation over-rode inhibition, this was my cock they were talking about, Damnit!

'You can't just fucking say it's defective. How?' and I held it out for inspection and debate. Well they were experts, so instead of passing up or sniffing at this free expertise, maybe I'd find out something worth knowing?

'What, what, what's defective about that?' I weighed my cock proudly, nearly adding, 'I mean, it's beautiful.'

'It's big, sure, it's big, but it's got skin', said shaven-head.

'Course it's got skin?' otherwise it'd be some agonising raw strip of bacon.

'Say, you Briddish?'

'Yes. Now what's this, "it's got skin" crap?'

Blond said, 'It's got a foreskin.'

'Yes?' It is a cock. Cocks have foreskin. This was just baffling.

Blond shook his head, 'Aw man,' and left.

Had I offended him? Actually I didn't care.

'That's a rare find these days,' said shaven, 'We don't have that here.'

'Foreskins? Are you all circumcised?'

'Yeah,' he replied, like I should know.

Was this a Jewish gay club?

'But I have to tell ya, it's impressive,' he continued. The third man nodded in agreement.

'Yeah?' I was genuinely pleased to hear that.

'Yeah', and shaven-head cocked an eyebrow. 'Is this foreskin a Briddish thing?'

'Well, we have foreskins,' but I was confused, I'd no idea what they did back home to compare with what they did here that was equally unknown. Then I remembered where I was, and, stuffing me bits away, said, 'OK thanks for that, I've got some dancing to do,' and I proceeded to shark-fin through the crowd towards the door, strutting assertively. 'Excuse me, gents.'

'See you later I hope,' someone said.

On the other side of dance floor was another bar, and at its far end I saw Christian, alone, nursing a drink. I'd half expected him to be doing what he claimed to do a lot of, namely doing some girl (Elly) from behind in a toilet cubicle, although then again, was having straight sex in a gay bog a faux pas?

I sat up beside him, asking the beef with gays and circumcision.

'It's a big hygiene issue. That's why Jews do it … so your nob is unhygienic,' he laughed. 'You're so cool, Jim,' he said, 'such a cool guy, and I'm really amazed at how you're taking this thing with Elly.'

I smiled and shrugged. Was he a bastard? He'd only taken what was on offer, what I'd missed out on, and we were all out here, in America, having a laugh, because of him. Maybe he wasn't totally terrible. We'd been very good friends only weeks ago, and a lot of that was due to his support for me about Elly.

But then he went and fucked her.

More than anything I was confused and just wanted a good time.

Then he said: 'The trouble is, I'm completely in love with Abigail,' and he looked like he might cry.

Abigail? A lovely girl back at uni, who Elly out-foxed by a country mile, and someone Christian would be living with next year, and who he'd said he had no chance with. I felt very sorry for him then, and glanced over to see Elly looking at us, wondering what our men's talk was about. There was a pang of relief when I realised he wasn't in love with Elly and probably wouldn't be, but Elly liked him. We were three broken hearts, thousands of miles from home, making a scene perfect for a film of maudlin late-night drunks in a bar.

It all got a bit bitty after that. There was something in a 24-hour convenience store, as we perused the aisles Greg stepped over to Elly, leaned close to her and said something, she nodded, his eyes widened and he smiled, and she carried on browsing.

Then we were in a breakfast burger joint and some bloke tried chatting me up in the loos, apparently he'd followed me from the club, so I gently told him to get lost.

Then as it began to get light we had a gorgeous drive home, me in the boot of the Pontiac, watching the Sun rise over Chicago, but got sad when thinking about what Christian said and what that meant for Elly. In the car park back at the flats I told her not to bust herself up over Christian, but she didn't really get it.

Then another beer.

Then out.

191

Boiling over

Saturday. Raw heat welcomed our hangovers as the Weather Channel said today would break the 100s. I was far from sober and in no mood to argue with the Sun which was making an angry claim to everything, with not one cloud to argue with it.

Yesterday was fry-day, today was die-day.

At the hanger, we pitched about coping in the heat versus the fortune we should rake in. Our ice-cream vans would be like ambulances to those frying outside, they'd queue around the block for treatment. Instead of kerb-crawling for kids, we'd just park up at a park, sell out by lunchtime and trundle home with a tray full of lettuce. That was the plan.

Instead, it was as hot as a desert, and couldn't have been more deserted. The yards, the parks were empty of barbecues, even Mexican picnics, any punters having cleared off back to seek shelter under the air-con. Nor would anyone would make the 20 yards walk down their drives to buy off us. We all boiled away, all day long, in our metal cabins, no fans, the breeze as hot as a sauna we couldn't escape. Very occasionally there was a punter wilting on the roadside, but otherwise the streets were empty, like some apocalyptic film like *The Swarm*, with killer heat instead of killer bees, and distant life proving just lies told by mirages. So I ground along, brewing up, images of Elly and Christian fucking, and fucking, and fucking, until my mind was itself one almighty heat shimmer.

I did find a boy and a girl dancing under a sprinkler, they started their ritualistic dead-eyed chant, 'I want … I want …', like the human sacrifice from *The Temple Of Doom*. Suddenly their toddler brother appeared at their front door, his face all excited, and he tottered down the black tarmac drive towards me. But he was barefoot, and halfway his face flipped from joy to confusion to pain, until his feet burning, he just stopped, plonked down on the path, bare legs frying on the hot plate, and he started howling. His siblings ignored this and continued their worship at the ice-cream altar, and, frightened this kid would burn and I'd be blamed, I jumped out with my water bottle and poured it over his legs and feet, before scraping him up like a burger and taking him back to the door, where his mother appeared looking unhappy, but grateful when I explained. His brother, who'd left him to fry, just called him 'stoopid'. The rest of the day was spent getting hot, hyper, angry and punching things.

I arrived back at the hanger glowing red from heat and frustration, shouting only 'diabolical!' at Hank, which made him really laugh, and counted up to barely $100, total. Shit all round for us all the colour of boiled lobsters.

We drove back in quiet, then decided for Dooley's for free air-con, where many others damp with sweat also sought cold beer away from the glowering landscape, so it was busy, even for a Saturday, and we guzzled pitchers. Elly was talking to two wiry-looking blokes at the bar, them in jeans and T-shirts, while I steadily got jealous, when Christian said quietly, 'they're off-duty cops.'

192

So? I sunk my soul in beer. Then Elly appeared, picked up the now-empty pitcher next to me, and asked, 'where's the pitcher I just bought?'

'Oh. Did you buy that?'

'Yeah. Where the fuck's it gone?'

I looked around for the 'guilty' party that'd stolen our beer, but she was having none of it.

'You drunk it all, didn't you?' she grinned, but it was an incredulous smile.

I pulled a 'what me?' face. No dice.

'Useless,' she spat, 'fucking useless'. The first time she'd said I was useless, 'you have no use,' was funny. This time she looked at me like I was shit on her shoe.

'Beer's supposed to be drunk!' I said, but she was strutting back to the bar. Jeez, what'd I do wrong? A weary path of thoughts and counter-arguments beckoned, until I concluded she was right, I was useless.

She went and lent on Christian's shoulder, to arrange a massive sweaty session later on, but just as a Hellish pit of self-loathing yawned wide open for me, I was distracted by a ruckus. From the middle of a crowd round the bar was a familiar Scottish voice, whacking out syllables with ever greater speed and harshness, shouting down the increasingly high-pitched voice of an American woman. As people backed away, I saw Greg, hammering one fist on the bar and wielding the other at the barmaid. The hubbub went quiet just as Greg shouted in furious Glaswegian: 'And it's nay fucking wonder you're such a fucking bitch with a fucking face like that, you fucking rancid cow!' which silenced her as well. He smashed a pitcher on the bar, spat, then spun round and brandished both fists. 'Come on you fucking cunts!' he yelled, muscles flexing. Punters tottered out the way as he lunged hither and thither towards the door, which he banged open, smashing a glass panel as he thundered into the car park.

Christian by now was standing on a table, singing, 'Give peace a chance', but the barmaid shouted 'call the police', and the two wiry guys in jeans, though several drinks down, darted out after Greg. Knowing Greg would beat them both up, or have a damn good go, I found myself pelting outside into the wall of heat, to find Greg all coiled up and about to spring on the two cops, now stalled by what confronted them, as he yelled, 'I'll kill yer fuckers!'. He was nanoseconds from launch.

'No Greg, no!' I jabbered, 'don't do it, don't do it! You'll kill them!'

'AYE!'

'Don't, Greg, the police are coming, *police*,' then I remembered but hardly managed to say, 'Greg - they *are* police! They are police! Don't do it! Calm down!'

Somehow that registered and he stopped, his face suddenly confused.

'They're police, Greg, just fuck off, go!'

'Shite!' he said, panicking as it hit him if he hit them he'd be in real trouble, and he wheeled around, seeking direction.

'That way! Go on, run!' I pointed towards the apartment and he barreled through the car-park hedge and trees. The two wires watched him pound into the darkness, but didn't chase, as faced with a pissed up skinhead Scot on the warpath when they were a skin-full down made them forget they too were police.

'He's really shit with drink, he'll be all right, really, he's OK,' I breathlessly explained, but they weren't interested.

'I'll get the squads in!' said one, and they went back inside, leaving me alone, so I decided to make a wobbly exit as well, pelting unsteadily after Greg, who I could hear effing and blinding as he floundered across the rubble and craters of the building site between the pub and the apartment. Reckoning that was a chance for him to calm down and flush some booze out of him, I slowed and started to pick across the rubble. Well, that, and I could barely bloody see, and didn't want to end up face-down in a crater.

In the middle of the site was one of those caterpillar-tracked scooper things with a big open-top cab, which struck me as a good vantage point from which to see if I could see Greg, or look out for squad cars coming our way. I climbed into the cab and tried to think through the haze of beer and adrenaline about this latest bout of bollockery.

Fucking typical, eh? Let's round off a shit day with a quiet night down the local, so I don't have to watch my love engage in some red-hot porn show under blue moonlight, nor duel with our lives with the Pontiac for the sake of buying beer, let's just have a night dahn the boozer, *standin' rahnd the ol' Joanna, capla pints Gor Blimey* – o look Greg's smashing it up and fighting the police. Fucking brilliant. Non-stop entertainment, all this.

But as I sat alone, and saw no flashing blue and red lights coming, I calmed down and thought the guys at the bar must have also calmed down, and seeing Greg for just a silly drunken sod, they'd probably cancelled the back-up, out of their own embarrassment. It would all have sorted itself out by now. I dismounted the scooper and headed to the pavement to go back to Dooley's, for more beer and laugh it all off, but saw two figures running towards the flats. Elly and Weird Adrian.

'Hey, yous, what's going on at the bar?' I shouted, and they slowed down to jog on the spot.

'Where the fuck is Greg?' Elly bawled.

'I've no idea. Hiding somewhere. Quite right too.'

'They're looking for him!'

'Who -'

'The police are fucking looking for him! And they're coming back to the apartment!' Now on the pavement, now I could see red and blue lights flashing up in Dooley's car-park. Oh shit, they'd come from the other direction.

'What? Why are they coming back? How do they know where we live?'

'Because Ben and Val had to fucking tell 'em, they've taken over the bar, the police, they're all in there.'

'Shit. How did you get out?'

'We came through the loo window,' said Adrian, pleased with himself, making me wonder what him and Elly were doing in the toilets together, but Elly repeated: 'The police are coming back to ours!'

Ours where there were no work permits to be found, but there was a ton of grass. Something heavy launched from my belly and I felt light-headed, before I heard myself say: 'Fuck, let's go.'

We pegged the final hundred yards to the apartment block's side door, where we all stopped and looked at one another for the key.

'So?' I said.

'So?' said Adrian.

'Yeah, so'?' said Elly.

'So no key!' I yelled, 'shit!' and Elly flapped her arms.

'Fucking idiots', said Freak.

'You've got the key, have you?' I said.

'I'm not the one in the shit cos of your -' he started, but just then the door opened and an elderly couple stepped through, saying goodbyes to two girls inside. We hopped past into the building, surprising the old lady. I shouted 'Sorry, bit of a rush, don't you know' in my bestest Briddish accent.

'You guys Briddish?' said one girl.

'Yes,' said the Freak.

'Wow that's so cool! What are you doing here in Shorewood?'

Good question, to which Freak stopped to chat with them. We didn't have time for this! Panic flushed through me, making me wobble. 'Adrian,' I said, but he only looked at them, his patter underway, 'Adrian, come on.'

'I'm talking with these girls,' Mutant replied.

And the cops are coming to fuck us, I nearly shouted. I wanted to hit him.

'Forget him, let's go,' Elly stage-whispered, pulling me away.

'See you later,' I said, then we hammered up the stairwell, into the corridor, to our front door – for which we *still* had no key! – but Elly just pushed it open.

'How the fuck come?' I asked, but my brain was racing and overtook – what the fuck do we do now?

'Get the drugs,' she hissed, and I lunged at the sideboard next to the sofa, yanked open the drawer, and under a quilt of skins I found the bag of grass.

'Thassit, thassit!' said Elly, but my heart leapt: instead of Satsuma-sized ball of grass was just a tight thumb's worth of knotty green seeds and leaves.

'Fucking Hell, there's not enough, there's not *enough*!' I said.

'Must be!'

'No! There's more than this. Much more! Where's the fucking rest of it! *Where is the fucking rest of it?*'

Where, where, where? Why have a drugs drawer – then stash half of it somewhere else? Who *does* this? It fucks the system, I wanted to yell, for sure as bastard fuck, if we couldn't find the stash, the cops would! I wrenched out the drawer and furiously scrunched up all the papers, roaches and dope into a ball and stuffed it in my pocket, but there was still a silt of dope dust and seeds in it, so I thrust the drawer at Elly.

'Hit it down the bog, down the bog! Then hoover the drawer!' I said.

'Why not chuck it all down?'

'It'll just float!' And it was the stash!

She ran to the bathroom, cracked the drawer against the bowl, flushed, while I clattered the hoover out of the cupboard, manically uncoiled the cable, stabbed the plug into a socket and turned it on as Elly appeared, she grabbed the hoover nozzle and frantically rammed its sucker all over the drawer.

'And the floor! The floor!' I said.

'I know, I know,' she said, while I starting hauling out the drawers under the TV to find the rest of the stash. Nothing. Then I looked on the coffee table, under the coffee table, under the sofa. Nothing!

Elly turned off the hoover, sirens were approaching.

'They're coming. *Shit!*' she said.

'Where's the rest of it?' My heart was in my mouth. 'Those fucking coppers'll will find it, right where I'm looking, shit, shit, shit'. I spun round and round, eyes and fingers darting into every nook and crevice. Under the cushions? Under the table? Behind the TV? Fridge? Sugar bowl? Coffee table? Sofa?

'It's not here.'

'Fuck it, let's just get out of here!' she said. She ripped the plug from the wall and crashed the hoover back into the cupboard, the cable whipping around her legs and nearly tripping her up while I jammed the drawer back in, then whirled around and saw I had to ram all the other open drawers back in so it didn't look like we'd burgled our own flat.

At the door, we glanced back into the room, 'it looks fine!' she said.

'Yep. Let's run'.

The door slammed, and the lock sprung. Now we were properly locked out. Then she asked, 'dope?'

'No I couldn't find it all, didn't you fucking understand any -'

'Where's the *stuff* you *did* get?!'

'Shit, sorry, yes,' but in my mind I saw that small ball of dope still on some surface in the flat, waiting for the police to arrive, and with desperate futility I padded my pockets for the door key I knew I didn't have - but instead found the blob of dope and skins, now damp from my sweat-soaked pocket.

'Got it'.

'Great!' She turned for the lifts far up the corridor, but I pulled her back to the stairs, 'We've got to get off this floor, now!' We clambered up the sweltering stairwell, and a couple of flights up, we crashed back into another long corridor of doors, when I twigged the drugs in my pocket were just waiting to be found in the police pat-down we knew was coming. I looked at the ceiling and its suspended polystyrene tiles, reached up, flicked up a tile and threw the blob of drugs stuff into the dusty dark gap, while Elly for want of any better random panic act again pelted for the lifts. I pounded after her, where she was at the lifts, hopping from foot to foot, whacking the call-lift button. We could hear the sirens louder now, and little flits of flashing blue light could be seen through the lift-hall window.

'Now what?' My mind was on pure turbo and going nowhere, 'where are we going?'

'Mike's flat! They're there, we'll have an alibi!' she said.

Except the fucking lift wasn't coming. We fought up the stairs next to the lift, hauling ourselves up the stiflingly hot chimney of a stairwell, up to the sixth floor, gasping through the door at the top, where a window allowed red and blue lights outside to flash hard and steady against the ceiling. The sirens had stopped; so must have the police cars. They'd be in the building in seconds. A new jag of adrenaline flooded into me and all weak-limbed I lolloped down the never-ending corridor to Dave's flat, our sanctuary, where we could jabber out a story, or just hide. We pounded on the door. No reply.

'Where the fuck are they?' I said, shaking, and looked at her for an answer, because this was her idea.

'He's in the bar with everyone else!' she yelled. Of course! Great Fuck! Her eyes rattled left to right, her hands held out, as if the one idea that might yet save us was going to fall from the ceiling.

'Give me your ID,' she said.

'Why?'

'Your student ID, it's fake, like mine! Just give it to me!' she hissed.

'Fuck, yeah!' I blurred through my wallet to find my crappy student ID, gave it to her, and she tried to put hers with it up through a polystyrene ceiling tile, but she wasn't tall enough and they fell back on her, so I did it.

'Thanks,' she said.

'Good thinking,' I replied.

'Let's just get the fuck out of here,' she said, repeating her first good idea. We ran back to the lifts, my legs now feeling like lead, as it struck me we'd been going flat out in all this heat, all on unknown reserves. We slapped the call-lift button but we decided to fuck it and just run down the stairs, ramming the stairs' door open and chopping and jumping down flight after flight, lurching around each landing, me catching an ankle by clanging it off the steel bannisters, and nearly falling down the final steps. Only at the bottom of the stairwell I thought the police would probably come through the side door that we were heading right towards - to escape we'd have to go out the exit at the other end of the building!

'Out the other end,' I said, 'come on, come on, we can do it!' I gasped at her as we pelted down the sweltering ground floor corridor.

'Yep, yep, yep' she gasped back. Maybe we were going to get away with this, the last desperate run down this corridor that ended still dozens of yards away with a big brown door, but beyond which I could already feel the cool breezy freedom of the Illinois night and its massive black sky, and surely to God for all the good work we'd done, we'd have to snog to celebrate.

We flailed into the reception foyer where the corridor carpet gave way to polished granite and we scrabbled like cats for grip, and I glanced at the large glass entrance doors and saw a row of dark silhouettes backlit by flashing blue and red. Then I saw Val among the shapes, looking sullen, and surrounded by three big guys in black outfits adorned with flashy bits of chrome. Elly saw them too and we dropped to a trot, waving and smiling, but one cop banged the door hard with something long and black, a horrible sound echoing off the stone floor and walls, and he scowled and yelled something we couldn't hear but was clearly something like 'open this Goddamn door or we'll break it down and kill you.'

Elly stopped. 'They're angry', she said, 'I think we have to let them in.'

My heart sank. 'Yep,' I said. Damn. After all that, we were caught. Only now it occurred to me, we were already at the far end of the building when we were outside Mike's flat, where there were stairs that end we could have taken, instead of doubling back, then doubling back again.

One flight of stairs from freedom.

And robbed of a snog.

Would this be a fatal blunder, or had we done enough? Like when the GIs in *The Bridge at Remagen* are desperately kicking dynamite off the underside of the bridge before the Germans blow it up?

So my mind read while I tried to look all matter-of-fact as Elly went to open the door. But then I felt calm. We'd done all we could. All we had to do now was stay calm and pretend, 'why officer, whatever could the matter be?'

I said to Elly, 'We didn't do anything wrong, did we?'

'No,' she replied dead-pan. In the car-park beyond I saw Ben, gesticulating in confused explanation to a crowd of men in black. But for all the frantic rushing around, up, down and along, it was this short, leaden walk to the door when time just slowed, and I began to feel woozy, sick, like at the end of a really long rollercoaster.

As Elly pulled the lock she winked at me. I blinked agreement.

'Oh, wow, Val! What are you doing here?' Elly said with ludicrous surprise as she opened the door. Val's face read entirely, *not-funny*, *not-now*, while the officers pushed her in.

'You were in the bar too, right, during the fight?' growled the burliest, a sergeant, at Elly and I.

'Yes.' I said.

'Why didn't you wait for us?' he barked.

'We didn't know you were coming. I was there during the fight, but went outside to calm Greg down, and I thought once he'd gone it was kind of all over.'

'Oh yeah? This is the Greg who caused criminal damage to the bar, threatened the barmaid and two officers?'

'Err...erm,' yes that's Greg, but I was panicking in my mind about agreeing with what he said in case he took it as a witness statement or whatever, 'if that's ... he's called Greg,' I said. Ah shit, Greg was in serious trouble. And so are we.

Another took Elly aside to ask questions, while my officer demanded,

'OK, empty your pockets,' which I did, hoping to God no remaining mash of skins and dope came out.

'Turn around and put your hands against the wall.' We did, and we were patted down.

'Leaving a crime scene ain't the thing to do,' another cop said.

'Well, er, we didn't think it was a police matter,' I said.

'Oh *no*?' said another. 'This girl's been telling us you all live in one apartment here. Guilt by association!'

Oh shit. What else had they said? Had Val and Ben already confessed everything, or not? We'd had no time to get our stories straight. With no idea what the police now knew, I wondered if it was a crime to lie to cops who already know better? Were any of us underage? Schaumberg's finest would quickly find out from our passports and bust us for boozing, then find the rest of the pot, find out we were all working illegally, fucking us and Hank's business, too. A good night's haul for bored cops, and not so much dollops of poo hitting a fan but a four-engined B-29 propeller-plane flying into a cumulus cloud of shit. We were all in real trouble, and I was two shades of shit away from crapping myself, as was Elly. But then I had no energy left to panic and even if I had I couldn't use it. Whatever would happen would happen, we were all going down together, and because there was nothing left to be done, I felt strangely relieved.

'You with the guy who wrecked the bar, yeah?' a cop asked me.

'Erm, the excited guy, yes.' Again I didn't want to confirm that in case it counted as evidence, but Elly just said 'yes.'

Fuck it. He smashed it up, not us. Dob the fucker.

'He ain't around?'

'Haven't seen him since the bar,' I said.

'We're going to your apartment where we'll wait for him.'

'OK,' I said.

Ben had been escorted inside by then and looked decidedly alarmed and sweaty, his pockets hanging out from the pat-down, he looked like a scared little boy. He looked how I felt.

Luckily there was no apartment night-manager to see all this and confirm who exactly the flat was rented to. Each of us escorted by our own officer, with a few more in tow, we traipsed back to the flat, hearts aflutter, legs of lead, my mind doing a wall of death with questions: Had we done enough? Had we cleaned it up? Or was a bucket of guilt-proving evidence poised precariously over the door to fall on our heads?

This was supposed to be a hilarious, fun-packed student working holiday. Really, it was fucking stupid.

Val put her key into the door lock.

'Hang on, Val -'

'Shuttup,' said a cop.

I'd wanted to ask, if she had a key to the flat, why hadn't she come through the side-door instead of wasting time going round to the front door ...

because she'd been playing for time. Nice one Val. Yeah, shuttup, me.

Val opened the door and trilled, 'Greg … we've got some people to see yers,' in the same sing-song sitcom 'hi honey, I'm home!' way. I wanted to laugh, but promised myself I'd personally smash my stupid face in if I did.

The flat, just hovered, sofa cushions all puffed up, looked quite well kempt. Greg couldn't be here without a key. All the police were piling in now, though, and one pushed past me, asking: 'Do you have any illegal substances here?' and before anyone could answer, with some uncanny sixth sense he aimed straight for the drugs drawer and pulled it out, holding it aloft … then he jimmied it back in its slot before untidying the sofa cushions as he searched for dope.

Another cop glanced into the kitchen, three took Ben into the bedrooms and bathrooms to see if Greg was lurking there, or whoever or whatever else might be.

'We're gonna need to see all your IDs. Fast.' With a cop posted in each room, we retrieved our passports, which were duly passed between a trio of police in the living room. One took Greg's passport and radioed back the details to base. 'None of these are old enough to drink,' commented one.

What? Bollocks. 'I am, and he is,' I said, pointing at Ben. So was Christian, but he wasn't here. Where was he?

'I'd only just arrived at the bar when it kicked off,' said Val, neither confirming nor denying she'd drunk anything.

'Nor me,' said Elly. She'd had a few at Hank's, hours before, but at Dooley's I'd finished the pitcher before she got any. Did she smell of it?

'You're the worker, right? You got a work permit?' one cop pointed at Val.

'That's me, yes. I'm a waitress,' said Val.

'And the rest of you are doing what?'

'Just visiting,' said Ben. Right, I thought, we're just visiting, praying that my face didn't betray the infinite calculations going on in my head. Had Elly picked up on the hint? Ben was drenched in sweat. For fucks' sake, man, look less worried and guilty, I thought.

'You got this apartment just for you tourists?' said the lead cop. Major plot flaw, we'd sailed into our own mine.

'Yeah really they're only here until more workers are coming from England. We're-'

'How?'

'It's through a visa exchange scheme between British universities and North American something or other, Corporation,' proffered Ben, betraying a little too much knowledge, surely? Was our story taking on too much water?

Val cut in, 'We're all British students, I've come here to work the summer as a waitress, and others are going to come to this apartment for work, but before they do these guys are visiting and sharing the rent cos it's much cheaper than a hotel for them.' A brilliant, brilliant elaboration of the truth that Val said with authority. I stared down at my feet and saw my khaki linen shirt

200

was dark with streaks of sweat. Cool, calm and innocent I so totally did not look. This was like walking in a minefield with flanking great clown boots on.

'And this Greg guy?'

A random nutter, officer.

'Another friend,' said Val.

The lead cop was about to say something when his radio crackled and he broke off. He went into the corridor with two others and they began conferring, while three more waited in the flat and looked stern, but asking not-so-unfriendly questions.

'What are they discussing?' Ben dared ask.

'Whether they can get a judge out tonight or whether we'll wait 'til tomorrow to have you arraigned,' and the cop smiled. Cop humour? Did he want me to shit myself there and then? Did these guys bust people for fun? What'd I do wrong? Everything felt airborne. My stomach was in free fall, my heart felt weightless. What felt like an eternity later, the lead cop came back in.

'The manager of the bar doesn't want to press charges, for some reason,' he eyed us suspiciously, 'what he wants is for this guy, Greg, to come in, tomorrow morning, apologise and pay for the door. If he doesn't, then we'll arrest him.'

'Blimey. That's, er, very generous of the bar manager.' I said.

'Yes, very generous,' said Ben. Another cop came in and called the sergeant away.

He came back in and looked at us one by one. 'You tell that Greg – pay up, fess up, or he's busted. Understand? You get that into his head when you see him, right?'

'Yes officer, and we're very sorry on his behalf for his behaviour tonight,' I said, then went overboard with the post-stress familiarity by saying, 'it's the Scots in him'.

'I'm a quarter Scots,' snapped the sergeant. Fuck. Then he laughed, and said: 'I never want to hear from this place again. Understand?'

We all meekly nodded and said 'Yes, sir.'

'Enjoy your stay in Illinois – don't make us come back!' he said, and they filed out, cackling and jingling their way downstairs. Ben saw them go, gently closed the door, eyes rattling with relief, then faced us as we all stood in pouring sweaty silence, then he summed it all up in a word: 'Fuck'.

In the following minutes, Christian reappeared from somewhere, then the other drivers at the bar came around, surveyed the scene, said 'fuck' a lot, lit up and opened beers. I swung in a haze of shock and relief, while the chatter got excited as everyone reconstructed events and exaggerated their own roles as the magnificently improvised lies were recounted. By some miracle we'd all just, just averted disaster.

'Why was the flat unlocked?' Ben said.

'I'd left it unlocked, as I was the last out and didn't know if anyone had a key so I left it on the latch,' said Elly.

'That was fucking lucky,' said Ben.

'Fucking lucky we weren't robbed,' said Christian. I thought 'don't have a fucking go, it's what saved us,' but the conversation had moved on.

'What about my lie? Wouldn't have taken anything for them to check the flat's rented by Hank, not my old employer,' said Val. 'That and the key I had has no fob. They were having a go at us at the front door why I couldn't get into my s'posed own blimming flat, and I was saying, "I haven't got the fob, this is the spare", luckily we argued about that instead of them askin' "so what were you going to do?" and going around the side-door. Fucking Hell.'

'It was a genius lie, Val, thank God you're legal anyway,' I said.

'No, not really, Jimbo. Don't forget my work permits only relate to that place in Missouri. I only still have my visa cos I did a runner here to Chicago,' she snorted with laughter, 'to safety.'

'Like some slave on the old moonlit escape trails,' said Ben.

'I don't know why the diner's not checked my visa properly,' she shrugged.

Then Christian jumped in: 'Why the fuck did you let the police into the flat in the first place?'

'Because they were coming in anyway? What do you mean?' said Ben.

'They'd no right to come in,' Christian said.

'Because they're cops, Christian, we're supposed to be kosher and if you give them just a flick of trouble they'd have been all over us,' Ben replied, with an edge to his voice.

'They don't have the right to come in without a warrant. You could have told them to get lost,' said Christian, emphatically, apparently expert on local cop law. Christian who'd done nothing but dance on a table, was now asking the questions from the fools who'd saved the day.

'And they'd have been back in an hour with a warrant, and pissed off with it. What fucking good would it have done to say "no you're not coming in, go away?"' Ben said, voice rising, 'because funnily enough Christian as half of bloody Illinois police department fleeced me in the car park and marched me through the front fucking door I was going to tell them exactly fucking that, "oh no, you're not coming in without a warrant." What are you on?'

'They're just small-town police, with no right, to come in here and do what they did. Searching the drawers was bang out of order!' Christian yelled.

'For fuck's sake!' I nearly screamed, 'they're small-town bored bloody cops but they're still the police! Why do you think so many came round here to find one drunk bloke who broke a door?'

'Fuck's sake Christian, you're talking shit!' Ben shouted. 'They were itching for a bust, you don't mess with cocks like that.'

'*Exactly*,' Christian sharply said to Ben, 'they're small-time and they over-stepped their rights. They had to be let in to get in and they knew it. They knew we didn't have to do that, in fact, we could sue them yet. They have to have a warrant to come in.'

Ben started shouting.

Then the door opened, and there stood Greg. I leapt up and lost it at him.

'Where the fuck have you been? You fucking idiot! You *fucking* idiot!' That he could have just lamped me across the room just didn't bother me right then. 'Are you trying to fucking get us all deported? For God's sakes, man!'

He actually looked like he was about … to cry, and in a hushed voice he said, 'I know, I know, I'm sorry, I'm really sorry.'

'Your fucking temper is out there! Fucking control it, for God's sake!'

'I know, I'm really sorry, I'm really sorry,' and he started to flap and blub. I felt sorry for him.

'Oh for fuck's sake. Sit down or something. Just … sit down. Have a beer.'

As Greg sat and buried his face in his hands, Val came over and took his arm, 'aww Greg man.'

Christian and Ben were still shouting.

'Jesus, not with the door open, everyone can hear you,' I said, 'sorry Christian, what? We could sue them? Sue the police? What are you, mental?'

Ben joined in. 'We're fucking illegal workers, *illegal*, by some fucking miracle they didn't find that out, or find the dope, or get Greg, but by luck, Christian, luck, if they'd found anything and asked, what, I don't know what questions, we'd have all been totally fucked over. We haven't got a leg to stand on about rights, or, or, or point out what crap they can or can't do.'

'They didn't have the right to come in!'

'We had to play their damn game!'

'They didn't have the fucking right to do it!'

'We don't have any rights! Every fucking thing we do is illegal because we are illegal!'

'But they need a fucking warrant!' Christian shouted.

'So they would have left five guys here, got the warrant, come back and turned this place and us over. We'd be in front of a fucking judge before dawn charged with everything they could find to fill out their fucking ticket book. Hank too. Fucking Hell, we had to look innocent, why can't you understand that?'

'They have to have a warrant. Right? For future reference, they have to have a warrant.' said Christian, retreating to the high ground he never held.

Future? Like this was going to happen again? Ben screamed at him: 'What? Future?' then choked off his words as he realised the futility of this debate. He looked angry enough to either hit someone or cry with frustration. 'Fuck this,' and he stormed out the flat.

This was too strange. I had to get out.

'I'm going to retrieve the dope,' I said.

'Good idea!' yelled Christian.

The stairs were like a furnace. I went up a floor and reached up to the ceiling and lifted the tile, and felt ahead, but couldn't feel the dope. I tried the next tile along, but nothing. And the one behind, and nothing. Then another, and another, then started again with the first tile, then all the other tiles from both directions. Had I thrown it further than I'd thought? Or was I simply rolling it back and forth between the tiles as I lifted them? O for fuck's sake, I thought, it'll be there tomorrow, and I went back down.

'Did you get the dope?' Christian asked.

'It's somewhere in the fourth floor ceiling. I think.'

'Where?' he said, his tone accusatory, suspecting I'd bungled.

'In the ceiling very close to the stairs,' as accurate as I could remember from the roasting panic. Although now I wasn't sure I'd even got the right floor.

'But you've looked and not found it?'

'I tried to save the dope, but really it was more important to get rid of it first, all right?'

'Well, either save the drugs or don't. Over fifty bucks' worth, and we need a spliff now.' I wanted to hit Mr Party.

'You mean you need a spliff, Christian?' Val spat.

'I, we,' he laughed. Val's eyes met mine, with a mutual look of dead-eyed disdain for this cretin. 'Christian, what did you do tonight, except stand on a table and did some cack impression of John Lennon? Not very effective, was it?' Val said.

'Would've been had anyone listened,' he smiled, pleased with himself, 'anyway the issue now is where are the drugs for which Jim is now responsible.' That son of a bitch.

'Mislaid. Anyway, what I took was only half of it. Where's the fucking rest? Nothing like enough in that drawer when I opened it, half-shat myself.'

'I sold a load to Jeff.'

'Oh. Right.' We all went quiet.

Then Christian said: 'Well there's nothing more to be done now, I'm going to bed.'

'The fuck you've done all ready, Christian', Val said. Only then I twigged there wasn't 50 fucking bucks' worth of dope, dope that we'd all paid for, but none of us had seen the money Christian got for selling some to Jeff, leaving an amount too small that led to the fucking panic. So we'd been ripped off and had the piss taken instead of praised. Wanker.

Elly had sat next to Christian throughout the row but said little. Now she leaned forward, hand extended out to me.

'Well done, Jim. We did really well.'

'We did, didn't we?'

'We were that close - ' and she did an air pinch.

'Yep. That fucking close.'

She didn't mean what I hoped, so I went for beer. It was getting light outside, but there was time for a couple more –I'd earned them.

Cunt

Sunday morning, we were still reeling from the night before.

Somehow we all made it into the car and got to work. Nobody spoke on the drive in and we all quickly split up at the hanger.

Someone asked me, 'Your mate all right today?'

'He's not my mate' then I felt bad him and the whole stupid episode, and just shook my head.

It was fucking baking out, I mean crazy bastard hot, and while we roamed around, the jingles banging my head, the thoughts of the previous night came and went, the van, the concrete sidewalks and white-painted houses, the tarmac, the brick-built shops, the metal of the cars, all glared with heat.

Everyone was still hidden indoors, under the aircon, next to the fan. The waterpark was rammed, but I couldn't stop there, while the parks and yards remained empty.

Sweat just boiled off leaving you dry with great scabby salt crusts on my T-shirt and even my black shorts. But my seat was damp, the soaked foam rehydrating years of other drivers' bum sweat. Oh God.

The heat sapped all strength, leaving me slumped over the steering wheel and bewildered, too hot even to get angry at the little shits who did dare come out and hopped from foot to foot like those lizards, as their feet baked on the tarmac. Even driving faster only blew more hot air through the cabin, like when you open an oven door to get the pizza out and the *wmmfff* of heat in your face causes you to lurch away.

'You must be doing good business today, man,' one sunglassed mother said.

'You what? Fucking diabolical, the whole place is dead,' I said, then looked at her and covered my mouth. I saw her look shocked, then she started laughing.

I knew there was shade around Joly's house, and out on the grass he was! I was pleased to see him, and he even asked me to stop and play ball, but I couldn't, I said I'd seen Eskimo beetling off in the direction of lucrative destinations, and business was so shit I really had to grind along, so I really couldn't hang out, all a crappy lie and it would have made no difference if I'd stopped for longer, so I don't know why I said it, because being with Joly I wasn't wound up about getting deported cos some bloke I happened to live with had smashed up a bar, or my so-called best mate fucking ... none of that shit mattered.

Anyway, I told him the appropriate bits, sold him a Snowcone, said sorry again I have to go, got ten yards away when he shouted, 'Cunt!'

So I stopped.

Leant out the cabin.

Looked at him.

Not really angry or upset, but stunned. 'What did you say?' I quietly asked, enunciating each word with particular precision.

'Cunt,' he replied, slightly hesitant as he realised the word was enough to stop vehicles.

My eyebrows wavered.

I got out and strolled over to him.

'Joly, that's a really bad word. Where did you hear that word, Joly?'

'I dunno, what's it mean, anyway?' he shrugged.

'It means', no, I couldn't explain this. But I couldn't leave him without an explanation either.

'What's it mean?'

'I can't tell you. Your parents wouldn't appreciate it. Just believe me, it's really, really bad. And you shouldn't say it to anyone.'

'But what's it mean though?'

'I'm not going to tell you. And don't ask your parents either. They might get real mad. Just don't use that word.'

'OK, but …' he was insistent, figuring if he was in trouble he had to know why.

'Nope! I'm not saying,' This wasn't going to work, but I endeavoured. 'Really, Joly, trust me,' but he looked like he was going to cry, 'no, no, it's OK, it's OK, I'm not angry, that's just not a good word and you shouldn't use it. All right?' Oh God, don't cry, I'll be hunted down for it by the whole neighbourhood. He nodded, top lip sunk behind his lower lip.

'Right. I've got to go. Take care now, see you about, OK, matey?' Another nod and he turned for home. All felt uneven, somehow. Not a happy situation.

So the day hauled along. Back at the hanger, everyone looked dead.

Jeff told us, 'I did pretty shitty business today, in the good spots too, til I rounded a corner and saw this fuckoff school bus, painted white, the driver on dead slow while one man leant from a window taking money, and two others chucked boxes of ice cream out the back. It was like a fucking battleship.'

'What did you do?'

'Drove oudda there, man, that shit scared me, dude.'

Elly looked forlorn.

'What's wrong?' I asked her.

'It's that man again, the one I told you about. I've told him I'm not interested, I've told him I've got a boyfriend, but he doesn't listen.'

'I'm sorry girl.' This wasn't good, I scrabbled to think of something to do about it. 'Do you want us to get a group together, go have a word?'

'What, with baseball bats?' Was she afraid of this escalation or spurning it?

'I dunno, er, yeah, why not?'

She looked down and sighed sharply.

'Or just tell him to piss off. You've told him you're not interested, so tell him to piss off. And I mean, *piss* off. Dead in the eye, "mate, piss off. Just piss off"'.

She looked at me sadly, then said, 'And the Italian men they won't get out of my van. They buy a lot but they tease and tease and won't leave me alone, today they were getting in the van again and hanging off it.'

I leaned and rubbed her forearm. 'Do you want a beer?'

She paused, then said, 'yeah'.

Christian leaned in, 'take it easy this evening. When we get back have a shower.'

She nodded.

On the drive back Ben said the others were taking the A-Team van into town to find a decent club, remarking that Greg was banned from coming.

I said 'yeah, great!'

'I think Val's got the evening off as well, I'll ask her.'

'Christian?' I asked, begging he'd say no. 'No, I'm OK, I'm going to chill out this evening, thanks.'

'Elly?', begging she'd say yes.

But Christian had already made her mind up for her.

'Nah. I'm not up for it. I'll stay in the flat and chill,' and looked at him keenly. Chill? Oh for God's sake, girl, don't start talking like him.

Val was up for it, Ben and I got ready, Greg was out somewhere so we didn't have to tell him he wasn't welcome. Christian and Elly were on the sofa, I saw Christian pick up a book as Elly turned her legs to brush against his, but he shifted an inch away.

'Do you want a beer?' she asked him meekly. He pursed his lips, nodded and glared pointedly at the book. Oddly cold.

I'd be on my back lapping out the ends of an empty beer bottle and *ZZ if Elly got her way, Christian would be on his back lapping out her end while she emptied his cock into her mouth ZZ.*

Anyway, out the door we went. We drove into town, dumped the van and walked along the baking pavement, past baking buildings, to a large square of wasteland between two towering buildings, a busted old car and bits of chain link fence, while into this square towards a single door in the side of one of the buildings was a line of people, headed off by two huge black bouncers.

The bouncers fussed over my driving licence, which was getting increasingly mashed up, but they let me in, only then it struck me, I hadn't seen any black guys around in, Jesus, ages. I really hadn't seen any in the suburbs. I said this to Ben and he just nodded, as did Mike.

It was a massive, multi-floored club that the side door gave no clue to, like the Tardis, loads of people but loads of space to dance, too.

For once I felt I looked good and for a second thought of Elly and Christian, then thought, 'fuck them, seriously, fuck them,' and started to dance. Strutting back and forth, turning, twirling, totally energised, until my linen shirt was black with sweat and then I danced all the more, even during the crappy songs when the floor cleared, just to out gun everyone else, just to say, 'I can go all night, and I am. Fuck you.'

'Fuckin' class dancing, Jimbo!' Val said on the way home. I smiled in victory.

Cracks

It was a day off, but as we were getting ready to do whatever we were doing the guys from the other flat came in and said the A-Team van was bust. Christian volunteered me to drive them in the Pontiac, great if it meant escaping that cunt for a few minutes.

I was driving, with Greg, Addy, Ali and a couple of others rammed in. It'd been raining hard and was still overcast, with that distinctly sharp smell of rainwater, tarmac and grease when it's not rained for ages then pisses down.

We bombed along as normal, but when we slew across the railway crossing just before the highway I felt the back of the car give out a shade, although no-one else noticed, and we hit the highway and got up some good speed. Soon enough we rounded a long bend and then a few hundred yards away was one the biggest junctions on the road, the lights green all the while we approached, but the longer that went on the sooner they'd change red, and we hit that weird void between knowing you'll need to brake soon, but you don't because they're still green and should make it through even on amber, but it's one or the other, and now you're too far away to even make it on amber, even if you floored it, but too close and too fast so you'll have to brake much sharper if they change.

These lights stayed green until we'd just moved out of the safe-to-brake-gently zone, but I was sure they'd go amber soon, so I began to brake anyway – but we didn't slow. At all. I pressed the brakes harder, no slowing whatsoever, closing the distance to the lights. I braked again with a bit more urgency as we sailed on, nothing, then the lights went amber just as I felt the car aquaplane, but it did so in a straight, straight line, like a missile, with neither the noise nor the shudder of a skid, so nobody else noticed we were gliding along out of control, not slowing an inch, to which Mike exclaimed, 'Jim the lights are going red!' as I pumped the brakes again, just as they turned red, with yards to go, and I said, 'I know, we're not stopping!' which I meant to mean, 'we can't stop', but they understood as 'to Hell with the lights', for as what were only a couple of seconds passed, but everything goes into fly-time, I realised there was no way we'd stop, or if we did we'd lock the wheels and spin out, careening into the box junction, if we hadn't gone into the trees. It was like in *The Cruel Sea* when Jack Hawkins is about to depth-charge a U-boat but in the water ahead are a load of survivors from a previous sinking, but he can't stop to pick them up or he'll get torpedoed and lose the sub, so he powers on and blows them all up, to his own horror.

It was do or die, so I floored it, the front rising as I did so, blasting the horn, causing everyone in the car to start shouting in panic – thank God our lane was clear and I could see the traffic about to cross the junction sides weren't moving yet, and we bounded through the lights, across this massive junction, to a chorus of horns, some having jolted forward a foot or so, and a chorus of 'Jesus Christ!', 'Fuck!', 'What the fuck are you doing?', 'Fucking idiot!' from within the car.

'I could not stop! We were aquaplaning! '

'Fucking Hell!'

'We were not stopping! It was too greasy, the brakes weren't stopping us at all.'

'You were going too fast!'

'I started slowing from miles ...'

'Idiot!'

The shouting abated a bit but I felt sick for it, got to Penguin and out they all got, with a few muttered curses levied my direction. I sat feeling pissed off and frustrated for a couple of minutes while having a smoke, then thought 'fuck this' and backed the Pontiac out, jacked it into DRIVE to bound across the gravel to drive me home, alone.

I drove slower just to make sure I didn't spin out or skid out of stupid anger, tracing along the railway towards the crossing point, where I slowly turned, then went to straighten up again to actually cross the rails, but the back end of the car just drifted on, like in a slow pirouette, now gliding toward the rails but almost side on, my side heading for the rails. I spun the wheel to the left, into the skid, and it caught just as we hit the rails with the engine almost pointing down the track, but the Pontiac straightened out too sharply, with the boot waltzing right round the other way so as we hit the second rail lines we were now pointing that way! I spun the wheel back the other way, and something gripped somewhere, then a skid, turn into it, a lesser skid, turn into that, a little skid, turn, and a few yards later it was all over, but I was fucking jacked.

'Jesus, Ponty, it's not funny, you fucking get.'

The car growled to itself in quiet humour. Bastard, if it'd done it earlier the others would have seen how slippery it all was.

Back at the flat, the plan for the day was, great, to go to the mall. I could have fucking wept.

'Let's go into town, do something in Chicago proper,'

'It's too far and the car's fucked,' said Christian.

'The car's always fucked.'

'All the more reason then not to drive it hours on the highway, then, fuckwit.'

'Fuck off!'

I seethed, Val looked at me in sympathy.

'I've not on 'til this arvo though, Jimbobs, I'll come with to the mall.'

'Great. We can go in the car that's fucked.'

I sulked all the way. With all of bloody Chicago to go see, we always ended up in the fucking Death Star, with no money.

Outside the mall was stood an elderly man with his Labrador. Immediately Elly went 'aw' and was straight over to the dog and was all over it, 'hello! hello!' in that over-excited, breathy way that people who like dogs talk to dogs, her hands stroking its back and shoulders as the dog nosed towards her, as her hands moved to its head and cheeks the dog clamouring left and right, tail wagging, 'ooh yezh you're a good boy, a good boy, a beautiful boy, aren't you yes yes you are yes you are aren't you yes,' as she squatted down to pet it and it licked her hands and face. She was absolutely gone with delight, nothing else mattered.

Christian lit up and asided to me, 'that conversation we had the other night at the gay club, it was brilliant, like something out of a film,' he said, then quieter he said, 'weird though, since I told you how I feel about Abigail, I've stopped thinking about her.'

'Maybe you just had to talk about it to stop thinking about it,' I said.

'Yeah, something like that. Anyway I'm slowing things down with Elly, she's getting quite heavy,' he said.

Inside we browsed stuff we couldn't afford.

Later at home, Christian was reading some brochure for radios and tape decks he'd got from an electronics shop, him showing the ones he liked to Ben who could have cared less, before he chucked it onto the coffee table and rolled up a fag. Then Elly picked up the brochure and flicked through it, flicking to the same pages at the same pieces and photos Christian was looking at. There was a weird, rattling urgency to her gaze. Was she gleaning together some point of interest to talk with Christian about? Days ago they'd been fucking each others' brains out. Now she was pretending to like tape-decks?

I was pretty sure I knew why Christian was putting it on ice. He'd split from his 'ex' only a few weeks before coming, and he was here to party as destructively as possible, with sex as an excellent extra, but no strings. If Elly had wanted that, the pillow talk had since got serious, too serious for Christian, who just wanted a holiday, but she wanted more, and now was ending up with nothing.

Had she tried too hard, to turn the fling into a relationship, too soon if at all? Shit. Had she told him the worst, and was he rejecting her for that? Yes or no, even if she only thought that, it didn't bode well for her at all. Did he know, and was that why she was being slowly dumped? All questions to torture herself with.

And oh God, resorting to reading some tatty tape-deck brochure, to impress him? Come on. But she was, poring over the hi-fis and pointing Christian to them. Then I realized, this is what I'd do with her. Nothing I'd ever done was enough to win her over, so I turned on it all, hated it all, and tried to rebuild my interests about whatever it was she thought was cool, or what I thought she thought was cool. I destroyed myself and tried to rebuild myself as what she wanted, which Elly saw for what it was: sad and pathetic, and rejected it thus. And she was right, it's a pitiful spectacle.

And now she was doing it. Did she seriously think he'd say, 'Oh, you're into radio tape-decks too, let's talk about them and relight the spark between us.' This didn't make sense. They were supposedly enamored already. She was a tungsten-scorching sexual Goddess, yet she scraping lower than Liz Taylor ever had to in *Cat on a Hot Tin Roof* where the whole audience was yelling Paul Newman had to be some kinda Goddamn faggot not to fuck her lights out!

'Since when have you been into or interested in hi-fis?' I asked.

'Since always'.

'Oh.'

'Fuck off.'

She knew I was onto her.

So: Christian really was calling the shots. Confirmed.

Christian really was cooling it off. Confirmed.

She wasn't happy about it. Confirmed.

If she wasn't in love with him, she sure as Hell was in something with him. Confirmed.

Now he was pushing her away, and she couldn't handle that. Strong suspicion.

In the car on the way home, Christian was in the passenger seat, Elly sitting behind him. She leaned forward and ferreted her hand around the edge of the front seat to take hold of Christian's hand, but he flinched sharply away, out of her range. He couldn't be clearer, and I could see out of the corner of my eye, her expression was between sad and confused. She was losing her grip.

I knew he was hurting inside for whatever reasons, but still, why be a cunt like that to someone else? She's stunning, inside and out.

Zz - and he knew what she was like inside - zz.

Val was at the flat, with Bobby and Sandy, nice to see again. Christian skinned up and Bobby was jabbering again, about politics.

'Clinton will not win next year, they'll get him for something.' he said.

'Who's they?'

'You heard about the Iranian hostage rescue in 1980?'

'Mmm … oh yes, when they sent the helicopters to go rescue the Americans, but they all crashed in the desert?'

'What Americans?' said Elly.

'During the Iranian revolution in 1979 when the Mullahs took over, they stormed the American embassy and took a load of us hostage. I mean this Ayatollah guy was incredible, this was Iran, which to then had been a real friend of the US cos of the Nazi-loving Shah we put in there to look after the oil, yet still out of nowhere this Khomeni comes and overnight smashes it up. He's a real hardliner anti-American but with Allah on his side, some holy Lenin, and like of course oil prices go mental and Carter got all uptight and put on sanctions and went to the UN and all, but the Iranians didn't care and had our guys chained to a radiator. So Carter sent helicopters to rescue them, flying at tree-top height over the desert – a brilliant plan, but they all crashed, and this was such a fuck up it screwed Carter completely, as the Iranians not only dared take these guys hostage, real 'fuck you America!', but then he fucks the rescue. Basically it cost him the 1980 election and Reagan won.'

Woah. I was impressed.

'Shit.'

'Yeah. But the real shit is, why did they all crash? They didn't have sand filters on them and the engines bunged up with sand.'

'That's insane. How could they not think of that?'

'Exactly, right, how could you not?'

'That's just mental. I remember pictures of Bf109s and Spitfires in the desert in World War Two, with fuck-off great big filters on the engines.'

'Exactly, right? Of course they thought of it, but the CIA wanted to screw Carter, so their agents at the helicopter bases took the filters *off* the choppers so they'd crash and fuck Carter. It was deliberate. He was a way better president than Reagan, for us, but the CIA wanted Reagan in to go kick ass in central America, so they arranged to fuck it up.'

'Bastards.'

'Yeah, and you saw the same day of Reagan's inauguration, the very same morning, the hostages were released! It was unbelievable! They showed on TV Reagan on one half taking office and on the other the hostages being released. It was the most obvious Goddamn fix. Someone had done some deal with the Iranians to get them released, great, that's what everyone wants, right? But to time the release for the day Reagan takes office? The hour he takes office? Why not weeks beforehand? Because it was about fucking Carter and boosting Reagan, it wasn't even about the fucking hostages, instead commentators are saying things 'somehow this guy gets things done, day one and the hostages are out', yeah, what a blast to start the new presidency, and no-one's like, what the fuck's going on here, who the fuck organized this behind Carter's back, because he was president up to that point, while our guys ass-deep in sewage fight off rats I some fucking cellar? The Iranians didn't suddenly decide to give them up that day. Un-fucking-believable.'

'But why did the CIA want Carter out?' asked Elly.

'Because they really wanted to get into central America and raise Hell there, but Carter wouldn't let them, and they knew Reagan would, all the Republicans were in favour of doing a number on the central Americans as they were all socialists and friends of Castro. El Salvador, Nicaragua, Grenada, Guatemala, Panama. We fucked them all in the 1980s.'

'Shit.'

'So … I don't know, is Clinton going to get re-elected?'

'That's a great question. Because he is a Democrat, right, and normally they don't like Democrats, they're usually the enemy, but there's no doubt he wouldn't have won in '92 if they hadn't wanted him in. They had more than enough to sink him what with Gennifer Flowers and all, that came up.'

'Oh yeah, Gennifer Flowers, forgot about her,' I said.

'Yes they did, the story was out there in the run-up to the election, there wasn't any suppression of it,' said Ben.

'Yeah but he was given a lot of room to kind of get out of it and present himself as a homely kinda guy in love with Hillary and all, and no-one kinda cared as a result. People in high places wanted him elected, how far the corruption goes is incredible, even the porn industry wanted Clinton in office, Flowers did a kiss 'n' tell in Penthouse that came out that could have done him real damage, but it was published *after* the election.'

'Do exposes in *Penthouse* really have that much sway on voters?' said Elly.

Bobby said, 'well no, but, the real big thing is you gotta remember Clinton would never have won without Ross Perot splitting the Republican vote, Perot got about a fifth of the vote and they'd have voted Bush otherwise. They never had a third party candidate before! Perot was the first ever! And they only had him on to fuck Bush. The point is the hardcore right-wingers put him there to get Bush out cos Bush was too shit, a wimp, and was too busy keeping things for his own faction.'

'I remember those debates,' I said, 'Both Perot and Clinton were attacking Bush. Bush was going off on one about Clinton protesting Vietnam, "I just think it's wrong to attack your country when it's at war, you gotta rally to the flag," and Clinton said "you're wrong to attack my patriotism, I lurve mah country," and Bush kind of wilted, he could see Clinton was right, and Perot wades in like an uncle, "he was a young man then, young men make mistakes!"'

'But why would the right nobble their own guy?' said Ben.

'Wad? Nob? Nob-wad?'

'Er, nobbling - stuffing, fucking. Why would they fuck their own guy?'

'Oh right. Well, the right was split, and Perot's a Texan, and they are different. They are so different. "You can have your 49 stars but we're the Lone Star state." They just do their own thing. They're Republicans not because they have to be or they're like that, but because the Republicans have, er, mutated themselves way more than the Democrats have in order to get Texas to vote for them. Texas doesn't care! All they're on is oil, and this whole country's dependent on oil, because that's what Texas wants. We could all have electric cars years ago if the car industry built them and the government could do it like they built all the highways and what Gore's doing now with the Internet, but they don't cos the oil industry – read, Texas – won't let either of them do it, basically Houston made Detroit and Washington makes the country drive on gas, so we took over the Middle East for the stuff. That's the reality.'

'Yes. Have you read *The Prize*?' I said.

'No.'

'Brilliant book about the history of the oil industry, starting with the discoveries in Pennsylvania. You know it, Elly, I lent you it.'

'Did you?'

'Yes I did. Well you obviously read it, eh.'

214

'All I know about Texas I know from Dallas.'

'Yeah! And it's the same for most Americans, and Texans hate that show not because it shows them in a bad light but it shows them for who they are! But really most of them don't care what anyone thinks anyway. You think America's up its own ass, you want to go to Texas, and they think the rest of America is up its ass as well. It's got like 32 electoral college votes, you know about the electoral college?'

'Yes,' hopefully he'd veer out of patronizing, 'but hang on, I don't get how the CIA allowed Bush to be brought down, if it's all about Texas and oil, I thought Bush was an oil-man, and that's what the Gulf War was about, not just liberating Kuwait but establishing the US in the Middle East now the Soviets were dead,' I said. Not everything he said stacked up.

'He is an oil-man through and through, but he was also trying to get the rabid Christian vote, the right-wing Church, which also scared off a lot of voters. I mean, the CIA has a lot of power, up to a point, but there's a limit to what they can do. They can bring down a president by wrecking what he tries to do, but internal party shit isn't their domain. And Bush going for the church vote, really pissed off the Texans, cos they hate the Church, cos they're all Masons, and so is Clinton, and so is the CIA. You see what they did at Waco? That's what they do to preachers there. Bill Hicks said that was the state versus freedom of belief, or federal versus state power, but it wasn't, it was Texan Masons vs. the Church. Hicks was also a loyal Texan though and he was as much anti-Church, and that's why they killed him.'

'Suck Satan's cock!' *hawwwwwwww-brrrrrrrrrrrrrgghghghgh*!' said Ben.

'Ha! you saw that?!' I squealed.

'Yeah! Channel 4 one night!'

'Oh my God that was killer, was that, this Hicks guy?'

'Yeah!'

Bobby looked amused, then carried on. 'But Kennedy got killed too in Texas, although that was the mob, but the Masons and the oil guys were in on the fix somehow. Probably Bush was involved somewhere. The oil men were already on a roll after Eisenhower built the highways, and Kennedy wasn't messing with that.'

'If Clinton's their man now, why would they bring him down?

'He's not warring enough.'

And so the evening wore on, Bobby pouring forth theory after theory, some of them making sense, some not quite, with Sandy nodding now and again or sometimes looking a bit quizzical, but being a nice bloke really. Things wrapped up, we said they were welcome anytime, Bobby said he'd take us to a bar, and then off into the night they went on Bobby's cute little old-school Italian scooter. I stayed up to watch *Mystery Science Fiction Theatre 3000*.

215

5 cent shots

I woke up on the sofa, but the Weather Channel was on and showed a lot of rain over Illinois this morning, map had all sorts of colourful arrows and fronts and fonts smothering Lake Michigan and the surrounding states. The mother of all Canadian storms had busted south to take the northern USA, meaning we could go outside without dying, but business would be dead, too.

Looking out from the apartment to the freeway, cars lost in plumes of spray, some swaying a shade on the oily roads. Rain, on an American scale, surely meaning fat chance of work. But Hank called us in, said the radio said it'd clear by midday and we'd have a shooting chance by then.

Everyone seemed as groggy and grey as the sky, as we traipsed down to the Ponty rainwater vomiting out of the apartment block's drain pipes, the car park gutters forming streams and rivulets. The car fished through the standing water on the roads, seemingly buffeted along by its own wave of after-spray such we could barely see out the back, like those cockerel tails on Formula 1 cars, and we slew into the vast gravel trap in front of Penguin, wheels bounding in the dunes as the car shook itself dry, like a big dog, but pitching into puddle after puddle, while a duckless pond besieged the hanger doors, big enough to soak our toes and heels as we tried to bound over it.

We started the whole bombing up thing and eventually Hank unloaded the dry ice. But it wasn't the usual big fat cubes, these were barely a third the normal size, and Hank was handling each segment with a giant's gentleness, great bear mittens protecting his paws.

'Hank, you're holding that like it's gold,' I said.

'It is, today, Jim. This is all we've got.'

'Yerrrp,' leered Charlie, 'cost nearly four times the price,' signing off with a bungee spit out the door.

'How so?'

Hank raised himself: 'You know it's been real hot these past days, before this rain?'

'Yeah, we sold loads more ice-cream, before it got too hot,' said Christian.

'Yep, hot weather sells ice-cream, that's the pro side of the equation,' he said, 'but the downside is it gets hottest before rain like this, where we sell nothing.' Hank paused, deftly moved the ice onto the anvil, then breathed in. 'We've had it worst, where it was so hot we sold nothing, and then the heat has caused power cuts that have knocked out a lot of businesses round here, as well as preceding this rain here.'

'Thing is, there are two dry ice plants we can get supply from, but one's out the action, and output from the other one is halved, and as he's the sole producer now, his prices have sky-rocketed.'

Everyone was quiet. Some dry ice flakes had chipped into the puddles at the hanger doors, bubbling and steaming furiously. I'd thought this biz was like cricket, hot days meant selling, while rain stopped play. Nothing's so simple.

'So – you're all getting far less freezer ice, and you've got to use it far better, although today we may sell fuck all,' I said.

We all looked at one another. Further to go with less to go on, while today's profits would be hammered by the rain. We finished bombing up, Charlie helping deploy the nuggets of dry-ice in the freezers to best effect. 'We'll sure get some spoilage as well,' he said to me, 'so if you're geddin' on and the money's poor and you think the stock's going, just come back.'

Jeez, I thought on the drive down, this is like in *The Battle of Britain* when the Luftwaffe turned on London, 'they'll have further to go - and go back, while their escorts will only have 10 minutes over London'. Those furthest from Penguin will have the highest risk of losing stock, while local sellers could clean up what's left. This was a compromise on the grand strategy.

There was no grand strategy today though. The cloud cover pretty much all day giving a mugginess to slow, grinding trade, finished off with an excursion to Bartlett. I got back to the hanger about 6, with most of the others back already, pissed off and bored.

'Hey Jim. Get this shit.' said Ben.

'What?'

'That heatwave. It has killed hundreds of people.'

'No way.'

'Yeah. Hundreds. Mostly old people it seems, in their homes, the power went and the air-con died, where there weren't power cuts they collapsed in the heat anyway.'

'How many?'

'It's estimated over 150 but the figure's rising.'

'I heard 200,' said Jason.

'Fucking Hell.' Everyone started commenting.

'People were talking about it on the rounds.'

'Yeah I heard a few things.'

'It was quiet those days, wasn't it.'

'Yeah - they were all dead.'

'Stayed indoors to keep cool, but it backfired for too many of them.'

'Dogs boiling to death in cars,' Elly winced.

'Fuck. And we wanted it hot to sell ice-cream. And we didn't sell shit.' I felt bad, as if I'd willed it upon them.

'Well, they died cos of the heat, we could have saved them, just one ice-cream could have done it, wasn't as if we didn't offer.'

'True.'

I got myself a beer and one for Elly.

Silence fell, 'til I said: 'Anyone got any heatwave jokes then?'

'Got some Challenger jokes!,' Ben said, 'what's the Challenger crew's favourite drink?'

'Dunno.'

'Seven up and a Teacher's on the rocks.'

'What were the last words from the Challenger captain? "What does this button do?" said Mike.

'Did you know that Christa McAuliffe was blue eyed? One blew left and one blew right,' said Jeff.

'Oh was that the teacher?' Ben said.

'Yeah. I mean we teachers were real proud of her. In over a decade of teaching, she only blew up in front of her class that one time!'

'What does NASA stand for? "Need Another Seven Astronauts"', said Ben.

'Talking of things blowing up, are we going to get shot of the Pontiac, Christian?' I said.

This jangled him. 'Addy's being a total arsehole. He knows we agreed to rotate them, it's what we agreed with Hank, in fact it was Hank's idea.' He paused. 'Fuck it, I'll speak to Hank about it.'

'I don't like him. The way he refers to himself, as "ickle" it's creepy. He's 30-something,' said Elly.

'Anyway let's not hang here too long,' said Christian, 'we're going out this evening. Val said Bobby wants to take us to a cool bar in town.'

Bobby and Sandy were at the flat with Val, then Mike and Jason came in. Christian then got out some pills, 'ephedril' he said, 'for asthmatics. Mix these with Pro Plus and beer and it's like speed.'

'Cool!' said Ben.

'I won't this time but thanks,' said Bobby.

'I'll be getting some more dope in a day or two as well,' he said, adding, 'seeing as Jim never found the stuff he threw away.'

'Get stuffed,' I said, 'you'd rather the police found it?'

'Haha!' he said.

Wanker.

At last we were going back into town, piling into the Pontiac for the long cruise in, the great city in Space finally looming into view. We passed turn off after turn off under great big green signs, then took a turn to some part of the city I'd never heard of, the streets not lined with cafes and bright lights nor the posh facades of City Hall, but away off the main drags, with narrow, badly lit streets, few people, then across a sturdy girder and rivet bridge spanning a narrow canal, its inky waters shimmering with city lights, the buildings around were warehouses with large arched windows or long, windowless walls of fine brickwork. Bobby said something about how the waterways used to flow with the blood and fat from the meatpacking district, like *Tintin In America*, and I said there was a feel to the area that reminded me of the old industrial parts around uni, which could be incredibly romantic.

'There are a lot of artists in this part of town, it's getting pretty cool,' he said, adding though that the artists were still heavily outnumbered by drug addicts.

Near another girder bridge we found an alley to stash the car, then walked to a single storey brick warehouse, with large, blacked out windows. It was $3 to get in, no ID checks, Bobby knew them on the door anyway, and incredibly the deal was that shots were 5 cents all night. Inside went back a long way, the near half being the bar that took up all of one side, all painted black and lit by strip lights under the drinks' shelves, opposite a line of big old motorcycles serving as bar tables of sorts, the mirrors converted into drinks' holders. The back half was brighter with a pool table and old arcade games. Groups and couples of Goths and punks dotted here and there, it had such a cool, friendly vibe to it. With drinks going at 5 cents each, how could it not?

One of the games was *Frogger* which I couldn't beat level 3. Then Christian, who was playing a loud and raucous game of pool – much to Elly's apparent delight – offered me the caffeine tablets and ephadril, and soon I was smashing *Frogger* on level 8, 9, 10. A good evening rolled out into the smallest hours.

We cruised past the Sears Tower, and I remembered how I used to think Crystal Palace tower had to be the tallest building it in the world. I was sat in the rear gunner seat, then Bobby turned around and said to me, 'You know the Sears Tower is a fascist building?'

'No?'

'Think of the structure. It's several blocks rising together, separate towers that are bound together in this 'bundle' - what's a bound bundle? A *fasces* – ergo, fascism. It's the ultimate corporate tower as corporations are fascist structures.'

He nodded sagely as I looked at him eyes wide, which I meant to mean, 'are you really sure of that?' but he understood as, 'wow - you've blown my mind again!'

As tail gunner I got to see the city narrow away, like one of those tracking shots out of *2001: A Space Odyssey*. It was about 4am and the sky was already no longer black but purple-blue, the stars all gone, leaving the bright red aircraft lights of the skyscrapers supreme. As the towers diminished in height, the horizon melded blue with grey with brown and red and gold, and those glass towers all stood to attention to reflect the rising Sun, a row of golden shielded warriors hailing the return of the Great Star.

Washi Mashi

Like the Weather Channel predicted, it was a shitty day with pissy weather, but not so much raining as threatening to, the air was sticky and pressure was high, giving me a headache.

Sometime in the afternoon I was flagged down by the woman who'd offered me a job some days before, and I told her I'd thought about it (which I hadn't really but didn't want to admit I'd forgotten almost as soon as she'd asked), but couldn't accept, but thanks.

'Oh that's disappointing. See, not only are you Cancer, and it was on the cards, that we'd have a Cancer come work for us, but the cards said that we'd meet a tall young man who'd come from afar, and he would prove very valuable.'

'Cards?'

'Tarot cards. We got a real good reading just after we met last time. You sure I can't persuade you? We had another young man like you come over to us, and he's doing very well indeed.'

I said no again, but thanks, it all seemed so bizarre. Although for £10 I'd had my cards read at uni, this woman said I'd go to the Land of Eagles with a man from the Land of David, which meant going to the US with Christian who's originally Scottish, she said. It was uncanny. She also said I'd meet my wife in the US ... which I thought would mean Elly. Boy was I lost.

As I drove off, a few streets later, I thought more about the offer. Maybe my wife wasn't going to be Elly. Oh for fuck's sake, Jim, of course it fucking isn't. It was Elly who'd recommended the tarot reader, who'd told her the man she'd marry was a few years away, information that led me to literally bang my head against my bedroom wall.

But I was being given an opportunity. Shit – what had I just turned down? Surely not, no ... had I turned down the chance to stay and meet the woman I'd marry? Happiness? But surely, if Fate had in store what it had in store, it didn't matter what I did?

This was all too much of a head fuck so I was glad to find myself in Joly's neck of the woods, but was then sad to see he wasn't out. This was strange, I hadn't seen him a few times now, although this time his baseball stuff was out on the hillock and a couple of his usual friends were loitering, but at a distance so I couldn't ask them if he was around.

Was he avoiding me?

The atmosphere at the hanger was dross, a dozen disgruntled faces on heads atop stinking bodies. A few rounds of 'wad?' 'wad?', before we traipsed back to the apartments, where Val was home.

'We keep on getting these phone calls from some woman goin' on about washing machines. You pick it up and she's going, "*washi'mashi, washi'mashi*", it's completely freak. She's Chinese or something, it's all she says, "washi'mashi", and I'm goin, "no we don't want a washing machine, we've got a launderette upstairs."' She's phoned like four times in the past couple of days.'

'What kind of bollocks hard-sell is that?' said Ben.

'The stain says hot, the label says not,' I said.

'It's the ultimate in shit door-to-door selling, random phone calls where you just say 'washing machine washing machine' over and over until they give in,' said Christian.

Ben made a finger phone, 'Hello?' "Brooms! Brooms! Brooms!" 'Stop calling me!'

Val continued, 'talking of which, I were on the phone to Aaron earlier, poor luv, he was out all day yesterday doing his Skyshot thing, and he fainted from the heat.'

'Who's Aaron?' Ben mouthed at me.

'Boyfriend,' I mouthed back.

'Oh,' he mouthed, grinned, then frowned.

'Said he rung some doorbell, then just everything went zonk, came around with these two folks standing over him and this dog licking his face.'

'Shit!'

'Them whose doorstep he collapsed on were dead nice, took him in to cool down and gave him water, he came around and felt all right, carried on a bit, then gave up and went home. Lucky he didn't hit his head or owt on the way down.'

'And that they were in. He could have lain there for hours,' said Elly.

'Shit, yeah.'

'They'd have come later to find this dead bloke on their doorstep.'

'Not fucking funny Jim!'

'All shrivelled up, like a prune.'

'Shurrup!'

Christian said, 'I said Skyshot was shit. He should have come and sold ice-cream.'

'Fuck off Christian,' said Val.

Christian could be so helpful in people I-told-you-so, even if he didn't really know them, and especially if they were having a bad time of it.

Greg came in from his day of painting, or non-painting as the weather had pissed on his plan to paint the front of a house.

The evening wore on. We caught a bit of the TV news that put the death count at over 300. No-one said much, too many people in one space, everyone was out of sorts for what to do, and it was hot and sticky. The cloud cover made it like a sauna outside and inside the air-con wasn't much better. Everyone stank. Some sitcom was rendered unwatchable by ad breaks every five seconds. Christian seemed to be studiously ignoring Elly, who was knocking down beers in a fashion, until he upped and went to read on his bed. Elly made a face of mock grimace. I went into my room to get something, and turned around to see her in the doorway, then she came to me and punched my arm, doing a *pch!* sound effect, like all the best TV show punch ups.

'Oi,' I said, and punched her back, playfully, then she punched me again in the arm and my back, then me to her belly, she hit me back, and I grabbed her wrists and we ended up wrestling on the floor.

Maybe because I was still in stinky work garb, she somehow thought it preferable to take my clothes off, anyway, somehow, I was quickly down to my pants, God they were beyond their best as well. I was filmed with sweat as we tussled on the floor, and I got this massive, obvious erection, but she carried on. Me in my pants, her pissed, us wrestling, me pinning her down. Then I tried to kiss her.

She said 'no!', pushed me off and left the room, but was soon coming back down the corridor, bouncing off the walls, swaying through the doorway brandishing a spatula, which she then tried to hit me with to no great effect, until I grabbed her wrists again and spun her round, her arms across her body and she was truly caught. I threw her on the bed and lay on top, turning her over. I was so turned on.

'I have you now!' I said, but she wasn't having it. She relaxed all over and looked away, as if bored, and I let her go. Then she went to the door, turned and said with this moll-like sultriness, 'I'm going to get some action.'

She wagged a finger at me, then, humming with an insouciant naughtiness, went into where Christian was reading, the closing door quietening her humming. I was livid. We'd gotten all worked up and now she was excited she was going to give Christian the benefit of it all. Un-fucking-believable! She's going in there to get fucked senseless, I thought, caught between the raw excitement of her being severely screwed, and the frustration of having charged her up, now Christian cashes in ZZ *spending his wad in her pouch* ZZ

Then Val appeared down the corridor, seeing me all sweaty and near nude.

'What you gonna do with that then, Jimbo?' she said, looking to my crotch and the screaming stiff within these sweaty pants, as the love of my life lined up for a serious fucking off my best mate.

But she was out in a few minutes, looking non-plussed, got another beer, chugged it, chugged another, then wandered from room to room until she ended up falling into the bath.

'Someone help me,' she said, pitifully, so I went to get her out, but in hoying her out of the bath from behind my hands slid up and grabbed her breasts. Genuine mistake, but she cried out, 'What you trying to do?'

I said, 'trying to get you out', but put her back down in the bath.

'Don't leave me!' she said, with exaggerated terror.

Christian meanwhile was now back in the living room, eyes fixed on the TV, and he started talking quietly to me.

'Elly's being a nightmare. She came in, lay on the bed, I turned away, and she reaches over to start undoing my belt, so I stopped her, but she still tried to reach over to get my cock,' he said with quiet, pained frustration. 'I had to throw her off.'

Whereupon Elly walked in, stuck out her tongue and swayed into the kitchen, from where we heard cans being jostled in the fridge and she reappeared downing a beer, waving a V-sign at me, putting her tongue out at Christian, before trouncing back to her room, declaring, 'I'm going to bed, dunno about you boring losers!'

'Nightmare,' was all Christian said. Yeah, thanks for the details, and that you turned her down?

I found Elly in the walk-in closet.

'Close the door,' she said, 'I'm going to sleep in here.'

Fuck this, I thought, and went and got shit-faced.

Shoot hoops

Obviously things happened between me getting up with a swollen tongue and eyes, and finding myself driving to Westie. Luckily Hank hadn't asked me anything, I couldn't string a sentence together, but if I aimed at something I could walk in a straight line and I'd bombed up and driven off without crashing so I still had a good half-hour's drive to sober up for what was an overcast non-day, humid, crap sales, thoughts of Elly and Christian fucking and hitting things. At the hanger over counting and beer the others told of bad days, too.

The death toll was nearing 500. 'Yeah, all on my route, business was dead,' I said, but no-one laughed.

At the flat, Christian was picking the seeds out of the weed on the coffee table. Elly sat next to him and put her head on his shoulder, but he leant forward quickly to dislodge her. She put a hand on his shoulder and took a sly sniff of his back, but he twitched, repelling her. I was glad they weren't all over each other, but to see her bash herself up over him, and look so lost, over a total fucking arsehole, ugh. A real fuck and chuck.

She turned to me balefully and asked, 'Do you want to shoot hoops?'

Me? And shit, she was sober.

'Yeah, sure,' I said, even though I'd never liked basketball. I went to change out of my jeans into shorts, but got this raging boner, whereupon Elly appeared in the bedroom, so I stood still at an odd angle, and she looked at me funny and asked, 'what are you doing?'

'Nothing, just give me a minute', hoping the gloom of the room and my black shorts obscured the rager.

'I can see what you've got,' she sighed, 'come on'.

Down on the basketball court next to the car park, we were lunging in and out at one another, one bouncing the ball with terrible skill towards the hoop, the other in front, hands up to block the shot, darting in a hand here, there, trying to grab the ball, grabbing the other to get the ball, wrestling both them and the ball, lots of puffing and panting and we both fast worked up a sweat in the heat. I then began to wonder if it wasn't possible that we might end up in a snog.

Then a voice called, 'hey you guys, time out!'

It was Jeff. We stopped and disentangled ourselves, he took the ball and hooped it first try.

'Basketball was my scholarship through college,' he said, 'I was lined up to go pro even but threw my right arm and the shoulder popped out, that was that. You play basketball in England? You play, Elly?'

'I used to play netball. Really, I was a swimmer. Swam for the school, counties.'

'Would love to see you in a swimsuit,' he said, and whistled.

She flicked a V at him, then said, 'let's go back in for a beer.'

As Elly walked away, her trousers tight around her gorgeous bum, I looked at the floor in exasperation, and Jeff asked teasingly, 'what's up, man, did I block your shot?'

I just grunted.

'Denied!' he said.

Bobby was now there, having a shouty discussion with Christian about something. 'Hi Elly!' he said over- enthusiastically, then said 'Hi Jim!' with as much excitement, but he'd already given himself away.

I introduced Jeff, who waded into the discussion, then I got straight back on the beer and spliff. It was a strong one, and their uninteresting chat saw my mind go off for a stroll. It wandered around the old haunts of North London where I'd lived, until it came to our lovely old house where I grew up, its lovely long garden heaving with trees, the home we'd left just a year before, the same day ma and pa split, when we moved in with her, and watched him drive away.

In my mind, at the end of garden, still stood our Edwardian greenhouse, somehow rebuilt after it was destroyed in the storm of '87. Through the dusty windows I could see some figures. This was so curious I had to go in. Inside there was me, me, me and now, me. All sharing a cold-pack of beer.

Hello, I ventured, expecting a barrage of abuse.

Hello, they (I) smiled back.

We all looked happy. No bruising? No one had been fighting? No demons? Odd. I took a beer and squatted in a cob-webbed corner. At first hesitant, they (we) then came forth with the questions.

So ... what are you going to do, go back to uni, repeat the first year?
Possibly.

Three years all over again. Will you finish?
I paused, then said lamely, 'don't know.'

We looked at me, unimpressed.

That's not good enough, one of me said, *but it says a lot about your commitment. It's fucking hard work, the degree's just the first stage for the job. No-one else has to work this hard, do you really want to work your guts out that much fucking harder for a degree while other tossers piss about?*

What else would I do?

Anything but what you're doing. You're not going to make it like this.
I could do something else, like art history.

You're not interested in art history.
I could do anthropology, with Elly.

Oh for God's sake. You're not interested in anthropology, you're just saying it because she's switched to that. And why did she do that?
To impress Richard.

And you'd switch to impress her, to be with her.
It'll be great.

It'll be Hell. You'll lose interest and she won't want to go out with you for doing the same course. Be serious.
I need to do something.

Listen to yourself. Look at yourself. What are you possibly going to stick at for three years, in this state? Nothing. You're clutching at anything, any

225

fucking reason to go back, and it's just to be with her. But she's not yours.

She could be.

She said no, Jim. She means it. Nothing'll change.

She needs me as a friend. I have to stay as her friend.

Can you accept that?

I couldn't answer.

Your cock will scream itself to death. You know that.

But I can't lose a friendship over that. I must be able to control how I feel, that's so shit to lose friends over that.

You can't control it though. And it's shit to lie to yourself and her. Not only will you never go out with her, she'll go out with other blokes, and all the time you'll be looking to see where the next competition is coming from, remaking yourself, modeling yourself on them, changing everything you do, your life, your interests, to be what you think she wants, or battle off whoever you think she's going for, to get into her pants. It'll never happen.

But I love her.

Yes. Which is why you have to leave her.

No.

Is she going to be yours?

No.

So what do you do? Hang around her waiting for the word to fuck? Is that really what either of you need? It's trust, Jim, trust, everything is based on trust. She can't trust you, can she? Not this way.

But she gets so much grief off blokes, I have to protect her.

You're one of those men, and you know it.

I'm not! I'm not!

She knows you're in love with her, and she loves you as a friend. She's not trying to hurt you but you're the last person to protect her. Think about it. One day you'll lose your cool, it'll wreck everything.

I'd never do that.

No, you probably wouldn't. But what will it take to blow that trust, to destroy it? What'll you do when it's gone?

It's not gone. I'll recover. I'll rejuvenate. I just need something to apply myself to. A serious pursuit. Something challenging. Anthropology could do it.

You are lost. You go back, it'll be another spiral of drugs and booze, seeing every conversation with her as a cliff-hanger for the fuck that'll never come, hanging off the phone making up jokes and shit to please her when she invites you to the pub, where she'll tell you about her latest exploits, after which you'll hanging out of some 20th floor window.

The drugs. They will wreck it all again.

And your life. Is she worth it?

'No' appeared large in my mind, but I couldn't say it.

What are the odds of you, seriously, surviving the year? How close did you come to total defeat, months ago? Weeks ago? While you've even been here?

226

You're having a little renaissance now, you've pulled off some top stuff, you're feeling more confident.

At fucking last.

But come Winter, can you imagine? Don't do it, Jim, don't do it. Just go.

But what about my friends, I'll miss them.

Your so-called best mate fucked her, now your other best mate's fucking her, everyone you meet will fuck her, and everybody else thinks you're crazy.

Because they don't understand it. I've never explained it to them. I've never explained why I'm in this fix with her. I love her, it's real now.

So why this isn't just a crush anymore?

Don't ask me to explain. Anyway, isn't it inevitable that if you start life with a crush on someone, it'll develop into love if you hang around long enough. Why doesn't anyone understand how I know her? I tell them again and again, 'you don't know her like I do,' but all they say is 'that's what people say when they're in love, but it's not true,' and they think I'm just crazy, even Christian one night just looked at me and said, 'Jim… Jim … she said no.'

I wanted to leave her when she shot me down that night, I wanted to get away but she told me her past, I couldn't leave her after that.

I knew it'd be Hell.

All the times we'd meet up and she'd tell me about her life, then and for hours after, everything she'd ever done, everything she'd ever do I could imagine in such colour, without closing my eyes, the visions were there in my mind crowding out all reality so I all I saw were her occasions from her past, present and future. Visions ravaged by the pain of not having been there, to hear, touch, smell, taste, experience it all, live it with her. All that had passed, all that would be, I wanted to be there, but someone else filled the space where I should have been, she took those lagoon-like eyes and cast them with all the passion and mystical power of her eternal love on someone else and the memories that would be built from that.

I'd go to sleep wanting her, dream of wanting her, wake up wanting her and wait on her call. Drink and spliff to knock out the days in between. The visions. The hallucinations. Was she a witch? A Goddess? I saw her face in every crowd, in every cloud, waiting around every door, every corner, just waiting for me to come across.

And the nights, the stars I could see, so many just the ghosts of stars that had been born and died, their stories that covered billions of years still being told to us, millions of light-years away, stories once told they'd be gone forever. Was anyone listening?

The time I saw the rings of Saturn with my telescope in the back garden, gosh, that was a night. So beautiful no-one could ever dare really write about them, no mere man's ideas or poems about this astonishing, astounding mass in space, such awesome vast, serene beauty, billions of miles away, billions of years old, could ever do it justice. And the photos from Voyager around

Neptune, so vast and cold, its great blue spot, its cirrus clouds, so far away on the very edge of darkness. Such, such wonder.

She made me feel like that. And she liked the friendship, but didn't understand the love. Why should she, as others said, it was just crazy. All the conversations I had in my head to make her understand. All the ways I wanted to put it, 'but don't you see? We're right for one another! Just give me this chance!' then the guilt, 'not giving me this chance is a waste! It's wrong! I could do so much!' 'You've got to!'

But who'd believe me, I can't explain why. I know her like they never, ever can. And they'll never know.

I was back in the greenhouse.

You called her a whore the other day, in your mind. Slut, harlot, fucking bitch. Just call her one of those names, see how she feels.

Listen to yourself. This isn't something you're driving. You're on a rollercoaster. Yes, she trusts you, and yet you think such things of her… if you ever were a couple, could you trust her? She's slept with two of your best friends.

She's free to. She's not my girlfriend.

But can you trust her not to fuck any of your other friends. You're worried she'll fuck your old friends, you're worried she'd fuck any new ones. Together or not, you'll spend your whole time looking over your shoulder. Comparing yourself with others, wondering who she's going to fuck.

She's not a whore. She's free. It's not my business to judge, she's not mine, never was.

And she never will be. Get away, with your honour intact. Get away before you strike. You'll destroy her and yourself.

I won't. I wouldn't. And where do I go? There's nowhere to go. I can't leave again. Back to London? There's nothing to do. There's nothing I can do. What am I supposed to do? Who'd employ me? I'm scared.

Of course you re scared. It's been an awful year. London's got money for one thing, damn sight more than anyone at uni. You don't know. You simply do not know. Maybe even stay here, if you like it so much. But face it, the game's up.

I love her. She needs me.

And she loves you. But not in the same way. Protect yourself, protect her. Leave her.

But what did I do wrong?

Nothing, Jim. You didn't do anything wrong. It's allright, you've not done anything wrong.

I love her.

Yes.

So I must leave her.

Yes.

228

Jim.

Jim.

Jim...

The greenhouse disappeared and was replaced by Christian and Ben on the sofa, staring at me.

'Jim ... the spliff,' said Ben. An eternity to register, I looked down and half the spliff's length was ash and cinder, waiting to spill onto my bare leg. I'd also nearly slipped off of the armchair. Bobby was laughing, Jeff was gone.

'Where are you, Jim?' Christian waved his arms. I tapped the ash and silently brandished the spliff at eye level to signify my present state, or lack of presence. At last, a decision about deciding.

Hell night

I woke up weirdly early, so I sneakily smashed one out then went to smoke on the balcony. Christian appeared, and I gave him a cig.

'Just to let you know, I've stopped it with Elly,' he said, 'she's getting too heavy.'

I suspected why, but just asked, 'when did this happen, last night?'

'Yeah. She wasn't happy about it' He looked out over the car park and shook his head. 'So, if it's all right with you, I'll come back to sleep in the bedroom with Ben and you go back to sleeping in the room with Elly, is that good?'

Muggins me shifted from room to room because of you two and your fucked up bollocks relationship, though I was relieved it was over. What I said was, 'yeah, fine', and with everyone up we swapped our stuff around, then from the corridor I saw Elly on the sofa, looking at her hands. Shit happens, but fuck all this. Most of all, fuck Christian. Then he padded up behind me and said, 'don't forget, I'm leaving in a few days, it'll be better then,' surprising me with his insight into how everyone felt about him.

Nobody spoke on the drive to the hanger, and we bombed up without a word.

I felt bad for Elly, but thank fuck, and the day passed without any images of them fucking or evil puns.

Back at the hanger, she looked upset.

'That man was after me again,' she said.

'O shit, really?'

'He came up again today, and put his hand on my leg, and I said, "no get off," but there were kids there and I couldn't drive off either. I really hate him. He won't leave me alone,' she said, her hands covering her face in exasperation.

I didn't know what to say. So I tried to change the subject and talked about some stupid child on the route, but she just glared at me, then looked away. She told Christian the same, and he said, 'take it easy,' then, 'the other flat are talking about going to this bar, we all up for that?'

We agreed that sounded good.

Back at the flat, Christian told Elly to 'have a shower and take it easy, then we'll go out.'

We got ready, and Elly put on the same outfit she had that first night with Christian, to no response from him, but she had an air to her, this stand-offish rigidity, sitting and smoking on the sofa, staring ahead, saying nothing.

The others banged on the door and down we went to the A-Team van, Christian, Ben and I in the front. The bar was this big place about 20 minutes away, double the size of Dooley's, and with an upstairs gallery looking over the main downstairs bar, all heaving with people drinking and laughing and shouting, not saddos like at Dooley's but fit-looking blokes with calves and biceps like bowling-pins in bright, tight T-shirts, and girls so tanned and slim and leggy, amazing teeth. Even cleaned up, we looked mucky in comparison. Or maybe just I did. My nice jeans and linen shirt were clean, but my armpits and my back were already black with patches of sweat.

We started on tequila shots, slam, lime, lick, the scrunched up face, the heave from the gut, the fumes out your nose. Cocktail waitresses were wandering around with test-tube racks of colourful shots, which we tried, supercharging our baseload of beer.

Elly meanwhile was at the bar, half-sat on a high stool as she chatted with this guy in a cowboy hat. She was leaning in real close to hear him, her body turned his way, pushing her hair over her ear, all those ticks she'd done with Christian weeks before. Christian watched for a while, then went over with his 'fun guy' jokey posturing. The cowboy hat guy pulled a narked smile at this bloke was muscling in. Christian leaned in on Elly and put his arm around her, but she shrugged him off and put her hand on cowboy's forearm, said something to Christian, he stepped back, then he leaned in again but she turned to him with a cold stare, he stopped dead, she nodded him in our direction, and back he came. That's you told, I thought. Cunt.

'Right we're moving on to another bar', Christian said, 'up the road.'

'What's wrong with here?' I said.

'It's cos Elly's going, with that guy.'

'What?'

'Yeah. She's being weird.'

I got this cold sense of dread that she was going to fuck this other guy, but his next comment diverted my panic in another direction, 'by the way he's an immigration officer!'

'Oh. Oh, shit.'

'Yeah.'

Ben came over.

'We're going to another bar. Get everyone together.'

'What? It's fun here,' he said.

'It'll be fun there,' he said, 'get the guys together. Elly's being fucking weird. She's going with that guy and I want to make sure she's all right.'

'Aw, what?' Ben scowled.

'Get the group together and I'll keep an eye on them,' he told me.

Yeah I'll just go herd cats, someone's in the toilet, someone's at the bar, someone's trying to chat up this gorgeous girl, everyone was arsey about leaving. Something also distracted Christian, so the upshot being by the time we were all ready to go, Elly and her mystery man had already fucked off.

The others were rowdy in the van while Christian and I sat in the front in seething silence to the next bar, which was very like where we'd just left, great big car park, people swilling and swinging in and around the place, huge open windows, like massive patio doors letting the party pour in and out. We parked up and jogged in to see where they were, unless they'd stopped off in some layby and he'd already cum in her mouth and then – no, thank fuck, there they were at the bar, standing, him one foot up on the foot ledge, head tilted, like he was trying to convince her while she looked appeasing, he looked like he was turning to go but before he could she wrapped her arms around his neck and hugged him, kissed him slowly on the mouth, then let go. He looked confused, then tipped his hat and went off. She then turned to the guy on her other side, a black dude in a black suit.

I went over and put a hand on her shoulder, 'Elly you made it, you good?'

She shot me a look and leaned in. 'The fuck that you care,' she hissed, eyes wide and angry, before she swiveled towards her new friend, took him by the arm and pushed her way through the heaving swirl of party people to the dance floor.

This wasn't good, but, several beers and tequila down, and with two colourful test-tube suddenly thrust at me by Mike, I was nearly mentally and physically anaesthetized enough to deal with her anger. Still, I wasn't drunk enough to think her last hiss wasn't a little out of order, and surely Christian was the one she'd chosen to 'care', and he didn't. I necked the shots and was about to clean up with a beer when Christian charged through the throng and shouted, 'she's gone outside with him, she's going for the car', and he'd yanked me from the bar and bustled me outside.

What on Earth was going on? Christian and I had not so lightly padded out the club in pursuit of her, and here we were propped against the bonnet of the A-Team van, keeping a not so low profile as we watched her cavort and flirt with this suited guy and, what the fuck, his 30-foot limo. What was he saying to her? What was she saying to him? It was all radiant smiles. He was trying to get her into the car, she was playing his game.

'Once she gets in, she's his', Christian said hoarsely to me. Then his voice took a man-of-the-world tone. 'She is absolutely out of control. And if she gets in, he can do what he likes'. I tried to get as good a look at the guy as I could, considering it was a dimly lit car-park, they were some yards away and I was getting hammered.

'She dozn't even know him', I mustered, slurring, 'first that other freak, now ziss fucker.' Damn, those shots were strong. Christian played out the scenario, his tone almost resigned to watching a train-wreck he couldn't stop.

'She gets in there, he'll fuck her one way or another. She can scream and fight, but no court would believe her, that's the thing. It'll be all about expectation, what she expected, what she did or didn't say or do in the back of that car. Everyone saw her arriving with another guy, everyone saw her go off with this one, getting in his car. He could rape her, no problem at all.' Then he paused. 'And she knows it.'

I felt sick, with my face and belly burning from shots, and sticky with sweat. She was still reeling round the Limo, as the driver hovered near its back door, hand near the handle. Christian was hunched forward, almost perched on the bonnet, staring at them.

'There's a condition I've read about to do with the psychology of rape victims. One really weird part of the trauma is that the victim can want to relive the experience, to re-enact it, somehow, and take it right up to the edge of when they were raped before, but then change it, take control, stop it from happening a second time,' he said.

So she'd told him. I wondered when she would.

Was that what he thought was her being heavy?

Was that what made him lost interest? Oh no, please, not that.

There was a strange pang of loss, now he knew as well, they were more intimate, she trusted him more than she did me, and I was no longer first in line of trust … but there was also relief that someone else finally knew.

She's told me within just a few weeks of us meeting. Having long blown my chances, we were hanging around as 'friends' getting dully drunk in some shitty student bar one Friday, when I said something stupidly accusatory to her, and she let rip, Jesus she could pull one out when she wanted to, how what a waste of time I was, that I didn't know her, how her ex really knew her, he was so much better anyway, so on and on, left me in bits. That was the night she 'danced' with Christian.

Anyway I went home in tears and woke up next day in Hell, thinking something was seriously, seriously up. I knew I liked her and was upset about missing out, and for some reason I couldn't give her up, but why was I getting so upset, so drunk, all the time? Something else was going on. Should I go home? But to what? The new house wasn't ready, pa wasn't in it. It was all too depressing and fucked up to even think of going back in this state. Was that what was really going on? I wondered in this hideous stupor on my cardboard prison bed.

Then Christian banged on my door, 'Elly's on the phone'. I went out to the single payphone they expected three dozen students to all share, and it was her: 'I just want to say sorry for last night.'

'What?'

'Sorry for leaving early without saying anything.'

'What? You said quite a lot.'

'What about?'

'You don't remember?' I couldn't believe this. She'd totally shot me down but didn't remember a thing about it. We argued a bit about what had or hadn't happened then she said come down to see her to talk about it.

Might as well, better than Death.

We ended up in a pub near her house, a big Victorian, sandstone place on the corner, bare floorboards. It was only just gone midday and I'd barely recovered from the night before when we got the first round of Guinness in.

'I can only say sorry. What else can I say?'

'And why should I forgive you?'

She looked at me, with a vague shrug, and said 'because we're good drinking partners?'

Damn. 'Drinking partner'. Someone to get pissed with, that was all.
But it meant I could hang out with her.

I mumbled something conciliatory and pathetic, 'you know I'll forgive you anyway.' I don't know why I thought that might be endearing, but there was a sadness to her, as she gazed dolefully out of the window and onto the street, with its finely ornate redbrick Victorian shops, dappled in autumnal sunlight.

We took in the pints, and pints, and some time on round five, she was talking full stride about her shitty student house and her shittier student housemates, all well away from my 'student village' and partly what lured me to her in the first place, I felt sorry she was alone and away from things, and felt a need to make sure she was all right. Don't know why. She wasn't just stunningly beautiful, but she had this sadness about her, like something had sucked all the life out of her, so I thought. Something about her that made me want to make sure she was all right, which I'd already told her and she really didn't understand, it freaked her out. But it just made sense to me. I just cared about her. I don't know why.

'I fucking hate my flatmate' ... she said, 'she gets so uptight about shit she gets off blokes. She keeps going on about it, how some bloke touched her up or some shitty comment some idiot taxi driver made to her, and it drives me mad. I've had it worse, much worse.'

'How much worse?'

'Much worse.' She paused. 'The worst'. I gave a sideways glance, hoping 'the worst' might suffice to cover that horror she was alluding to, or that 'worse' might mean a hand up the skirt, but she left me under no illusion.

'I've been raped,' she said, voice without any tremor of emotion, but tears suddenly falling from her eyes. I held her gaze, saying nothing, mouth ajar. Rape. That shattering, terrifying word the newscasters said with the same sombreness as murder, the word that brought visions of violence, lonely screams in rainy back alleys and women cast into a living Hell. The word that referred to the night, the dark, cold parts of cities usually far, far away where evil lurked. Yet here was the most beautiful girl I'd ever, ever met – and someone had raped her.

She nodded so slowly to confirm my disbelief. I moved my hand to take hers but then moved it away, unsure if she wanted to be touched, even in solace, at this appalling confession. 'And the feeling of shame burns and burns,' she said, as more tears fell and she cupped her face with one hand and gazed out the window. My own question *what do I say? What do I say?* translated first into 'Who? When?'

She cut me off. 'I don't want to think about it.' My mind went into numb shock, and I glanced from her to the table before rearing back slightly, looking at her almost side-on, in panic, at the unfathomable pain before me, but she looked worried: 'Why are you looking at me like that?'

'Like what?' My mind battled for clarity. 'Like nothing, I'm not looking at you like anything. I ... I don't know what to say, that's horrible. Oh no.'

'There's nothing to say,' she replied with such bitter sadness.

'It's horrible ... Who would ... ub ... blum ... You know it's not your fault, don't you?' She looked unconvinced, but nodded, probably to stop me going off on one about the complexity of her pain that I had absolutely no idea about.

'It'd kill my dad if he found out. I couldn't go to the police, couldn't have a trial. In court, all those people ... Standing there, with some lawyer tearing me apart ... it'd kill my dad, I know it. But the day after it happened, I was so cruel to him, shouted at him, everything he did, every tiny thing, I just lost it at him. It's so unfair. ... ' and she covered her mouth and stared at the table as more tears fell, and by then I realised I was crying too. So we sat there, silently crying, as young and old men and women drank and laughed and pointed and shouted about the football on the big telly, shielded off in their innocent Saturday afternoon world. We sat at the table at the window, looking out at the handsome but long-neglected Victorian street, the puddles in the potholes reflecting the maudlin autumnal sunshine, the small dunes of red, brown and gold leaves that weeks before had died and departed the trees on which they'd bloomed so vibrantly green.

You know nothing, I told myself. *You're now really in the unknown. This is what grown-ups deal with.*

One of us must have got the next round in, but everything was somehow both very sharp and yet very blurry. How the conversation then steered away from what she'd said, I don't recall, but we both stayed, as if weighed down by Guinness, talking with a strange but beautiful intensity as we both knew the worst now, and yet neither had frightened the other away, that was the touch point of trust. What could possibly stop us telling everything else there was to tell, and we talked, listened, told stories, debated, laughed and sang until sometime, hours after the dying sun outside had been replaced by pools of inert orange streetlight against a black-brown sky, we were both out of money, and neither knew of a cashpoint we could reach without fear of getting mugged. So we staggered and weaved back to her little house a couple of terraced streets away.

She retrieved a bottle of cooking sherry she'd found in the cupboard when she moved in, and we took pained-face-inducing shots in the gloomy back room, a pitiful side lamp's light all absorbed by a horrible purple shag-carpet and a big, bulky black vinyl sofa which I lolled upon while she cooked pasta shells dumped in some gooey, lumpy salt mixture. The shells were soft and then hard and crunchy, but it was cooked with a drunken, loving care.

Then we watched some utterly inane TV while I cracked crap jokes, before I upped, we hugged, said some tender goodbye, I'd arranged to meet Peter of all people and go to some party, and felt I couldn't break the date, although on the doorstep Elly looked sad that I was leaving, and I made some strange reassurance, then wandered the long miles back to halls, mulling over her beauty and thinking how right I was to fall for someone so fantastically perfect, yet deep, someone to spend endless golden hours together with. And yet someone who I now couldn't leave, not after she'd told me that. I had an idea that knowing she wasn't going to be mine, and fancied Mark, and would probably end up with him ... yet now I couldn't leave her.

A voice in my head said, *this is going to be Hell. Make no mistake.*

And I said, 'but I can't not be friends with her now, can I?'

And the voice replied, '*She's going to go out with Mark. And it's going to be Hell.*'

And I met Pete, and went to the party, and got more drunk, and he started talking shit and I shouted at him, and got thrown out, and wandered home in quite a good mood for having shouted at him, and only when I got into my room did it come back to me what she'd told me, and the shock of realising someone so beautiful could be hurt so deliberately, so violently, all came over me, and I wept for hours. Never cried so hard, so long, about anything. I absolutely wept, until I passed out.

'The victim deliberately sets up close encounters and then re-takes control at the final moment,' Christian said, 'like they're regaining control of what happened when they were raped.' So he knew, too. At last, someone else who understood. I felt tears welling up.

What were we doing here?

'It's about control, staying in control.'

'Do you fink zat's her game now?'

He paused, and I got scared. For the first time in weeks, I really wanted, really needed him to have an answer. 'It seems to fit. That and her being so angry about shit, that she's trying to punish us. I mean, fuck's sake, she can't want this to happen, she knows we're here, does she want us to fucking rescue her?'

'Zass not being in control,' I said, trying to sound more sober than I was.

'Not really, but if she's trying to push us to rescue her, that, for her, is control.' He ran with the thought. 'This is what she wants, to make us rescue her.'

We carried on watching, waiting for calamity as Elly wavered back and forth from the back of the car, the door now open, the driver smiling and gently waving her towards him. Why was she doing this? Didn't the cow know I loved her?

'She's lost it. This is going to get really fucked up, really fucked up,' Christian hissed. Then he straightened up sharply. She was getting into the car, he got in after, and the door slammed.

'Fuck it, that's it, let's go, let's go, we've got to stop her!' Christian's voice rose in alarm, then he said 'I'm gonna get the others,' and ran towards the club. My legs felt wobbly and I felt in no state to run anywhere, and that there was no time to get the others. Something would have to be done right now, but there was only me to do it, whatever the fuck it was. The thought made me feel sick. Focusing as hard as I could, I began walking, staggering more like, towards the Limo, with some blurry intent on intervening in some way, but what did I think I was going to do? God I wanted to puke. I didn't want to do this. With each slow, unwieldy step, a new thought typed into my mind about what was horribly imminent. What do you say to a massive guy with a probably massive, screaming cock as he's about to fuck a girl out of her mind, 'oi please don't do that!'? And what if in fact she was up for it? My skin felt tingly all over. If I open that door, and they're just talking and stuff, how stupid am I going to look, too far gone to think up some back-up excuse and thereby doomed to say 'shit, sorry, I thought you might be being raped.' Cos that's what big black men do with white women in the back of cars, the driver would exclaim sarcastically, before ripping my face off in indignation.

The Limo was a few yards away. There were hundreds of people in that club, and only me here trying to stop this, but what was this?

Were me and Christian wrong?

Was this simply nothing?

But I'm gonna get killed, I thought, wanting to stop and sit, drink and think, but my legs somehow were taking me to the Limo. If I open that door, and he's fucking her, how do I stop him? Muffled sounds from the car were audible, a voice rising to high pitch. Was she flirting? Moaning? Having sex?

If this is rape, I'm going to see it, and I'm fucked.

A couple more steps.

If they're fucking, and she's loving it, I'm fucked.

Nothing was visible through the Limo's blacked-out windows, which I could nearly touch.

If I open that door, and they're screwing, either way, it's going to blow my mind and I'll get my head mashed in.

The back door handle was within reach.

And if they're not fucking, I'm going to look a fucking idiot. Every fucking which way, I'm fucked.

I don't want to see this.

I don't want to do this.

Why is she doing this?

I have to do this.

And on that note, I opened the door and she was there on the back seat, fully clothed and giggling, and she looked up at me in surprise, smiling, her beautiful blue eyes wide and friendly as we locked looks. The driver leaned towards her, I saw the lower half of his face as he smiled and said 'hello, can I help you at all? Do you want something?' and he was smiling too, like he wasn't about to kill me for intruding.

My head was a swirl and I said something like 'Elly what you doing, come back with us,' and she said, 'I'm just having a chat.'

'Yeah man, what's up?' he said, puzzled. But before I could say more, the others turned up, and I found myself at the back of a scrum of us ice-cream men, Mike doing the persuading to get Elly out of the car and to come back with us.

237

That poor dude thought he was going to get laid, now this Brit lynch mob turn up. Shit. But it was all just words, trying to get Elly to come with us.

I slouched back, bewildered at what I'd thought I'd see, what I got, what it meant, the whole stupid fucking evening. What the fucking fuck.

They tried for a long time, but couldn't persuade her, and the evening was over for us, as she was driven off in this limo. As we got into the A-Team van, and the others were now wound up with concern about Elly and where she'd gone, and all of that, then it sank in. It'd been a wind-up. She'd gone out on this suicide run to get everyone worried about her, and she'd succeeded.

Everyone was talking ten to the dozen, speculating about this, or that, what was wrong, what was she doing, why, and so on. I sat in the front, saying nothing, now feeling increasingly sober and stoned with anger as it sank in, the stupid fucking cow had done it all just to get attention. Attention from me, or from Christian, or us both? God only knew if we'd see her back at the flat within the hour, or we'd ever see her again. But we would all be utterly freaked out one way or another, all of us already were. It was all for attention and she'd got the attention of all.

All for attention.

All for attention.

All for attention.

Everything went white, then the lads in the back of the van were shouting at me to stop and calm down as my fist piled over and over onto the dashboard. What did I have to endure from this cow? What? What had I fucking done to deserve this? Nothing.

I stood at the flat window staring out, waiting for her to come back, and lo! Into the car park swung a long black limo and swept right up to the main entrance, just out of sight. Very shortly, the door buzzer buzzed, and it was her, and in a drunken, tittering manner she said, 'can you let me in? I'm locked out!', like the total Hell of the evening just hadn't happened, or was nothing to do with her.

'Fuck's sake!' I said, buzzing her in and leaving the door to, then sat down and waited for her to stagger in, as I heard her giggling down the corridor, so pleased with herself.

'Did you have a good night Elly?' I said.

'Aye, fucking champion! You missed out!' she giggled, heading towards the bedroom.

'You stupid girl,' I said.

'Fuck off,' she said, tottering off, but a seconds later she come back, and, smiling, she beckoned me over, 'come here, come on,' she said, and so I went right up close, and said in my face she said, quietly, but without a glint of boozy slurring, which such cold anger, 'the absolute fuck you, or Christian care. Nobody fucking cares. Everyone wants to fuck me and that's it! Fuck you.' And with that she stomped off to the bedroom and threw herself onto the bed, face into the pillow.

I stormed after her and shouted 'don't you fucking talk to me like that. Get up. Get up! I'm not taking that from you, you little cow! Get the fuck up, now!'

'Fuck off!'

'No! You don't tell me I don't fucking care and you don't go and do what you did tonight you epically stupid cow!'

She sat up, her face coming out of the shadow and it was rage, but then a voice from over the corner said 'Jesus guys, can you keep it down? We're trying to sleep.' It was Val.

'Shit. Sorry Val,' I said.

'Sorry,' said Elly, and I motioned to her to come with me into the other room, 'let's talk in there.'

'OK. Get some beer.'

'Good idea, can you get an ashtray?'

'Yep,' she said, while I went and got four cans.

'I've got ciggies, you got a light?' she said.

'Yep,' but the box of matches in my pocket was mashed with sweat, but she saw a lighter on the sideboard and lit us up both a smoke, while I handed her a can, then opened mine.

'Right. So. What the fuck was that about?

'None of you lot fucking care! That freak on my route touched me today and I tried to tell you about it and you didn't listen.'

'Yes I did.'

'You didn't, you started talking about some other crap, because you don't care.'

'I didn't know what to say. I thought you didn't want to talk about it.'

'I just told you!'

'Yeah but, but I didn't think you wanted to dwell on it.'

'I wanted to talk about it!'

'Fucking OK but what are we supposed to do about it, I said do you want us to come with baseball bats and fuck him over, or something, I don't know. I've said that.'

'Oh yeah you and everyone come along like bouncers? Just burst out at him?'

'Maybe not quite,' I tried not to laugh, as did she, 'but why can't you just not go down that road?'

'The money's good and there are nice people down there.'

'But why stop at his house?'

'I don't, it's other kids I stop for but he appears.'

'Tell him just to fuck off. Just fuck off, yeah? Just piss off. Anyway what's that got to do with your fucked up behaviour tonight?'

'I was having fun.'

'Fun! Did you have to go in his car? Did you have to go in that limo?'

'You don't care. Nobody fucking cares! Everybody wants to fuck me. You, Christian, Bobby, Greg, that bloke.'

'Nobody cares? Did you see the whole of fucking Penguin come out to get you out of that limo? Did you see me there?'

'Penguin. Even fucking Charlie. You were there on Independence day when he came and said he'd chase me round the world.'

'He also gave you truck 16 which is the best truck, the most reliable truck, which as he said he did so just so that you wouldn't break down and so that he wouldn't have to come rescue you from somefuckingwhere. So I think he does give a shit.'

'Fuck.'

'But why didn't you say you were pissed off, instead of going off with two total bastard strangers?'

'I did tell you, I told you at Penguin, you changed the fucking subject, started talking shit about shit. You don't listen!'

I had. Shit.

'I got it wrong. I didn't know what to say or do so I started ... started talking about other stuff to get your mind off it.'

'Well it's stupid.'

'But even so, you can't just tell me you're upset? Instead you have to fuck off into the night with some bloke from immigration, then follow up with some guy in a limo? What the fuck did you think would happen? What were you thinking?

She reared up on the bed and pointed to herself, her face all rage.

'So what, whatever happened, it's my fault. Is that what you're telling me? It's my fault. It's my fault? Is that it?'

Like she'd wanted someone to accuse her of that, and it was me. I felt panicky.

'No it's not your fault, I'm not saying it was or it is or whatever, no, no I'm not! But you put yourself in such a dangerous position! What do you think could have happened? And who would have been believed?'

We toed and froed, until the bedroom door opened and Val came in, slowly, as if cowed.

'Could you please stop arguing? This is horrible.'

She looked really quite upset.

'Oh,' I said. 'Sorry Val, we'll be done soon.'

'Yeah, sorry Val. Were we shouting?'

'Yes.'

We all paused a moment, then I said, 'OK we'll quieten down.'

'Just stop it!' she said, turned to go out, where I saw Greg waiting and she went and hugged him.

Both Elly and I sighed, slugged the beer, drew on our smokes,

'Wait, what's Greg done?'

'Asked me for a blow job.'

'When?'

'On your birthday.'

Was that in the shop?

'And what did you say?'

'Of course.'

Eh? Then we carried on the row.

'What kind of fucking point are you trying to make, by going and doing that?

'You and Mags are the same, you both worry like mad about what I do. You've got to learn to trust me.'

'Trust you? How can I do that? How am I supposed to fucking trust you when you do stuff like tonight?'

And so it went on, until we ran out of steam at some point, laughing really, and I heard the front door go so Christian was back from wherever, and then it went surreal, as I went to go sleep in the walk-in cupboard, Elly coming to tuck me in, and I asked her, 'Do you want a snog?'

She looked pissed off, and went to go row with Christian.

Hours later in the grey light of a pissy morning, the sidelights still on in the living room, I was smoking and staring when I heard the toilet go.

'Who's that?' I said.

Christian padded into the room and said slowly, 'What the fuck happened last night?'

I just nodded at him.

He collapsed onto the sofa, he looked exhausted, as I felt, then he said, 'I spoke with her last night.'

'So did I.'

'What did she say?'

'A lot of shit. I hadn't realised how much this guy on her route had pissed her off. That and loads of shit. But what the fuck she was doing with that limo. And that immigration officer. Fuck knows what could have happened.'

'Yeah.'

'What did you talk about?'

'Same shit, but a lot of bullshit about us, and it's like, fucking Hell, we're finished, and was she actually trying to get herself raped? She said that first guy had asked if he could fuck her, and she'd said no, and he'd not pushed it, but ... she'd gone with him in that car, no fucking court would look at her.'

'Shit.'

'Yeah, lucky he didn't push it. And she admitted she knew he probably would do something. I told her she needs help. Proper help. She's fucked.'

I lit two cigs and passed one to him. We stared at one another in silence for a moment.

'And what the fuck is this shit she has for this guy Richard?' he said.

'Does she go on about him with you?'

'Fuck yeah. OK they had this great romance, but it's over, woman, he dumped you.'

I smiled to myself. Holy shit, Richard this, that, and everything. It probably didn't torture Christian like it did me, but she did it nonetheless.

'I'll be glad to get the fuck out of here,' he said.

'When are you leaving?'

'Three or four days, max.'

'That soon?'

'Yeah. Fuck this.'

Then I remembered what a bastard he was, but couldn't be bothered to have a go at him. Now I felt like I needed him.

'You know, I'm thinking of not coming back to college.'

'Really?'

'I don't know if I want to do the first year again. So what's the point?' I wanted to say, I'm in love with this girl who terrifies me, who's determined to fuck all my friends, including you, bastard. But I didn't.

'It'd be sad not to have you, but you might be right. You've not enjoyed this year at all have you really?'

I paused, then admitted it: 'Nah.'

'She was telling me the other night, you were this close to having her. I see why you went mad.'

Genuine words of consolation and understanding, from the guy I'd confided in most, who'd then fucker her in the mouth.

We burned our smokes down to the butts, until he said, so sadly, 'this was supposed to fun.' I wanted to say it wasn't all bad, but it was. I didn't know what to think. I didn't want to think. So I just nodded, then he went back to bed.

That chat was the most coherent bit of a day that passed in a blur as I was in fact still pissed and up on adrenaline, before the submarine of my mind submerged to murky depths. A blur to the hanger, a blur at the hanger, I probably stank, fuck knows, I only woke up a bit when taking a corner too fast and the freezer shifted.

As many kids said no thanks as yes please, some 'get losts', one 'fuck off'. For about an hour in the afternoon it just pissed down, so I just parked up with a big bottle of coke and smoked.

I felt weirdly betrayed, not by her fucking everyone but ignoring everything I'd done for her.

Worst, I realised, I couldn't help her. All that tip-toeing around, feeling like I was carrying her whole being, like a bowl of boiling water, scalding me, but I couldn't drop as it destroy her. None of that had mattered, and last night I'd been scalded and scared beyond belief. Nothing I'd done mattered, and now I didn't know what to do. I'd never known what to do. I'd been panicking ever since she'd told me. What she'd done, she'd said, knocked me sideways, and though we'd sorted it out then, now it really felt like it was over, and that stoned me some more.

Some kid said something like 'what's wrong with you ice-cream man, you look like fucking shit,' and laughed, and I just stared at him, until he shut up and walked away, looking over his shoulder every so often in case I was coming for him.

The only good bit was this almighty bang and sudden, horrible rattling under the van, and the engine hadn't fallen out again but the muffler end of the exhaust was half hanging off and scraping the floor. I groaned at having to call Charlie a-fucking-gain, but then thought I could fix it. Inspired, I took the straps off my khaki rucksack, with those little metal loop buckles, and strapped the muffler back onto the chassis. It held, and I was so chuffed with my work with the Sun now out I got some sales in before the rain started battering down again, strafing into huge puddles on the road like 20 mm cannon fire.

Back at the hanger Charlie flagged me into position and I told him about the muffler, he said he'd have a look, while the 20 yard dash inside still left me soaked as was everyone in there, you could almost smell the steam coming off them. The heavy rain battering on the metal roof drowned out any banter, and everyone had earned fuck all, and me and a few others were still *what the fuck* from the night before. It was like in the *Battle of Britain* with the Luftwaffe fighter pilots, who started out off so chirpy and confident and flushed with success from having shot down everything over Europe, and were going to hunt the RAF out of the skies. But by now they've lost loads of pilots, and they're sitting at the dinner table in silence, staring at their plates, more candle-lit wreaths in the table places of yet more missing.

Even crap Adrian picked up that something was up and didn't do his usual simpering spazzery.

I was reeling, and didn't want to talk to anyone, not least Elly who looked winded, and wasn't looking anyone in the eye. Christian was pointedly ignoring her. I felt sorry for her, but counted up and drank in silence.

'Are you all right?' she said, turning to me, and I tilted my head and said 'yeah' with false jollity.

So it all passed, in a daze.

243

Cunts

Woke up in a weird world, dazed. Nope, nothing to be done. Christian was right, she needed help. I was out of my depth.

I sat on the sofa smoking with Ben and Greg, loading on coffee. Elly walked in so I went and smoked on the balcony.

At the hanger she put her hand on my arm, 'are you OK?'

'No, no, all's fine. Just a bit tired,' I said, and walked away.

The 'well done' I'd hoped for off Charlie about the muffler as I asked for my bag straps back was 'they were burned right through. You were damn lucky you didn't have a fire.'

Piss, felt like a little boy.

On the drive to Westie I thought again. *You stopped that little boy being run over. It was Christian who crashed the lights. You saved us all from the police raiding the flat, when Christian just fucked about. You went in first to stop Elly with that limo when Christian ran off. He's the arsehole, everyone thinks so. You're not the bad guy. You're the guy with nothing who's doing all the fighting back. There's nothing you can't do.*

Except save her.

Yeah, but what.

What.

Wad?

I didn't see Eskimo or any others, not that many kids either, some enthusiastic ones, but most weren't jumping up and down or running in for money or waiting to beg for a free one, weren't even acknowledging me as I passed all the slower to get any reaction at all, which felt like proper pervy kerb crawling.

I neared the basin where Joly hung out, but he wasn't there, a group of women and their children were picnicking on the hillock. A handful came over as I slewed up in the truck. I served these mothers and children, and turned to the last woman, somewhere in her late thirties, long black hair sternly bunched up, and large bee-like sunglasses.

'Are you the British ice-cream guy?', she asked straight out. British, she said, not *Briddish*.

Yes, I replied, wondering what was coming.

'I have a question to ask you,' she said, coolly, ominously, 'about what you think you are doing teaching my son disgusting language, and upsetting him.'

She said it quietly enough so as not to attract attention, but there was angry menace in her voice.

'What? What do you mean?' I racked my brain for the last time I'd really lost it with any of the children in these parts, wondering when I'd last been effing and blinding to wake the dead. Not here, I positively looked forward to driving to this bit, not least to see Joly. Ah! Her accent wasn't American, it was too flat, was she British? Was this Joly's mum? He'd said something about her being from England, hence she'd know a certain word that only a British guy would know.

'Ah, wait, wait, wait. Are you Joly's mum?'

'Yes.'

'Right, and the language in question, four letters, begins with c,' she had her arms folded tightly across her chest, she was nodding agreement, lips taut, 'ends in t, incredibly rude,' I said.

'Yep.'

Joly did ask her then, and must have said I'd told him it when she asked where he'd heard it. Now she was gunning for me.

'Well, I remember it now. Did he say I'd told it to him?'

'Yes he did, and he was upset that day.'

Ah, shit.

'I thought he was. But it's a very British word that only a British person would use, kids around here would have no way of knowing it.' She nodded. 'And so the only person he could have heard it from is a Brit, i.e. me.'

She nodded.

'Right. Really, I didn't tell him it. He'd actually shouted that word at me as I was leaving, and I stopped and asked him how he knew it, for all you know what I've just said, and he said he didn't know nor knew what it meant..'

'But where could he have heard it?' she countered, not with a backhand manner, 'that's just not language he'd know from round here.'

'No I know, and that's why I was so surprised when he said it, and it makes total sense that I'd told him it, but I didn't. I can totally see how it kind of must have been me, but it wasn't.'

'But he said he got it from you.' Oh God, I don't want to call him a liar. She cocked her head slightly, her expression saying, 'and'?

'I talked to him about it, yeah, but I've honestly no idea where he got it. On that day, he said it and then when I stopped, you know, like, "what?", he asked me what it meant. I didn't tell him because it is, err...' I sniggered, 'quite rude. So that's why I didn't tell him and that's why he possibly got upset, cos he thought he was in trouble, and it makes perfect sense that he got the word from me, but I stopped and asked him because I was so shocked that he, you know, him, here, would know it. But I really didn't say it to him first.'

'Well I was shocked too, believe me,' she cut in, almost smiling.

'I can imagine,' I allowed myself a laugh. She seemed to be buying it. 'But also it's not something I'd use for children here.'

'What would you use?' she was suddenly very intrigued.

'I mean, if a kid here, if he was really winding me up, I'd call him a shit. And I have done that once or twice, not with Joly, no, he's lovely, that's why we chat as and when we do because he's the nicest kid I've met, but I wouldn't use the c-that word,' a small girl was hovering next to the cabin, 'because it's too strong to use for children, they're not evil enough to warrant it. Certainly not

Joly, I chat to him because he's normal.'

She took off her glasses, and her large brown eyes were passive, sincere.

'But also for being too harsh for kids, American kids because don't know what it means. It's doesn't mean anything to them so it's pointless.' She laughed at this, possibly envisaging the poor ice-cream man screaming You little CUNTS! while all the children look at each other confusedly, impervious to the ice-cream man's violent rage because they don't know what the Hell he's saying. 'Wad?', they'd say, while they stole his money, let down the tires then overturned the van. She seemed convinced, and we wound down the debate, until she asked, 'Where are you from exactly, anyhow?'

Phew. Honour intact. Normalcy preserved.

Somehow some British culture did make the jump. But how?

We all cashed up quickly at the hanger to get out from the pall hanging there, said little driving to the flat where we padded around aimlessly. As I sat in the armchair Elly looked at me, her face concerned, and mouthed, 'you all right?' I smiled unconvincingly, then went to smoke on the balcony and admire the car park and its sodium lighting. Val joined me.

'I reckon Elly should go home. Did you see her the other day with that dog? Oh my God it was so sad to see, she's so homesick. , and what with Christian being a total dick, she should go.'

This was terrible. If Elly went it meant the whole thing was a total disaster. What would I do here without her? But if it was right for her, then she should. I felt so sad and shit. Also now we all knew Christian was leaving soon, we just wanted him to go, stop this stinking the place out, pissing about with Elly.

Plus what the fuck would I do now I wasn't going back to uni. But for that, instead of beating myself up, instead of Demons screaming at me, I felt ... all right. Like amid all this shit, I'd made the right decision, again amid so much shit others had created.

For which I got to leave uni, my course, my friends.

Hang on, what friends?

What fucking friends?

Mocking

A non day except for meeting up with Joly, and all lovely banter was restored. Didn't see Eskimo or anyone, made a few dollars.

Christian said we had to get back sharp to the flats where we'd meet Appalling Paul and two other Brits he was going travelling with.

They were there in the car park, two lads, with most of the Penguin drivers and beers all round. These guys seemed nice enough, one was a big lad, taller than me which always freaks me out, and he had a rugby player's build. Elly was looking at him, and looking back at Val with an expression of 'phwoar'. Fuck, was there anyone she didn't fancy? One day I manage not to think about her and Christian fucking, now I'm thinking she'll cop off with this bloke. I used to play rugby, shit, if I'd carried on playing would she fancy me and not him? all these fucking muscleheads and my skinniness, my arms should be rippling from driving that truck around all day. Bollocks.

It ended up as a party at our flat, all us Penguiners, and these two new dudes and Paul, drinking and spliffing, and it was quite fun, until Elly, slugging on yet another beer, took the phone, dialled, then exclaimed 'Mags!', her partner in crime at home. Elly was pissed and loud, hanging off the telephone, swinging in and out of the kitchen into the living area like one of those shutter doors at a cowboy saloon. Her gaze fixed on Christian, and soon his name came up again and again, her voice increasingly mocking, biting, 'and then Christian did this!' Christian sat on the sofa, staring back at her through squinted eyes, seething as she dissed him, in front of everyone, as well as her mate thousands of miles away.

My name come up a couple of times, sandwiched by hoots and shrieks of laughter. 'Fuck this,' I said to Christian, 'let's go somewhere else.'

He flinched, his head shook 'no', determined to hear every bitchy word as Elly's laugh got louder, his name said with a nastier tone. So he sat and stared.

'Come on mate, this is bollocks, she's off on one.'

'No. I want to hear this.'

Others were going to Dooley's, Mike said.

'Hear that mate? Come on. Fuck this.'

But he stayed and stared, she continued to mock.

Half an hour later or so, she appeared at Dooley's, calm as, asking where Christian was.

'Is he not with you?' I asked.

'No, he went out after you did.' She looked puzzled.

We didn't see him that night, then he came back after we'd all gone to bed, sleeping on the sofa, he told me later, as I told Elly. She was surprised.

Breakdown at the fun bar

Coffee and fags for breakfast. Ben looked irritated when Christian came into the living room, Val muttered 'fuckin' 'ell', when he walked out.

At the hanger I saw him with an ice-cream box, standing next to his van with Elly, her looking confused, pleading, him looking like he wanted her to go.

Eventually he put the box down, and they hugged, but neither of them looked happy. All day I felt hatred towards him, sadness for her, thinking, 'why can't he just fuck off?' But the way she spoke about him last night, if it wasn't over before it was sure as fuck over now.

But he still had a leaving do to do, for which we all went to the 5 cents a shot bar, all ice-creamers, Val, Appalling Paul and Christian's two chums, Bobby, Sandy and crew, and Mike's mates Dave and fat Glen, and everyone took turns at pool, Frogger, riding the motorbikes, then treating everyone to another effectively free round of shots from the bar. The relief of Christian leaving made for a great party mood, so people were willing to do shots with him, while Mike and Jason and I tapped him for ephedril and caffeine tablets so we could cane Frogger, my linen shirt streaked black with sweat. Val came over – 'watch this skill, Val!' *waggle-waggle-waggle* of the joystick, *bap-bap-bap-bap* on the buttons, another level cleared.

'Skill,' I said.

'Yeah that's great Jimbobs,' she said, then started talking about Elly and Christian, asking how I felt with Christian leaving.

'Thank fuck.'

'I'm so glad he's going, can't stand how he looks at my arse.'

I groaned at his tacky behaviour, 'that wanker was supposed to be with Elly.' Tacky two-timing – oh fucking Christ I wanted to play Frogger. Then Val said, 'I think Bobby's lining up to try and ask her out.'

'What? How do you know?'

'Oh come on Jimbobs, you must have seen he's got a crush on her, anyways he's just asked us if Elly's said owt about him, with Christian going off scene could he ask her out. Look over there, how he's looking at her.'

Elly was at the bar, trying to talk to Christian, while Bobby was leaning against the bar a yard down from her, looking towards her ... longingly ... before he tapped her shoulder and she turned and I saw her mouth 'Bobby!' with a smile – oh no, not of lust?

Bobby cocked his head and then leaned in to say something to her. I felt sick, whether she liked it or not there were blokes queuing around the block. I looked back at Frogger, where I'd hit level 12, but saw I'd died. Something the fuck in me broke, and I started crying.

And crying and crying.

'Oh, Jimbobs! What's wrong? Come here for fuck's sake, man.'

'No, go away, go away, leave me alone...'

'No man. It's Elly isn't it? You upset about her?'

'Yeah, oh leave me alone.' Not now, not now to make a scene, not again, like all those months before on how many nights out, Val, Elly, the others, getting shit-faced and then blubbing how I still liked her, Elly pissed off with me getting 'heavy', ... so I'd learned to keep a lid on it. Until it all burst out now. Val led me to a small table in a corner, sat me down, went and got me a beer and a shot, then said, 'you and Els have got to sort yourselves out, I'm going to go get her.'

'Oh fuck no Val, don't! Don't! I'll be all right,' not wanting another 'heavy' evening, but too late, I was burying my face in my hands, another evening ruined, then I opened them to see Elly sitting opposite, and Val saying something to her, and she was looking at me not with bored derision, but concern.

Ah crap.

'What's the matter?'

'Nothing, go away.'

'No come on, what's the matter?'

Val was still in range and said, 'come on Jimbobs, out with it,' then she went off.

'I don't want you to see this,' I said, trying to wave her away.

She looked at me sadly. 'What's wrong?'

And all the shit poured out. how I felt about her and Christian, how I felt about her, about her being dumped, how wonderful I thought she was, how I wanted to protect her but also to fuck her but she made me so happy in so many ways, I thought she was amazing, not in a crush but what now seemed like genuine love, but I couldn't stand this endless line of men, and it'd never be me, and that was the shitty shitty reason I felt I had to leave.

All this shit I'd not even thought I was thinking, and never wanted to say to her, rehashed crap from months before when pissed and it pissed her off, and made no sense, and I was begging her to go out with me. Now it all did make sense, and I wasn't begging her so much as ... fuck what was I trying to do? Nothing. I hadn't even wanted her to come over.

'Does any of this this mean anything to you?' in this pleading voice, expecting her to say 'fuck this' as she'd done before.

Instead, she said 'Yes ... yes it does mean something to me. It means a lot.'

I asked her if she was interested in Bobby.

'Bobby? He did ask me, if there was a chance after Christian had gone, but I said I wasn't interested.'

I sighed in relief.

'Some day, some man will come along like some knight on a horse and whisk you away and you'll be gone and it'll be incredible love forever, and it won't be me.'

She looked sad, 'no, that dream's died for me. That won't happen.'

She put her hand over mine, then walked off.

Mike came over and started consoling me.

'It's obvious mate, there's something between you, the way you two talk to one another, confiding, there's some deep connection.'

'I can't even be in the same city as her. Totally fucked up the last year at college. Why I'm leaving,' I said, but more normally. Just saying it all aloud felt lighter.

'Talk to Glen about it.'

'Glen?' Fat Glen, the beer and chips mechanic? He had a heart?

'Reason he's here and going across the US, it's the first leg of a world trip, had to leave Leeds after a year, like you, in love with a girl, got nothing but total heartbreak for it.'

I scanned around for Glen, and there he was at the pool table, cue in one hand, pint in the other, laughing with a couple of the others. I'd just taken him for a slob. Oh no.

'What's he going to do?'

'Teach English. He's got one of those teaching certs you can do over a month, means you get proper teaching work and not just bum about Thailand taking the piss.'

I'd not even noticed that I'd finished my beer or the shot til Greg appeared with more each. Drained of emotion, I saw Christian riding one of the motorbikes, but Elly had gotten onto the back and was hugging him from behind, to which he didn't look happy. Meanwhile I saw Bobby look over to them then look away, then he turned at waved at the bar tender for more booze.

'He just wants rid, don't he?' said Mike.

She'd broke her heart on trash, but the poor sod was in love with someone else.

Everyone's in love with someone else.

Maybe I had to go see the world, get out of this shitty trap, I'd never travelled and only seen my own little world collapse, while she was out seeing real things far, far away, really living. Uni was miserable anyway, getting drunk with people who'd nothing to say for themselves while outside it rained all the fucking time, and no-one saw the romance in its old redbrick warehouses, mills, the canals.

Unknown number of drinks later, I was in the boot of the Pontiac with a panoramic surround of a beautiful purple and pink dawn, reflected with a wavy grey tint by the towering shafts of glass buildings, evenly festooned with red lights. Elly was in the rear passenger seat, hankering for Christian in the front.

Hiding

Fucking Hell, Christian. Just leave.

Why was it so painful and grinding along?

The weather was clammy and the jingle bothersome. Some days I forgot it was there, some days it was all I could concentrate on, that and seeing Elly being fucked from behind. But not today.

There were a couple of boys in a front yard who'd not reacted to the jingle. I slowed, then one saw me and said, 'no we don't want any, go away.'

Then I went down a street so tightly packed with parked cars I was wary of taking wing mirrors off, but there was no gap to pull into, and it was a dead end. I executed a frustrated eight-point turn and floored it back up the road to the junction, prompting some dad to shout, 'SLOW DOWN!' Ah fuck off to yers.

At the hanger there was something of a hubbub, the usuals were hunched over and whispering, glancing back at Hank in his office corner as he spoke with a driver I recognised but didn't know. Hank wasn't leaning back in his chair but was standing, while this driver flustered, hands to head and then out wide again.

'What's the score?' I said, squeezing a seat.

'Big hoo-ha, Dave caught Gary in his town today,' said Ben.

'Who's Dave?'

'That guy there in the baseball cap, with the tache? Ben pointed to a guy sat next to the tarped car, one of the Americans who didn't mix with us Brits.

'Gary's patch is 10 miles from Dave's, so what the fuck Gary was doing in the middle of it? Caught, red-handed,' said Ben.

'Oh dear.'

'Yep. He's not happy, and nor is Hank. Apparently, Dave'd seen and heard another Penguin van around there before, and had even asked Gary if he'd had the same problem cos Gary's close by, but Gary said no. So he knows it's been going on a while, and it was Gary all along. Probably sack him.'

'Is it that serious?' said Elly.

'It's not on, is it? Working an area without a permit isn't legal. And working your mate's patch? No fucking way. And Gary lied. It's trust.'

'I'd be fucking furious,' said Mike.

Oh dear.

We ended up at Dooley's, Elly and Christian notably absent, but I had to get more cash from the flat and went back with trepidation in case I either walked in on a row, or worse, them having some end-of-days fuck, them writhing in an island of thrusting porn in middle of the living room in love juices lapping against its walls, 'just for old times' sake' or whatever the fuck these fuckers would say, their falling out giving the fucking a ruthless edginess that just made them fuck like rabbits all the more.

But the living room was empty, the sidelights on, but the flat eerily quiet. I got some lettuce, then went to listen at the bedroom door in case the smutty bastards were at it in there, but there was nothing. But the door was locked. Were they having a silent last flurry of fucking, to cap all that had passed between them, that could not be disturbed?

I scooted back to Dooley's for beer to wipe out the pain – then saw Elly in the car park with Mike.

'Where've you been?' she asked.

'At the flat, getting money.'

'Did you see Christian there?'

'No? Why, is he not here?'

'Was he not in the flat?'

'Didn't see him. I tried his bedroom door but it was locked, and I couldn't hear anything either.' Oh shit, don't say you were listening at the door!

'The door was locked?'

'Yeah. He must have been in there. But it's so early.'

It wasn't even 10:30. He was hiding.

'I'm quite glad if he is in there, to be honest. I'm sick of his shit,' Ben had appeared.

'So am I,' I said.

Elly looked so sad. I sighed for what I was about to say.

'Do you want to see if we can get him out?

'Christian? You in there mate? You coming to Dooley's?'

No reply. I looked at Elly, she looked at me, I knocked again.

'Christian? What you doing, you coming out or what?' No reply. 'He must be in there though.' I put my hands up in a shrug, mouthing at Elly 'what the fuck', then said, 'Shall we go?'

'He doesn't even want to say goodbye, after what we had together?'

I wanted to say he fucked her and chucked her, which was true, but it was really because he thought she was damaged goods, which would have been too painful, and for which I truly hated him. I'd told her be careful, he was up for a fuck and nothing more. She said she was too, but the stupid cow had fallen for him. Still I felt sorry for Christian, so hated he'd had to hide, much as I was offended that he'd done so.

We all hated him, we all wanted him to leave, but there was no need to be anti-social. Anyway it was obvious there was only one person he was locking out.

'Bastard!' she exclaimed back at Dooley's. Yep.

Christian leaves

Next day, we came down to find the Pontiac had gone, as had Christian and Ben, and we all piled into the A-Team van.

While bombing up Ben came over. 'Christian's gonna leave soon if you want to see him go,' he said, 'we didn't speak on the drive in.'

'Things that good between you?'

He shook his head and went off.

Back across the gravel I saw a rusted and patched silver Chevrolet, that I somehow knew but couldn't think where from. It was a fucking wreck that at home wouldn't be allowed on the road, but for here it was a touring car in good nick.

I walked over. Christian was in the passenger seat, smoking. I looked at him, he looked defeated.

'So you're off in a bit?'

'Yeah,' he said. 'It's good that I'm going, it'll be better.'

I didn't deny it.

'Whose car is this?'

'Paul's.'

I didn't know what to say. I felt bad for him. This had all been his idea, and we were all supposed to have fun. But he really had been a total dick, especially to Elly, and for fucking her, and being so patronising about it, and he'd pissed off everyone, like he'd gone mad. Now he knew everyone hated him.

I put my hand out for him to shake, and he took it, 'good luck man', I said, 'safe journey'.

'Yeah, you too, look after Elly.'

'Yeah. Sorry it didn't work out so well.'

He shrugged. 'See you back at uni.'

I left, then thought the bastard knows I'm not going back. He doesn't fucking care.

Is he a just a fucked up bastard, or just a complete bastard?

I went back to the hanger as the others in Christian's party came out, waving, 'see ya later suckers!' And when I came back out with my float and stock list they'd already backed out and were crunching away to the highway, whereupon Elly appeared: 'Have you seen Christian?'

I pointed at the car now turning off the gravel and out of sight towards the highway.

'He's fucking gone and left,' she said.

I held her elbow, 'fuck him' and took to turn her back. But she wasn't coming.

'No, it's all right,' she said, and she stood there, shoulders slumped, hands open in exasperation then clenched in anger, staring towards the lane, then staring at the floor.

Hank caught me in the hanger.

'Hey Jim, you're not going to West Chicago today.'

'No?' Fucking A.

'No. It's Wayne's day off, and he normally does Crystal Lake, so you're going there.' he pointed to a spattering of lakes in the north-west, Twin Lakes, Fox Lake, Wonder Lake - Wonder Lake?

'It is a nice earner, so don't run over any kids and get Penguin a bad name.'

'Do what? What have you heard?'

'Jus' pullin, Jim!' he said. He gave me the map and permits, and off I went.

Crystal Lake was exactly that, a fabulously clear lake, bottomed with pebbles, ringed with gentle hills and old trees and houses, the hilliest and woodiest bit of Illinois I'd seen. The large, lush greenness around the houses somehow made for a deceptive appearance of wealth - there was a lot of unused land, with thick, proper grass, not scrubweed, and a few of the houses were creaky and cracked, as if surrendered in the battle against the smothering embrace of bushes and mosses.

There was shade and water, the air was cool and refreshing, even with the sunshine, and because it all looked lived in, it seemed human, in contrast with the soulless islands of the new estates with their plastic houses, plastic grass, plastic people. Crystal Lake was like an oasis in comparison, and as I pootled the van along roads that bowed out from the lake like a ribcage of old fish bones, there was a light breeze that smelt not of dry dust or hot tarmac, but sodden leaves and rich vegetation.

Business was steady, no competition I saw, there may've been a whole squadron of them 10 minutes ahead clearing up, but ignorance is bliss.

I pulled up for two boys.

'Hey chaps, what can I do you for?'

'Hey ice-cream man, we don't have no money,' said one, for which they were about to get a cloud of exhaust fumes instead of ice-cream, but he said, 'we can do trade, if you want.'

Such budding entrepreneurialism was interesting.

'Hm! Trade what?'

One felt into the pockets of his shorts, all spattered with fruit juice, then asked his friend, 'you got 'em? Got the heads?' and the other boy started ferreting in his pockets, then said, 'yeah I got 'em,' and he offered up to me his open hand, in the palm of which lay a half-dozen little V-shaped stones.

'They're old Injun arrow heads. We can trade you these for ice-cream.'

Indian arrow heads. I reached down and picked out a polished grey stone head as large as the end of my thumb, and was so evenly shaped and smooth. There was also another smaller but much sharper head of some kind of flint, like a roughly hewn black diamond, with two tiny indents for binding to the fuselage or stick of the arrow.

I looked closely at these beautiful, simple little fossilised hearts from a lost civilisation, a world killed off only a century or so before. A breeze lifted my fringe and gently felt out my face and head, like ghostly fingers touching me from beyond, as a dollar bill blew loose and flitted inside the van. Somehow these arrowheads, there was something so poignant my eyes nearly welled, I felt like Dan Dare, in *The Man From Nowhere*, when this buttoned up true-Brit hero pilot totally trips out for a few seconds, saying to himself, 'Far, far away, I hear the music of the stars.'

'We got 'em out the lake,' said the bigger boy. Down on the lake where Braves hunted and killed fish and rabbits for themselves and their families to feed only a few generations before, when people actually lived off the land and the water. Now those arrowheads were currency for ice-cream for children living around the lake that was a pretty backdrop for people to simply exist in.

Maybe that was too harsh. These were nice children living in big houses and who could play in the lake, or in the woods, and who could find things like these heartrending little things … and just trade them for ice-cream.

'That's a deal, ice-cream man,' smiled the bigger boy.

'Are there a lot of these arrowheads around?'

'Yeah we get loads all the time in the lake,' said the smaller boy.

'You should collect them.'

'I got a drawer full of 'em at home, but they ain' worth nothing. They're everywhere,' he said. Boy, if only you knew.

I drove off, down a long, gravelled road, a narrow lane really with creaky looking clapperboard houses either side, big birch trees, fir trees, a great Ash like we'd had in the back garden, with a tree house, at our lovely old home.

Outside a house with scaffolding around it, a couple of chunky guys were going back and forth, and one saw me and hoyed me to stop, and this bloke in a dirty white t-shirt and jeans came over and ordered about five Choco-Tacos.

We talked a bit and he asked where I was from, what was I doing, then soon enough where I was going and then my answers got vague, probably mentioned leaving uni and Elly and crap, but I really don't know.

And he's a big guy, a working man, but he was really, I don't know, something really clear about how he spoke and intense, and he was very nice, and he suddenly said, 'wait here, I'm going to get you something,' and so I did, and he came out with a load of tapes, with these blue covers, with a white circle on them, and titled, 'Discovering You – how to reinvent yourself and succeed'.

'These are self-help tapes. I used to be like you, but I listened to these, and now I have this company, this truck, these guys working for me. I turned it all around,' and he turned to look at them, and one in a hard hat smiled and shouted 'hey Gary!' and he shouted back, 'you doing good there Jeff?'

'These tapes really helped me, and I think they'd work for you, and what I want you to do is listen to them, and then I'd like to talk to you about them. Would you like that?'

255

What the Hell did he want to talk to me about? 'Yes, sure,' I said anyway, trying not to be rude but really wondering why he was so interested in me.

'You sure about that? I want you to be sure,' and he smiled.

'Yeah, yeah, great!' I said as enthused as could be.

'So if I give you these tapes, and I give you my number, but I really want to talk with you about this. What is your number?'

He seemed genuinely nice, but what did he want from me?

I just felt overwhelmed. I told him when was good to call and he said he'd call then.

I looked at the tapes, and saw the illustration was like the Moon over the sea, but not, it was a bit mystic and dream-like, and thought of playing them there and then but the tape cassette machine batteries were flat.

But what the Hell, my haul was about $190, and I did another few hours before heading home. A different route to the hanger, I saw signs for a roadside café and being starved I pulled in to this roadside gaff, not a shitty caravan like in British laybys, but a big, brightly lit bungalow, with a smiley man behind the counter wearing a Thunderbird hat who pointed out the special offer of two hot dogs, fries and drink for $3 – class. Then I saw this *Simple Simon* type game, a quarter a go, with a free meal if you beat it and burned a dollar on that.

At the hanger I sat next to Elly and got out the arrowheads, and I dropped them into her open palm, 'old Indian arrowheads. See this little black one – it's quite sharp, but I thought it could make a lovely pendant.'

She took in a sharp intake of breath, mouth open as she looked at it and then me and said, 'they're beautiful! Are they for me?'

'Yeah, yeah, real arrowheads. Fragments of a lost world there,' I said, and she got it, and stroked the heads gently with one finger.

We cashed up, fucked off home, then Val got back and told us Aaron was coming up for a couple of nights, and she hoped we were OK with that, cos he was coming now so we could all fucking lump it, anyway it'd be good to see Aaron, hear about Skyshit. Greg came back, Mike came down, Bobby turned up, we got pissed and stoned and had a really funny evening, Bobby inviting us all to a party in a few days' time,

Grand evening all round.

The atmosphere was lighter.

Because Christian was gone.

Brewing up

I got up to find Val on the phone, detailing Aaron about getting to ours the next day, then Mike turned up and we piled down to the Pontiac.

Ben drove, as he started the engine, noted the rev counter dallying up and down and the speedometer creeping up, but the petrol gauge was asleep in its corner.

'We have got fuel though, haven't we?' I said.

'Yes, filled it two days ago,' Ben said.

'Right.'

'You've jinxed it now,' said Elly.

It was a lovely morning, sunny but not evil hot, and we cruised along, breeze dancing through the half-open windows. As we neared a gas station, Elly said, 'last chance for petrol!'

'Right. We're fine,' said Ben.

Lo and fucking behold, five miles further on, doing best part of 60 in the middle lane, the engine's roar quietened, then died. 'Aw fuck it's done it again,' Ben shouted.

'OK, OK, pull over,' I said.

'Pulling over,' and we slew rapidly right across the slow lane to the hard shoulder.

'How's the steering'

'Fine – no it's not, it's getting heavy. And the brakes are going!'

Going up a slight hill helped slow us, while a car behind us beeped loudly as it had to jack around in front.

'God, I see what you mean, the brakes are like they're locked off. Can you help steer?' he said, and I leaned over as he tried to straighten onto the hard shoulder, the wheel all ground up, and we coasted to a stop.

'Well this is just fucked, isn't it?' said Ben.

'Where's that fucking gas can?'

'We're near Hank's aren't we?'

'I've got his number.'

'There's a phone 100 yards back there,' said Elly.

Ben went and phoned, we had a smoke on the roadside, then he came back, 'Hank'll be along soon as. He's just going to pick us up and Charlie'll come get the car later.'

'Fuck this car.'

'It was like a missile back there.'

'It's a fucking beast.'

We looked at it, the rotted and furled wood veneer, the rust along the passenger door, the dead bolt keeping the door closed.

'Let's call it the Beast!' said Elly.

'The Beast, yeah,' Ben let out this horrible cartoon-cat miaow-like roar, sounded like *Charlie's Cat*. "*Rwwarrrr* you fuckers trying to get to work, eh? We'll see about that."

'All three tons of him'.

It was quite nice playing by the road, and we cheered when Hank arrived.

'Any chance of Charlie fixing a new petrol gauge in,' Ben said to Hank.

'We've kept it filled up as best we can,' said Elly, 'it's not that we're not taking care.'

'Might be a leak somewhere,' said Hank. 'Charlie will give it a proper look.'

In Westie, morning merged into midday into afternoon, now overcast and muggy, making me sweat and stink, then a breeze blew into a light wind, making me cold. Rain was coming, but the weather was being indecisive, and at around 5 I shouted skyward, 'either rain, or piss off,' which baffled the child I was serving, the only sale I made in nearly an hour, with the whole 'I want ... I want ... wad? Wad?' shit.

How was it not possible just for him to stop the van, say, 'hey, ice-cream man, I'd like an ice-cream.'

'$1, please.'

'Thank you very much.'

'Pleasure, have a nice day now.'

Something as simple and civil as that a few hundred times to sundown, and we all fuck off home happy. Not this epic indecision, every fucking time.

This was bollocks. I had to do Bartlett, so pulled into a '76 station off the highway for gas, fags and Coke, but as I reached back in for money, a guy at the next pump shouted, 'hey mac, your engine's dripping!'

Wad?

'It's dripping! Look under!' he said urgently.

So I looked under, and shit! Black-grey stuff was dripping onto the concrete. I undid the rubber ties on the bonnet, but it was scalding hot, and smoke was seeping out, so I grabbed some hand-wipe papers and tried to lift it, but they kept slipping, so I had to hit it upwards to reveal grey-blue flames dancing all over the battery and flaming droplets of black and silver plastic raining onto the forecourt.

'Fuck! Fire!' I shouted, 'fire!' then I blew on the fire, did nothing, then tried to smother the flames by hitting at them with the hand-wipe papers, but they caught fire so I stamped them out, shouting 'fire!' as little black wisps of burning paper, tiny waves of gold shooting across them, floated around and stung my legs. As I wondered whether just to leg it before the whole gas station went up, an old man toddled over from the shop, like he had all the time in the world. I told myself not to blast my water bottle at the fire, then remembered a big towel I'd put in the freezer, which I hastily retrieved with a banged knee and smothered the battery with this ice-cold towel seething with CO_2, killing the fire.

'You OK?' said the old man, now at the van.

Having saved the day again, I beamed, 'yes. Now I am!' then grimaced, 'fucking Hell', as I padded down the smoking black battery box and my knee began to hurt.

'Ah, you had a short-circuit,' he said, pointing to a long bolt stuck into the black melted plastic.

'What the fuck?' I said, then apologised.

'This bolt shorted it and set it on fire. But where did this bolt come from, hmm. Ain't that something? I think you need a new battery.'

'Double fuck.' He was right, the starter motor wouldn't turn. Just stony silence.

'Yep, that's dead,' he said. 'We got new ones on sale, but those cables are scorched through.'

That was that. My earnings for the day were finished, and I'd barely hit $90. With the weather in full wank mode there was another three hours of scrabbling about, burning fuel, to reap probably $40 max, $13 to me, to pay for the gas and fags and cans I'd just bought. I gave up. The old man helped push the van to the side and let me call Hank, refused an ice-cream, then I sat and revelled in my heroism for stopping a fire that could have blown up half the highway.

Jess turned up instead and wasn't up for covering my lost earnings, so we argued and haggled and agreed I'd get back the cost of fuel and fags, before we both sighed at the pettiness of it all.

At the hanger I cadged note paper, grabbed some beers and wrote letters for a couple of hours, until the others traipsed in.

'Did you have a good day Jim? Much excitement?' said Jason.

'So-so. Pissed about. Takings were low. Oh yeah, the van caught fire while I was at the petrol station, that ended the afternoon.'

'That's a new one.'

'Yeah. The battery short-circuited and it was raining liquid fire out the engine. Makes a change,' I said.

'Probably been getting ideas off the Beast,' said Ben, '"Rwaoarrr! You wanna hang out with me, ice-cream van? Why don't you set yourself on fire? In a gas station? *Rwaaroorrr*!"'

'Like some appalling initiation.'

'Yeah, your van's got low self-esteem, will do anything to fit in and make friends.'

'You had a good one, Elly?' I said.

She shrugged.

Crap Adrian came in.

'Hello, Elly,' he said in his cringeworthy, 'I have a crush' way.

'Hello Adrian,' she said, subtext clear: 'Shuttup, child.' Everyone sniggered.

He then started talking to Jason about bollocks, taking corners too fast, his competitor, kids climbing in the van – still? Should have stopped that ages ago. Ben rolled his eyes. Fucking amateur.

259

Hank came over to say the Beast was fixed, with the petrol tank now in the boot, the rear gunner seat replaced by this massive steel suitcase, which to look at was unnerving, you never normally see the gas tank. Mike and Jason came with us back to the flat.

'Crap Adrian really is crap,' I said.

'Us, we're veterans,' said Ben.

'Veterans! Hard bitten danger men,' I said, 'and women,' nodding to Elly, 'we take no prisoners.'

'Like in *Platoon*, fresh-faced rookies like Crap Adrian filing past us battle-hardened, hard-bitten veterans who stare blankly back at them and the Hell they're about to face.'

'Gnarled and embittered, no time for that rookie shit!' said Mike.

'I take no shit!' I said.

'You take no shit!' Ben said.

'We take no shit!' Mike said.

E-party

The day started non, and ended non, a few dollars, no incidents, so I cheered myself up with a hot dog meal and *Simple Simon*, improving my game.

Back at the hanger Elly reminded me that we had to get back to see Aaron. Ah shit, it was also Bobby's party tonight. Would Aaron come?

'Come on,' said Elly, 'Val wouldn't let him out even if he wanted to. Which he won't.'

And there in the flat was good old Aaron! Handsome dude, on the sofa, Val on his lap, and we all cheered, even Ben was putting a brave face on it.

Aaron told us about his job, door-to-door selling of aerial photos of people's houses, which sounds exotic, but some bloke turns up on your door saying, 'we've been flying over your house taking photos of you in your back garden, do you want to see what we found?', they don't sell well.

Other than that, though, Aaron hadn't a lot to say. I was glad to see him, a nice guy, but apart from the course, we didn't have a massive amount in common. We first started hanging out when the course started, he was another good-looking dude from the south and by that odd mutual attraction we became friends.

The chat trundled on, although I think Val and Aaron were itching to fuck, if they hadn't already.

'I never liked Christian,' Aaron said.

'Did you meet him?'

'Yeah, couple of times. A few months back I was telling him about Skyshot, and he said it was a load of shit and no-one ever made any money. And he was right, but he didn't have to be such a dick about it.'

'Everyone, and I mean everyone, hates him,' Val said to him.

Course they'd bloody met, that night Elly bawled me out for one, Aaron and Christian were there but had nothing in common, which helped the evening drag. Housemates and coursemates don't' mix, they either don't get on or got along too well and I'm left out. That was the evening Christian gave me a big sell to Elly, but she shot me down and then rubbed herself off on him on the dance floor.

The doorbell went, it was Bobby. Fuck, I felt guilty and divided, should we go with Bobby or send him away, spurned, and hang with Aaron who'd come all this way?

Put it to the people! 'Bobby's party! Who's up for it?'

'No way, Jimbo, we've got some things to catch up on,' said Val, wrapping her arms around Aaron's neck. Aaron smiled. Elly'd been right. No guilt!

'Elly?'

'Staying here.'

To do what, listen to them fucking? She would as well. Once we'd walked past some student room and we'd heard fucking going on, and she got on her knees to spy through the keyhole.

Ben was smoking in an armchair, notably staring ahead and not at the sofa.

'You coming to the party, Ben?'

'Yeah, what the fuck eh?'

Either that or stay here and listen to them fucking. And with Aaron and Val itching to get it on, we all found ourselves itching to get out.

Bobby gave us directions and scooted off, but while driving around identikit estates was bad enough in daylight, by night it was a joke, the darkness smothering the ludicrously high-numbered houses and all Bobby's helpfully listed landmarks, like 'really big oak tree'.

We crawled, turned around, and turned around, three times passing a couple out walking their dog, who I stared at to see if it was the same couple, so they stared back, suspicious of my staring at them from this knackered vehicle that kept circling them, but we were driving on fumes and they turned out to be very pleasant when we told we were lost, and Briddish, and not drive-by shooters. We made it to No 487, an indistinct 1970s bungalow, atop a long, sloping drive, with a real stone chimney as the centre piece of the house.

'Bit quiet.'

'Yeah. Hmmm.' We got out and weaved towards the front door, looking and listening for any clue of a riotous party within.

'Shit, what if it's the wrong one and the hick inside thinks we're Japanese students?'

'It's a risk!' I replied, standing behind him as he rang the doorbell.

Bobby hoyed open the door, stripped to the waist, sweat pouring down his body.

'Dudes! Great!' he beamed, overly serenely, 'come-on-in.'

There was about a dozen people in the fairy-lighted front-room, then more in the next knock-through room. There was a snogging couple in the corner, not in a furiously drunk-fuelled clench, but holding each other lightly, just brushing lips and fingers. They were inches from a trio of rippling youths wearing only baggy shorts, sweat flying off them as they punted and chopped lividly to this trance music. In the other room and into the kitchen were chattering pockets of people who greeted us, strangers, with deft kisses, hugs, in free and breezy effortlessness.

'These are my *English* friends,' Bobby said proudly.

'English ... that's so ... cool,' one fit girl replied, nodding, looking us up and down through half-closed eyes.

This was all a bit too civilised. Where were the crates of beer? The screaming? The vomit? Newcomers would float in and be greeted by the same serene friendliness, with Bobby always retreating to watch the party from a corner, gazing around with a this-is-how-it-should-be look in his eyes, underlined by a fixed smirk, and toking from a water bottle. As was everyone.

Ah shit, it was a pissing Ecstasy party. The boring shite fashion-victim bastards. He came over.

'Jimbo, my fine English friend, how goes this fair night of entertainment for you?' Why do people think drugs make them more eloquent?

'All-righty,' I said, 'it's good fun,' though I wished I was at the flat.

Nothing worse than house parties with bloody students on E, already tripped out on their own flaming sense of self-importance, self-satisfied bastards gathering in some ramshackle Victorian villa to twat about with how liberated and brilliant and special and relaxed and open and uninhibited and sophisticated and advanced and superior they were just because they'd taken an aspirin with an apple stamped onto it. I mean, piss off.

If they were all seven-foot tall, bald, and wearing silver suits and talked about eight-dimension mathematics and shit, because they were from Space or the future, then yeah, I'd say they were genuinely superior. But not these cunts, who the next day would either be crashed out or emerging from some flea-pit room as the unreasonable, snap-tempered, grabby little shits they really were.

Fuck 'em, fuck 'em all. Beer and spliff took you to Planet Zog, but you'd never be fooled into thinking you came from there, and you'd shit yourself laughing if you believed you were. Getting pissed or stoned only ever made people stupidly free enough to snog randoms, fall off roofs or start fights with massive fuckers. It'd shut down your organs and make the veins in your face explode, as was your choice. But if anyone got kidney failure off E, this trendy drug of collective ease and social advancement, it was a bad pill, or the dealer's fault – although up to then they were the coolest person to know until he sold you a load of Vim. 'Dove', 'apple', gah, Yoko bloody Ono in a pill. Crap. It's got to burn up something in your mind, burn up some neurons, they'd all get Alzheimer's. But with no scientifically-backed proof beyond killjoy government lies, people would only know E posed any danger until they themselves showed damage, and they'd be too damaged to know what'd happened anyway.

A real party was the Friday night student Bop. Hundreds of hopeless youth from all over Britain crowded into the ground floor of a shabby 70s' tower block, with its office-like steel and Formica tables, polystyrene ceiling tiles, everyone armed with 10 Silk Cut and a tenner for booze at a Pound a plastic pint, a gallon for you and a couple for your mates. It was so crap it was great. By 1am, the boys' toilets had like an inch of watery piss on the floor, that soaked through the splits in your shoes, the lake later breaking its banks to leak into the main hall and seep into the swirly carpet. The overflow came from the slash wall dammed with fag packets and bog roll, while smashed blokes needing both hands to lean against the wall left their cocks to hose a pressured gallon of piss about, blowing back on their trousers and onto the floor. Even with one hand holding their aim true, they might stagger back and forth, all message going floorwards, or a comment from a mate may cause them to turn unwittingly and hose their neighbours to shouts and screams. The girls' bogs were also pressured to the brink of a riot, so pissing refugees came into the boys' cubicles or stuff themselves into the sinks and taunt the drunker chaps wading in with bits already flopped out.

Now that's a proper, unpretentious party, so gross that I felt better about myself if I hadn't pulled, because no-one in there was likely to either. The trendier students would abandon this place after the first or second visit, preferring to spend £20 on pills and bottled beer in piss-artist nonce joints in town, queues round the block, arseholes on the door and super-arseholes inside. But for half the price, 100 yards from home, same time each week was this real entertainment, with the same faces, same fights, same piss on tap then on the floor. Like the best TV jokes are the ones where you know exactly what they're going to say. That was the Bop.

Students on E, Yankees on E, wankers on E.

'Yes, yes it is, it's ... fun,' Bobby said, half-closing his eyes and nodding in approval, his mind a universe of mind-blowing concepts accessible only to those in the E know. He offered me a pill to help me cross over to the enlightened side, but I declined and plonked onto the sofa with beer and dope as Bobby watched the room, nodding slowly with approval. Ben was off getting pilled up and would soon be as space-aged as these buggers, so a really tedious evening looked likely, until I remembered that E apparently made people randy as fuck.

'Do you reckon any of them are up for a snog?' I yelled at Bobby.

He smiled approvingly. 'You are my fine English friend,' he said, 'and as my guest, I shall help you in this quest,' he said calmly, and sauntered off into the couples.

He found a stick-thin girl, very pretty with clear skin and large dark eyes, with bum-length crimped hair. I couldn't hear what he was saying but his hand gestures had a peculiar ease to them, his speech punctuated by flicks and rolls of his eyebrows, all part of this wondrous language he had brilliantly mastered. Soon he brought her glidingly over, his hand delicately cupping her elbow, but I cut him off before he could launch a cringingly verbose introduction. 'Hello, I'm Jim.'

'Hey, I'm Sandy. He he he he he he he!' she replied in an absurdly high-pitched tone, clapping her hands like a seal but gaining only smiles and approving nods from onlookers because she could enjoy herself and her space so freely, as one the initiated into being uninhibited.

She is free. So are we. Cos we're on E. Wankers.

'Jim is a fine English gentleman,' announced Bobby, obviously being English was a selling point.

'English? He he he he he he he!' the girl squealed and clapped.

'Now if you'll excuse, I must tend elsewhere,' and off Bobby went.

'Err, yeah, cheers Bobby. So what do you do, Sandy?'

'I'm a hair transplanter. He he he he!' Clap-clap-clap-clap.

'Oh, right. Great.' The girl was an idiot, yet I was baffled. 'What kind of hair? From where to where?'

'He he he he he!' and she clapped away.

That was that. So I got hammered and stoned alone on the sofa, while I dwelt upon the gang of buffoons before me. I had a great time, but no snog.

Much later, we came in gingerly, seeing the silhouettes of Aaron and Val over by the French windows, and sneaked to bed.

Blues Brothers

Surfacing with a foggy head, I saw Aaron and Val in an embrace on the living room floor in front of the French windows.

'Morning you two,' I said. They only replied 'mmmmm', and carried on doing what they were doing, as far into the corner as they could get, fucking basically, not stopping for me, and I studiously hung out in the kitchen to make coffee, then took the end of the sofa furthest from them, and turned on the TV.

'Turn it down, Jimbob,' said Val, 'it's distracting.'

'Well I was ... trying to distract the noise from over there.'

'Fair enough.'

Feeling out of sorts, I tried to make conversation.

'Part of our daily ritual, Aaron, is to watch the Weather Channel, I guess you do too if you're out on your feet all day?'

No reply.

'Mate?'

'He can't fuckin' talk right now, shurrup!' said Val, on her back, her head tilted back, Aaron out of sight – oh right, yeah.

Ben walked in.

'Ben!' I said in a loud whisper, 'coffee's in the kitchen!' and I waved him towards the kitchen, he looked at me puzzled then heard a groan from Val, double took, then walked out again. I wanted to shield his gaze from them as much as not disturb those two.

The Weather Channel predicted the rain we could see out the window, it was still raining as we trotted to the Beast, us all hunched over in that lame way that doesn't stop you getting wet.

As we drove past Hank Towers the rain worsened, like we'd just driven into a car wash, and I batted the windscreen wiper paddle, but nothing happened, so I hit another paddle, nothing happened, then looked all over the steering column and dash and pulled this nob and hit that button, and nothing happened, as the road disappeared from view.

'Which fucking paddle is for the wipers?'

'Er, left one I think,' Ben said, pointing to the first paddle I'd hit, which I batted up and down, then back and forth, before hitting everything else all over again.

'Nothing's happening!' I braked slightly as we couldn't see shit, and now the windows were fogging up. Bollocks!

'Is there a button instead?'

'I've hit everything already, do you want a go?', I said, dropping speed.

'It's definitely one of those paddles, they worked the other day.'

'Can't see anywhere to stop,' I said, suddenly seeing two blurred blobs of red light in front, making me brake sharply, which the Beast ignored, but the tail lights were rear lights, not brake lights.

'Can't see fuck all.'

266

'Shit.' We slowed to about 20 or so on a road made for 50, luckily other cars had slowed as well, and putting my shades on I stuck my head out my side, as did Ben his side, like the *Blues Brothers* without being funny, and rain hitting sunglasses was almost as bad as hitting the windscreen, but at least it wasn't going so badly in our eyes.

'OK people we need good communications on this!'

'You're doing well, going straight, not hitting the trees,' shouted Elly, her head half out as well.

All the spray from cars in front and passing, like a bad Formula 1 race, made it treacherous. I cocked my head so I was half looking ahead to keep the spray off my specs and my eyes, while also trying to follow the centre-line with peripheral vision.

We were going slow, this car behind beeped and beeped, prompting Ben to look back and shout, 'fuck off!'. Then this guy, still beeping, overtook, doing a double-take as he as he drew alongside and passed.

It was like this for the whole drive, until we bounded across the gravel in front of the hanger, great pools of water already formed, when the wipers suddenly came on.

'That's fucking hilarious, Beast. Fuck you,' I said, killing the engine.

'Rwaaaaaaa-ahahahahahaha!!!!' said Ben.

'Sick of your shit, Beast.'

'Rwaaaaaaaa!' Ben replied, rolling his eyes and slobbering his tongue outside his mouth.

'I'm not taking, your shit, anymore.'

'You're not taking its shit.'

'You're darn tooting,' said Elly.

As the rain hammered the metal roof of the hanger, we were all gathered in suspense, waiting for Hank to call it off. But he was sure there'd be enough sunshine later to make it worthwhile. Our petrol gambled against his dry ice.

It binned it down all the way to Westie, these epic flashes of lightning kept smashing the sky, great jagged cracks pulsing from sky to land, others more sheet-like out the corner of the eye, and booms of thunder, doors sealed against the wind and spray, windscreen wipers just about clearing the windscreen but nothing for the mist in front, everyone on the highway at half-speed, half-lights on. Today would be a joke for business, but at least the weather was impressively shit.

Along the suburban avenues, the gardens were as empty as the sidewalks. Maybe the rapids in the gutters had washed all the little buggers away. One person shouted something about 'being optimistic', then I gave up, parked up for a couple of hours, put my feet up on the steering wheel for added effect and played a bluesy saxophone in my head, the rain rushing and pulsing on the roof of the cabin in jazzy percussion as I filled the van with ciggy smoke.

It was great, there was absolutely no point, nought but to enjoy watching God smash the skies, shattering the black horizon into brilliant shards, then counting off the seconds before the boom enveloped the van. Me, Coke, ciggies, some money, no thoughts of Christian and Elly. It was allright, really. A few thoughts about what next life wise, but I felt energized. Could I seriously switch courses, or take a year off, go travelling like I should have done, across South America for months and months?

Eventually the rain stopped, but the cloud cover remained so nothing dried and no kids came out. They'd only churn up their lawns and redecorate the house with mud. Ah, this was so shit it was funny.

Back at the hanger, the atmosphere was boisterous, but Elly was quiet. 'You all right?'

'That man came out today. Even in the fucking rain. He went to put his hand on my leg and I kicked out, and told him to piss off. Just stared at him and told him "piss off". I was so angry.'

'What did he do?'

'He stopped. I said "piss off,"' and she showed me – wow, the anger in those eyes and her hissed voice. '"I don't like you, I don't want you around me, just – piss – off." And then he went off,' she said.

'Brilliant. Fucking brilliant, well done, good work.' I grabbed her hand and squeezed it, she sighed, smiled and looked at me with tenderness, a job well done and toasted with two fresh beers. Go Elly!

Aaron was at the flat for one more night, and after the chat about tutors and shit ran out, Mike and Jason turned up, so we played party games, *Give Us A Clue*, *I am a household appliance*, 20 Questions, which fizzled but the banter was good by then. It ended up with Aaron and Val and Ben on the sofa, and myself on an armchair with Elly on my lap, side-saddle, and talk of planning next year's adventure, and with her arms around my neck she said to me in this ludicrously sweet way, 'can I come?' and I said, 'yes of course', thrilled that she'd want to come do something different and not shit, and she grinned and looked dolefully into my eyes with her beautiful blue eyes, and she said, 'don't leave uni,' but I said nothing. And I could smell her and her breath and the warmth of her arms on me and the incredible feel of her bum on my legs, she smelt, looked, sounded and felt amazing, all mine, in my arms.

We stayed like that a while until she got up and went to bed, and Aaron remarked 'Jimbobs, you could have had her.'

He was right. But I didn't want to spoil it by kissing her.

Another time.

Uphill

Another sunny morning, we said goodbye to Aaron. Greg came with us in the Beast to talk to Hank about getting more painting work, but along the highway, touching 60 uphill, the Beast's engine went quiet, roared, choked, and died.

'OK it's dead,' I said, 'we got 10 seconds. Ben, could you indicate?'

Ben stuck his arm out the right side, as I crossed the lanes towards the verge, luckily no other cars in the way, with the Beast still doing good speed with momentum, I could feel the brake pedal falling away. The hard shoulder was more like a cycle lane, far too narrow for us, then further along the embankment tracing the road I saw a tiny lane coming up.

'Can't we stop?' said Elly.

'I'll get it in that lane ahead,' I said.

'Are you sure?' said Greg.

'Yeah.'

Pumping the brakes for what it was worth, with the hill the Beast slowed. 'I'll need your help on the turn,' I said to Ben.

'Aye aye.'

I gave one last pump then with all my strength yanked the wheel right, 'Now!' and Ben leant over and with all four hands, me pushing the wheel up, him pulling it down, like a fucking bell ringer, the car mounted the lane, slowed and stopped, its boot just clearing the road, and I yanked on the handbrake.

'Bravo!' said Greg.

Elly got the gas can out the boot, showed a bit of leg and quickly enough we got a lift to a gas station, from where she flirted us a lift back as well.

At the hanger we argued with Charlie about letting it run dry while we said it had a leak. Goddamn lazy pisshead bastard.

On the rounds, takings were slightly buoyed by the better weather but I was consistently a quarter down on when we'd all started. But instead of thinking of Christian and Elly fucking, I was worried about her, she seemed wan. She was wearing the same clothes from day to day, and had begun sleeping in them. Sleeping in her clothes. Just like me when my mind collapsed those months before.

At the hanger, we talked about her day, and I felt I was her confidant again, and her mine.

That evening the self-help-tape man called like he'd threatened to, ah shit! Ben took the call as I was getting pissed and having not listened to the tapes I didn't really want to talk to him about how to make myself into a better person or whatever while sounding pissed, so I told Ben to tell him I was out, but he said, 'I can't tell him that as he knows I've just asked you,' but he wasn't covering the mouthpiece.

'Tell him I'll call him back.'

269

O well. Even if I remembered to bring the tapes to work, I never went back to Crystal Lake, and wouldn't ever have listened to them. So I felt a bit bad, but not really.

Next day was a day off for most of the cool ice-cream men, so I drove the unlucky ones to the hanger, Elly came for the ride, again in yesterday's clothes.

It was drizzling on the way back, but our mood was good, then as we neared the apartment, Elly said, 'the Beast's not done anything.'

So of course, as I slowed right down off the highway and made the final left turn into the car-park, the passenger door Elly was leaning on flew open, she squealed as she swivelled on the seat, feet out scraping the tarmac, her barely grabbing the door frame to stop being completely thrown out.

'Nice one, Beast. We wondered where you'd gone.'

Back in the flat I remembered we still hadn't got flights home. Checking our stashes of notes I had somewhere over $250, Elly a bit less. We found the numbers of a couple of travel agents to phone about flights and prices. Elly had a wedding to attend on August 20, so we agreed to leave at least two days before.

'You don't have to come,' she said.

'I have to escort you safely out the country.'

She looked at me so lovingly.

Getting all the options of dates, times, direct, stop over, costs on the phone took ages. Another overnight in New York with taxis and all was too costly, so flying out August 17, Chicago-JFK-LHR was best. But we were about $100 short, and with no-one else to borrow off – fuck, had I even paid Christian back? Oh no I'd have to see him again ... we couldn't go that day to buy the tickets, while my shitty Solo card didn't work out here. We resolved to go in next Monday, make a day of it and hope they hadn't sold out, and settled in to write postcards, watch TV, piss about. I suggested we get pissed but she didn't want to, scuppering an outlying plan to snog her. Then Mike came and said they were all bored, too, so we opted to go see *Waterworld*.

We had some beers each, I loaded up on the ephedril and caffeine Christian had left, but they backfired, even before the film was halfway I was nodding off and just when Costner took some woman down into the depths in this diving bell, and Mike said 'oh fuck that', everything went black until the credits when I was prodded awake with severe neck ache from my head lolling around.

The reviews poured out.

'What a load of shit.'

'That stupid shoot out with all the bullet holes conveniently lined up for Fishhead to climb up.'

'When they were driving that old car on the Exxon Valdez, to underscore, "these people are environmentally unfriendly", you know', "boo hiss". Fuck's sake.'

'Yes, their cavalier driving so angered me, I had to restrain my fist I so nearly shook it.'

'Bit bloody late to care anyway, the world's flooded and we're supposed to say "oh no gas guzzler going 50 yards back and forth." I mean it's happened already.'

'When the world flooded at the start, that was good.'

'Yeah. Downhill after that.'

'I thought if Fishhead takes that woman past the Statue of Liberty I'm bloody well leaving.'

'And what the fuck the ending, they just find that island in the mist?' "oh phew, good navigating, nice work".'

'I didn't miss much then,' I said.

'No, your coma was a good idea,' said Mike.

I smiled, then went and threw up behind a pillar.

A haze of hours and some beer. Elly went to bed early, on top of the bed, still in her clothes. Oh, stop it woman, please stop it.

Sat back in the living room, Greg said to me, 'I can see why you like her so much.' There was something very, very conciliatory in his tone.

'You haven't fallen for her as well?'

He half-smiled. 'I could. But I've got a girl.'

'Yeah? Since when?'

'Just over a week. Maybe that's too soon to say "I've got a girl" but she is lush. Met her through the work and we've been out a couple of times, last time we were necking outside her house like a couple of teenagers, it was braw.'

'Yay,' I said, and punched the air.

'Ha! Aye. To be honest it's spared us your fate, my poor friend!'

'Yeah,' I sighed. He laughed.

'Sometimes, though, she sits on the sofa like this,' I hiked my feet onto the sofa, tucking them right up almost under my bum, and pushed my knees out, with my bits pushed out towards the edge of the sofa, 'and I'm like, I really, really wish she wouldn't do it. Drives me up the wall.'

'Yeah. I can see that, too.'

I began to feel a bit sick, with … longing. I wanted her so bad.

Dog

The next morning Elly appeared in the living room in the clothes she slept in. Enough already.

'Elly, you're sleeping in your clothes.'

'Yes.'

'Have you showered?'

'No.'

I was going to jibe her about how she stank, although she smelt of all wonderful mysteries, but she looked so distant.

'What's up?' I asked.

'I don't know.'

'It's like you've got no self-esteem.'

She looked at me, as if stunned.

'You haven't, have you?'

'No. No, I haven't.' Shit, was she going to cry? I gave her a hug and she held me tight.

'Come on,' I said, 'come on, it's all right.'

She held on. We held on to one another for a while, me telling her how much we all liked her, how good she looked, how Christian was an arsehole, and she had to forget him. She seemed to cheer up and I said 'change your clothes,' but she had none that were clean.

'Have a shower, though. Sort your bleeding life out!' as they said in the cadets. 'We got time, ain't we Ben, for Elly to shower?'

'Course.'

So she did, and got a clean top off Val. She was first up for the door as we went to leave, but upon opening it she screamed and leapt backwards.

'What the fuck!' said Ben.

Elly held onto the kitchen door frame, gasping for breath as she laughed.

'Els, it's a Chihuahua,' said Val, and there was tiny dog, the size of a small loaf, with massive bulging eyes sticking out of its tiny head, like Crap Adrian, jiggling like on drugs, then this Spanish woman picked it up, said something and stomped away.

'I thought you liked dogs,' I said.

'Not a dog, more like a rat,' Elly said.

'Fuck you, rat-dog,' Ben said, 'I'm not taking your shit.'

'You're not taking its shit!'

'I'm not taking its shit!

'What?' said Elly.

'Wad?'

'Wad?'

'Wad?'

272

Yet as soon as we hit the hanger, my mood binned, and all the drive down to Westie, I asked myself, what am I going to do back home? Did I really have to give up the course?

Then there was anger about not being with Elly. She could have had anyone, just not me. She'd had Mark, then Christian, all those times tapping me for information about them, getting me to get them out with us.

She'd known how I felt. And what did I get for it?

Nothing.

Fucking nothing.

Even fucked my degree.

I braked sharply to avoid smashing into the stopped traffic in front, not bad enough for the freezer to slam into my back, but the driver in front yelled, 'Jesus H, asshole, be careful!'. Instead of letting fly I just nodded and said sorry.

What was I thinking?

Why was I thinking this?

Stop it. She's a free bird, she never asked you to love her, she didn't ask you to be jealous. And you're rebuilding yourself.

But what am I going to do? I could teach English, go off for a year, see the world. Amazing experiences and amazing stories.

But what if I ended up torturing myself in some shithole, missing everyone back at uni?

Who'd you miss? They're all bastards.

I stashed those thoughts and decided, if I could make Elly happy, somehow, put it all behind us, that'd be enough.

At the *Shaved Snizz* shop where I'd go for smokes and Coke, they also sold toy cars, including one of a black limousine. So I bought one and put on the dash, looking at it all day in anticipation of Elly's face when I gave it to her, cheering me even when the kids were crappy.

And when I gave it to her at the hanger her face lit up with delight. I'd made light of that horrible night, and now she was smiling.

Then we got home and minutes later, we heard a buzzing outside, then the front door buzzer. It was Bobby.

'Oh yeah, come on up,' I said, too late Elly grabbed my arm, mouthing, 'no'. As I hung up she said, 'Bobby's got a crush on me. I don't really like it.'

'Right. Shall I tell him to not come around anymore?'

'No it's all right, he's nice, it's just a bit intense.'

Bobby arrived, we opened a beer, Elly went to bed quite quickly though, Ben and Greg weren't around, so it was just me and him.

I got to the point, 'you've got a crush on Elly, haven't you?'

He grinned and blushed.

'But you know she's not interested?'

'Yeah … I hope I might persuade her. But …'

273

'Go with the "but" on that one,' I said, 'this one's got no wings.'

'Anyway, I know you like her,' said Bobby.

I just rolled my eyes and shrugged. 'Yep. And I have no chance.'

He smiled again as if not to be put off by a rival, but he could tell I wasn't just warding him off for my sake.

'She'll be "the one that got away". Your life's a film, man, you're Hollywood.'

'Thank you. I always thought I looked like Colin Firth.'

'Who's he?'

'He was in *A Month in the Country* with Natasha Richardson, who is lush.'

'Who? Oh, yeah, did I tell you, you know the guy who made *Clerks*? Kevin Smith, also made *Mallrats*, right?'

'I've seen *Clerks*.'

'Well some people say the mall up the road is where they filmed some of *Mallrats*. It's a lie, it's all filmed in New Jersey.'

'Oh.'

'But you haven't seen it so it doesn't matter to you does it?' he said.

With the air cleared, we fugged it up with spliff, and talked, him going on about the Internet, this Windows 90 thing, then I said about how around here without a car you're absolutely fucked, the whole country's built around cars, hence its addiction to oil, and all the war and political ramifications of it.

Then he blew my mind, telling me that all the crap we'd had off the police, the original highway patrols and obsession with ID, all went back to road patrols to stop slaves escaping from plantations. Now, instead of plantations were Mexican estates, while the whites, refugees from Chicago city that they'd abandoned to the blacks, were now locked in their own gated communities. These estates were all still linked by highways guarded by police, and without a car, or the means to own one, you weren't going anywhere – hence wrecks like the Beast being so common, which the police used to identify the poor, criminal types, blacks, with dead cert arrests for broken tail lights, open beer bottles and pot. The 'freedom' of having a car was really the salvation of being trapped without one, but a car brought a whole load of other shit with police patrols and traps on every road in the country.

'Illinois Nazis, man,' he said, laughing.

I gawped at him like that elderly Ewok whose pipe falls from his mouth in awe at C3PO's story telling.

Then we talked about feeding the world and the causes of famine, what agriculture was supposed to do, what capitalism was really about, about Adam Smith meaning this while people warped his ideas to their own ends, capitalism being as warped an ideology as communism, Smith's tome on morality no-one had ever read.

It was wonderful, we talked until the horizon turned pink again, then he scooted off and I went to go to bed for the few hours before work. Felt like a real meeting of minds.

Incontinent Beast

Elly finally had cleaner clothes on.

The day passed in a dream. Customers were thin, well they were fat, but thin on the ground, a lot of me being ignored. Bartlett barely made up the difference, especially as I keenly felt the need to make up the flight money.

We cashed up and fucked off, filling up on the highway, but the car absolutely stank of fuel. I mean it did most of the time, but this was full on.

'Did you get any gas on yourself, Ben?'

'No,' he said, 'Fucking stinks, though. Can you light us a cig please?'

I did him one and me at the same time.

'God, it reeks of petrol,' I said.

We bounded over the railway crossing, then Elly said, 'I can hear the petrol sloshing it the tank.'

'Shit, so can I,' said I.

Then she leaned over the back seat to look into the boot, then whirled around and said quickly, 'stop, stop, the tank's leaked all over the boot, pull over, put your fags out. The boot's full of petrol.'

Ben rammed his into the ashtray and I just threw mine out the window, and saw it zip towards the back window that was open, but it flew past, ricocheting off the boot.

We pulled over and then with the engine off we could hear clearly the *wub-bwub* of the petrol sloshing back and forth. We got into the back seat and looked onto the horrible tank, now sitting in pool of petrol inches deep, with the filling up pipe half off where it connected to the tank.

'Fucking Hell. Did any of it actually go into the tank when I filled up or did it just all piss into the boot direct?' said Ben.

'This is so fucking dangerous. Oh my God,' said Elly.

The smell was intense.

'I normally like the smell of petrol,' I said.

'Me too! That and Swarfege.'

'Oh! That green jelly to clean grease, it's such a dad smell,' I said.

'Yes!'

'Fucking Beast.'

'We had it fixed. It's like it's trying to outdo us every time!' said Elly.

'*Rwararrrrrrrrrrrrr*! Thought you'd fixed me, motherfuckers? Put a new tank in me would yers? RWAAAAAAARRRRRRR, I'LL FUCKING BLOW YOU UP!' screeched Ben.

We opened all the windows and the boot, and with a cola bottle tried to bail some out, and hoped the rest might evaporate. We found a couple of rags and tried to stuff them into where we thought the leak was, feeling like great mechanics but it was decorative really, but we were only a mile from another petrol station, so we convinced ourselves that simply starting the car wouldn't blow us all up – although they left it to me to start the engine while they both stood a few yards away, my door open for a sharp exit. Then I got out, Ben and

Elly got into the front seat to be as far away from the leak as possible, although as Ben said later Elly was trapped by the bust passenger door, anyway with all the windows down we pressed on to the next garage, filled up and the spare can and drove home, dispatching Elly to the other flat to say we had to come in the A-Team van in the morning, while we'd phone Hank first thing to stress the urgency of it. We could have blown up, for fuck's sake.

I got a crate of beer from Dogface then got back to find Val home, on the sofa. 'Post for you Jimbo, from Bobby. He delivered it to me today,' handing me a tiny envelope padded out with a many folded letter on blue paper. Elly and Ben looked excited, Elly saying 'ooo! A letter!'

Val added, 'He's been a bit funny last couple of days though, Jimbobs. He keeps going on about his IQ being so high, like the other day it was 135, today it were 142. It's like, Bobby man, which is it?'

I read the letter:

Jim Respect to you! I'm writing this in the hopes that it can inspire you whenever you question why the Hell you came to America, or what the Hell you are doing in life. It is a HUGE thank you for the lot of last night. You may never come to the full realization of what you did, but the skinny of it is this & You have shown me, and given me the confidence that All humanity Does live by the same ideals. The full jist of my meaning is too complex for this letter, certainly, but I hope you can understand, it was sort of a final frontier in my confidence and understanding of self-worth that you have brought to me imported from Europe. I suppose what I am saying is that the few doubts and fears that I have had were utterly annihilated last night by the 'intense understanding' (for lack of a better term) that took place in our conversation. It has enlightened me in ways that I hope you can understand. It has given me the confidence that my ideals will come to light, and that it IS people like us that WILL change this place. Thank you sooo much! Utter respect, Bobby.

What a sweet young man.

'What does it say?' said Elly, amused and enthused.

'It's private,' I said.

'What did you two do last night?' said Ben, lasciviously.

'Talked! Got stoned!'

'Oh aye,' said Val, unconvinced.

'He's got a crush on you,' said Elly.

'No, he's got a crush on you,' I retorted.

Fucking Hell. Finally I have someone I can actually talk to, who Elly's not going to fuck, and they make out it's some homo thing. Bastards.

Still, Elly didn't go to bed in her clothes, a good sign.

Fighting over nothing

Hank said not to worry about the Beast, we could all use the van for now – although that's been a fight in itself, said I, but he said it'd be fine. Meanwhile the Beast would stay in the car-park. Ben went down to the car park to remind the others we were coming in the van, apparently Addy was a bit arsey about it, 'and I was like, "Elly told you, the Beast is fucked, so we go in the van. It's not an issue."' Ben paused. '"It's not your van," I should have said.' We crammed into the A-Team van, leaving the Beast as punishment for misbehaving.

It wasn't a completely shit day. The weather was sunny enough to be outside, but not so bad you'd get skin cancer, and business was good, I knew I'd be able to squirrel some aside. A couple of police cars were trundling around, looking for people to bust on suspicion of being alive, but not me so I felt fine.

With business done in Westie, I headed for Bartlett, feeling a brief chill of nerves, but forgot them as I made a tidy pile kerb-crawling the wide, well-kempt avenues.

An hour in, I saw three kids fifty yards away jumping up and down and waving. Business. But rolling up outside the house, they'd suddenly disappeared.

'Where've you gone?' I said as I dismounted the van. No sounds of begging money from mom. Nothing. Suddenly, two huge blasts of disgusting lukewarm water strafed my shirt and face, while a third winged my nuts as it battered my shorts. Ambushed!

'Motherfuckers' I nearly yelled, but screamed, 'Aghgh', then 'assholes' I mutilated into 'Assassins!', then leapt into the van for my water-rifle, squealing children zipping behind me. When I turned two small boys were clamouring in two directions, but a third was side-winding down the side of his house into his back garden, and with him in the cross-hairs I gave chase.

The garden was a fenceless lawn that sloped gently down towards a lake the size of a couple of an American football pitch, one half of its curvy shores edged with gardens, while the far side was traced by a road one could placidly drive along and admire the view, without driving into the water.

A great gob of warm water filled my right ear. I shrieked and started hacking bushes with the water gun, totally unconcerned about what house-proud parents might think of a six-foot-one trespasser violently hacking at their plants, screaming for their children.

Then I heard it, a distant but distinct, *Baa..da.. de-der, de-der, de-derrrrr....* of *The Entertainer*. I'd definitely turned my jingle off. Had the bastards taken over the van, was this ambush a brilliant diversion while one of them robbed all my money? As I was impressed with the sophistication of this heist, a bush to my right jostled and I fired at it, then a boy bowled through it at me, writhing in feint pain as I blasted away at him, then jabbed the sky with my rifle, doing the Sand People's warrior cry URRR-UH-UH-UH!, instead of shouting 'have some motherfucker!'

Then I heard the jingle again, louder, and I glanced across the lake, and saw winding its leisurely way in our direction was a white van, with markings like on mine, but a far heftier vehicle. I could just about make out the guy behind the wheel, black hair, penny glasses – oh by Fuck, it's Ali! I span around and sprinted back round the house, into another brilliantly executed ambush of water. No time to return fire. I had to go, or Ali catching me there would mean big trouble. Gunning the engine and hoiking the wheel round, the kids lowered their weapons, calling, 'Hey ice-cream man, we want ice-cream too!'

But too late. I U-turned desperately, back toward the highway, glimpsing left through the houses as Ali's bus trundled round the lake towards where I'd just been. God, please don't let the kids talk. Two or three more groups of kids and parents stood on the sidewalk, hands up, bills waving, but I had to make my getaway.

That evening, as I bounded the van back across the gravel towards the hanger, I saw the Beast, hoyed up high off the back of the pick-up, like it was really ill. Ben and others were in the hanger already, as I asked, 'how come the Beast's here?'

'Bit of a problem,' said Hank. 'Val called, its tank was leaking all over the car park, so we had to go pick it up. It'll be fixed in a couple of days.'

I cashed up, beered up, chatted with the others, but felt sick about Ali coming back. He duly did, and walked straight over to Hank and started talking, pointing at the map, at Bartlett, and surrounding towns.

Mike came over from having cashed up with Jess, and said, 'Ali's asking Hank who else works down around Bartlett.'

Then Ali came over, face impassive, with his Himmler glasses. 'I know Steve works around Bartlett, you're down there too, no?' he asked me.

'Bartlett? No, I'm West Chicago.'

'Right, just down from Bartlett.'

'I know it's there, yeah, I've passed it'. Shit, I so nearly said through it. 'It's up the road.'

'Have you seen another Penguin truck around yours?'

'Mmm, I've seen other vans very like mine, but never thought they were Penguin. Why?'

'I just saw a van around that looked like a Penguin van, and Hank told me there's only you and Steve near there.'

'I'm near there, but I'm only in West Chicago. My main enemy is Eskimo and he's in some blue thing. Actually that's not true, there are others I've heard of and I've seen a distance away, and I've definitely seen a van I thought was ours, but wasn't.'

'Right.' Had I convinced him to doubt himself?

'An ice-cream truck is an ice-cream truck.'

'Yeah,' he said, turning away.

If you're going to call me a liar, mate, just do it.

Back at the flat Val filled us in on the Beast's accident. 'After you lot had gone to work, and I was just gettin' ready to go off, about midday when I really need to be getting going, and I heard sirens, right, and thought o well, summink's

279

going on somewhere, then I looked out the window and saw the fire brigade in the car park, right, and saw they had the fuckin' Beast chained up, they were going to tow it away! I ran down screaming, "what you doing, that's my mate's car", didn't tell 'em it was mine, not my bloody car I'm not fucking responsible for it. They said it'd been pissing petrol all over the car park and they'd had to lance the tank, there was all this sand they'd put down the soak up the petrol, detergent all over, and car all up in chains on the tow, and I had to persuade 'em I'd call the owner and he'd come and get it, and they were like well dubious about that, but I persuaded them and got Hank and told him owt and they were like here so damn quick, you know how laid back Hank is but he wasn't when he got here, him and Charlie, and they towed it back to Penguin.'

'So the damn thing pissed itself, ends up sitting in a pool of its own petrol in tinder dry heat, just waiting to take out itself and everyone around it,' said Ben.

'I'm not kiddin', right, you should have seen the spears they used to lance the tanks, 10-foot fuckers. One of them said they were going to push it into the pond over there.'

'Jesus H,' I said.

'You should've heard them, Jimbo. They were laughing at the state of the car, they could not believe it, even the deadbolts on the door one of them pointed out and said weren't we afraid the car would get nicked, I said "are you fucking kidding? Who'd nick this?" They pissed themselves. You can't even leave it in a car park without it blowing up. Anyway wouldn't get very far now you've drained it of petrol. Oh, Elly, you should've seen the firemen, couple of them were lush, like the fuckin' Chippendales, I am not kidding you.'

'I was going to ask!'

Ben started giggling. 'That fucking car,' he said, and put his Beast screech, 'Goddamn fucking assholes think you can goddamn leave me here? FUCK you! I'm just gonna … gonna BLOW MYSELF UP! ROAAR!'. Kind of funny, but not.

'This is obscene. I'm sick of this. Right – they can fix the car and then Addy's lot get it and we get the van. Fuck this,' I said.

'Agreed. Fuck this,' said Ben.

Fix

Next morning in the car-park, Ben told Addy the handover for the van would be when the car was fixed, to which he said 'aye,' then changed the subject.

It was hot. We bombed up, sold some ice-cream, didn't run anyone over, didn't crash and die, got back to find the car was fixed, but the van was gone, with a couple of others from the other flats still at the hanger.

'Where's the van?' I said.

'Addy's fucked off with it, said he needed it to go somewhere,' said Jason.

'We fucking need it to go somewhere. Everybody needs it to go somewhere.'

'Well shit, you're coming with us then,' said Ben.

'Fuck this.'

'Can't believe he just fucked off like that,' he said.

'Wanker.'

'I've had enough of this.'

'Yeah,' I said.

'I have had enough of this,' he said, jaw clenched, and said nothing for the drive home.

Val was already back.

'Fucking Hell. Bobby, right? He is fucking *on* something. His IQ's now like 164.'

'I thought it was 142?'

'Going on and on about how intelligent he is. I don't want him around anymore, he's givin' me the creeps.'

The phone rang.

'Better not be that bloody washing-machine woman,' said Val, going to answer it. 'Hello? … oh right, Bobby,' she said loud enough so we'd see her pained expression. 'Er, hang on let me look.' She covered the mouthpiece and mouthed at me, 'Jim, Bobby wants you,' then said to Bobby, 'yeah hold the fuck on mate, I'm looking,'

'That's given the game away,' said Ben.

'Me?' I mouthed at her. She glared. I shrugged. She waved at me to come over, before saying to Bobby 'yes, yes, shurrup, he's coming,' muttering to me, 'fucking take the phone and talk to your mental boyfriend.'

'Hi Bobby?' I said, as Val grumbled away, 'I can't get away from the fucking nutter, at the diner, callin' us here, comin' over, fuckin' sick of him. Give us a cig, Ben.'

Bobby was gabbling, and kept asking to come over, but I firmly said no, 'I'll see you at the bar in a few, yep? OK cool, bye.'

As I walked into Dooley's he hopped off a seat at the bar and dashed over to me, hand out to shake, eyes wide.

'Hi man,' I said, 'you got a drink?'

'Just a soda.'

Soda what? Anyway I got one for him and a large beer for me and with a suspicious glance at the barmaid, he took me to a corner table.

'How's things?' I asked.

He leant his forearms on the table, looked at his hands, then turned his gaze upon me.

'Jim, what you said the other night. That's it.'

'What's it?'

'What you said. It's, it. Everything. It was incredible. Everything ... makes sense.'

'What makes sense?'

'All the things we discussed.'

Shit, what did we discuss? 'Oil, food, politics, er ....'

'Yeah. What you said was incredible. That's it.' He said it with this quiet passion, all the while staring at me without blinking, this great smile on his face. 'You're a genius. You must understand, you are a genius.'

'Ha well, erm,' I flustered. This was flattering, or it would have been if I could remember what I'd said that was supposedly so incredible.

'And there's been a development.' He fumbled into his jacket pocket and brought out a slightly damp piece of folded paper, which he excitedly thrust to me.

'Here's a letter I've written to the President. Read it.'

'The President? President Clinton?'

'Yeah, Clinton.'

'What about?' I half-laughed.

'Just read it! It's all in the words!'

'OK.'

I carefully unfolded this letter, thinking it might rip. Handwritten, the writing not joined up.

Mr President Utter respect to you, Sir I understand. If you are actually reading this then you already know that I have a small record in IL. So I'm assuming (assume everything) you'll take care of all that in due time (just for the incredible feeling it would give you). Apoligies for such a crude style of communication (since comm. is everything), but that is exactly the point. (you do know what I'mean) If you want to know more (we both know you do) simply give me a call at home and we'll set a meet. We'll do it however you want it (we both know how important it is) Respect! Analyze this however you would like. We both know my intentions are good and we both know the implications. I just want a meet. Bobby Fulcox

Between the paragraphs, as afterthoughts, he'd written diagonally, 'CALL ME', and, 'it's in the words!'

It made absolutely no sense, but Bobby's mouth was wide open in joyful expectation of me saying Clinton would *love* it.

'Well? Well?' he cried, while I tried to look anything but worried or amused.

'You're going to send this to President Clinton?'

'Yes, Damnit!'

'Mmm. Yes, it's interesting.'

'Isn't it?'

'But,' but, *shit, you've flipped.*

'What?'

'You mention your record. Are you sure he'll actually get the letter if you point that out?'

'He'll get it. He will. I'll arrange for him to meet you, too.'

Don't fucking drag me into this!

His phone rang, he answered, then said, 'I gotta go. But this is what I'm sending him. Thank you Jim, I'll never forget what you said. The world will change.'

I thought he was going to kiss me, but he just got up and left, leaving the drink I'd spent money on barely touched. He'd also left the letter, so I read it again, and again, over my beer, before ordering another.

This was fucking weird. But I was dealing with it. Like when Greg smashed up the bar, the times Christian nearly fucked it for all of us, Limo night, picking up the kid from the road, even this crazy Bobby shit, I was dealing with it. Me. Propping Elly up after everything, and realising I could live without her. I'd solved so much shit others had started, pulled it back enough times, surely I wasn't such a bad guy. What next though, teaching, where, how, or uni – still? Really? Doing what? – leave Elly or could it, could it actually work between us? My mind swirled.

I drank up and went back to the flat. Val joined me for a smoke on the balcony.

'About Els,' she said. Oh fuck what? She's leaving? She's in love with someone? 'She said you've been getting on much better, seems like your thing for her has gone, says you're so much cooler.'

I remembered though when my 'thing' for her was at its height, Val told me Elly'd said she loved me, *so* much, but we were friends, and that was it.

'Are you definitely leavin' uni then?'

'Think so.'

'We'll miss you, Jim.' Really?

'I'll miss you lot, too,' I said, but unconvincingly.

'You've really turned around these last few weeks, n'all.'

Now that was true.

Ben came out.

'We've got to resolve this car situation.'

'The Beast is all right now, isn't it?'

'Is it shit. I'm sick of it. Addy's been a dick all this time and I've had enough of it. I'm sorting it out tomorrow.'

'OK ... I agree, but ... fuck it you're right.'

Negotiations

'You all right to deal with Addy?' I said to Ben over morning coffee.

'Yeah,' he said, putting his shades on with theatrical bravado. I didn't envy him.

At the hanger, I bombed up and drove off sharp, on the way out seeing Ben talking with Addy outside the hanger door, Ben looking not happy.

Fucking weather couldn't make up its mind all bastard day between being pissy, grey, drizzly, muggy, and cold.

At a big junction in Westie I pulled up at the lights alongside another white van adorned with ice-cream stickers. Its driver was like me, youngish, T-shirt, shorts, cap, hunched over the steering wheel. He saw me and I anticipated a load of abuse.

Then he shouted, 'pretty shitty, huh?'

'Bloody awful!' I yelled back. He smiled. The lights changed, he went off left as I drove on, me giving a toot goodbye.

The takings were shit, as was Ben's mood at the hanger, as he was already one of the last there when I got in.

'How'd it go with Addy earlier?'

'As expected. He is being a fucking knobhead.'

'What do we do?'

'Talk to Hank?'

'OK, I will.'

I asked Hank for a chat, outside, explained the situation, and in his lovely, avuncular way said Addy's behaviour was that of someone in their early 30s who thinks they're somehow higher than the others just cos they're older, and also, while it was pissing everyone off, it was up to us to sort out.

'But they're his vehicles, his flats, this is ... how can he stand off like that?' Ben said as I cashed up.

I found myself defending Hank, then said, 'no shit, you're right, his cars and his workforce yet here we all are, arguing among ourselves. And he's OK with that?'

'Guess so,' Ben said. 'So. What now?'

'Flatten Addy.'

'What do you mean?'

'Beat him up and take the keys off him?' I said, hoping someone else would do it. 'He's outnumbered. Mike's had run-ins with them. The other flat are pissed off as well.'

'Jason's lot?'

'Yeah cos Addy uses the van like his own. They never get to use it.'

'I even heard Weird Adrian complaining the other day.'

'Hmm...'

We fucked off home, Greg there already.

'Call Mike and Jason, we need a house meeting,' I said to Ben. They were down in minutes with some of the others, and we talked about the cars. All agreed it was shit.

'We need to get the van off him,' said Ben.

'But how, do we just take the keys?' I said.

'If that's what it takes,' said Ben.

'Isn't that theft?' I said.

'It's not his van,' Mike said.

'No, you're right. Why would I even think it was?' Weird.

'I'll do it now,' said Jason.

We all looked at him. 'I'll go get some beer, now, in the van, and ask Addy for the key, assuming the cunt's in.'

'He was when I left,' said Mike.

'OK, and if I tell him it's only out of his fucking precious possession for only five fucking minutes, he'll agree. Then when I get back, you get the keys.'

'Wow,' Ben said.

'Then give the Pontiac keys to Mike, who can give them to Addy, and say it's under duress.'

'I don't have to give them to him at all, they're not his to replace,' Mike said.

'No, but you know what I mean?'

'Yeah.'

Jason – what a dude. Off he went on his solo mission, Ben skinned up and we carried on with what beers we had. The game was on.

Val came in and went off on one before she'd closed the door.

'Bobby's going fucking mad and driving me fucking mad. His IQ is now a hundred and fucking eighty. He's got a fucking screw loose, I'm telling yers.'

'Oh God,' I said. Elly looked worried.

'Today he spent like three hours in the diner, all that time he's got one drink, I said to him, "you got to get more than that luv," he says, "no I don't need to, I've more important stuff to do than talk with you."'

'Arrogant little fuck!' said Ben.

Val nodded, 'I said, dead calm, "Bobby mate, please don't talk to me like that," but I was this close to doing him,' she pinched the air, 'then, right, in the kitchen the manager has a go at us, cos Bobby's my mate and he's hanging out for hours without ordering shit, and I said, "no, I've told him he can't hang out with one drink, I've said it, and he won't listen," and the manager was "all right", and was going to throw him out basically, but just then Bobby got up and left anyway. Fucking wanker.'

'Jesus, what a dick!' I said.

'And I've been slimed.'

'Do what?'

286

'Do what? Do what? Do what do what do what?' Mike and me yelled.

'This geezer's come in now for the last five days runnin', this bloke who always asks for me to serve him and no-one else. He's not nasty or nothing, it's just he looks like a bit of a mummy's boy, kind of well dressed in jumper and shirt but when you look closer the jumper's a bit grubby 'n' that, and his trousers are stained and I'm not sure if it's always the same outfit. I can feel him just starin' at me all the time, and when I look over he looks away too late and smiles to himself.'

'He's got a crush on you. Cute!'

'Bollocks, he looks about 30. He's 'orrible. I can't really tell me boss cos he's not done nothing, but,' and she shivered.

'Do you want us to go and sort him out?'

'Ben'll shave his head, we'll stick on the shades and roll up in the Beast. That'll scare the shit out of him.'

'Scare the whole fucking place,' Val said. Ben smiled at me, and I smiled at Greg. Triumph - we were hard men, not to be fucked with. We had arrived.

'Thanks but no, me boss'd have something to say about that. But today, right, he's give us this letter. Have a read.'

Scanning through it, Val helpfully pointed out the misspellings. - DEAR VAL, I HOPE I'M NOT BEING TWO FORWORD IN WRITING THIS NOTE TO YOU, BUT I HAVE TO TELL YOU HOW I FEEL. YOU ARE A VERY PRITTY GIRL AND I WOULD, IF YOU WANT TO, LIKE TO MEET UP WITH YOU FOR A COFFEE OR SOMETHING, WHEREVER YOU WOULD LIKE TO GO, JUST TO TALK ABOT THINGS IN THE WORLD. I KNOW A VERY NICE PLACE NOT FAR FROM HERE, THE RISTAURANT CALLED WENDY'S.

'Wendy's, he's got class,' I exclaimed.

She nodded, aghast.

I handed it to Ben, and Greg leaned over to view. They snickered between themselves.

'S'not bad though, Val, he just wants a date. I think it's cute.'

'Jim! He's 'orrible, he just sits there for hours. He's after me always, and when I ask him what he wants he takes ages and ages to choose, and then he always orders a coffee, one fucking coffee right, all that time wasted and he thinks it's cute, when it's not cos I've got fuckin' other customers to serve who tip decent and you get fuck all tip for a coffee and it pisses me off, cos he's not only sad, he costs me money.'

I frowned an apology.

'And he's slimy.'

'Why's he written the whole thing in capitals?' said Greg.

'You should reply in kind,' said Ben.

'What, write "NO" on an A2 size bit of paper?'

'Do one of those notes with all the letters cut out of newspapers,' I said.

'But he'll know it was from me.'

'Course he will! It's not supposed to be anonymous, it's supposed to freak him out.'

'He'd just think I was trying to engage with him on 'is level, or summink.'

'Ah say we go round and fuck this cunt over!' Greg said with full Glaswegian vigour.

'Kick down his door.'

'Stick a burning crucifix onto his lawn.'

'We can do that burning bag of shit on his door, ring the bell and run like fuck, he comes out and stamps it out,' said Greg, and he guffawed.

'But he won't know what it's about, though.'

'So? It'll be funny!' Greg yelled.

'It's just your favourite all-time trick, isn't it?' Ben's voice wavered, as Greg's face went red. Ben started to skin up.

There was a knock at the door, 'Better not be fuckin' Bobby,' said Val. But it was Jason, returned with a load of beer – and the van keys.

'I've done it. I've got the van keys.'

'You fucking star.'

Ben put the Beast's keys ceremoniously into Mike's hands. We divvied out the beers and started sending the spliff around.

'Right – better tell Addy!' said Jason, 'What's your number again Mike?'

Mike dialled it for him.

'Hi this is Jason, is Addy there?'

We all shushed ourselves to listen in.

'Hi Addy ... Yep ... There's been a bit of a change of plan and I've given the van keys to Jim's lot.'

I flinched – the bomb was dropped. Ben's mouth fell open.

'Well, that's what was agreed all along and ... Addy, you get to use the Pontiac, so it's all OK.'

Addy said something.

'It works fine,' Jason replied, 'you can get to use the Pontiac like the others do.'

Addy was saying something that made Jason nod and smile widely.

'The van's bigger and others need it more than you.'

'Good stuff Jason,' I whispered, Elly looked at me in agreement.

Jason responded again, 'but Addy, Addy mate, it's not ... no, no, listen, listen, ... come on Addy man, listen, shouting'll do no good.'

'Wooohoo!' we scoffed.

'But you'll be able to use the Pontiac, like we all will ... no, no, Addy, it's not theft ... No it's not ... No ... it's not your van, Addy, Addy mate shop shouting – it's not your van, so no-one stole it, no-one can steal something you don't own.'

'Good lad!' said Greg.

'It's not your van, it's not even your car, mate. Fact.'

'Get in there!' said Elly.

Jason's eyes widened and he breathed in, then said, 'You'll what? Fucking smash my face in?'

That got a very loud 'ooooooh', from all of us, as Jason wonderfully replied, 'Come on Addy, that's not really going to solve anything.'

Oh, this was a wonderful wind-up.

Then again, 'Addy, Addy, no, no, come on man, come on ... you're not going to fucking smash my face in. No you're not. Because there's no need for it.'

Another great 'Way-hay!' and laughing from all of us, which Jason held the phone up for Addy to better hear.

'No, no ... I'm sorry mate, I can't have you talking to me like that. ... you'll be able to use the Pontiac, if everyone agrees, the van's downstairs, I'm sure they'll lend it out ... no, no, you won't, Addy. I've got to go. Bye.'

He hung up and we cheered, laughed and cheered some more, slapping Jason on the back, even Val gave him a hug.

'O come on it wasn't that big a deal,' he said, almost blushing.

'You all right with this, Mike?'

'Fucking no skin off my nose, he'll probably be a dick about the Pontiac as well, but it's Jason he'll be after.'

'Fuck him, he's full of it,' said Jason.

'He'll have to take us on as well!' I said, 'what the fuck threatening Jason?'

'We don't take no shit,' shouted Ben.

'We don't take no shit!' I shouted back, leaping from the sofa and jabbing myself in the chest, shouting in his face, and he shouted back, 'we don't take no shit!'

'Jason doesn't take any shit!' Elly yelled.

'I don't take any shit!' Jason yelled back.

Then it was we four were jabbing at one another, shouting about how much shit none of us or the other would take , then everyone was at it, 'are you taking any shit?' 'I'm not taking any shit!' 'what about my shit, you taking any of my shit?' 'I'm not taking any of your shit, of your shit, or yours,' and so on.

'Veterans!' I said to Ben.

'Veterans! Ben replied.

We drank on, then I said, 'what else can we blow up?'

'Let's get that jakie who slimed Val,' said Greg.

'Class! Val, give us the number.'

I phoned it, an answerphone started after three rings, 'This is Andy, I can't come to the phone right now, but I'm very glad you called and please do call,' then the beep, and I yelled in my worst Michael Caine voice, 'If I ever see you round the diner talking to my girlfriend ever again I'll fuck you up, and I know where you live, you fucking cunt! Cut your balls off!' and hung up to a chorus of raucous laughter.

More beer, spliff and song, then someone suggested I needed my hair cut, so Greg got out his clippers and shaved my head.

Did a good job too.

Jason slept on the sofa.

Get out of this place

Today, our day off, was the day to get the plane tickets out of here. We took the van into Chicago proper, with the aquarium and Sears Tower on our hit-list, the one time we'd hit town in daylight. We hadn't even seen a baseball game, like the others had, and then when we'd got the plane tickets from the travel agent, then ate at a cool burger joint, somehow the other stuff wasn't going to happen.

It didn't matter though, just us alone, in town, such a handsome city by day, yet felt so different to only eight weeks before. I felt different. I felt good, for all the shit I'd dealt with. And now it was just me and her, no threats from anyone else. Just us. All I wanted.

There was a vague plan to meet at Dooley's later. I remembered the phone message from the night before and how that bloke sounded on the voicemail, bit sad really, poor bastard obviously didn't have much by way of social skills, and I might have really scared him, all for a laugh.

Val came back and said 'that message must have worked, I've not seen slimy today.'

'Hah!' Ben said, while I smiled, but actually felt terrible.

'Oh God it's not funny, he's probably never going to leave his house again.'

'Good!' said Val.

Around 8pm or so the door buzzer went, and we all looked at one another askance.

'Are we not going to meet them there?' Elly said.

'They don't ring the door, they just come,' said Ben, 'it must be Bobby.'

'Pretend we're not in?' I said.

'No, he'll see the lights are on, he did that the other night.'

'Fuck him, he's not welcome.'

'He's disturbed.'

The buzzer went again.

'Bollocks,' said Ben.

'I don't want to let him in, but he might not go away,' I said.

Elly looked panicked and started looking around.

'Tell him to fuck off,' said Ben.

'I will but I'll do it nicely. Ben, he's mental.'

The buzzer went again.

'Wanker's not going away. Hang on, if you're ready to go, then go now out the side, I'll talk with him for a bit, then come over. Go now,' I said.

'Plan!' said Ben, and Elly nodded.

I picked up the door phone. 'Hi?'

'Hi, Bobby here!'

'Bobby! Sorry mate, I was in the shower, I'll just buzz you in,' I said loudly as Elly and Ben went out the door, Elly whispering, 'quick!', to which Ben replied with conspiratorial glee, 'Quick, quick!'

I threw some water over my head as if I'd had a shower. Then after just a few seconds, Bobby appeared at the door.

'Hey Jim!'

'Hey Bobby, sorry about that, I …' my shower story didn't work as I realised I still stank from the day. 'I was just dozing.' One bad lie after another.

'Your hair's wet.'

'Yeah, yeah, just waking myself up. The others have gone out, and I'm going to bed soon.'

'Oh yeah really where? They not here?' he looked startled if not sad. 'Did they go out? Can we go too? Are you going by car? Is Elly with them?'

'No,' I said, barely bothering to hide my tiredness at all this weirdness, 'they've gone into town. What's up?' I sat on the sofa to keep him here instead of going off and searching Dooley's, before realising we might be here a while. He sat in the armchair, leaning forward, hands telling the story as much as his staring eyes.

'I was sitting in Denny's. There was this feeling, this buzz going around the entire restaurant that only a very, very few could pick up on. Most of them weren't ready to understand it but as I was looking to see who was channelling in I saw this kid, must have been about five years old, a little girl, and she looked at me and I looked at her and I could see in her eyes, she knew. It was like electricity coming between us, just her eyes were full of understanding and wisdom. She knew, and I mean, she knew, and I thought, yes, I am succeeding, my work in finding the others is succeeding, my work is being done.'

I was afraid that, as I sat gazing at Bobby's face, if I looked away from that pasty mass of cheeks and wild eyes, I'd find this maniac hysterically funny. His eyes were ringed and puffy, as if he hadn't slept for days, but he was talking so quickly. He must have been on speed or something.

'I continued to stare around the bar and see who else understood, but this girl looked at me again, and she said, "don't over-reach yourself Bobby. I understand. That is enough for now. Your time is soon."'

'She said this to you?' I couldn't contain my incredulity.

'With her eyes,' and then he nodded.

He was jabbering like Jeff Goldblum in *The Fly*, but somehow this was more sinister. Then it clicked who Bobby really reminded me of, that nuts ventriloquist Anthony Hopkins played in *Magic*. Any second Bobby seemed about to get out a dummy and let it do all the talking. This was both terrifying and funny. Stare at his eyes, he's scary, not funny, I told myself, feeling great weights of mirth catapult up into the vaults of my mind, clanging off the bells of the steeple up there. When would they scream back down and smash me into the floor with laughter?

292

This was like the ending of *Moonraker*, a multi-million-pound film that climaxes with Roger Moore looking at a crap Atari game, saying 'steady, steady,' in his wonderful bass voice, and it was brilliant, edge-of-the-seat stuff, yet all he was doing was saying 'steady … steady …'

I couldn't be bothered to look interested and my eyes flitted around the room.

'Hey man, you look tired,' he said.

'Yep.'

'OK … I'll leave you alone, but we gotta talk again soon. We got things we gotta do!' he said.

'Yep,' my stomach rising, heart sinking.

Then he left. I heard the buzzing of his scooter engine then hoped he didn't see the Beast or the A-Team van and twig I'd lied, but then I thought, oh, fuck him if he does.

Sick of this shit.

Maniacs fawning all over the place.

Fuck off.

Close shave

I walked into the hanger, feeling spruce. Hank saw my hair and said, 'you look different, tough!'

'Tough! Ha!'

'Lemme feel,' and I bent my head down and he pawed my hair, 'it's like a little carpet,' he said and chuckled.

'The carpet look, it's all the rage,' I said.

Bombed up, fucked off, sold some ice-cream, thought about shit. For the first time in a while serving some child, I got a vision of Elly and Christian fucking, and I flinched. Just a thought, but enough to give me a rager and piss me off so much the next child asked, 'are you OK? You look angry.'

'Do I? Sorry,' I said, and carried on serving.

Most of us were back and counted up before the others. Jason sat with us, Addy and Ali sat apart from everyone.

Crap Adrian came in, did his pathetic 'hello Elly' thing, but before he started counting up he said to me, 'oo, I've not been able to find my driving licence, it might be in the van, can I borrow the key to get it?'

Berk.

'Yeah, sure.'

'Great, see you in a sec.'

Ali got up and moved out, Addy went with him, a couple of other ice-creamers as well.

I knocked down another beer, then said to Ben, 'you done mate? Elly?'

'Yep. Right, do we take anyone in the van or just us?'

'Oh shit, not thought of that.'

'Hang on, I gave Adrian the key,' and I looked around and he was back, counting up.

'Mate, you got the van key?'

'No?'

'No? I gave it to you two minutes ago.'

'Ali's got it.'

'Why?'

'He asked for it.'

'What?' Ben yelled and we stalked outside. The Beast and the van were still there, Addy was getting not into the Beast, but the van, Ali already in the front.

'What you doing? You got the Pontiac now,' I said.

'We're not driving it, it's bust,' said Addy. 'It's broken down, we can't drive it, so we're all going in the van.'

'Is it fuck!' said Ben, storming back to the hanger.

'When was it bust?' I asked Addy.

'I told Hank this morning it was bust, he's got the key.'

'He's said nothing.'

'It's fucked, Charlie said he'd fix it but he hasn't, so we're taking the van.'

'Not fucking without us,' I said, confused, then Ben came back, holding the keys to the Beast aloft, his face like thunder, 'it's not broken down. Hank and Charlie just told me, it's driveable and they said you said whatever you said about it being bust wasn't the case,' his voice rising, and he looked like he was going to jump into the van and do them there. 'It's perfectly fucking driveable!'

'Is it now?' said Addy, 'well you're good to drive it then. Come on Ali, off we go,' and he leaned forward, and tried to hoy the slide door shut even while Aidan and others were standing, waiting to get in, and they pushed their way in barely before the van started to pull away.

'Arsehole! Fucking arsehole!' Ben shouted, kicking the side of the van.

'Cunt!' I shouted.

'Wankers!' shouted Elly, as gravel sprayed back at us.

Ben was apoplectic, and he started to kick other cars, hanger doors.

'Ben, Ben, Ben Ben, stop it, stop it,' I said. He screamed.

'Let's just go, fuck this, let's fucking go,' he said, calming down.

Mike appeared at the hanger door, 'fuck's going on?' then said, 'oi, where's the van gone?'

'That cunt Addy just drove off with it.'

'What? He's supposed to drive us back.'

'Well he's fucked off, lied to us the Beast was bust, he was going to drive off anyway and has taken the van again!'

Mike shouted back into the hanger, 'oi – Adrians! Hurry up, we're going in the Pontiac.'

Ben was too angry to drive, so I did.

'That lying bastard,' I said.

'Better get some fuel,' Ben said.

'Adrian – yes you, boggle eyes, were you in on this?'

'In on what?' he sounded surprised.

'In on getting the van back to Addy.'

'No? He just asked for the keys? I don't understand.'

Mike filled him in on all the hoo-ha about the car and the van.

We pulled into a gas station, but as I filled up, my legs, my hands were shaking with rage, so badly I spilt gas back onto my shorts.

Crap Adrian said, 'it does sound really unfair, if he's gone back on the deal that's not good. I can see why you're so angry.' Was there in fact a solid young man lurking under that dickheaded exterior?

We stormed from the car back to our flat and hit the fridge, us both downing two beers, glowering. Greg was home, 'what's up you with you twos?'

We told him as best we could between us, although Ben kept suddenly shouting, 'arsehole!'

Then I said, 'fuck this, we're going to go up there and have this out. I'm not having this cunt lie to me.'

'Nor me.'

'I'll come! Just you talking about him, I hate him too!' said Greg.

I glared at Elly. 'Well?'

'I'm coming, but don't drink too much, you'll bugger up the argument.'

With great speed and even more anger we rehearsed what we would say, recapping what we'd ranted about in the car now with Greg, prepping like in *A Few Good Men*, but not quite as coherently. All went quiet for a couple of moments, then I launched out of my armchair, 'let's get the bastard!'

The four of us steamed up to Addy's apartment, striding down the corridors, getting more and more pumped as the distance narrowed, 'til there, I pushed open the door and we powered in and I said aloud to Addy and Ali, both on the sofa, 'we want to fucking to talk to you' as I went and stood in front of them, Ben to my side, Greg plonking down next to Ali, one or either of them going 'what the fuck' 'don't come barging in here, what the Hell are you doing?'

'Shuddup!', I felt dazed with rage, then as I was about to go off, Crap Adrian said, 'oo wow, it's a posse!' causing me to glance at him in a second of distracted rage, and Addy say 'what the fuck's this then eh?' with this withering calm tone to his voice.

'There's nothing wrong with the Pontiac! We said it was fixed and it was fixed! It was never fucking bust! You said it was bust and it wasn't and you took the van when the car was fine and so you lied and it's fine,' as I felt myself berate into incoherence, legs shaking, pointed finger shaking.

'Don't shout at me. Who said it wasn't fixed?'

'You did!'

'I never. Anyway it's a death trap and I'm not driving it.'

'It's your turn – yes it is, yes it bloody is fixed.'

'Fuck the turns, it's bust, it's a death trap, and –

'We've had it for months - '

'And you can have it some more, seeing as it works fine like was said earlier,' the bastard wasn't flinching, and I felt myself flailing.

Ben cut in, 'You agreed to take it back and we'd get the van. You said that time and again.'

'Who to?'

'Christian.'

'He's not here.'

'But we are! That car is fine to drive, you agreed to take it, now this evening you said you weren't taking it because it was broken down , you said Charlie said – but it fucking well isn't broken down.'

'So what's the problem?'

I nearly screamed, 'you lied!'

'Don't call me a liar!'

'You are a liar!'

'You are out of order, calling me a liar, coming in here, mob handed - '

'You're out of order! All this shit! Threatening Jason! You are bang out of order!' I yelled, still pointing at him.

'Don't point at me.'

'I'm pointing at you, you're a liar and you're out of order!'

'Call me that again and I'll slap you!'

'It wasn't broken down, you just said it cos you don't want it. That's a lie, you are a liar.'

'And you left us there tonight,' Mike said.

'What? No I didn't.'

'Oh yes you bloody did,' he said, real anger, but said with such calm. 'You took off without me and Adrian over there. And even though the van's supposed to be for the flat, you act like it's yours.'

'No I don't.'

'You do, Addy, you do, and we're talked about this before.'

Meanwhile Greg was sat eyeing Ali up, 'you looking at me funny, mate?', then even Weird Adrian, who'd I'd not seen turn up, joined in at Addy.

'What about that time I wanted to take the van and you said I couldn't have it, and then you said you'd pick me up but you didn't bloody turn up, left us to make my own fucking way back.'

'Fuck off did I!' said Addy, then Mike backed up Weird Adrian and started off himself, Addy's head turning this way and that as he was getting it all sides from four blokes standing over him. Mike's voice rising, Weird Adrian's voice rising, Ben's, Addy shouting back but ever more beleaguered, it was great, everyone was on him, everyone backing us up, then Aidan walked in, 'please stop this shouting, please, it's doing me head in.'

'See,' I said, 'you fucked this up. You're a liar.'

'Call me a liar again and I'll give you a slap.'

'Come on then! Stop saying it and just do it!' He could have knocked me across the room, but I was so, so stoked, I wanted it just to mark the occasion.

He stopped short.

'We're taking the van, you're getting the Beast,' said Ben. Addy just looked agog, as Mike picked the van keys off the kitchen table and swapped them for the Beast's keys with Ben.

'Gottit? Fair's fucking fair,' I said, and we steamed out, back to the flat, almost literally steaming as we were cloaked in sweat, the corridors long and hot like a steel mill, Greg and Ben in front, me behind with Elly trotting alongside me, powering back down the corridor, all of us absolutely pumped.

'I fucking told him, did you see Ali, he was shitting it' said Greg.

'I heard you fucking telling him,' said Ben.

'Shitting himself,' Greg said.

'Fucking yeah! They all were!'

'How do you think that went?' I asked Elly.

'You sure told them.'

'Yep. I fucking did,' although I knew I'd stumbled, probably the beer, the stress, Crap Adrian starting up when we walked in, felt like it'd all come out in a stupid jumble.

But we'd won. Everyone else waded in.

I felt like grabbing her, holding her against the wall and snogging her, but didn't.

Val had come back, saw us charge in, red-faced, sweaty, she seemed to pick up on the vibe.

'Everything all right?'

Ben yelled from the kitchen, 'no fucking beer!'

Greg, dead happy at playing the heavy, unloaded on Val all that happened with the same excitement that I'd gone blasting in with, although he was more coherent than I'd been. Suddenly, really weirdly, I felt tired, and this strange sense of shame, like I'd done something wrong, and slumped into an armchair, Ben repeating aloud, 'no fucking beer!', Greg carrying on with who'd said what and how they'd won each trick or blow, a lot about me, 'you should have seen him!'

Elly knelt beside me and put her hand on my forearm, 'you all right?'

I took her hand and kissed it. She smiled so coyly, then I said, 'well fuck this, I'm gonna get pissed somehow,' got some money off her and Ben, and went off to see Dogface, the walk cooling me a bit, there I hauled two big boxes of cans out of the chill cabinets, then heard this English voice behind me say camply, 'ooo! Fancy meeting you here!'

It was Crap Adrian, eyes a-bug like he's so fucking hilarious.

I just started shouting.

'Shut the fuck up! You little cunt! What the fuck was that back there? "Ooo look out it's a posse!"'

'I –'

'Shuddup wanker! We told you we were coming, you knew we were upset, you fucking sat with us and talked with us all about it, then we come over and you, you take the piss!'

Now his eyes were a-bug for real, he tried to speak again.

'Shuttup! You got nothing to say! You fucking take the piss!'

He just stared.

'What have they said?'

'Um ...'

'What did they say after we left? Tell me dickhead, you were there.'

'Nothing. they didn't say –'

'Nothing? Nothing? Really? Sure you weren't in another room, wanking?' A surge of rage came through me, 'you little bastard, getting the key off us to get your driving licence, what about that, were you fucking in on it?' I wanted to take him by the throat.

'What?'

Just as I was going to drop the beers and slap the bastard he said, 'my licence was in the van, like I thought, I found it, I found it.'

It sounded just, just truthful enough. I paused.

Nonethefuckingless:'You were with us, you agreed with us, but you took the piss, "oo oo here they come all hard and big". Fuck you. All right? Fuck you.'

'Sorry.'

'Damn fucking right,' I said, somehow the sorry had an effect and I felt myself blow out, my voice dropped.

'They've said nothing? Fine. You say nothing, right? Nothing! Go back to your flat and you say nothing. This conversation didn't happen, geddit?'

'OK.'

'Now fuck off.'

No comment from Dogface, nicely enough.

Back home, everyone was still around, and we clanged cans as we continued to pick over the rubble of the fight.

'All this fighting among ourselves, do you know why?' said Ben.

Elly spotted it: 'The Beast! Even when we're not driving it, it manages to raise Hell, among us all.'

'I can hear it now, laughing to itself,' said Ben.

'It's the ultimate stirrer!' said Elly.

'I'm not taking its shit,' I said.

'Anyways, Jim,' said Val, 'I was telling them when you were at the shop. You know Sandy, Bobby's mate? He was in today asking if he could talk to you, and he is upset, and I mean, upset. He was tellin' me, right, the other night he was drivin' Bobby home from a party and Bobby was just goin' on and on about this seriously crazed stuff, just fucked up stuff, no sense to any of it. Sandy got so scared he said he was crying while driving, because he just couldn't understand what the fuck Bobby was on about. It were bad, Jimbo.'

'Christ, like what?'

'It's hard to say, I mean, there was something Sandy said about Bobby wantin' to kill himself as a martyr.'

Had Sandy said this or was Val filling in the gaps of her report to make it all the more exciting?

'Kill himself?'

'Yeah, for the cause in order to connect people but I weren't sure why, only that that stuck out as one of Bobby's worse ideas.' Suppose he had said that, then.

'I'm not jokin', Jimbo, you should have seen him. You know Sandy right, he's the quiet one, at first you think he's a bit awkward or aloof, but actually he's just really a sweet bright guy, so to see him in the state he came to the diner in

299

today was just shocking, but what Sandy said was Bobby keeps referring to what you and him talked about the other night.'

'I didn't say anything! We talked about oil, roads, farming, about all sorts of stuff – '

'Feel like I missed out,' said Elly.

'Val, if Sandy comes into the diner again, can you tell him Bobby's not welcome here anymore,' I said.

'I've told him. I've said it, nicely, you know me, and Sandy don't want Bobby comin' round anymore anyway cos he thinks Jimbo's gone and possessed him with some demons.'

'Oh fucking great. Class! This is all my fault!'

'You put voodoo on him!' Ben screamed.

Oh God this isn't funny!

Fuck me

Next morning we piled into the A-Team van. The Beast was gone.

We got to the hanger, I flinched a bit when I saw Addy, but he was moving fast and his pace skipped a beat and he looked away when he saw me, almost scurrying. Was he afraid of me?

I felt bad. Me shouting down some bloke in his 30s with my gang, about a van. Just shit. This was supposed to be fun.

Mostly ignored on the rounds, except one girl who said, 'no thanks, we had ice-cream already!'

'O, right. Who off? Eskimo?'

'Who's Eskimo?'

'He's a fat man in a blue truck.'

'Mm? No. This truck was yellow.'

'Yeah she's not called Eskimo, she's called Glacier,' said her friend.

'Yeah it's a she!!' she said, 'She's a she-e-e-e-e!'

'She's a she.'

'O right.' A yellow truck? Glacier? Who the fuck were they talking about? How many others were down here?

A couple more 'go aways', from kids. At the hanger, others said similar.

Val was already home, and I dreaded the latest news on Bobby, which she served up pronto.

'News for you, Jim, Bobby's mum's been into the café, too. She really wants to speak to you, wants to know what the Hell you've been saying to Bobby.'

'I've not said anything!' I shouted, 'I've not said anything!'

'You told Sandy Bobby's not to come round anymore.'

'Aye. I've told him already, but he's so fucking worried about him, he wants us to help Bobby.'

'I thought Sandy didn't want him coming round either!' I shouted.

'Oh he doesn't, but he's fucked as well. But I'm worried about him being with us. He's so not making sense. Sandy's right. But, this is crazy.'

'I fucking know …'

'Voodoo! Someone's put voodoo in my son!' Ben screeched in a Nigerian accent, 'You put demons in my son's mind!'

'No I didn't! It was the Beast! The Beast has possessed Bobby!' I shouted back.

'The demon has realised its host is dead and has taken over Bobby, he's now the Beast in human form!' Elly said.

Ben stood up and in a great southern preacher-style voice, declared, 'There shall come a time when that which drives among us shall die, and become He who scoots among us. The Beast shall become the Bobby – all hail the

Bobby!'.

Elly and Val started 'o hailing' and waving their arms at him, while I did a crucifix with my fingers, saying 'Hail Mary, full of grace, Hail Mary, full of grace,' like Robert Redford crossing the Rhine, then the fucking doorbell went and we all screamed.

'Nobody move! Everybody shuddup and get down!' I said. Ben lunged to turn off the side lamp as we hit the carpet.

It buzzed again.

We stayed down.

'Is he going to fuck off or what?' whispered Ben.

Then the phone started ringing.

'Jesus, take the hint, motherfucker,' I said.

We all lay on the floor, trying not to laugh, even though Bobby wasn't even in the building to hear us, or so we thought.

'What did I do? What did I do?' I whimpered.

The phone stopped ringing, but we stayed down. Val whispered, 'If he knocks on that fuckin' door I'm jumping off the balcony.'

No knock came, we picked ourselves up, and sat in the dark, like the cabin scene in *Jaws* when they're all getting shitfaced, then Jaws turns up.

'He ate the light'.

Then we heard a scooter start up and buzz away.

He'd gone, it seemed.

Jesus shat.

After some pissing about people drifted off to bed, leaving just me and Val.

'Like I was saying, Elly, she said, you're so much cooler now it's like your thing for her has gone.'

My 'thing for her'. Thing. Not a thing. I had to tell her anyway.

'It hasn't gone, well, not really. I'd marry her tomorrow if she wanted. I've never met anyone I've ever loved so much.'

Val looked at me like I was crazed. 'She loves you too, so much, but only as a mate, she wants you as a mate. She's said so, so many times.'

That look. That fucking look. How many times had I had it the year past, or people said it, 'she doesn't want you, give it up, it's crazy, you're crazy.' Me saying, 'you don't know her like I do,' them saying, 'that's what people think when they're in love,' while she was there, on my course, with my friends, fucking my other friends, me knowing what I knew, no-one else, except Christian, and look what he did.

Instead I said: 'I know. And I don't think I can stand it, I've got to leave uni. She can have anyone, and she does. Mark, Christian. Bobby if she wanted, although she said no, apparently even Greg asked for a blow job.'

302

'But come on Jim, you know what she's like, if she'd really fancied Greg she'd have been in his pants the second he'd made a move on her. Even if he hadn't.'

We talked on and on, until Val eventually went to bed. I carried my can and ciggy, wondering if there was anything on telly, when I looked up and saw Elly at the opening of the corridor, glaring at me.

'It's fascinating listening to what people really think of you,' she said, her voice loaded with emotion. 'Absolutely fascinating.'

There was no point denying anything, but I asked, 'What did you hear?'
'Everything.'

'Did you hear when I said I loved you and wanted to marry you?'

No reply to that, but her gaze flicked to the kitchen, then down to the floor, and her shoulders slumped.

'I hate this place,' she said, 'I hate it. There's no privacy, no escape at all.'

'Come on, sit down, let's talk.'

She looked at the sofa but didn't move. I went and got her a beer, lit up two cigs, sat on the sofa and patted the cushion next to me. She came over and we started talking openly.

'I probably would have gone with Greg, if Christian hadn't done what he did to me.'

'But you didn't use any protection with Christian.'

'I panicked,' she said, her voice with a flash of defensiveness, 'I said no, but he was just kept going and I just, I just panicked, so we did it.'

She'd told Val they'd just got too carried away, but I didn't pick on that. She said, 'I told him about me. Did he say?'

'Yes. Did you tell Mark any of that?'

'No, we were never that close.'

'Not much to him is there?'

'No. No, not at all.' Mark was as deep as a piece of paper, who only wanted to blow up people he'd never met. But you can't hear that from a spurned lover.

Then she looked afraid, 'do you think that's why Christian dumped me?'

Yes, but I couldn't say that. 'I think he just wanted a fun time, he was always going to go travelling so there was a time limit on it.'

'But we had a fun time. All I wanted was fun.'

Why am I having to listen to this?

'He'd only just dumped his previous girlfriend of what, three years? I think he was, fuck knows what, worn out?'

'Do you think he wants to see me again?'

'I don't know. I've not spoken with him. I thought he was an arsehole when you two got together and then the way he carried on, like that night we got raided, then with you, how he treated you, and he pissed everyone off.'

'Did Mark ever tell you why he dumped me?'

Please stop asking me. All those times you hung out with me to get to them, and now they're gone, you're still asking? 'No idea. He's a shallow bastard,' and then I told her, 'Anyway we stopped talking when you two started going out. I couldn't stand it.'

She looked sad. 'I didn't know that.'

Yes you bloody did! You used to say 'you're just jealous' with fucking glee on your face, knowing what jealousy felt like, if not knowing I wanted to fucking kill myself. But I didn't want to burden her with guilt. So I jokingly asked, 'Any more of my friends you want to fuck?'

She chuckled, said 'no', then added, 'they didn't work out well anyway.'

'Could have had me all along.'

'I know. You were too strange though, going out and you'd get so drunk and then you'd get so heavy, crying, ruining shit.'

'I know. I don't know why I was getting so upset, and so upset. I wondered the other day if it was cos of ma and pa splitting up and the house being sold. Maybe even the meningitis from last year. But all that stuff happens, you know, you carry on.'

'When did you have meningitis again?'

'At Leicester. Fucking nought to Death's Door in 12 hours. It's why I left there and moved over to ours.' As I said this, it struck me, it'd been a year since I'd seen pa drive away that day, all alone. A cold wind of sorrow blew through me. 'I told you this. I had the headache from Hell. I lost a stone in a week. If you want to go on a diet, get bacterial meningitis.'

She smiled, sadly.

'I don't know why I was such a fucking mess, why I was doing like you said, I hated myself for it. I didn't understand it either.'

'I do love you. So much. You do really listen.'

'Not as much as Richard though.'

'No, more than him. You're better than him. That book you bought me about the gap year, it was amazing, I identified with everything she wrote.'

This was amazing to hear. Absolutely amazing, when all those months ago the worst thing she'd ever said, 'I don't need you, you don't know me, you don't know me at all'.

We talked on, about hopes for the future, marriage, children, with whomsoever, and she said, 'I'd make a terrible mother.'

'I think you'd make a great mother.'

'Really? Why?' she looked genuinely surprised.

'Because you're so worried about being a bad one, it's obvious, you don't want to be crap at it.'

'I can't even look after my dog properly.'

'But you do, you love it to bits. That dog you were with outside the mall the other day, you were all over it, and again, it's like, you're so worried about looking after your dog you actually do look after it, it's just so obvious how much you love dogs, really love them. Kids will be the same.'

304

She looked at me like she could cry, saying quietly, 'no-one's ever told me that before. Everyone's always been "Elly? With kids? Fuck no, keep them away they'll end up in the bin or falling out the window."'

'Nah. They're wrong. You'd be great. '

She got up and kissed me on the forehead, before saying she had to go to bed, then added, 'please don't leave uni'.

What was I going to do without her? Why wasn't I with her? Couldn't I just forget it all, forgive it all? Be with her? Why'd she fucked all my friends but not me, even now?

All bloody day

At the hanger, as I was bombing up, Elly came over to my van.

'You good?' I said.

'Just want a cig, and to see you,' she said.

I lit two and gave her one.

'All been a bit wild, eh?'

'It has. And it's been you dealing with it.'

I was pleased she noticed, 'I've surprised myself, to be honest.'

'When your back's to the wall, that's when the real fighters show themselves, what my gran used to say.'

For no reason I started to sing the tune from the end of *The Empire Strikes Back*, and she looked at me, wistfully, then I said, 'come on, work to do'.

But. All the round around, I kept getting images back of Elly and Christian. Rage at them. Then I'd think about leaving uni, and going abroad, and hope it'd all be amazing ... then think I was leaving a professional course, cos of my so-called friends, Mark, who I was supposed to be sharing a house with, and Christian, mates with all my other mates.

Best friends, yeah.

I found myself with that thousand yard stare thing like GIs, then a voice said,

Put it behind you, Jim, you've done so well. You don't need any of them.

But I'm leaving the woman I love. Who'll protect her? She needs me. She loves me. We need to fuck.

No, she said no. Just get out of here, make her happy these last days, and go.

I remembered the sound of her cumming.

All day this cycled through my mind, all day the jingle, all day kids saying 'I want ... I want ... ', or, 'get lost'.

At the hanger I went and talked with Elly, all that mattered to me was that her day was fine. As we parked back home we queried the beer situation, so Ben went in and shouted from the balcony, 'Oi! – No fucking beer'.

I gave him a thumbs up, Elly and I drove off to Dogface for a couple of boxes, rolled back, killed the engine, I passed a can to her in the back and one for me.

'I'm really going to miss you,' I said.

'Well don't leave then.'

'Nothing for me at uni though. I fucked up the year, I don't know if I want to go back.' I wanted to say, I have no friends I trust not to fuck you, or you them, and break my fucking heart. But I didn't.

'What am I going to do at uni without you?' she sounded almost tearful.

'You'll be all right. You'll have Val, Aaron, Ben, you're living with Jim as well. You've got the whole lot.' She had as well. My gang, before we incorporated her into it, at my doing, cos I thought she was lonely and I wanted her around.

'But you're the one I love,' she said.

I reached back and scratched her head.

'I love you too.' Damn, I was in the wrong seat to kiss her.

We said nothing for a while.

'Do you ever think, when looking at the stars, so many of them, what, we can see about 3,000 in the sky on a clear night, how many of them are dead already? Have been dead for years, but we don't see that yet because they're millions of light years away? The stories they're telling us now are from years and years and years ago. The sky is full of ghosts.'

'Why are you talking about this?'

'I just remember the wonder of when at school I opened a book and saw these beautiful, glossy photos of Neptune from Voyager 2, showing it had bands, and a great blue spot, like Jupiter. It wasn't that vague blue blob we'd seen it to be as children, we finally knew what it looked like, it even has cirrus clouds, the clouds on the border of day and night on the planet, and I thought how cold and dark and far would it feel to be on the planet as it turned to night. It was stunning.'

I looked in the rear view mirror and she was looking out the side window.

I mumbled something about astronomers reading their stories, epics of scale in time and distance, formed by forces beyond our imagination, played out eons before mankind even existed as a twinkle in God's eye.

She wasn't listening and I'd bored myself by then.

But she'd told me she loved me. Wow. How good did I feel.

We went to get out, then she said, 'oo, don't leave the can in here, the police will find it and fuck us.'

'Oh God yeah.' We scanned the foot wells for any other contraband and went back to the flat, where Val was.

'Anyways Jimbo, there's a development with Bobby.'

'Oh fuck, what now?' I must have snapped, as Val stalled, looked surprised, then asked, 'shall I tell you later?'

'No. What's he done, blown himself up?' I tried to make light of it.

'No. Not quite. Sandy came in though, right. He wants us to go see Bobby. He said his mum wants it too. To square things.'

'What the fuck?'

'Go round and talk to him, and her.'

I groaned. 'Can't he just fuck off?'

'Not nastily, Jim, just go round and talk to him. He was a nice bloke, he just went stupid, but anyway it's not just him that wants it, it's his mate, and his mum.'

'It's fair enough in a way,' said Elly, 'I mean, if it were just Bobby I'd be thinking, "fuck him", but Sandy and his mum are upset, if it helps them, maybe we should.'

'That's what I think,' Val said.

'Balls,' I said.

'When?' said Ben.

'Well, shall we just get it done? Go round tomorrow?'

I sighed loudly.

'You don't have to do it, Jim, just come with us. Sandy's give us his address, just take us to work, right, go to Bobby's first, then we all go to work.'

'Sounds fair.'

'Yeah, and that's better in the morning cos work means we can't stay long. Evening'd be open for him to want a beer or something, and we don't want to, that's the point,' said Elly.

'Cool. Honestly I'll do the talking, you just back me up,' Val said.

'I don't want to see him,' I said, and Elly agreed.

'I'll go in. Just be ready to kick the door down in case he takes us hostage.'

'Had you already agreed to do this?' I said to Val.

She paused, then said, 'yeah, I said to Sandy it were a good idea and Bobby's mum should see us tomorrow morning. It is a good idea, Jimbo. If anything saying summink in front of his mum will seal it for Bobby that he can't come around anymore, but we're not cunts about it, it's a good thing.'

'OK.'

'Good. Don't get too pissed tonight, you got to look good.'

'I'm not going in! You said!'

'I know, just saying.'

I felt like crying, then laughed instead. 'When, when is this shit going to end? When? Someone tell me, when will this shit end?'

Val looked at me with sympathy.

'Sorry I snapped, Val.'

'S'all right, Jimbo.'

Bye bye Bobby

Next morning we were all up early, and garbed up in our cleanest clothes. Elly with her layered look, jacket over shirt over T-shirt, a long-sleeved T-shirt tied around her waist. She dressed like a boy.

Ben drove the van, me in the middle, Val in passenger, Elly in the back, ready to jump out the back doors and machine gun whoever's behind us, not actually hit anyone but cause them to crash without being injured, and are so demoralised they give up.

We drove into leafy suburbs, and counting off post-boxes at the end of drives, we saw Bobby's scooter parked up at a house, then rolled on some yards before parking up so Bobby couldn't see us in the front, but we could use the wing mirrors to see the house.

All of us with our shades on, combining cool with incognito, Val said, 'Right. If I'm not out in five minutes, call the police. And fucking come in for us.' She got out the van, neatened up her top and looked at us, eyebrows arching up over her shades with a 'here we go' frown, and we gave her the thumbs up as she went.

Ben lit up three cigs, passed them around and we sat smoking in silence, til I asked, 'does anyone else feel tense?'

Ben and Elly affirmed.

'She'll be in the dungeon by now,' Ben said.

'In some pit, like *Silence of the Lambs*.'

'Stuffed birds everywhere, Bobby's going on about his mom wanting to talk to her in the cellar.'

'Shuddup!' said Elly. We smoked on.

'Has five minutes passed?'

'I don't know, wasn't anyone timing it?'

'Shit, do we call the police?'

'They'll arrest us before they arrest him.'

Then Val appeared at the front door, walked down the drive onto the sidewalk, all calm as you like, til with 20 yards to go Ben gunned the engine and Val first trotted then ran to the van, barely getting in the back doors before we tried to screech away, and she sprawled on the floor.

'Fuck that,' she said, 'just drive.'

'How did it go?'

'Oh God. Nah, weren't that bad really, his mum's real nice. I spoke with Bobby, in his room, right, bit of a midden but not vile. He was really quite subdued. So anyways, overall, right, I said he was a really nice guy and we liked him, but his behaviour lately was just too odd for us, just too way out there, and that's why we didn't want to hang out with him for now. And he seemed to accept that. And his mom nodded. And I said Jim's really sorry but he doesn't know what he said, he thinks it was just a stoner chat, and that we all really want him to be OK and sorry it's come to this, but I've come here cos we like you. If we didn't like you, we'd just told you to fuck off or ignored yers, or both.'

'Did you say that?'

'No not quite fuck off, I said we'd just let you suffer without telling yers, which would be unfair.'

'How'd he take it?'

'Yeah, he seemed really cool with it. He didn't say much which for him is unusual, but I think he got it, he'd fucked up but we didn't hate him for it. Kind of nice again, the bloke we all liked at the start. He did ask to come round and so on, but I said, Jim and Elly are leaving in a couple of days and they've got a lot of shit going on.'

'Right.'

'I thought I'd remove that incentive for him, if you're gone I doubt he'll come to see me or Ben to be honest.'

'Ha, he doesn't like you as much as us.'

'Too blimmin' right, thank fuck for that. Anyways, right, his mum, was there throughout, didn't say much, but she saw where I was coming from and was really nice seeing me out, said thanks for coming, she appreciated it, Jim shouldn't worry, and hopefully it'll be water under the bridge.'

'Aww.'

'Yeah. But he's not fucking coming back into the diner when I'm on.'

'Not taking his shit,' I said.

'Veterans!' said Ben.

'Veterans!' I said. 'You know I'm actually enjoying all this shit.'

'I know what you mean. Doesn't bloody stop does it?'

'Fucking Hell I sound like wots-his-face Attenborough in *The Great Escape*, he's telling Gordon Jackson how much all the escaping stuff, the plotting, the planning, he absolutely loves it. Then they all got shot.'

'Yeah.'

'And it's like every day, flying into the Death Star in *Return of the Jedi*.'

'In the Millennium Beast!'

'Shame we've got the van now. I actually miss the Beast.'

We rolled up to the diner and went in for coffee and pancakes, a lateish start at the hanger wouldn't kill us. A booth of girls already planted for the day gawped at us when we walked in. We were just too fucking cool.

'I'll take you to the table, no messing about, or you're out the door,' said Val.

A day of fair weather and fair takings. Back at the hanger, Addy appeared at our table. We were all quiet with apprehension.

'Why don't you come up to ours later?' he said.

I flicked a glance at Ben, who shrugged.

'Have a smoke. Pipe of peace,' he said.

'Erm ... OK. Yeah, OK.' I smiled.

'All right,' he said.

We drove home, mostly quiet.

'Pipe of peace,' said Ben.

'He seemed sad,' I said.

'I know!'

'I don't want to go,' I said, feeling ashamed of the whole stupid row.

'Know what you mean.'

'You coming, Elly?'

'No, I'm washing my hair.'

'Ha, good one. I might try that.'

'You can't, you shaved it all off.'

'Oh, shit.'

We got in, went up to their flat, where they had a couple of spliffs ready and beer. It was quite sweet really. We didn't talk about the cars, none of us knew what to say, it was awkward at first. Addy looked so crestfallen. I felt bad for making him feel bad. He'd been a tosser but I wished it hadn't really lost it over a fucking wreck of a car. But it was nice of them, we left friendlily.

What a boatload. Grown men rowing about shit like that.

Red handed

A long, slow day. With a cig I pondered over the map trying parts of Westie I'd not done, maybe a fresh approach would crack it, then thought of Bartlett, then Ali, then thought, fuck it, it's worth the risk.

Business in Bartlett was good, the Sun kept everything well lit as it descended. In the middle of the estate I crossed over a large, empty junction, atop one of the very few hills in the entire state, with a downhill view of houses in all directions. There was a big green on one side, and houses placed further back, no big trees crowding the space or blocking the view. It was all open, I couldn't have been in plainer sight, like one of the tanks atop the dyke road in *A Bridge Too Far*.

I crossed the junction and put on the jingle, looking left and right down the long wide roads for customers, then saw about 80 yards down on the left another ice-cream van, a big van like Christian's, this gangly kinda guy leaning out to a couple of kids. As he turned to look up in my direction, I saw sunlight glint off his glasses. Ali! And he'd fucking well seen me!

I turned off the jingle, absolutely floored it out of the estate, past jumping kids, jacking out of that junction where the police had done me, and belted back towards the hanger, panicking to think of an excuse, anything other than I'd been in Bartlett that day or any day, or just get back to base so fast there was no way I could have been in Bartlett at the time. Any fucking bullshit lie.

Oh my God. Maybe I'd driven off quick enough that he'd not identified me – but driving off like that was guilty as, a legit ice-cream seller wouldn't have panicked.

It was obviously me.

I would be totally humiliated and embarrassed.

Hank would realise how I made my money and decide I was an arsehole. I'd be fired.

Ali and Addy would take the moral high ground and I'd lose everything. Everyone would turn on me.

Shit, shit, shit, shit.

This rattled through my mind, back and forth, as I drove on and on. What if I somehow could meet up with Elly, make up an alibi with her? I looked at the map; her town was only 10 minutes away, but there she was nowhere in sight, and I realised she obviously wouldn't be, this was fucking stupid. With the Sun behind the trees, I turned away back towards the hanger, only to see in front a small white van with SLOW CHILDREN written on the back. A clean van, with very little rust, I pulled alongside and saw Elly driving! I beeped and shouted and she waved, then I waved at her to pull over and we did, right at the *Simple Simon* café.

'What are you doing here?' she trilled, before seeing my face twisted with panic, and I was soaked in sweat.

'I'm fucked. I was in Bartlett.'

'Where's that?'

'It's near West Chicago, I have to go there to make money, but it's Ali's patch, and Ali's seen me!'

'Shit!'

'I've totally lost the moral high ground, I'm fucked.'

She inhaled sharply, then said 'You fucking idiot!'

'I know, I know!'

'You're fucked.'

'Say I was with you.'

'What?'

'If we come back in together, say I drove over earlier to meet up with you for dinner or something, so I wasn't in Bartlett at the time.'

'Do you think that'll work?'

'Fucking better! Hank will know I've been lying all along as well.'

'God you fucked this up,' and she sighed.

Then I said, 'Do you want a hot dog? This place does hot dog and chips for like $3 and there's a great game like *Simple Simon*.'

She wrinkled her nose, and said, 'it's late enough, let's get back. How long you been doing this Bartlett thing?'

'Since the beginning. West Chicago's shit, and I honestly didn't think there was a problem going to Bartlett to make money, but by the time I found out I wasn't supposed to be there, it was my only real money maker.'

'You should have taken over Christian's route.'

That stunned me a second. 'Yeah. Shit. I should have. Who did take it over?'

'Don't know. Anyway we got to go. Come on, face the music.'

We drove back in tandem, me with a rising sense of feeling sick. Charlie waved us in, plugged in our vans, my stomach rolling and my heart beating fast as I expected to walk in and have Hank, everyone in fact turn and denounce me en masse.

But they didn't. Ali hadn't come back yet. The shit had yet to hit the fan.

We started to count up, but my gaze was locked towards the hanger door, as others slushed past on the gravel, me wondering 'was that Ali? Was that Ali?'

Then a larger van came in, at speed, then a horrible scrunching sound of a van sliding to a stop, then shouting and banging.

Oh shit that's Ali – and boy did he sound angry! Then more shouting and Hank jumped up and ran out, then came back in, reached behind the car under the tarp and hauled out a fire extinguisher, as the shouting continued and we could see black smoke billowing back across the gravel.

We barrelled out and stopped in our tracks to see Ali's van truly on fire, flames fingering up from out the bonnet, out the vents, up the windscreen, black smoke piling out. Ali jumped back in and got his tray out as smoke began to billow out the cabin, Hank yelled at Charlie to flip the bonnet up, Charlie just coming from the back of the hanger with a hose and was starting to blast at the van, then he hoofed the bonnet up with an amazing kick, and a great casket of

313

flame arose out of the engine block, a real *wmmff*, and burning plastic showered onto the gravel and front tyre, Hank and Charlie bowed away from this wall of heat we all felt, then Charlie was hosing and Hank blasting, as Dylan appeared with another extinguisher and Ali stood there breathing heavily, staring at the flames and smoke as they obscured a gorgeous purple dusk.

Had Ali been driving with such rage he'd blown up his van?

Soon enough, in place of flames was steam, a couple more blasts off the extinguishers to cool the whole thing down, then Ali, Charlie and Dylan slowly converged and talked.

Hank came over and said, 'well, that was exciting,' and we laughed nervously.

'You didn't get burned at all, Hank?' Elly said.

He felt the side of his face, one side of his beard was crispy and crumbly, and he smelt his hand, 'uh yeah, gee, smells like burning ants', and Elly asked him to look up in to the light, looked all over his head but saw no actual burns.

Ali came in and said, 'I'm sure I saw another Penguin truck in Bartlett' but as he did so, Charlie shouted from outside and Hank went straight out and stood talking with Dylan and Charlie, then Ali's mates asked him about the fire, he forgot about seeing anyone else and the van going up was all they talked about.

I said to Ben and Elly, 'shall we go?'

Ben said aye. 'OK, everyone coming in the A-Team van, are you ready?'

A few ayes, we all piled in and drove off, me next to Elly in the front.

'That was lucky,' she said.

'Yep,' I said, and amid chatter about the fire, we said nothing more.

Jason and Mike came back to ours, Greg was there, we had beers, told stories, played games, then Elly and Jason started play fighting on the floor and we were all shouting at them. By the end, it was just Ben with Val on the sofa, me in an armchair and Elly draped across my lap, arms around my neck. I wanted to kiss her but didn't want to wreck the moment of having her here, on me, all to myself.

Ultimately she got up and went to bed, giving me a long look as she left. I followed her as she flumped onto the bed, still in her clothes, and I said, 'I'd chase you around the world for a body like yours.'

'You sound like Charlie,' she said.

Then I went back into the living room and had another beer.

'You could have had her, Jim,' Val said. I nodded and guzzled.

314

Asshole

We went to work, it was overcast, more kids waved me away than jumped.

Well fuck you too, you little critters.

On the map was a whole grid of streets on the edge of town I'd only gone down once, and somehow wrote it off in my mind. They were on the other side of the highway, behind a thick wall of trees. So I went for another look and found loads of houses, along narrow streets, curvy, dense with trees and high hedges, like the Ewok planet, you often couldn't see the gardens until you were right on top of them and by then you were passing. One child bought something, another said, 'go away, we don't want any'.

Around one tight corner I nearly drove into the rusty white butt of a van hanging over the end of a steep drive, as if it were having a shit in the street. It was an ice-cream van, ex-postal like mine, SLOW CHILDREN written in red on the back. I stopped and stared at it. With Eskimo, the 'shitty weather' one, the yellow one, me, this one and that battleship at least, made six of us crawling Westie's streets. No wonder none of us made any money and the kids were sick of us. No wonder that bloke leaned out and shouted 'turn that shit off!' Fucking hell.

I was glad this was all ending soon. I'd had enough, and wanted to leave these people for who this was really a way of life to carry on. I got out and lit up, when a man came down the drive, stopped and stared at me.

'What are you doing here?' he said.

'Selling ice-cream, or trying to,' I said.

'Asshole,' he said, and went back up the drive.

Cunt.

I gave up early and stopped off for my hot-dog and *Simple Simon*, then rolled back to the hanger, an hour early, but everyone was back.

'Pffffffff…' I said to Hank. He laughed. Despite the low takings, there was a cheery sense of 'ahh, what the Hell, eh?', and the chatter got onto films, and who would play us when someone made the film about this place.

'Someone on the route said I look like Hugh Grant,' I said.

'But he's a pervert,' said Mike.

'No, he's been with a prostitute, that's-'

'Bad enough!' said Elly, 'I'd be that girl from that film with Jeremy Irons, that French girl, Juliet Binoche.'

'*Damage*?' I said.

'Yes. It's such an erotic film.'

'The girl no one can resist, a femme fatale,' said Mike.

I'd seen *Damage* at the Ritzy. People had laughed during the sex scenes, one where they're fucking and Irons bangs her head against the floor. One guy threw a beer-can in mock protest at his waste of money.

315

'I think you're much more Liz Taylor in *National Velvet*, or Eva Gardner in *55 Days in Peking*,' I said. Gardner, complete slut with a butt.

'Don't know any of those films.'

'Liz is too old and Eva's dead,' said Ben.

'If we had flashback scenes, for my youthful character I'd be played by Colin Firth and for my old-age I'd be Sean Connery. Liz Taylor for Elly in fifty years.'

She tutted, 'fuck off.'

'At times this job is less like selling ice-cream than carting explosives, like in *The Wages of Fear*.'

'I've seen that!' exclaimed Ben. 'When they're taking nitro-glycerine across the jungle. And for two hours you're on the edge of your seat watching these guys driving trucks at 5 mph, waiting for them to blow up!'

'What about just filling one of the van freezers with explosives?' said Aidan.

'Charlie could do that,' I said.

'Repaint it like an Eskimo van and roll it into Eskimo's depot and blow the whole lot sky high.'

'Or phone up Eskimo and pretend we're one of his lot and we're broken down somewhere, and while he's out we go in and torch his place.'

'Lure him into a trap, get him into some darkened alley somewhere and at the right moment we all turn on our headlights and box him in with our vans.'

'Do what they did in *Grease*, put those twirly blade things on the van wheels, drive alongside their trucks and carve them to shreds, blow out all their tyres.'

'It's a shame we don't have open-top vans, then we could really duel on the road like in *Ben Hur*.'

'I've had that anyway, when that Iceberg cunt drove alongside with a baseball bat.'

'Oh yeah. Fucking Hell.'

'That's the most dastardly, evil, underhand trick I've ever heard ... when do we start?' As we plotted, Hank was looking at us with the proudest, most avuncular grin his slightly burned beard could reveal. I nodded to Elly to have a look at the boss, and she grinned too.

'What do you think of our plans, Hank? Some of them are a long shot, but they might just work.'

'Inerestin',' he drawled, chuckling.

'Come on Hank, this is a golden opportunity, you've assembled a crack unit of loyal, veteran ice-cream men, your British contingent of renegade mercenaries.'

'Renegade, sure!' Hank laughed.

'A battle-hardened bunch of desperadoes, capable of the most cunning and cruel deeds. We only await your command to strike down your villainous former employees.'

'*The Dirty Dozen* of ice-cream.'

'*The Wild Geese* of Chicago's long, bitter, protracted ice-cream wars, sent out on a suicide mission into the depths of Shorewood to take out the evil Eskimo and his bloodthirsty cohorts.'

'Oo yeah, bagsy being Roger Moore.'

'Nah, it's much more Mafiosi. This is *The Godfather*. Hank's obviously got to be Marlon Brando, wotsit Corleone'.

'You're right. Jess is very, very much Michael Corleone, y'know, hard-nosed, business down the line.' Hank guffawed at that. 'Brilliant. We all have those round-barrelled machine guns.'

'That'd fuck up Eskimo big-time. *BRG-RG-RG-RG-RG-RG-RG-*!'

'A chance to reclaim your empire, *The Penguin Strikes Back*.'

'With Hank as Darth Vader.'

Ben talked into a beer can, '*Coh-sss, coh-sss*, murr you guys, *coh-sss, coh-sss*'.

'Well, pretty radical. So long as you get Eskimo, anything goes,' Hank said. We cheered, banged the table and punched the air in tribute.

We trundled back to the flat, and milled around. Ben pointed in the guidebook to a boat ride on the lake we could do tomorrow if we got time off. Seemed like a good idea.

I walked into the bedroom and Elly was lying on her bed, reading. 'Do you want a fight?' I said.

She flipped from her front and sat up, waved me closer, then punched my right arm. I punched hers back. She stood up and we were punching each other's arms, then ribs, chest, not punching but jabbing with pointed fingers, grabbing, wrestling, and ended up on the bed, then onto the floor, legs intertwined, using arms and legs to lever ourselves onto one another and lever the other one off, lots of huffing and puffing, it was sweaty, grimy. Then I lunged for her, tried to kiss her and she turned her head up and away and I got her on the neck, her arms went limp as if she wasn't interested, and I let go, went into the living room, and got pissed.

317

The Projects

Over morning smokes I said to Elly, 'I'm not sure about the fight we had last night.'

'No I'm not either.'

We both seemed embarrassed.

Some of the others came in the van, we got to the hanger and saw Addy getting out the Beast.

'It's actually quite fun to drive,' said Addy.

I asked Hank if Ben, Elly and I could finish a couple of hours early to have a last trip around Chicago, and he was totally cool with it, I got the Beast keys off Addy, he gave the A-Team keys to Mike, as if making a point, and I told Mike to meet us at the 5 cent bar later.

So the day passed, warm but not killing, I just wanted my hot dog and fries, and I beat *Simple Simon*! Then back, got the others, got Val and on to Chicago we went.

Somewhere up one of the canals in the posh part, we got a tour boat, going under the many little girder bridges, so many amazing buildings from the water line, and we couldn't get any lower so they were all as tall as could be. It was astounding, as the Sun lowered and the older, shorter buildings fronted with stone took different shades and tones of colour until they sank under the shadows, as the younger, taller buildings of glass vied for light and reflected the dying sunset.

As the dusk evaporated, the boat headed out onto the lake and we had an hour of taking in the skyline, spaciously laid out, proud, like the skyscrapers all felt room to stand alone and even admire one another.

Val and Ben were getting along very well indeed, and I was alone with Elly a lot. Surely I'd get a snog?

After the boat ride we found our way to the grimier end of town to the 5 cent bar and the others, we all got hammered, playing pool, Frogger, playing on the bikes.

Then I found myself with Elly in front of me, looking pleading.

'You can't leave uni. What will you do?'

'Go travelling. Maybe teach English, people have done that.'

'You'll be a nothing, a nobody. You'll end up like Appalling Paul, pissing around for your life.'

I liked her concern, but couldn't see an alternative. I couldn't go back.

'For God's sake man, you've got to come back, or you'll be nothing. Please. I'll be in tears soon if I go on like this, but you've got to come back.'

I really didn't know she cared so much.

'Please.'

I just smiled and went to play Frogger. A wave of anger shivered through me. She was going back, they were all going back, and I wasn't. It was all going to be over, very soon.

I had to get another drink. As I stood at the bar to get another shot I felt two hands pinch my arse, but not a pinch but more like an amazing deep stroke that almost immediately gave me a boner. I turned and saw Elly sauntering away.

Oh my God. Was she coming on to me? Was this it? Were we finally going to get it together?

'Did you just pinch my bum?'

'Maybe.'

I leaned against the bar side-on in what seemed like a manly pose, while I deliberated on making a move on her. But she'd been putting me off so long, I didn't know what to do.

'Do you want to do something about it?' I asked.

'Just having a laugh, man.'

The rug pulled again. I wanted her to do it again, and again, and again, but if it went nowhere I couldn't stand it as a wind-up. 'Don't then if you're just having a laugh, it's not funny,' I just about managed to say, regretting every word as I said it. I went to the bog and punched a wall – why is she doing this, now?

Just fuck her.

What? No.

Fuck her. Everyone else has.

I left the bog, found her, gave her a hug.

The evening idled to an end, the others pitched into the van, we took the Beast. Ben drove, he hadn't drunk that much, but somehow we missed the turning for whichever highway we needed, and were still grinding round some strange part of town as the girls dozed in the back.

'Loads of waste ground,' I said.

'What are these fucking horrible flats?'

Traffic lights half a block ahead turned red, and the pick-up truck some yards in front slowed for a few seconds, then gunned it through the red.

'Did you see that? He just went straight through!'

'Cheeky get!' and Ben tooted the horn as the light turned green. Further ahead was another set of lights that went red long before the pick-up got to them, but again he slowed only a second, then sailed on through.

'Is he pissed or what?' said Ben. Those lights were still against us and we slowed down to the junction, dilapidated old buildings on one side, waste ground and chicken-wire on the other. On a corner of the waste ground was a bashed up post box and a man, who turned and looked at us as we stopped. And didn't look away.

'There's a bloke staring at us,' I said, then looked back towards this guy, who was still staring, our gazes met, then he started walking towards us.

'Fuck, he's coming over!'

The lights changed and Ben floored it away, as this bloke raised his arm and shouted something.

'That was well leery.'

In the far distance we saw more lights, red and green, and we could just make out the pick-up barrelling away whatever was showing.

'Jesus, you know where we are?' said Ben, his tone hushed. 'We're in the Projects.'

I looked around. There was a distinct lack of street lighting and less light coming from the apartment blocks beyond the waste ground, flats that even in the dim gloom we could see were in a completely shit state, while the open spaces were strewn with rubbish and smashed up cars.

'Oh shit. Yes we are,' I said.

'We're in the fucking projects.'

'I don't think this is a good development.'

'No it's not!'

'Fuck, what do we do?'

'Well we better get out the fucking projects!' he said as I reached for the map, not that I could read it in the dark, even if we knew where we were on it. I was going to ask Ben to slow down so I could see a street-sign, but thought better of it, then reached up to turn on the inside light, but stopped myself.

'Beast – do not run out of gas, or you die with us!' I said.

'Yeah, car, trust us on this one,' added Ben, his voice quivering as if laughing, 'Where do we go? Where the fuck are we going?'

'I don't know! Just keep going! Don't slow down,' I said, just as the next set of lights turned red, and a group of men on the pavement started moving as we drew near, we were convinced they were taking an interest in us.

'Fuck it! Crash 'em!' I said, and Ben agreed, saying, 'I think that pick-up guy had a point.'

As we bounded over the crossing I glanced around for a street sign and caught a glimpse of something very tall, far away.

'Town's that way! Next junction go left and floor it.'

Back at the flat Ben and Val went to bed, while Elly was about to, I'd knocked down a couple more beers, then I said to Elly, 'we should sleep together'.

She stood still, and looked at me.

Then I said, 'as friends', and she came and hugged me tight, and we ended up lying on the sofa, me holding her from behind, just talking about how much I liked her which might have been all right but I got too excited and started going on about the crush I'd had on her months before, which always freaked her out, but surely she felt differently now, but no, it freaked her out, and before I knew it she'd wriggled free, said 'no', and went to her bed. Fuck.

Last push

Today was the last day. We got up early to clean our bit of the apartment, all a bit futile as the others were still there and going to trash it all over again. I was assigned to clean up the bathroom. I scanned the surfaces for my stuff, then opened the cupboard below the sink, expecting to find a wall of girly crap. But it was empty, except for a slim, pale-coloured oblong box.

A pregnancy test kit.

Suddenly I felt winded.

She'd be an amazing mother, to Christian's child, and she'd probably keep it, just to keep him hanging around. And he'd come over and they'd fuck again. And she'd every day give that child that incredible look of love, the child she'd had with him. I wanted to smash my fist into the mirror.

Fuck her. Just fuck her. When are you going to see her again?

She was in the living room, going through one of the drawers.

'Are you pregnant?'

She froze, didn't look at me, and said quietly, 'no'.

I wanted to ask, 'you left that kit for me to find, though, didn't you?' but didn't.

We drove to the hanger and we chatted a bit with Hank, and Charlie, and thanked them for everything, although we'd see Hank later in any case, and he gave us both a hug cos he's just a lovely guy.

The last day's takings were so-so, somehow I made enough to counter the loss of Bartlett. I drove slow around Joly's place, but he wasn't there. Maybe he'd gone on camp or something, but I didn't know which was his house and felt sad I couldn't say goodbye to him or his mum.

More so though I kept getting images of Christian and Elly fucking, and the idea of her being pregnant.

Back at the hanger Mike said we'd all be going out to a bar they knew, because it was our last night, which was really sweet. We went back and smartened up, Elly put on the same outfit that first night she'd fucked Christian. Or he'd fucked her.

We met with the others and went to this bar, a massive place, heaving, like the one where Elly had gone crazy. I was driving at this point but not drinking, but they were all caning the beers with shots and tequilas, and when we left the bar I got into the front seat of the Beast only to see Aidan in the back suddenly lurch towards the door, throwing up as he did so, some out the door, some on him, some on the back seat. 'Oh my God!' I said. It wasn't carrot chunk sick, though, mainly beer, as Mike got napkins to try and clean Aidan up a bit, but before they could do the backseat Addy got in. 'Addy no, don't get in! No no no,' I shouted, but too late.

'Oh God what's this?' he said, smelt his hand, 'ah no, agh,' he said, and got out. 'Oh bloody Hell, I hadn't done anything wrong tonight, either.'

'I'm sorry,' I said, 'seriously mate I said don't get in, I wasn't having a go, oh no.'

We went to Dooley's, somehow Elly and I were outside, then when we went in the others, all at the bar, turned and cheered us, a real roof-raiser, clapping, back slapping, it felt amazing, hugging everyone. I felt like the boss as I toasted us all: 'It's been a ride, it really has. Some real battles but it's been a fucking ride. Cheers everyone! Here's to all our futures!'

Then I caught myself. What future?

People were buying me drinks and I was downing them, downing them, downing them. I was soon pissed, and I mean, pissed. Ben said something about Christian, and then it all went black, until I came round, raging, raging, against Christian, against everyone, Ben now defending him, 'but she was never yours.'

'He knew I liked her,'

'But why is this all on him, she went out with him, she went out with Mark, why aren't you blaming her?'

'No – she's not to blame, she does what she does,' I was shouting through tears.

Raging, raging, raging. I remember Ben looked shocked, then Val coming over, said something like 'Jesus, are you all right?'

Elly was at the other end of the bar, talking to some loser bastard in a cowboy hat. What the fuck?

I waved her over, angrily, why wasn't she with us, with me? I stormed over to her to get her back to us. She didn't say anything but nodded, with a fearful look to her, must have seen my eyes all swollen, faced streaked with tears.

I think I shouted at someone at the bar to go fuck themselves.

Something about the other guys trying to calm the situation.

Me shouting about where Elly had gone.

I don't remember getting back to the flat, I just remember being slumped in an armchair while the party carried on around me, knocking down some spirit, 'til I thought Elly must be in the flat, in our room.

The bedroom door was closed, so I went in, there she already was, face down on the bed, in her clothes. I fumblingly took off all of mine, falling over, and stood there in these tatty boxer shorts.

Go for it. Just go for it.

I taggled her awake, and said, 'Elly, we need to make love.'

'I'm happy as we are,' she said.

'No, we need to. I love you and you love me, and it's what we must do.'

'No man, it's fine as it is.'

I grabbed her arm to turn her over, but she resisted, and wouldn't turn, saying 'no, we're good as we are, no.'

I tried to reach under to turn her over, but she was resisting. I kept pushing my hand and arm under her chest but she wouldn't turn. With some effort I managed to hoick her top up, and expose part of her lower back which I started to kiss. Great wet, slovenly smackers up and down her back. No response.

Mike came in half round the door and turned on the light, me in my boxers, head stooped by booze, barely able to speak, and eyes half closed from the bright light, he said, almost laughing from embarrassment, 'what are you doing?'

'Go away', I slurred.

'Give it up mate, come back out,' he said, then left, and said something to someone else.

I turned off the light but same thing happened minutes later with Jason, then again minutes or ages later it was Ben, who told me to pack it the fuck in, then he left, as I saw Greg stifling embarrassed laughter.

I was hammered, but tried again with Elly, pleading with her to fuck. Now she was on her back and I fumbled down her body, trying to hoick up her top and kiss her belly, then I put my hands up around the waist of her knickers and started to kiss down towards the gap in her legs, tugging the knickers lightly, whereupon with sudden, frightening speed, she sat up and thumped me on the side of the head, then pushed me back. She thrust her within inches of mine.

'Piss off!' she hissed. 'Piss off! Just *piss* off!'

I couldn't take this in. We were supposed to be having it off. I got off the bed and stood swaying next to it, and said, 'o come on,' but she flipped back over, then flipped back, again saying 'piss off', as I went to touch her she slapped my hand away with a real sting.

'Oh fuck this,' I muttered, and wondered whether to go get another beer, but ended up collapsed in the walk-in closet.

I woke up myself only a few hours later in the thickest alcoholic fog. Heard Elly say, 'and he was kissing my back'.

'Ugh!' Val said, as Elly continued, not sounding happy. But I somehow felt jubilant, like I'd achieved something.

I bounced from room to room, saw Val, saw Ben, both of them looking shocked. Something amused me about it all. Val said quietly, 'Jim. She doesn't think it's funny Jim.'

I knocked on the door of the bathroom. Elly opened it a slither, dressed in a white bathrobe, towel wrapped around her head. It was a vision of heaven, almost angelic, if not that her blue eyes were boring into me with something between cold disdain, but also, pain? Fear? Anger? No smile, no frown. Just a cold, frightened stare of broken trust. Still pissed, I laughed, and then staggered off.

Ben and Val drove us to the airport, Elly with them in the front, me slumped in the back. No-one spoke. We got out. Even I could tell my breath stank.

Val hugged me but she had this look on her face, fear shot through me. 'I think you're going to fall out. Big time,' she said.

I turned to Ben. He hugged me, but said nothing, just shook his head.

We ground through the check-in queue. She wouldn't talk to me, nor look at me. I began to feel a bit sick, partly by hangover, but more as the previous night's events flitted into my mind.

'Am I in disgrace?' I said at one point.

'Yes.'

'Can we talk about it?'

'No.'

The sickness turned to dread. I had to explain myself. But I couldn't think how. Of all the people she wanted as a friend, I'd been closest, the keeper of her secrets. Now one night had blown it all. One drunken night, and I'd never even shagged her. Panic vied with frustration. Anger battled.

'Why can't we talk about it?'

'We're not going to talk about it.'

'Come on, please, please.'

'No.'

'You're going to hate me.'

'We're not going to talk about it.'

'How, how can we not talk about it? How can you - '

'We are not going talk about it. Shut up. Shut up.'

So I did. And the sense of dread, the feeling sick, got worse and worse.

The connection involved a few hours at New York, we split up. Alone, waves of panic rising, I wondered if I should abandon the flight, head back to Chicago, try to find that woman who'd offered me a job. Something totally radical, but my luggage was already gone through to London.

Elly was nowhere to be seen.

Only on board the flight to Heathrow were we reunited next to one another, her stopping dead as she found me in the seat next to her. She asked a stewardess about moving, but was told it wasn't possible. We didn't speak. This sense of nausea kept rising up, then going away, then anger, 'why wouldn't she fuck me? She fucked all my friends, but not me.' Then panic, 'it wasn't what it seemed, I wasn't doing what it looked like, I ...' but I didn't believe it. Then I felt sick again. Each time it was longer and more intense, me stuck in the window seat, Elly beside me, asleep, for the whole five hours.

Oh God.

Memories of the guys coming in and seeing it all, laughing, flitted in and out, stinging me more and more with each recollection.

Then Elly's response. 'Piss off.' 'Piss off.'

My stomach burned, dread, panic, and anger.

I'd blown it.

I'd blown it all.

Absolutely humiliated myself.

Absolutely humiliated her.

She was right next to me, smelling so good, her skin so incredibly smooth and clear to see, my Goddess, right next to me, me the one she'd trusted, above all others.

Nearing London, she awoke.

'It's all over isn't it?'

'We're not going to talk about it.'

'Please.'

'We are not going to talk about it.'

'You'll hate me.'

'Shuttup,' she said, then turned and with that same anger, she hissed, 'shuttup. Just shuttup. Shuttup.'

My mind swung from thinking it'd all blow over, to it was so all over, and I might as well be dead. I had to squeeze past her to get to the bog, I thought of opening the back door and sucking me out - *zz not her sucking you off zz* - down into the ocean. But I didn't, instead having to clamber past her again to my seat, the window I wanted to smash and be sucked out, to be asphyxiated in seconds, I'd never feel the impact of hitting the water miles below.

My mind lurched in every direction.

Why couldn't she just laugh it off?

Why wouldn't she just fuck me?

What was I going to do?

How could I make this up to her?

How could I explain it to her? Surely I could say it was a mistake. I hadn't meant to do anything, it wasn't what I'd meant, it wasn't that bad.

But over and over I realised, we were so over.

And it wasn't the demons telling me this. This was me telling me this.

Down through landing.

Down through passports.

Down through luggage.

Down through customs.

She looked around at the many yellow and black signs, saw the one for the bus station, saw it, and started to walk away.

'Elly.'

She turned, again, with that stare, loaded with distrust, humiliation, hate.

'This is it. You hate me.'

'Come here, man,' she said, pulling me in for a hug.

'It's all over, I know it.'

'Don't be silly,' she said, then pushed me off, 'I'm going. Don't follow me.'

And off she walked.

Everything was over.

It was all over.

Everything.

I'd failed.
Failed the lot.
Fucked it all to Hell.
Oh fuck ... what now?
What now?
What now?

Printed in Great Britain
by Amazon

59368636R00185